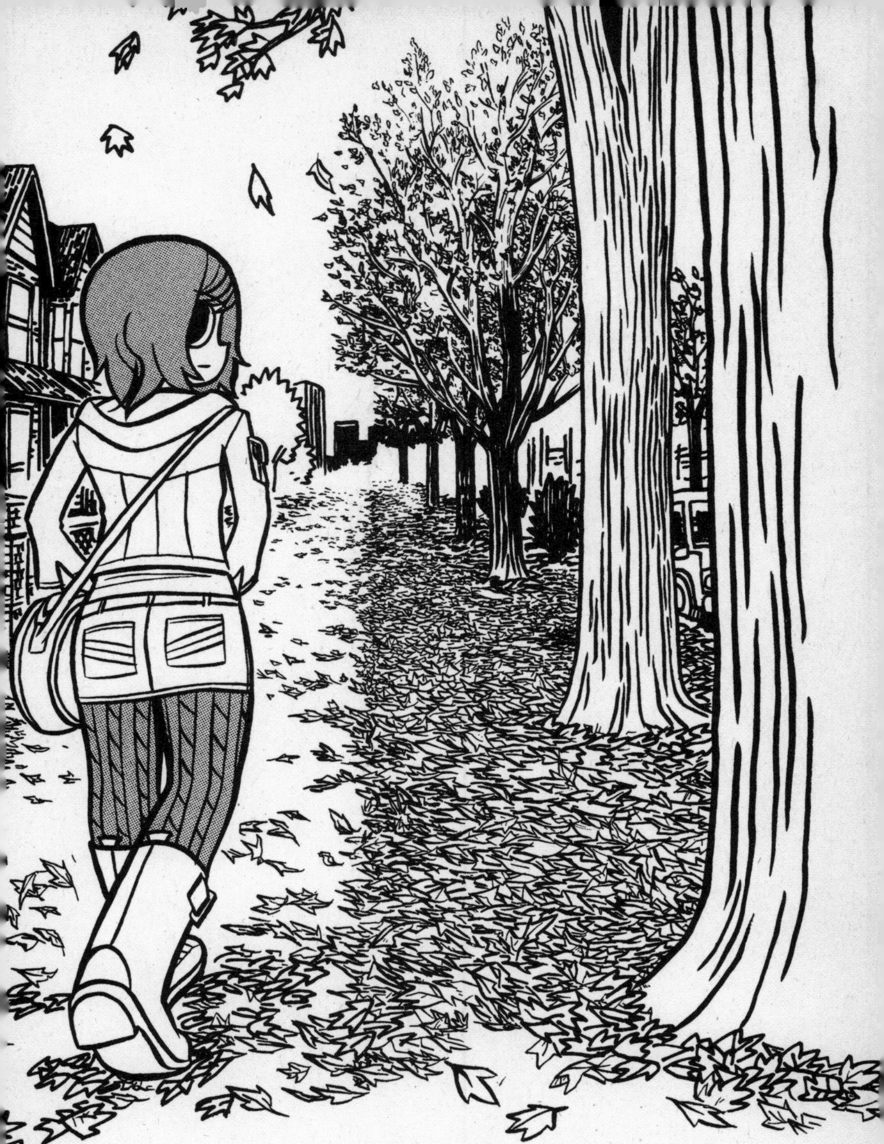

ONI PRESS *presents*
BRYAN LEE O'MALLEY'S

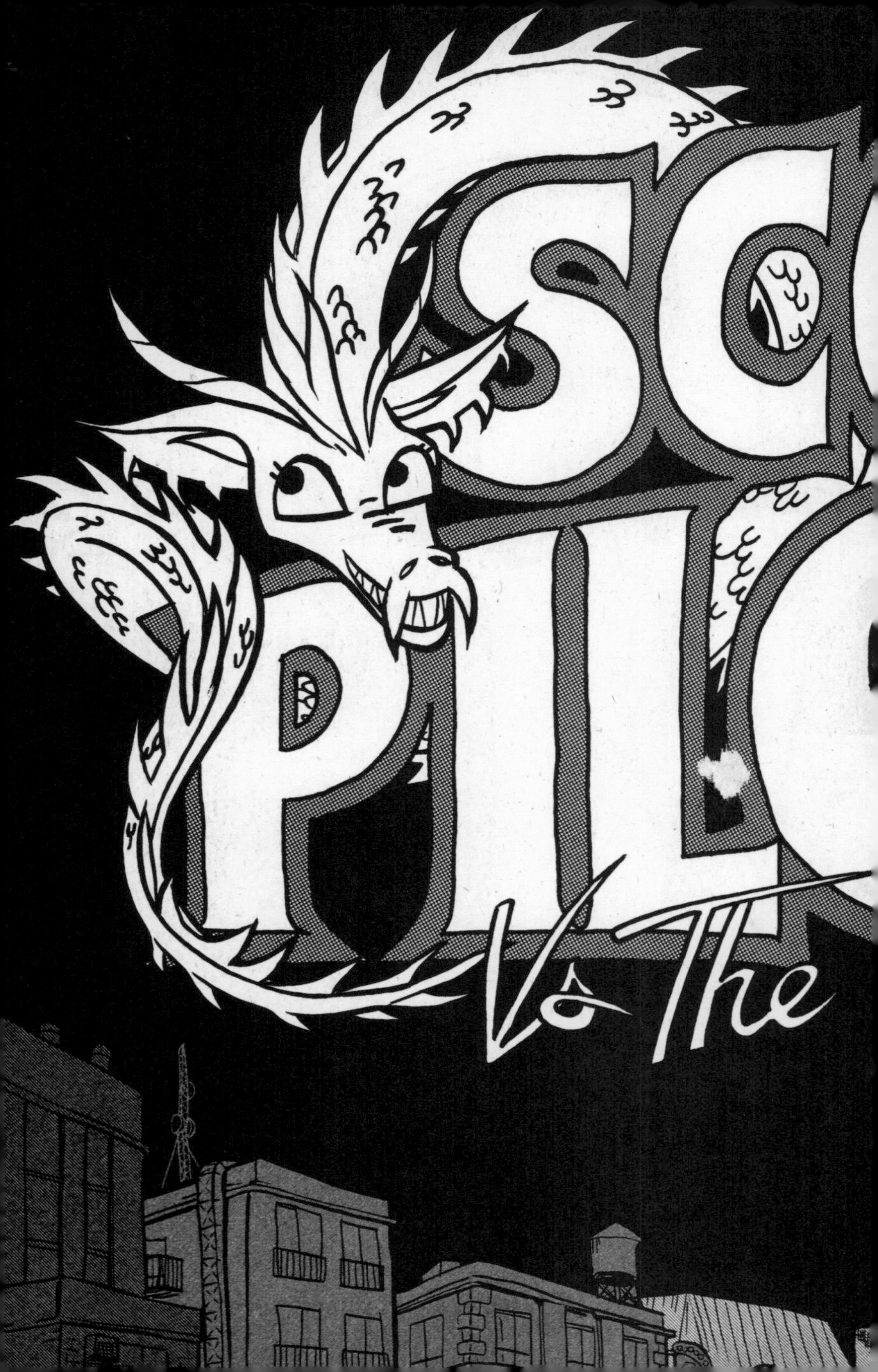
Vs The

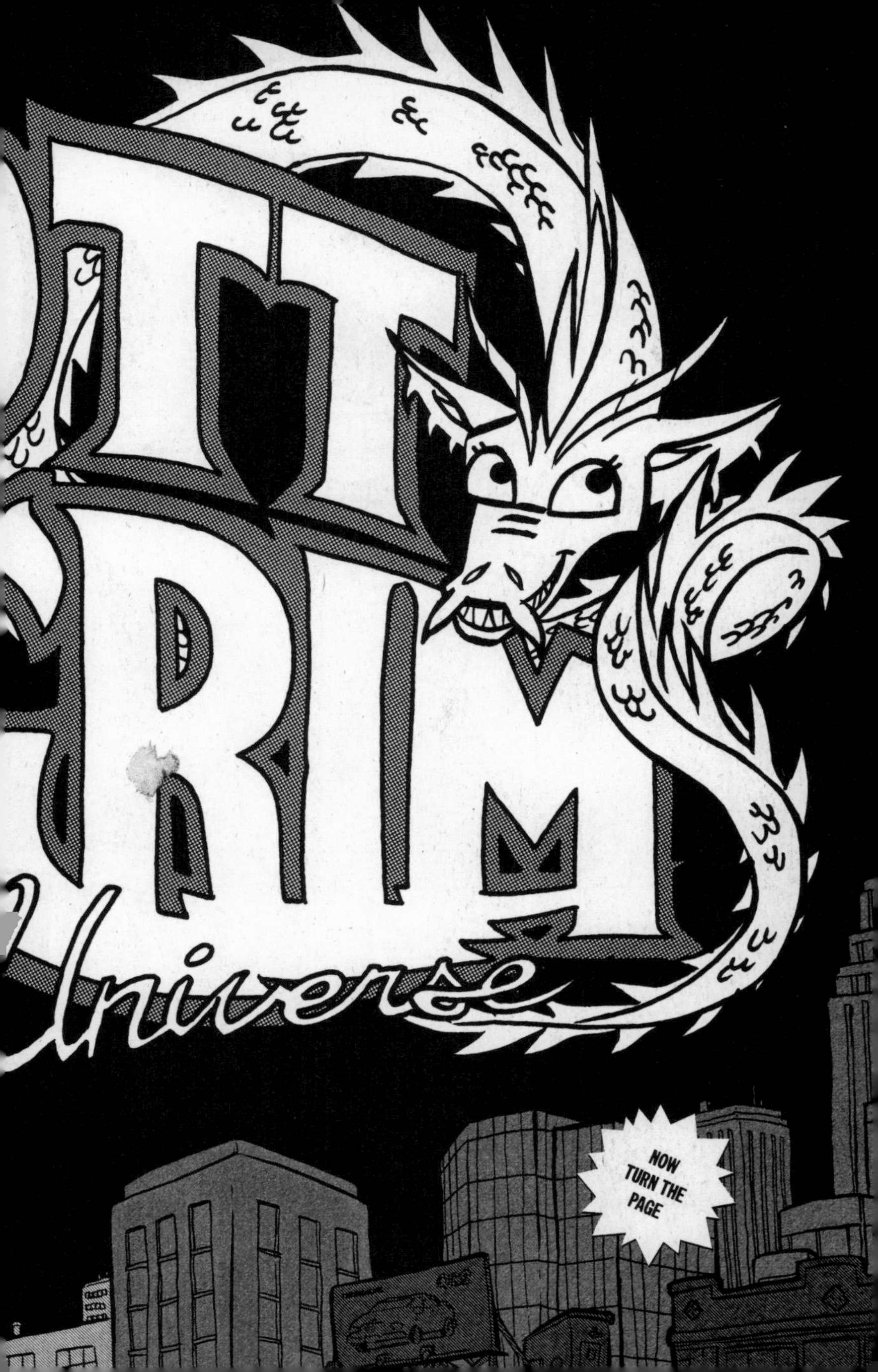
Universe
NOW TURN THE PAGE

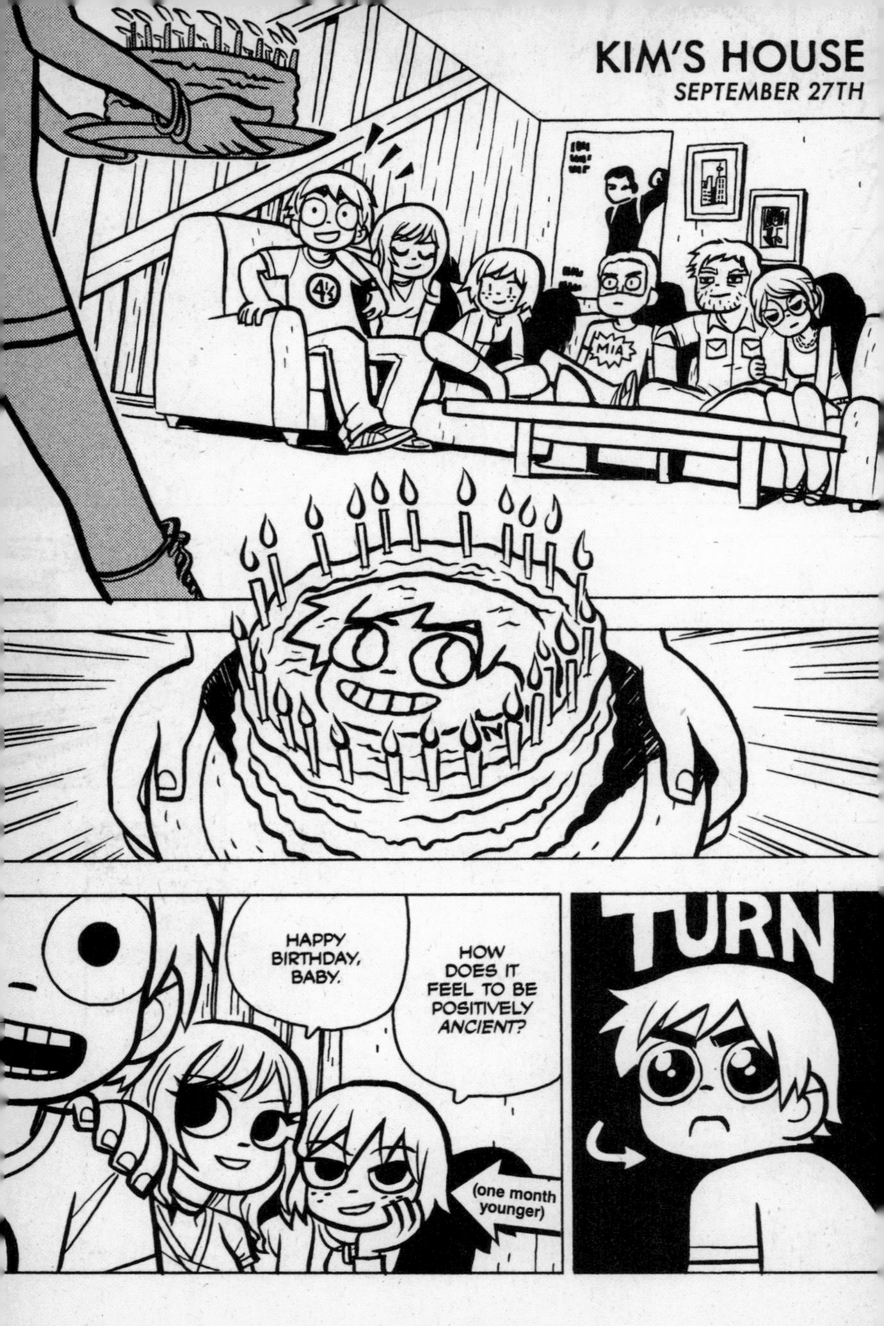
KIM'S HOUSE
SEPTEMBER 27TH
MIA
HAPPY BIRTHDAY, BABY.
HOW DOES IT FEEL TO BE POSITIVELY *ANCIENT?*
(one month younger)
TURN

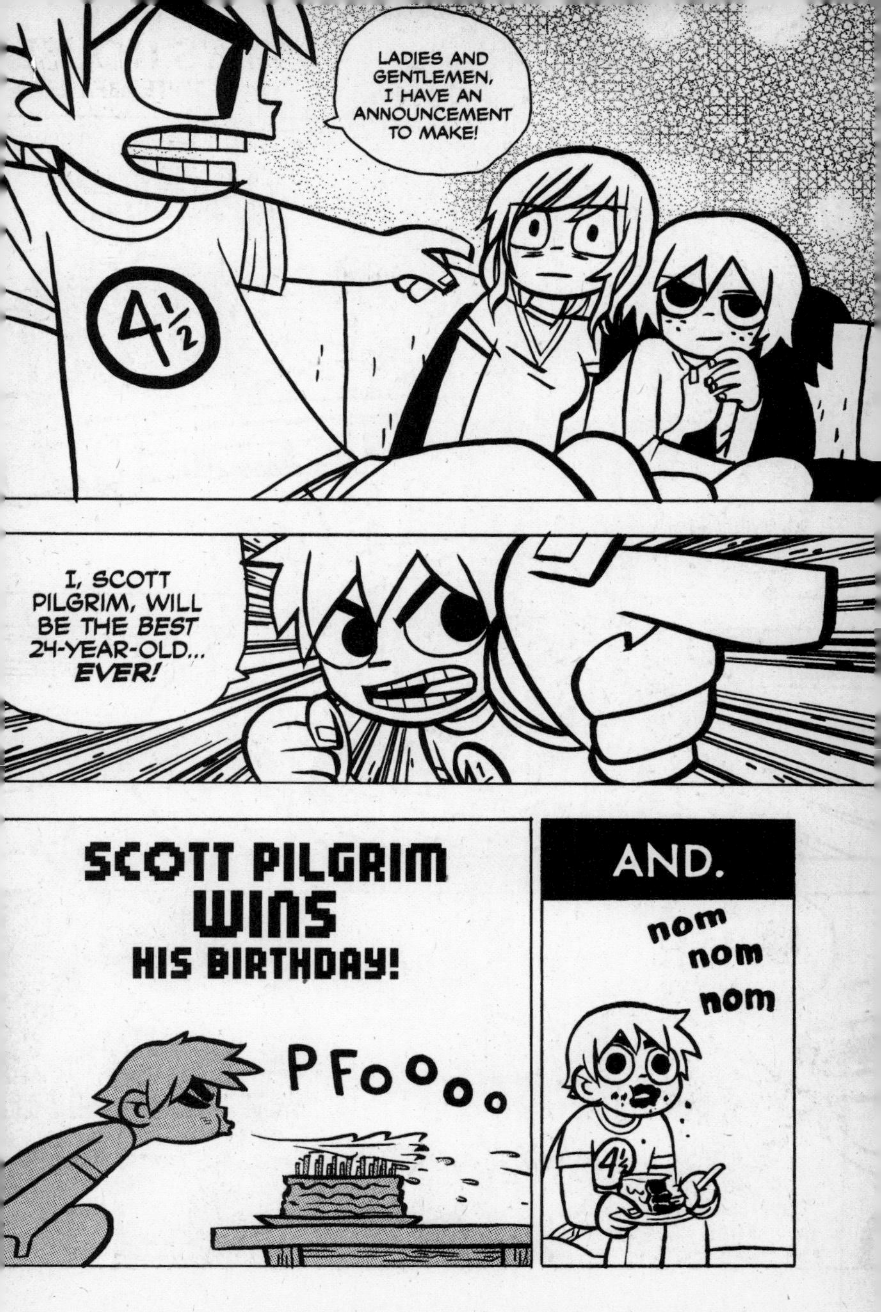

LADIES AND GENTLEMEN, I HAVE AN ANNOUNCEMENT TO MAKE!
I, SCOTT PILGRIM, WILL BE THE *BEST* 24-YEAR-OLD... ***EVER!***
SCOTT PILGRIM WINS HIS BIRTHDAY!
PFOoooo
AND.
nom nom nom

26

PRECIOUS LITTLE LIFE

JULIE'S NEW APARTMENT
A studio loft in what was once a warehouse or something. Julie shares the small apartment with three other girls because, although it is out of their price range, they knew it'd be the BEST place to throw the COOLEST parties.

Design by **Bryan Lee O'Malley** with **Keith Wood** | Back cover pixel art by **BEN BERNTSEN**

Published by **Oni Press, Inc.**
Joe Nozemack publisher | **James Lucas Jones** editor in chief
Randal C. Jarrell managing editor | **Cory Casoni** marketing director | **Keith Wood** art director
Jill Beaton assistant editor | **Douglas E. Sherwood** production assistant

www.onipress.com | www.scottpilgrim.com | www.radiomaru.com

Special thanks to:
Hope Larson
Intern Evan
TV's Matt Watts
Hugh Stewart
Shigeharu Kobayash
Kanye West
...AND YOU

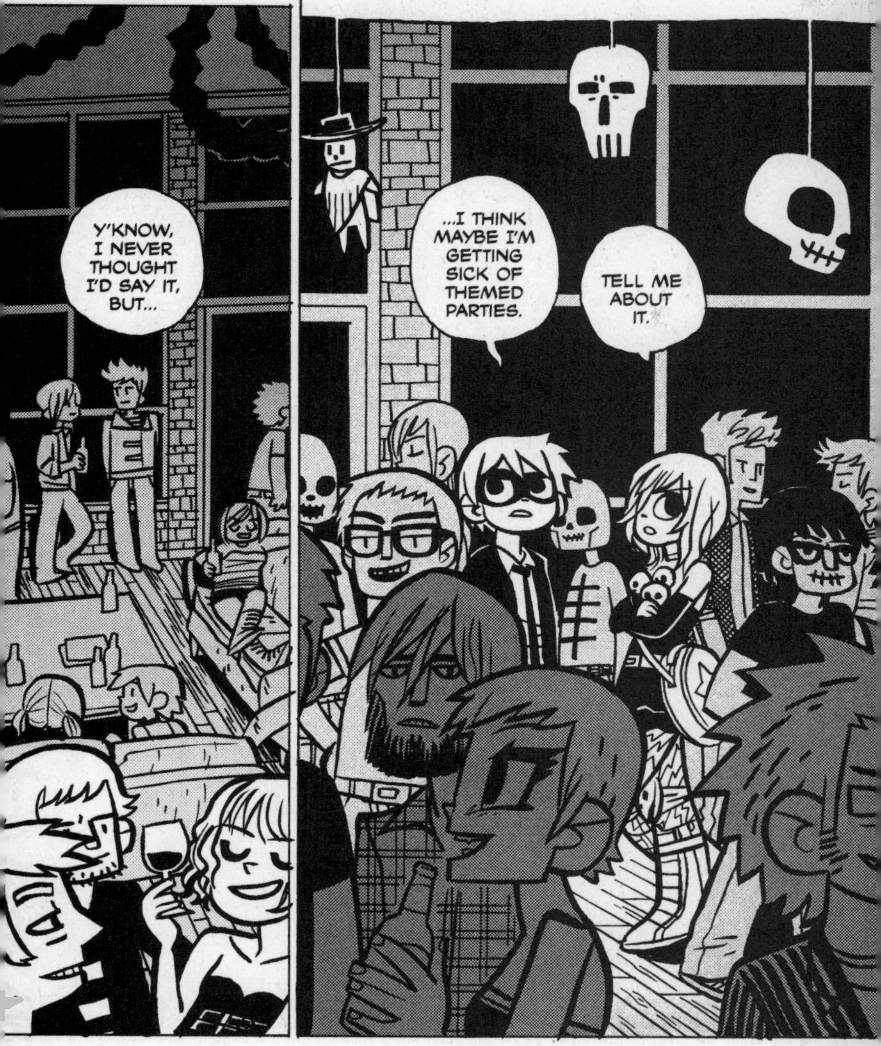
Y'KNOW, I NEVER THOUGHT I'D SAY IT, BUT...
...I THINK MAYBE I'M GETTING SICK OF THEMED PARTIES.
TELL ME ABOUT IT.

ONI PRESS, INC.
1305 SE Martin Luther King Jr. Blvd.
Suite A
Portland, OR 97214
USA

rst edition: February 2009
3N 978-1-934964-10-1

10 9 8 7
PRINTED IN THE U.S.A.

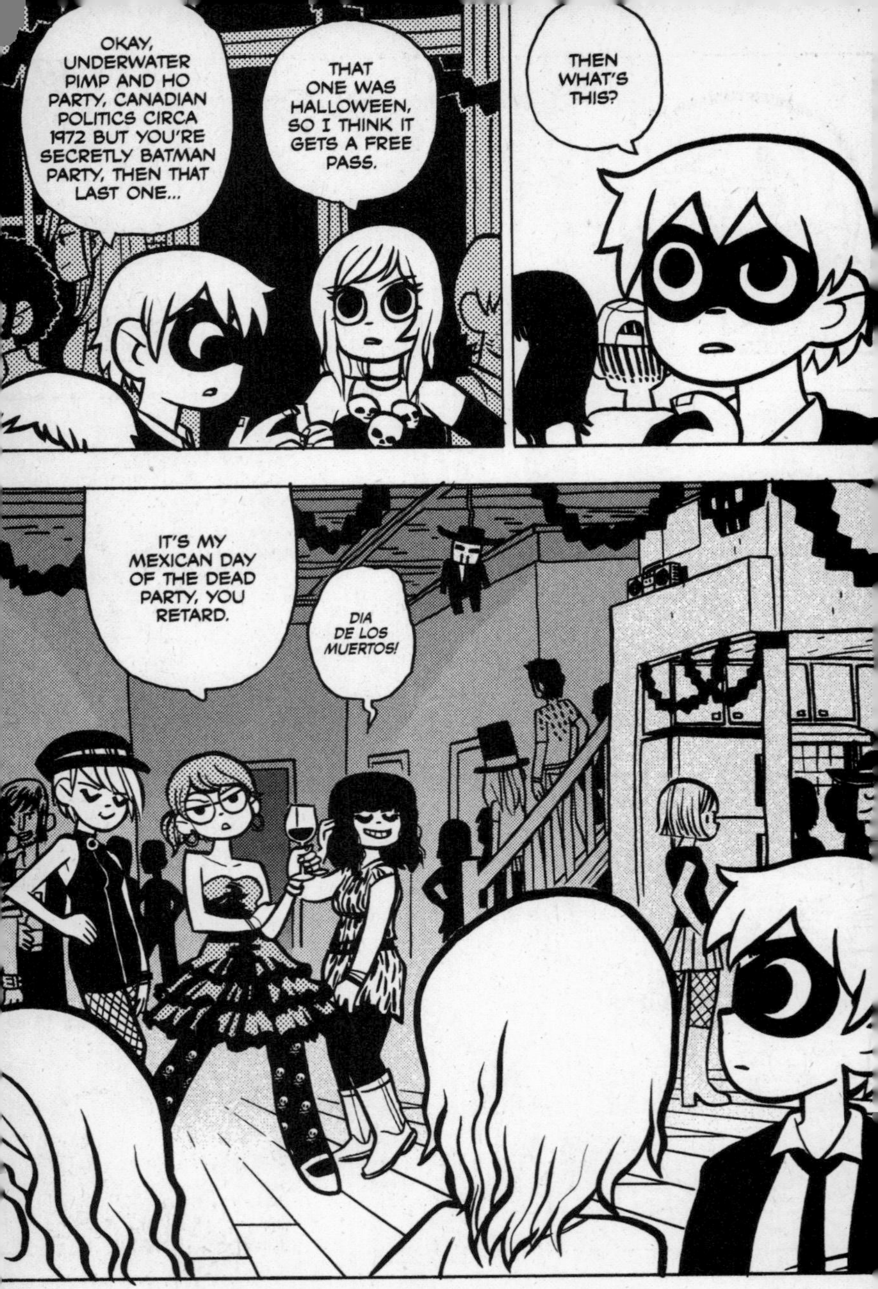
OKAY, UNDERWATER PIMP AND HO PARTY, CANADIAN POLITICS CIRCA 1972 BUT YOU'RE SECRETLY BATMAN PARTY, THEN THAT LAST ONE...
THAT ONE WAS HALLOWEEN, SO I THINK IT GETS A FREE PASS.
THEN WHAT'S THIS?
IT'S MY MEXICAN DAY OF THE DEAD PARTY, YOU RETARD.
DIA DE LOS MUERTOS!

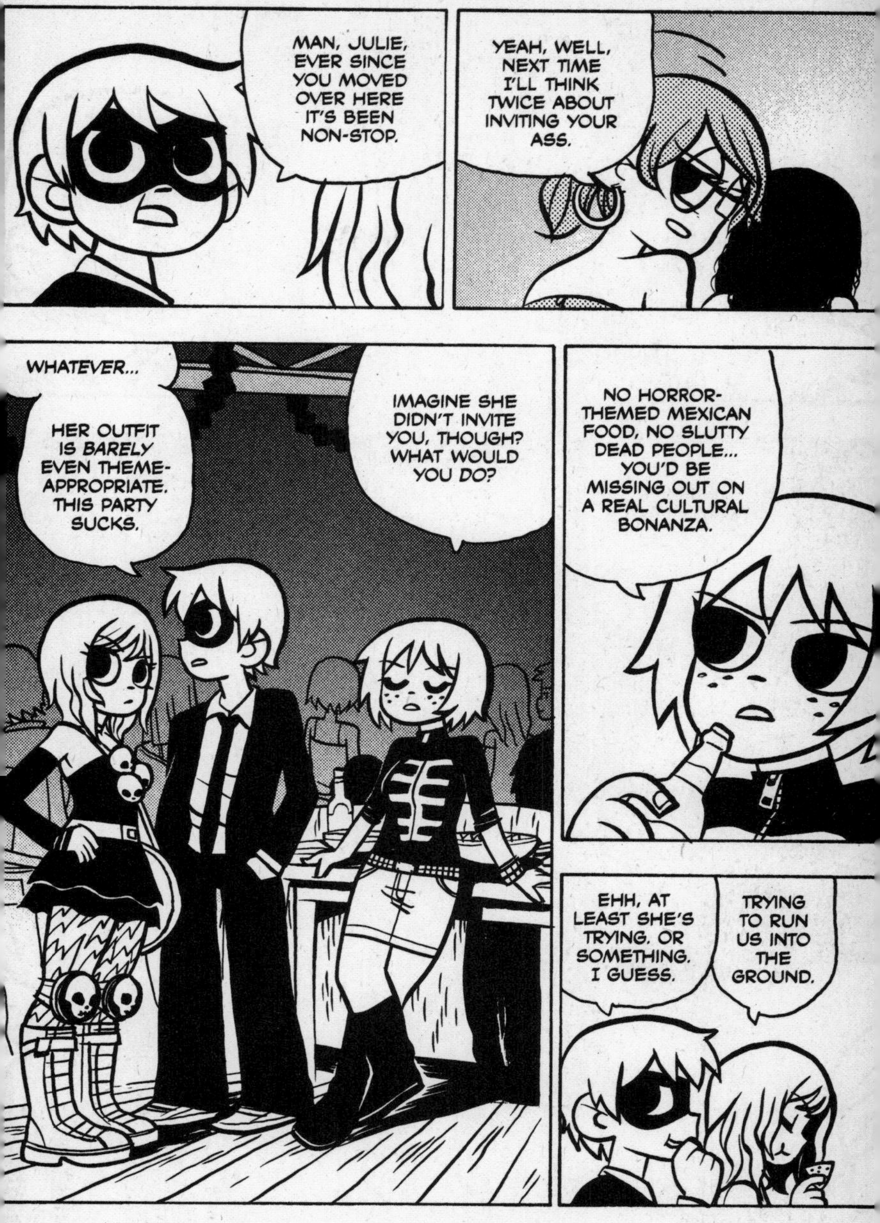
MAN, JULIE, EVER SINCE YOU MOVED OVER HERE IT'S BEEN NON-STOP.
YEAH, WELL, NEXT TIME I'LL THINK TWICE ABOUT INVITING YOUR ASS.
WHATEVER...
HER OUTFIT IS BARELY EVEN THEME-APPROPRIATE. THIS PARTY SUCKS.
IMAGINE SHE DIDN'T INVITE YOU, THOUGH? WHAT WOULD YOU DO?
NO HORROR-THEMED MEXICAN FOOD, NO SLUTTY DEAD PEOPLE... YOU'D BE MISSING OUT ON A REAL CULTURAL BONANZA.
EHH, AT LEAST SHE'S TRYING. OR SOMETHING. I GUESS.
TRYING TO RUN US INTO THE GROUND.

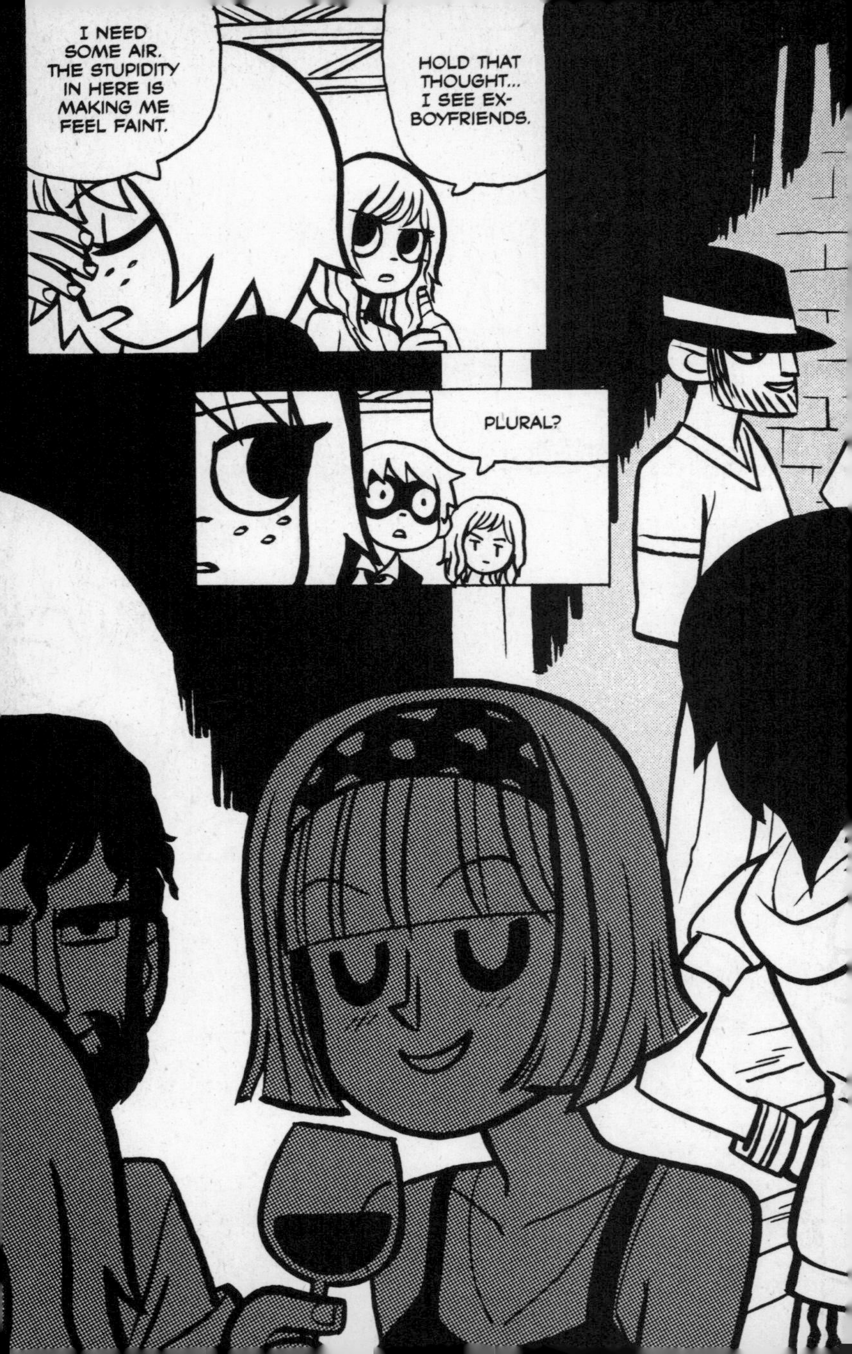
I NEED SOME AIR. THE STUPIDITY IN HERE IS MAKING ME FEEL FAINT.
HOLD THAT THOUGHT... I SEE EX-BOYFRIENDS.
PLURAL?

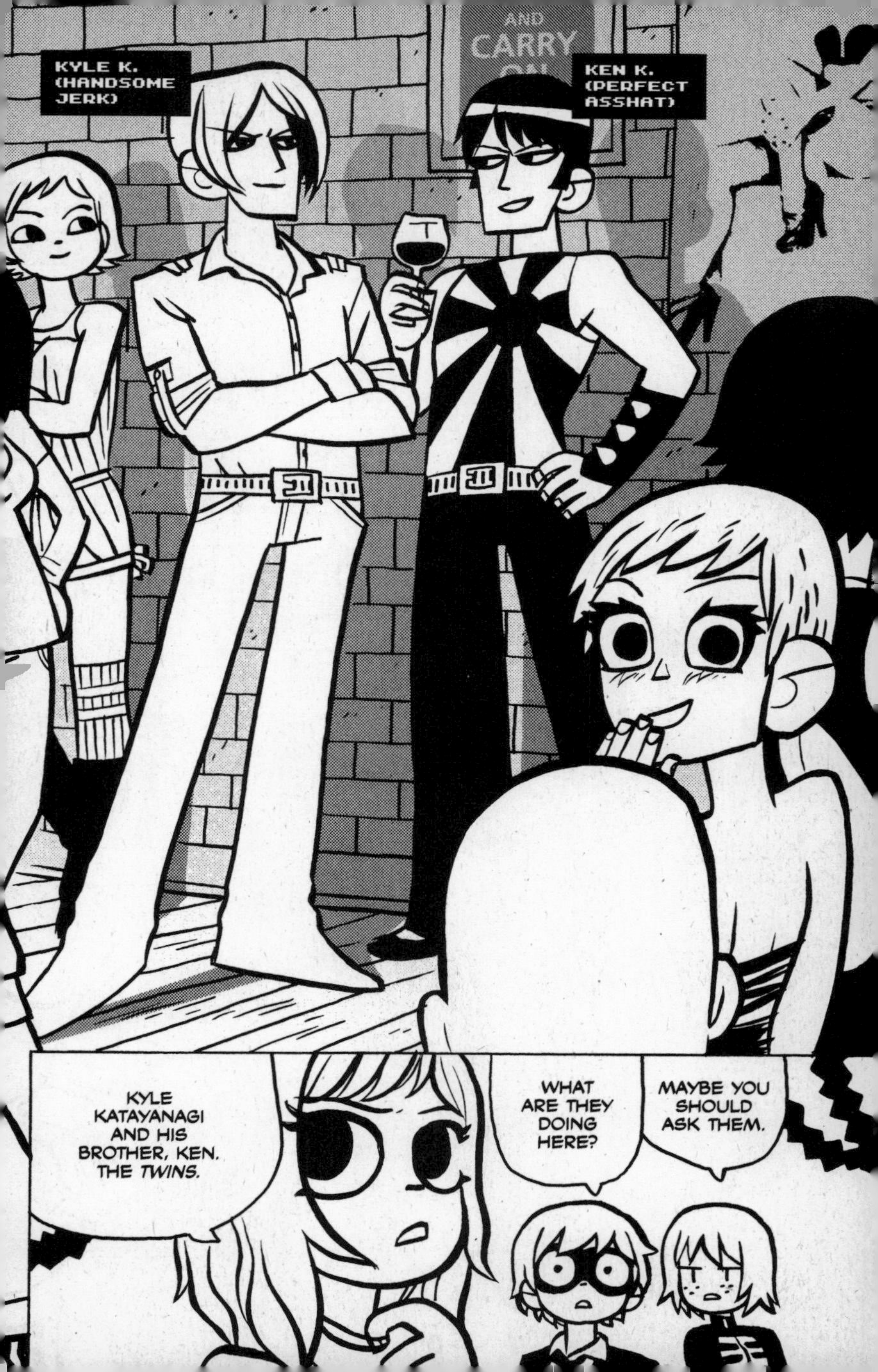
AND
CARRY
KYLE K. (HANDSOME JERK)
KEN K. (PERFECT ASSHAT)
KYLE KATAYANAGI AND HIS BROTHER, KEN. THE *TWINS.*
WHAT ARE THEY DOING HERE?
MAYBE YOU SHOULD ASK THEM.

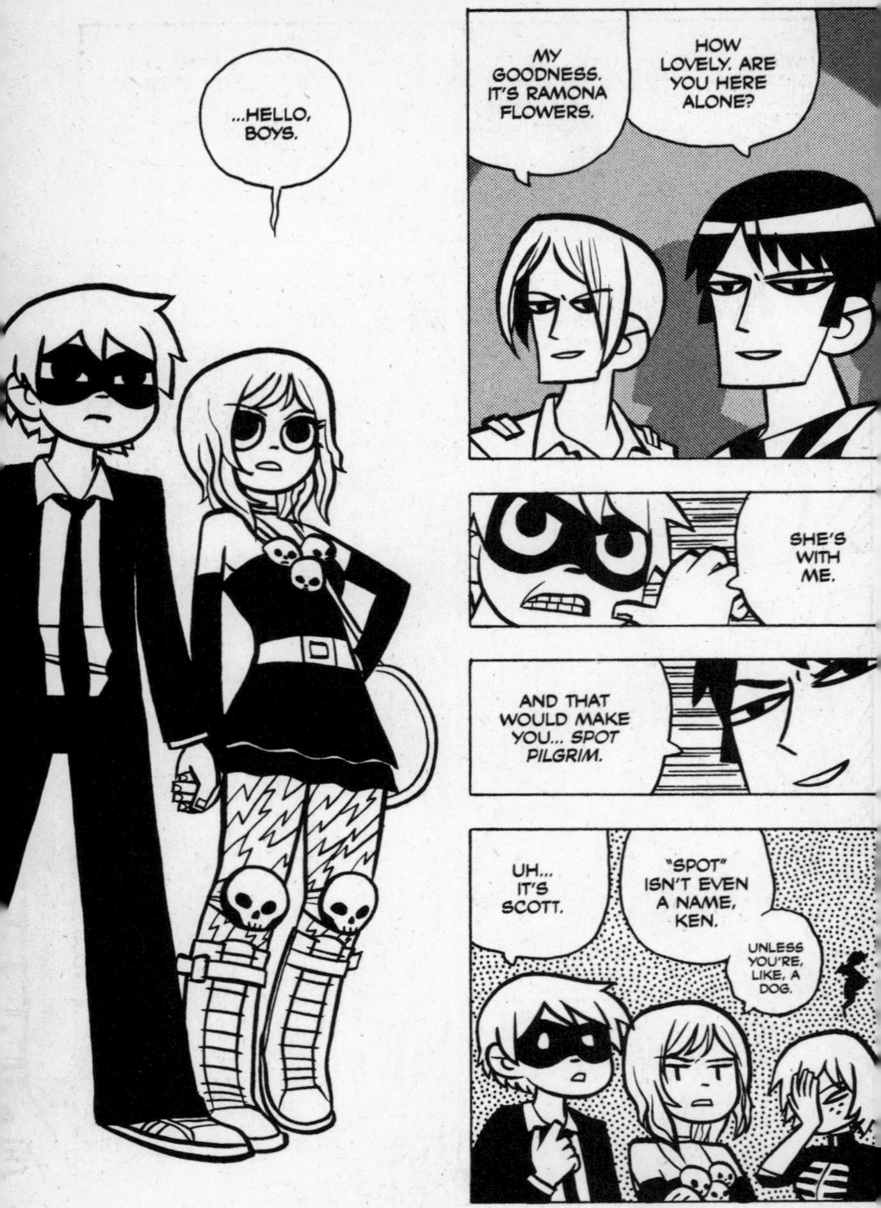
...HELLO, BOYS.
MY GOODNESS. IT'S RAMONA FLOWERS.
HOW LOVELY. ARE YOU HERE ALONE?
SHE'S WITH ME.
AND THAT WOULD MAKE YOU... *SPOT PILGRIM.*
UH... IT'S SCOTT.
"SPOT" ISN'T EVEN A NAME, KEN.
UNLESS YOU'RE, LIKE, A DOG.

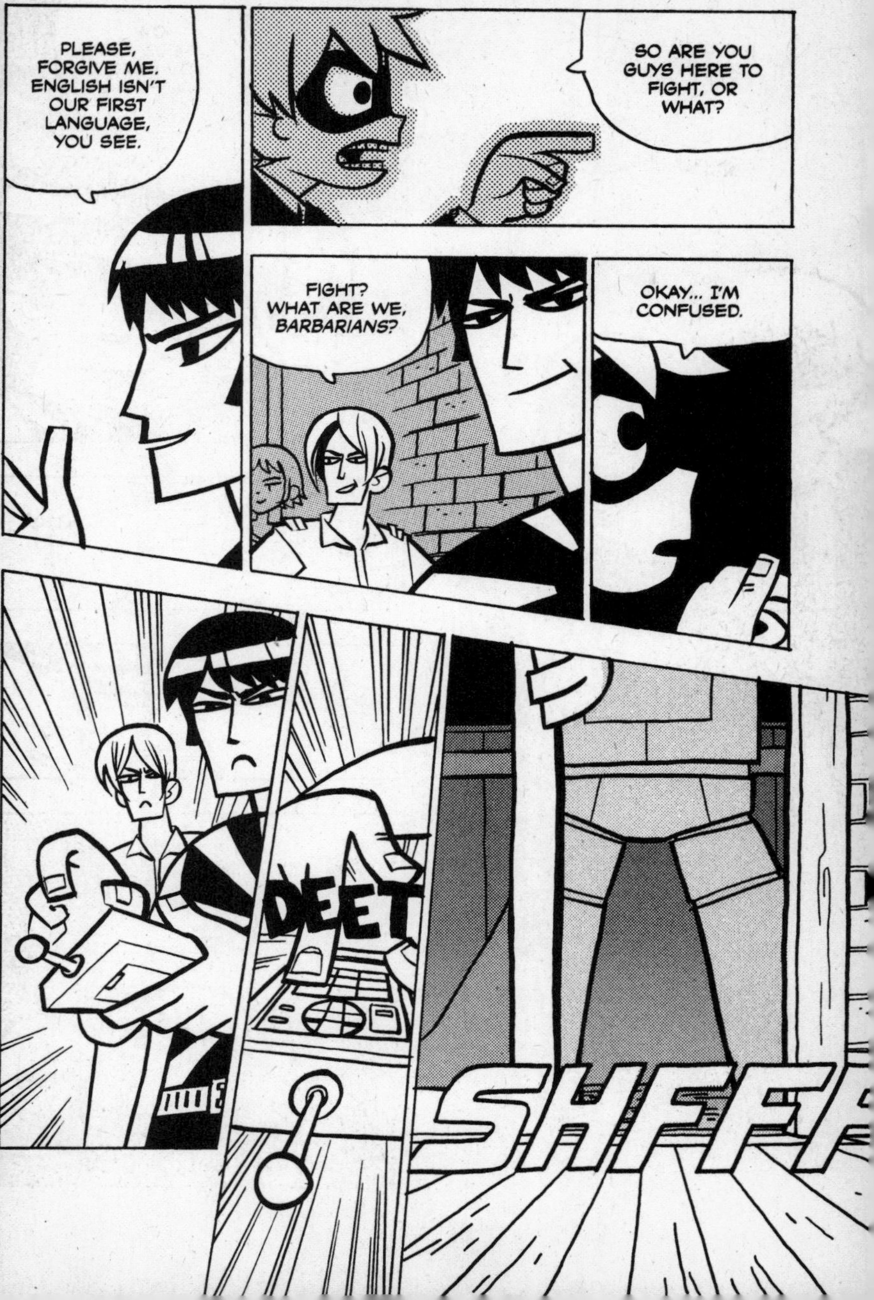
PLEASE, FORGIVE ME. ENGLISH ISN'T OUR FIRST LANGUAGE, YOU SEE.
SO ARE YOU GUYS HERE TO FIGHT, OR WHAT?
FIGHT? WHAT ARE WE, BARBARIANS?
OKAY... I'M CONFUSED.
DEET
SHFFF

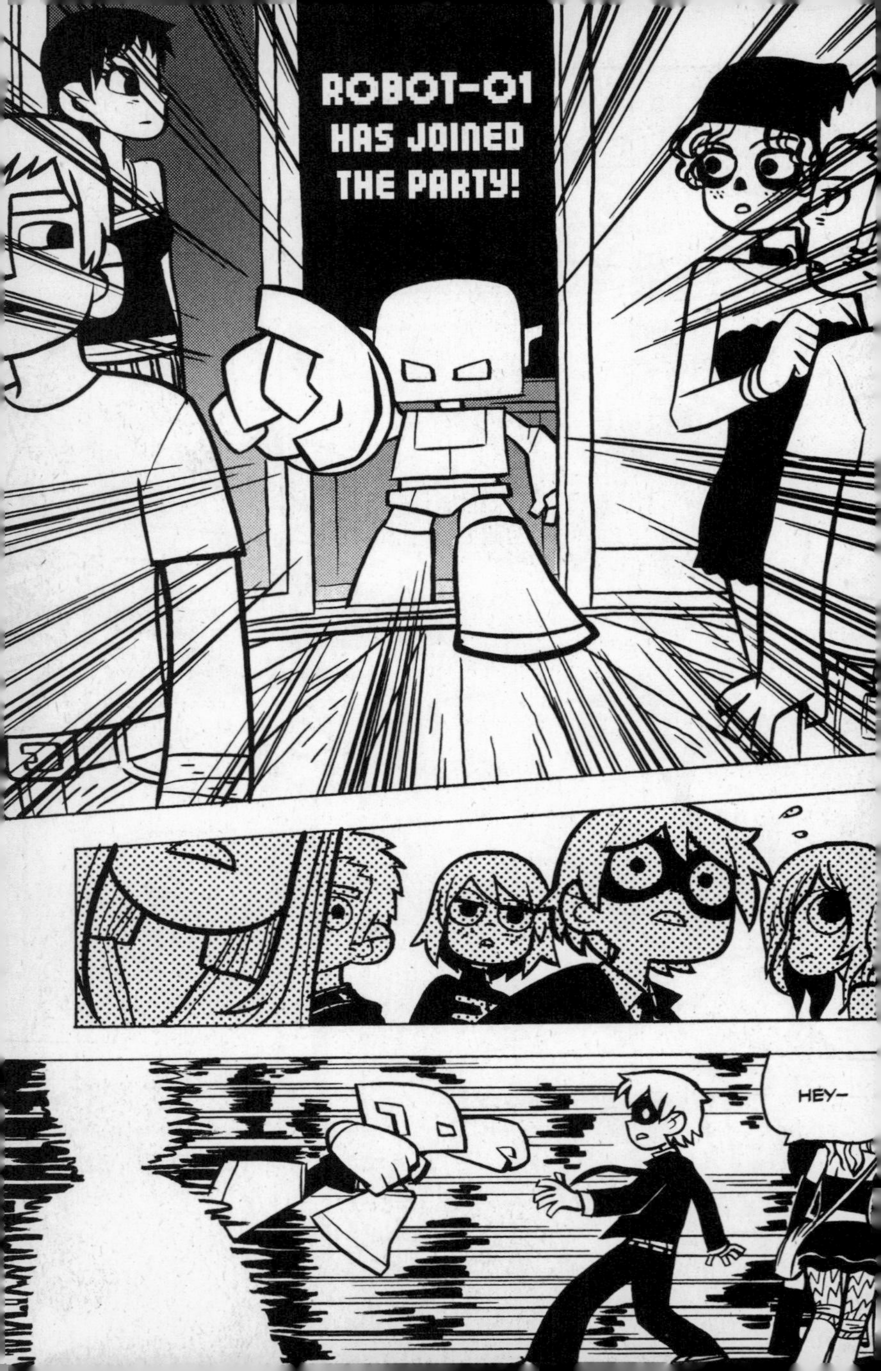
ROBOT-01 HAS JOINED THE PARTY!
HEY–

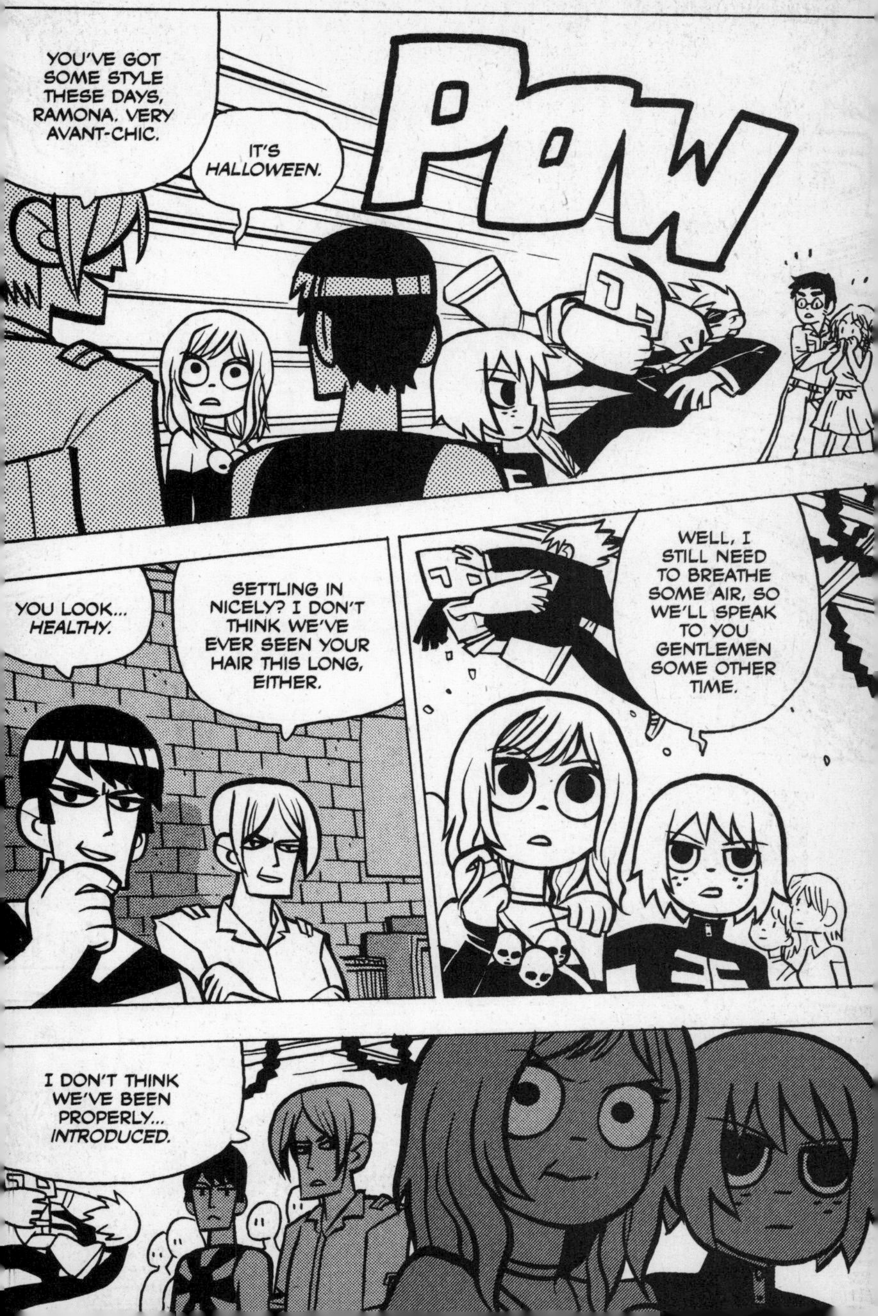
YOU'VE GOT SOME STYLE THESE DAYS, RAMONA. VERY AVANT-CHIC.
IT'S HALLOWEEN.
POW
YOU LOOK... *HEALTHY.*
SETTLING IN NICELY? I DON'T THINK WE'VE EVER SEEN YOUR HAIR THIS LONG, EITHER.
WELL, I STILL NEED TO BREATHE SOME AIR, SO WE'LL SPEAK TO YOU GENTLEMEN SOME OTHER TIME.
I DON'T THINK WE'VE BEEN PROPERLY... *INTRODUCED.*

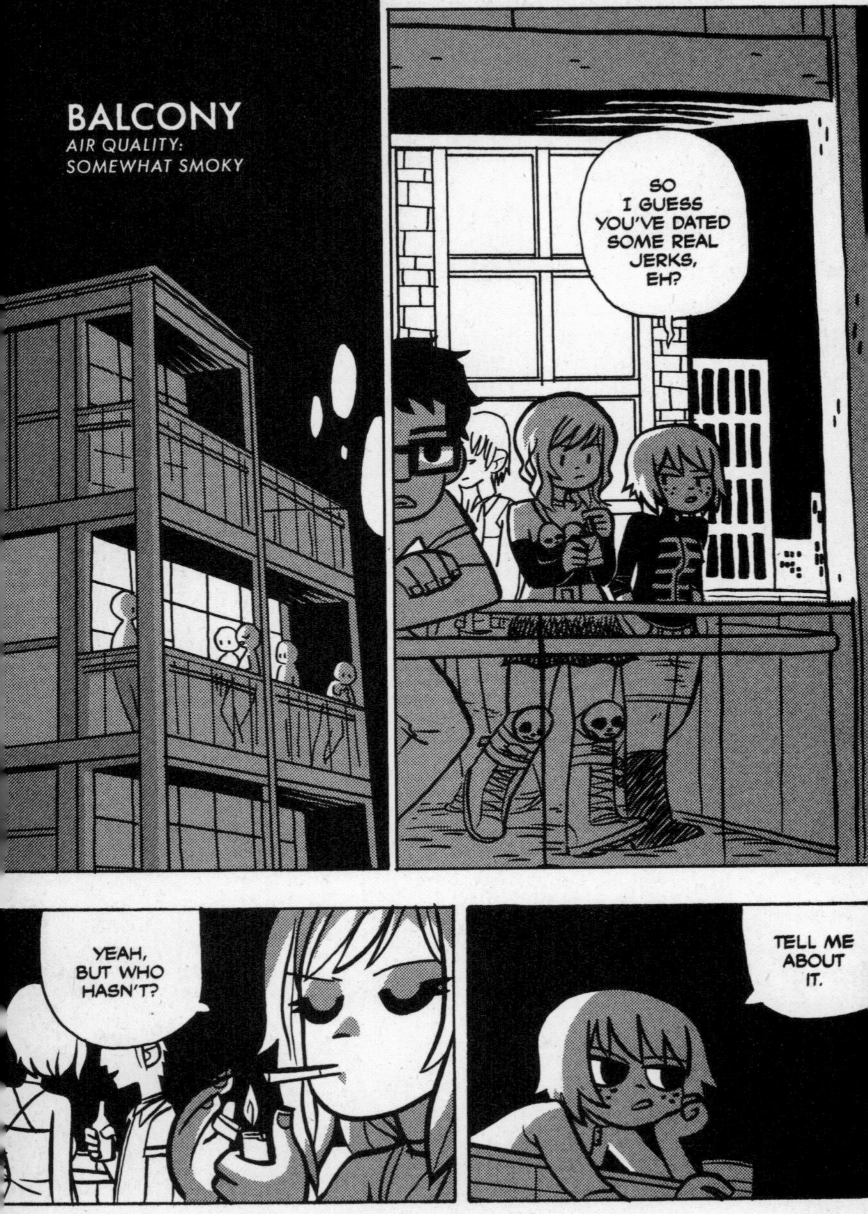
BALCONY
AIR QUALITY: SOMEWHAT SMOKY
SO I GUESS YOU'VE DATED SOME REAL JERKS, EH?
YEAH, BUT WHO HASN'T?
TELL ME ABOUT IT.

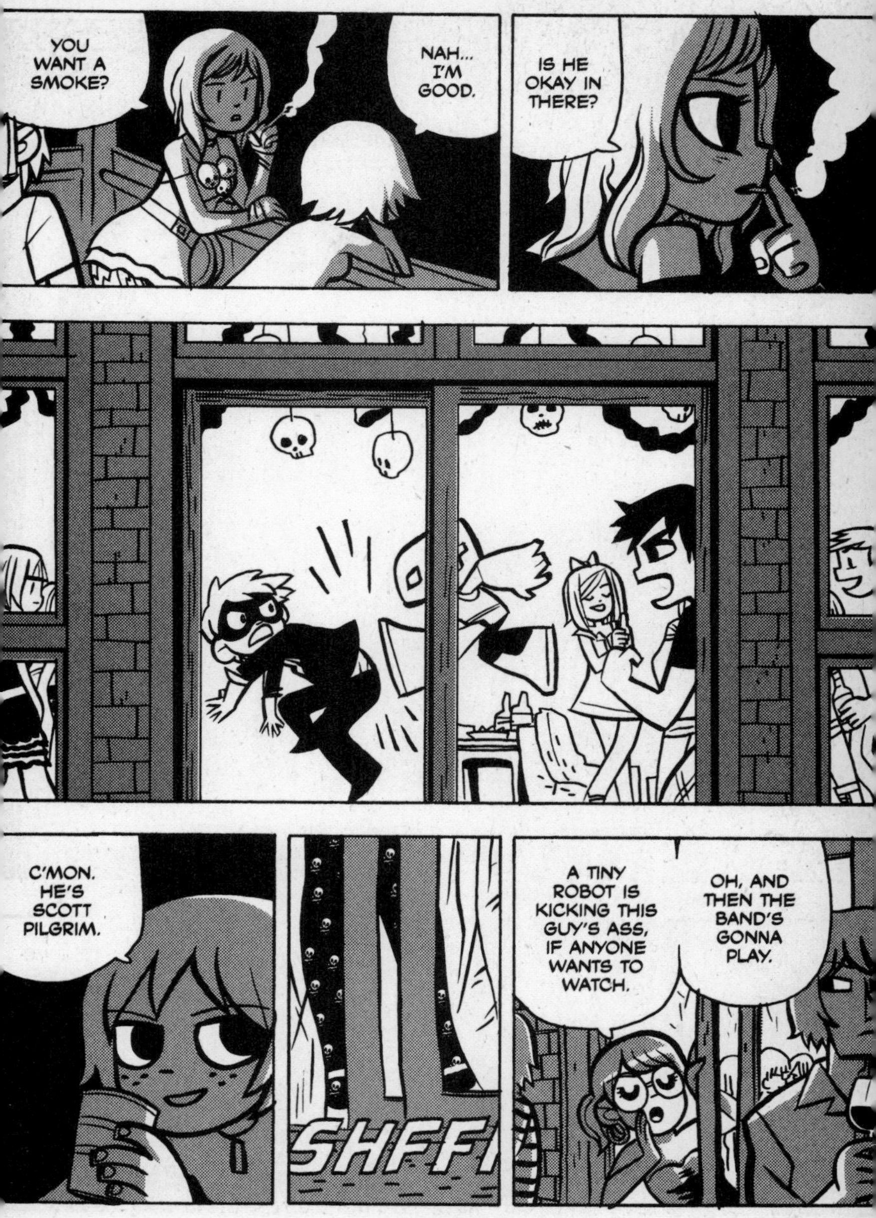
YOU WANT A SMOKE?
NAH... I'M GOOD.
IS HE OKAY IN THERE?
C'MON. HE'S SCOTT PILGRIM.
SHFFI
A TINY ROBOT IS KICKING THIS GUY'S ASS, IF ANYONE WANTS TO WATCH.
OH, AND THEN THE BAND'S GONNA PLAY.

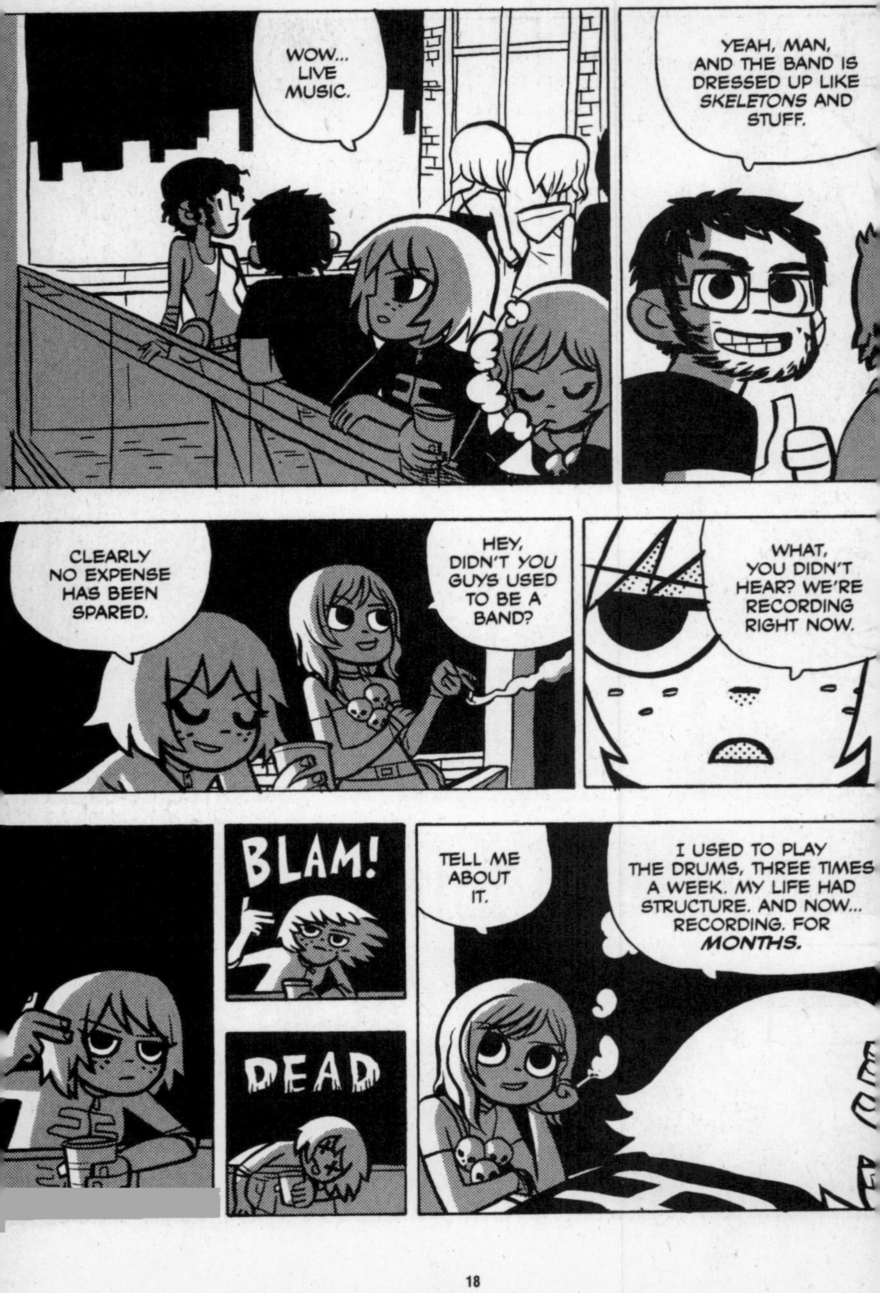
WOW... LIVE MUSIC.
YEAH, MAN, AND THE BAND IS DRESSED UP LIKE SKELETONS AND STUFF.
CLEARLY NO EXPENSE HAS BEEN SPARED.
HEY, DIDN'T YOU GUYS USED TO BE A BAND?
WHAT, YOU DIDN'T HEAR? WE'RE RECORDING RIGHT NOW.
BLAM!
DEAD
TELL ME ABOUT IT.
I USED TO PLAY THE DRUMS, THREE TIMES A WEEK. MY LIFE HAD STRUCTURE. AND NOW... RECORDING. FOR MONTHS.

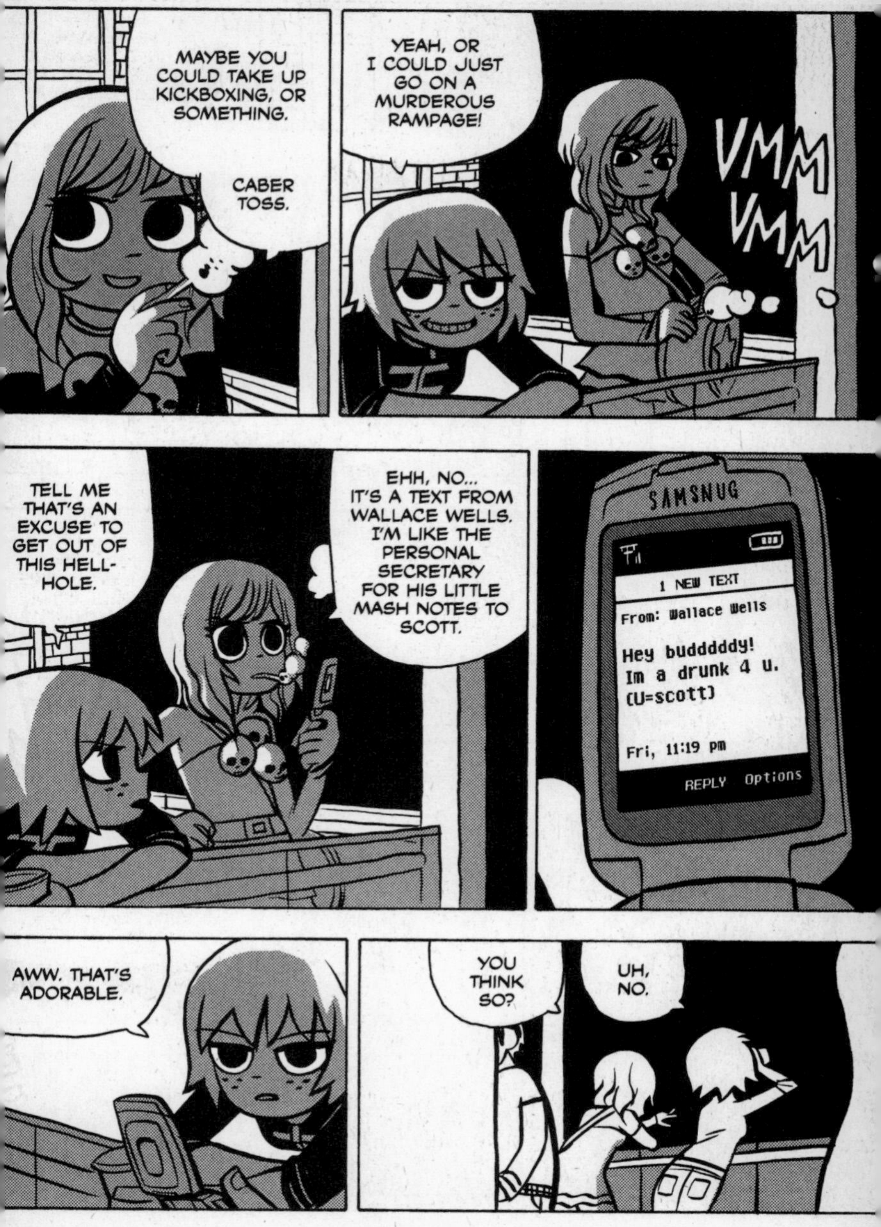
MAYBE YOU COULD TAKE UP KICKBOXING, OR SOMETHING.
CABER TOSS.
YEAH, OR I COULD JUST GO ON A MURDEROUS RAMPAGE!
VMM VMM
TELL ME THAT'S AN EXCUSE TO GET OUT OF THIS HELL-HOLE.
EHH, NO... IT'S A TEXT FROM WALLACE WELLS. I'M LIKE THE PERSONAL SECRETARY FOR HIS LITTLE MASH NOTES TO SCOTT.
SAMSNUG
1 NEW TEXT
From: Wallace Wells
Hey budddddy!
Im a drunk 4 u.
(U=scott)
Fri, 11:19 pm
REPLY
Options
AWW. THAT'S ADORABLE.
YOU THINK SO?
UH, NO.

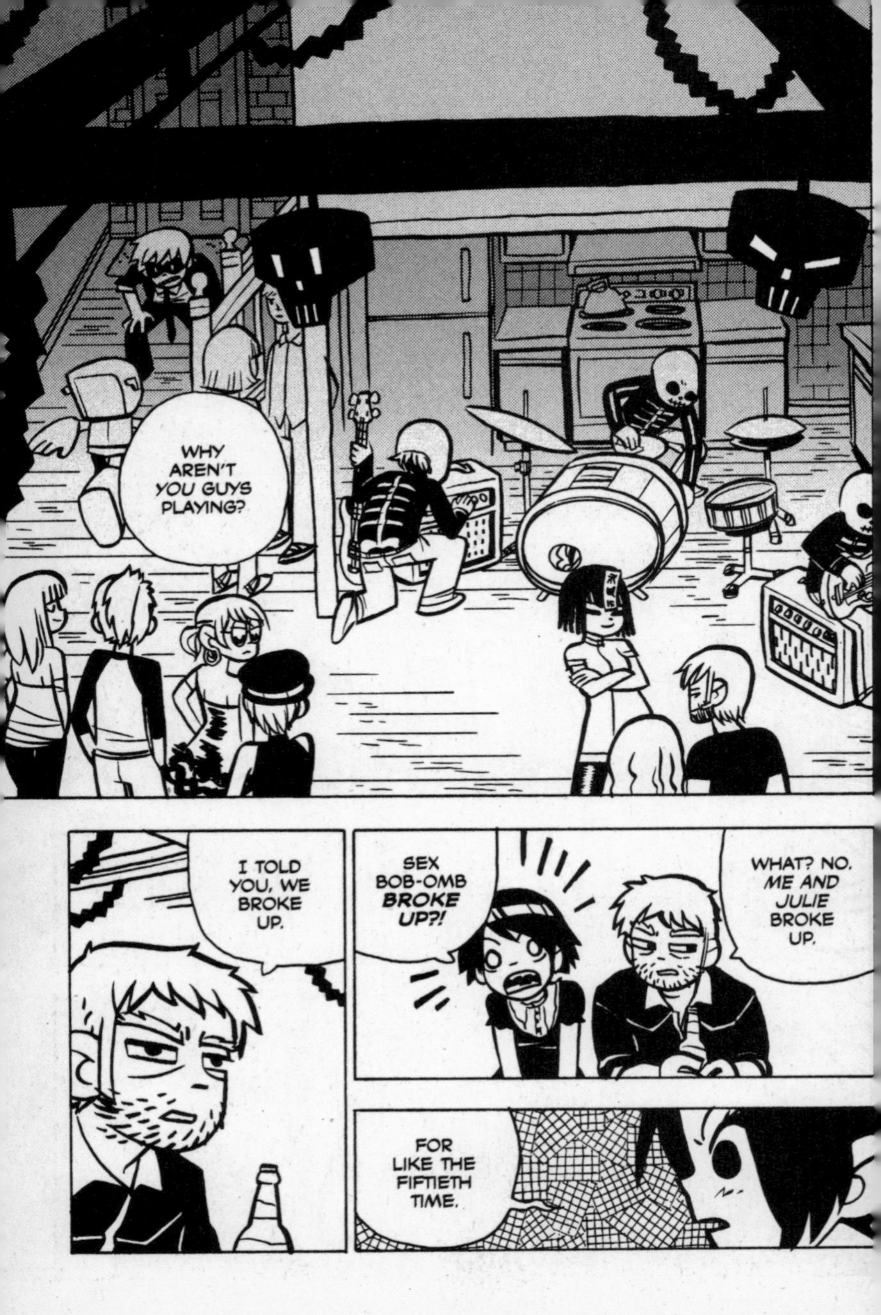
WHY AREN'T YOU GUYS PLAYING?
I TOLD YOU, WE BROKE UP.
SEX BOB-OMB BROKE UP?!
WHAT? NO. ME AND JULIE BROKE UP.
FOR LIKE THE FIFTIETH TIME.

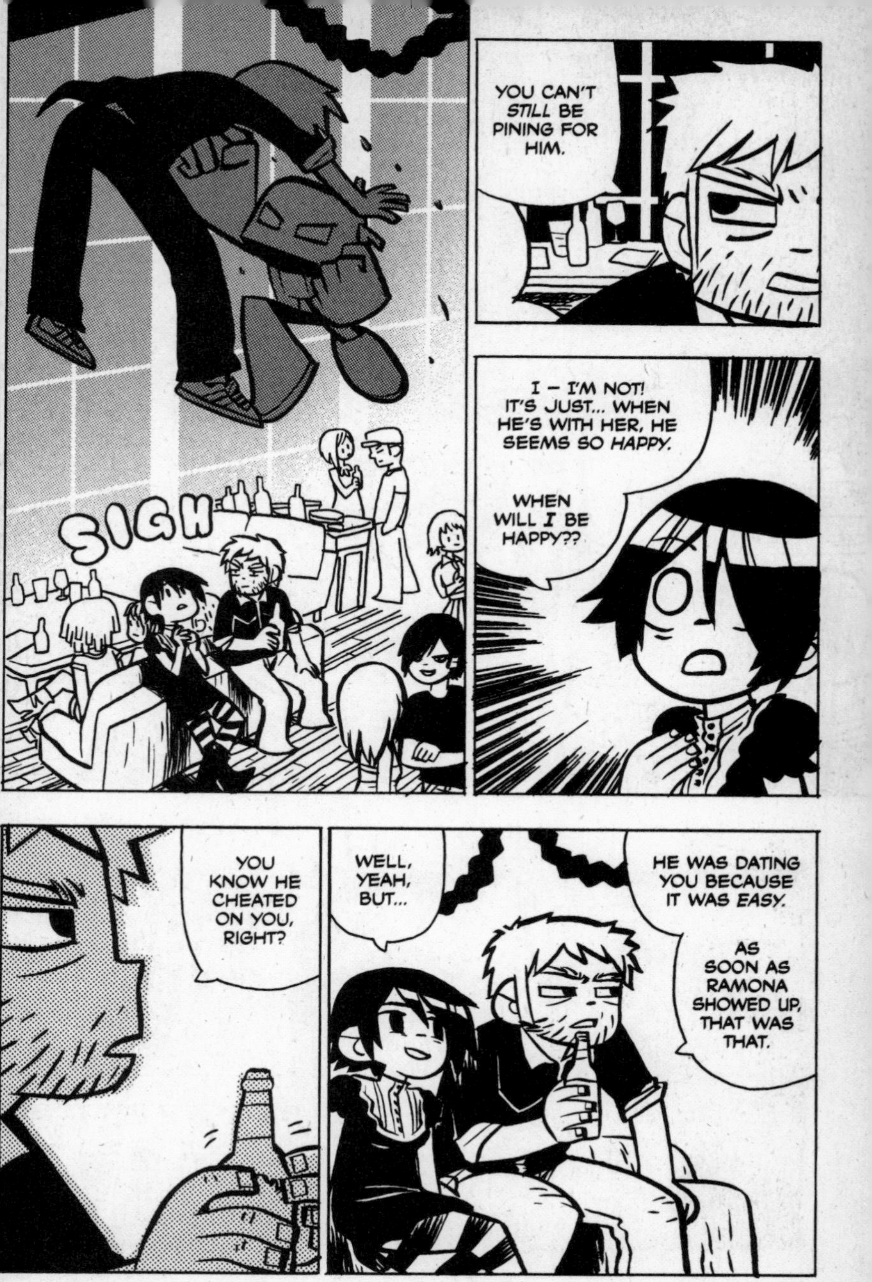
YOU CAN'T STILL BE PINING FOR HIM.
SIGH
I – I'M NOT! IT'S JUST... WHEN HE'S WITH HER, HE SEEMS SO HAPPY.
WHEN WILL I BE HAPPY??
YOU KNOW HE CHEATED ON YOU, RIGHT?
WELL, YEAH, BUT...
HE WAS DATING YOU BECAUSE IT WAS EASY.
AS SOON AS RAMONA SHOWED UP, THAT WAS THAT.

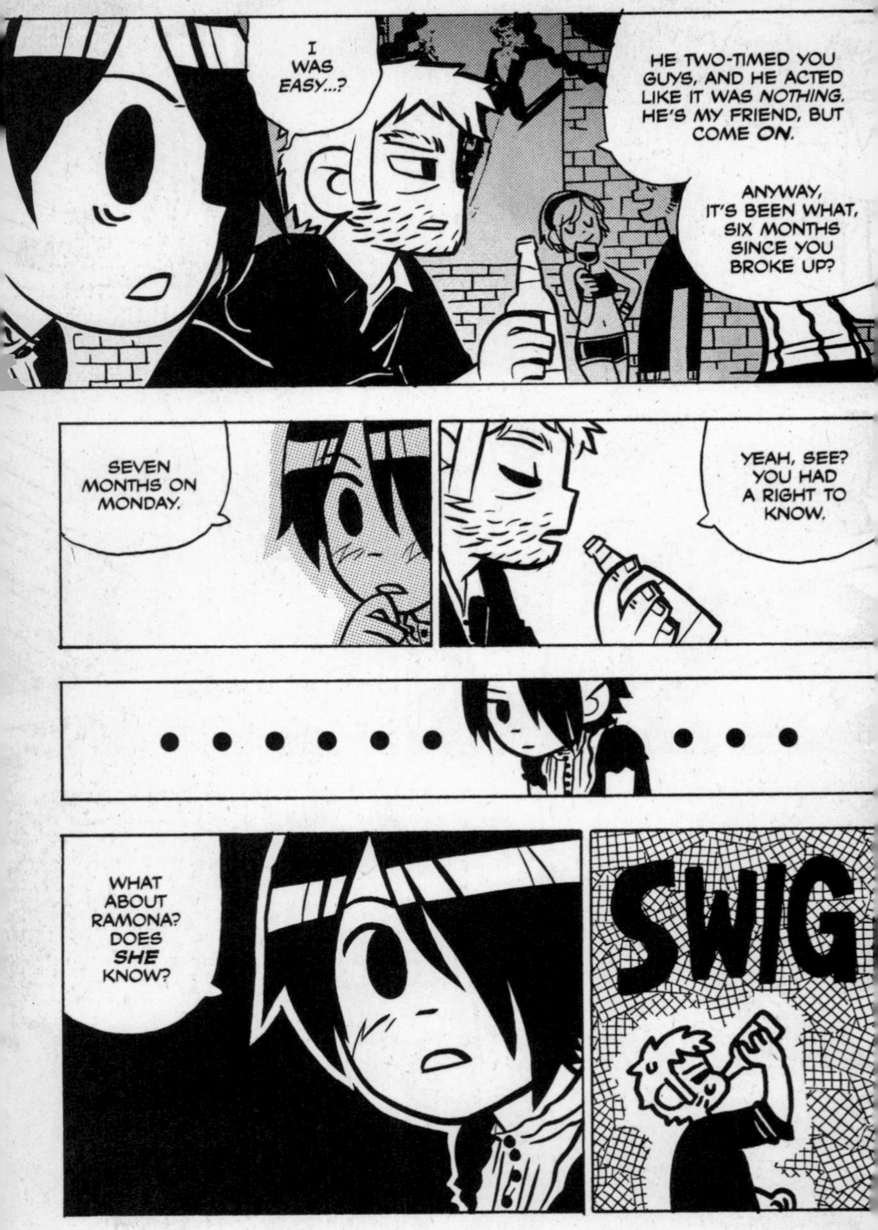
I WAS EASY...?
HE TWO-TIMED YOU GUYS, AND HE ACTED LIKE IT WAS NOTHING. HE'S MY FRIEND, BUT COME ON.
ANYWAY, IT'S BEEN WHAT, SIX MONTHS SINCE YOU BROKE UP?
SEVEN MONTHS ON MONDAY.
YEAH, SEE? YOU HAD A RIGHT TO KNOW.
WHAT ABOUT RAMONA? DOES SHE KNOW?
SWIG

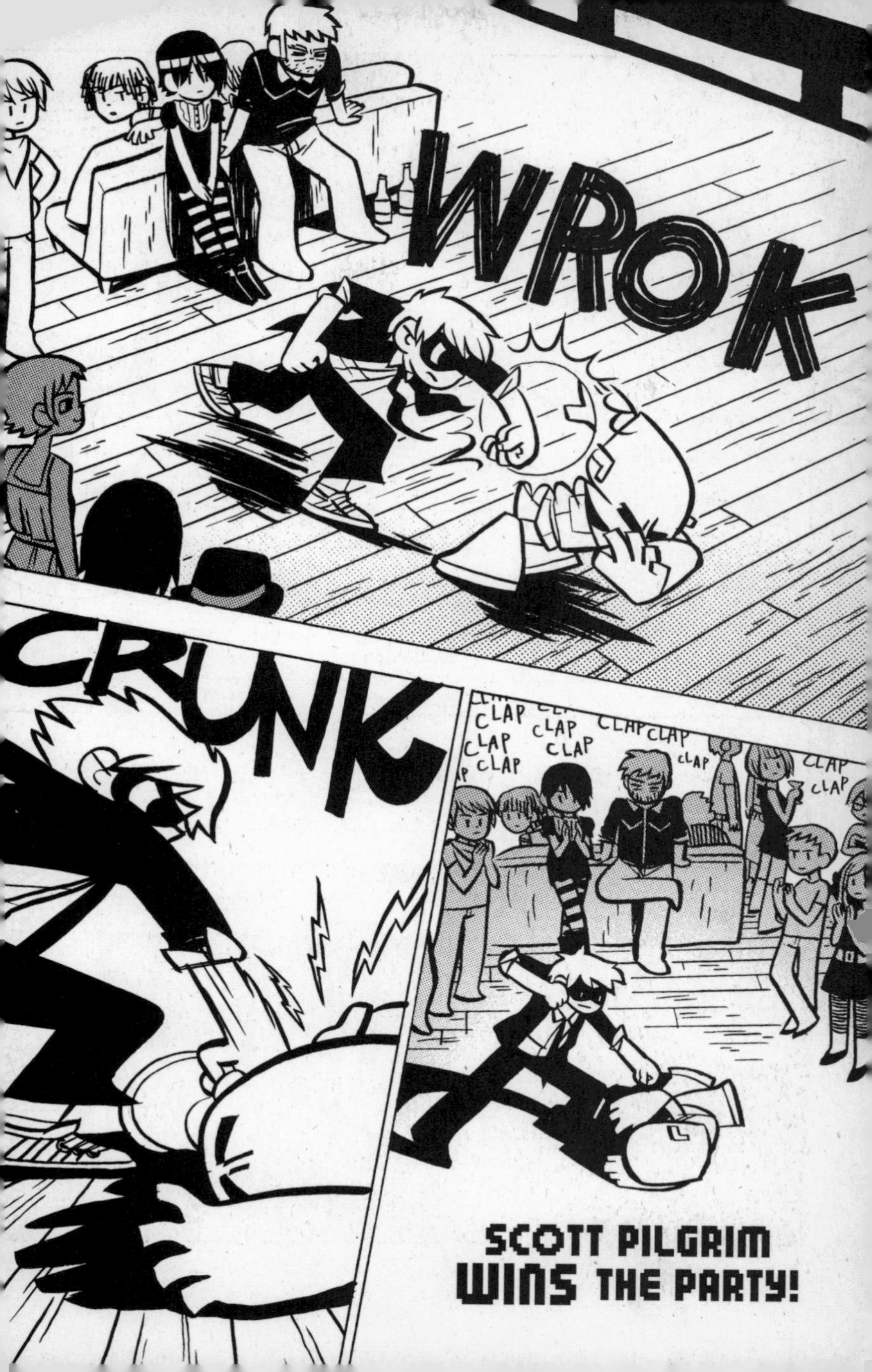
WROK
CRUNK
CLAP CLAP CLAP CLAP CLAP CLAP CLAP CLAP CLAP CLAP
SCOTT PILGRIM WINS THE PARTY!

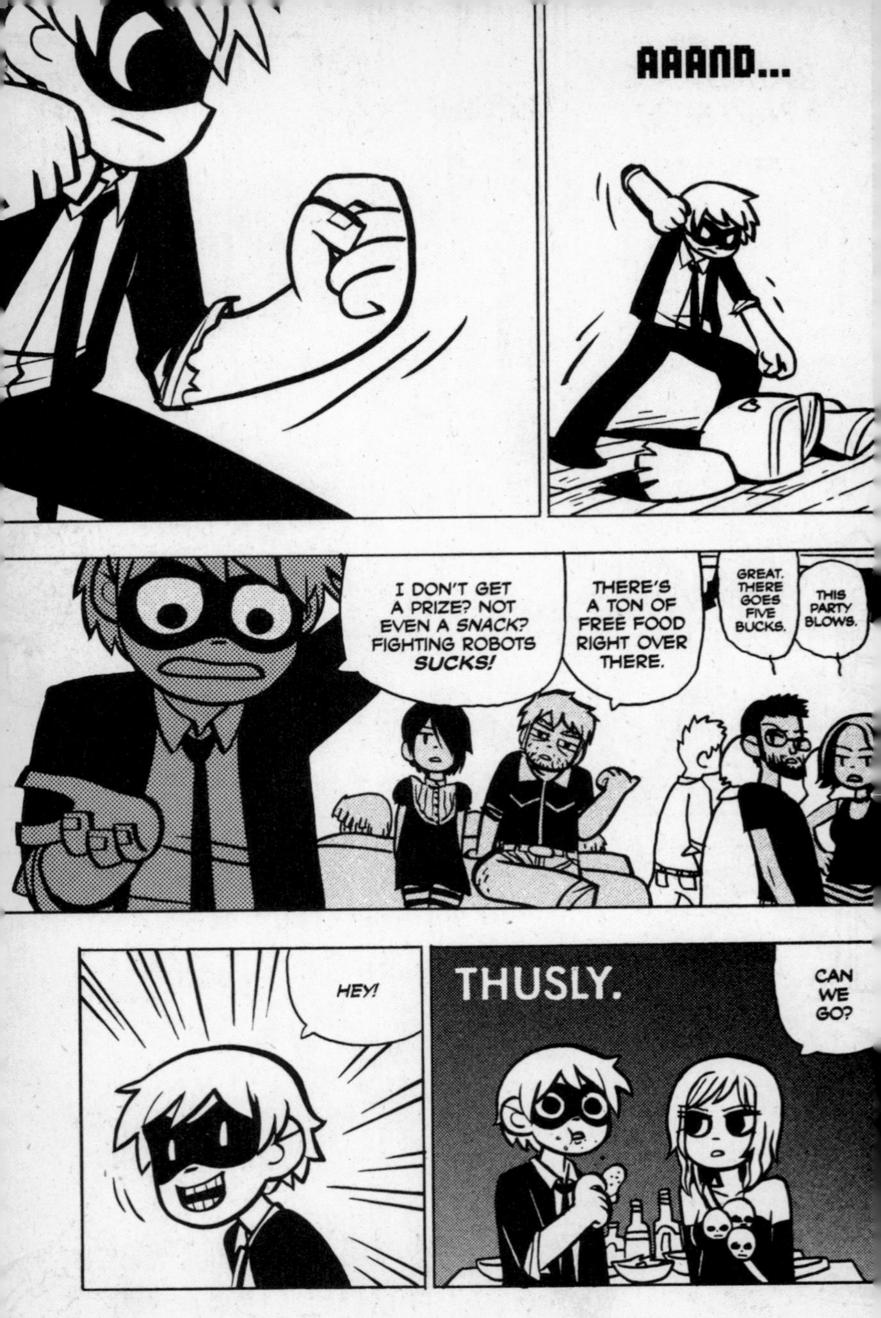
AAAND...
I DON'T GET A PRIZE? NOT EVEN A *SNACK*? FIGHTING ROBOTS *SUCKS!*
THERE'S A TON OF FREE FOOD RIGHT OVER THERE.
GREAT. THERE GOES FIVE BUCKS.
THIS PARTY BLOWS.
HEY!
THUSLY.
CAN WE GO?

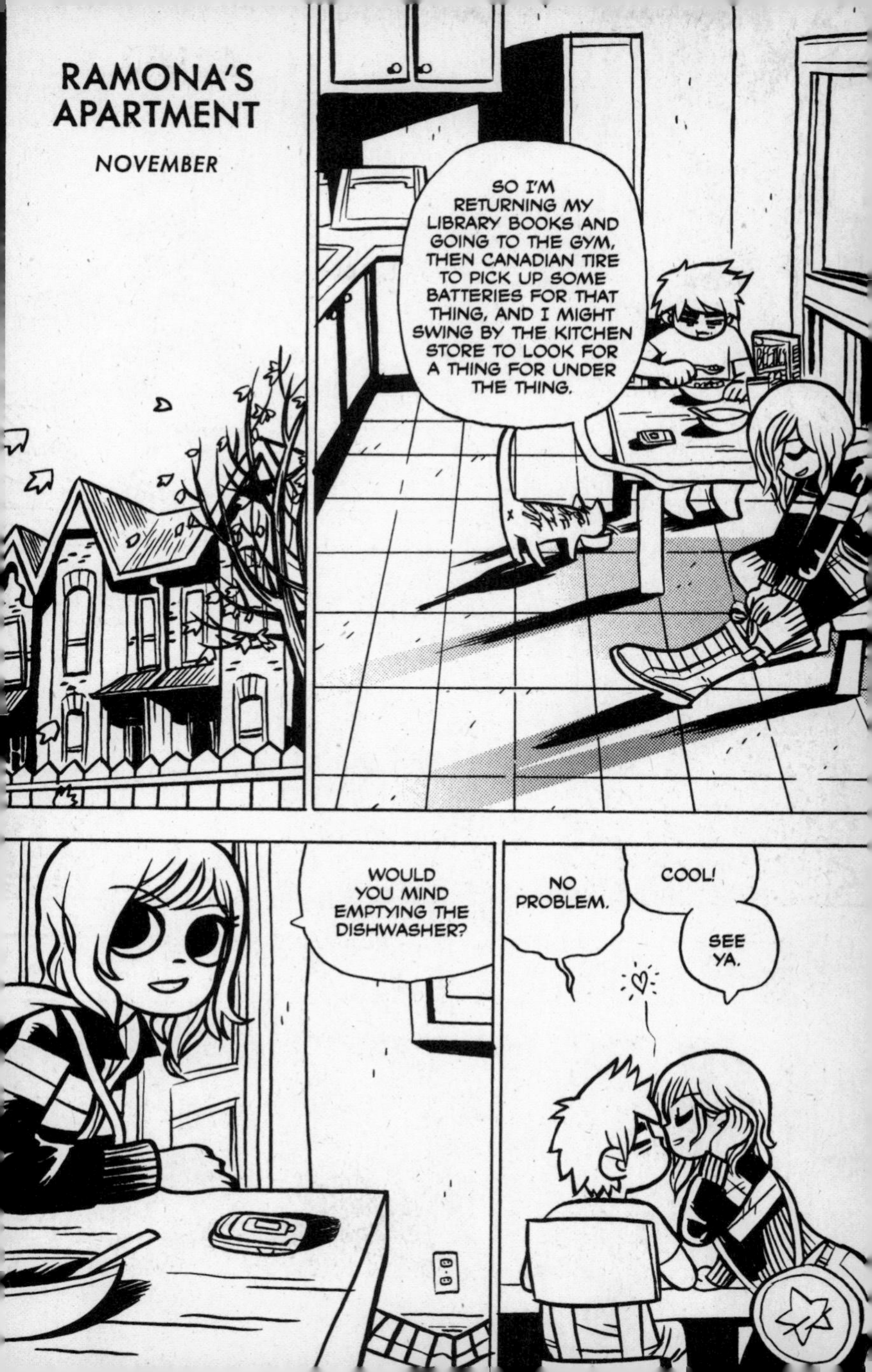
RAMONA'S APARTMENT
NOVEMBER
SO I'M RETURNING MY LIBRARY BOOKS AND GOING TO THE GYM, THEN CANADIAN TIRE TO PICK UP SOME BATTERIES FOR THAT THING, AND I MIGHT SWING BY THE KITCHEN STORE TO LOOK FOR A THING FOR UNDER THE THING.
WOULD YOU MIND EMPTYING THE DISHWASHER?
NO PROBLEM.
COOL!
SEE YA.

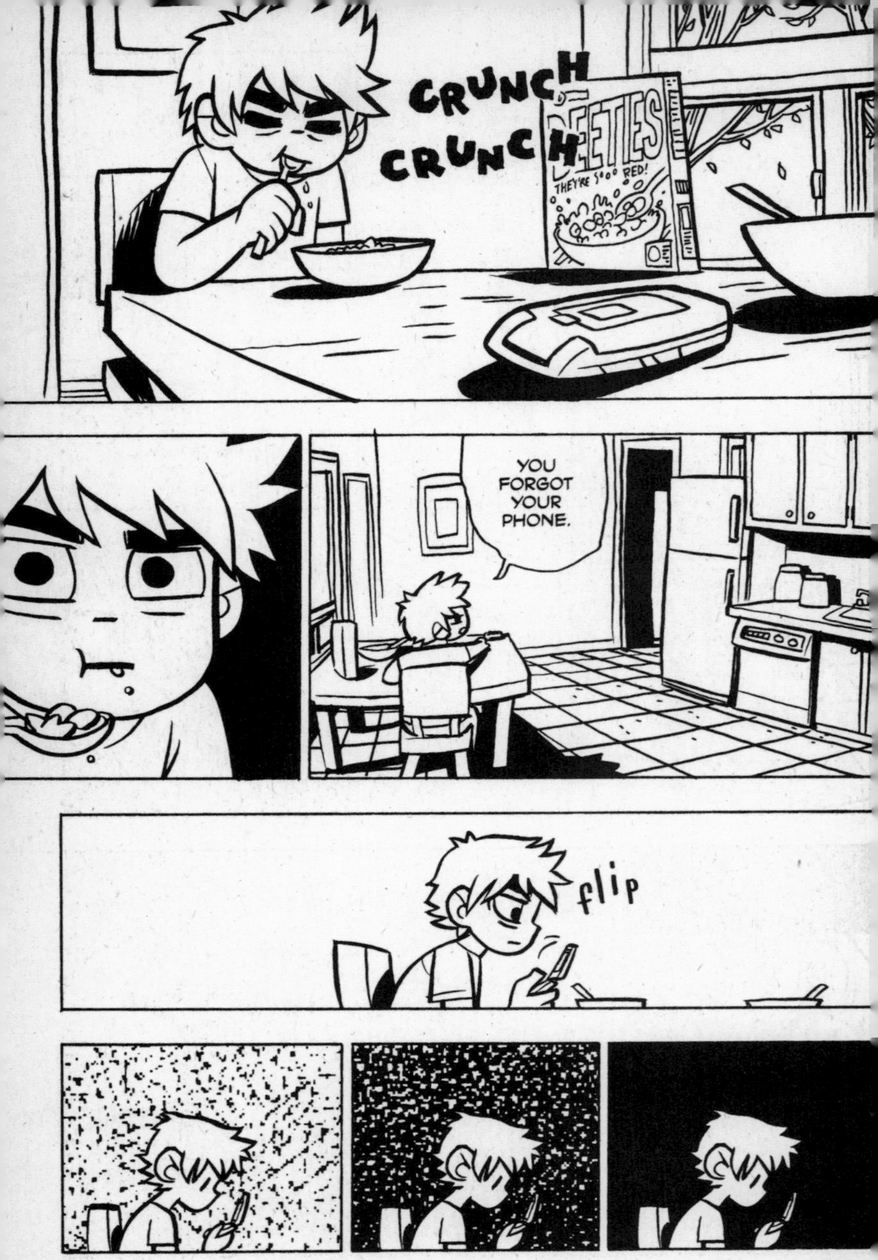
CRUNCH
CRUNCH
BEETIES
THEY'RE SOOO RED!
YOU FORGOT YOUR PHONE.
flip

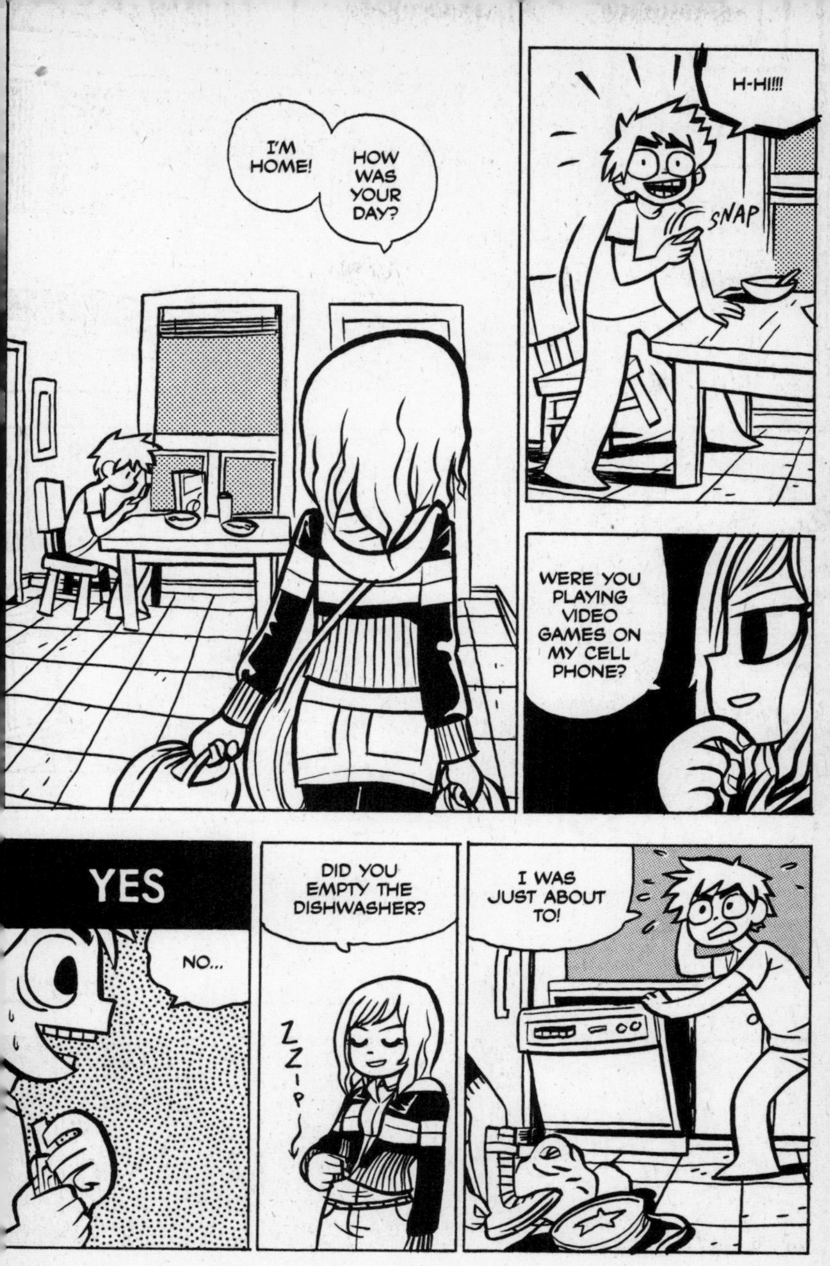
I'M HOME!
HOW WAS YOUR DAY?
H-HI!!!
SNAP
WERE YOU PLAYING VIDEO GAMES ON MY CELL PHONE?
YES
NO...
DID YOU EMPTY THE DISHWASHER?
ZZIP
I WAS JUST ABOUT TO!

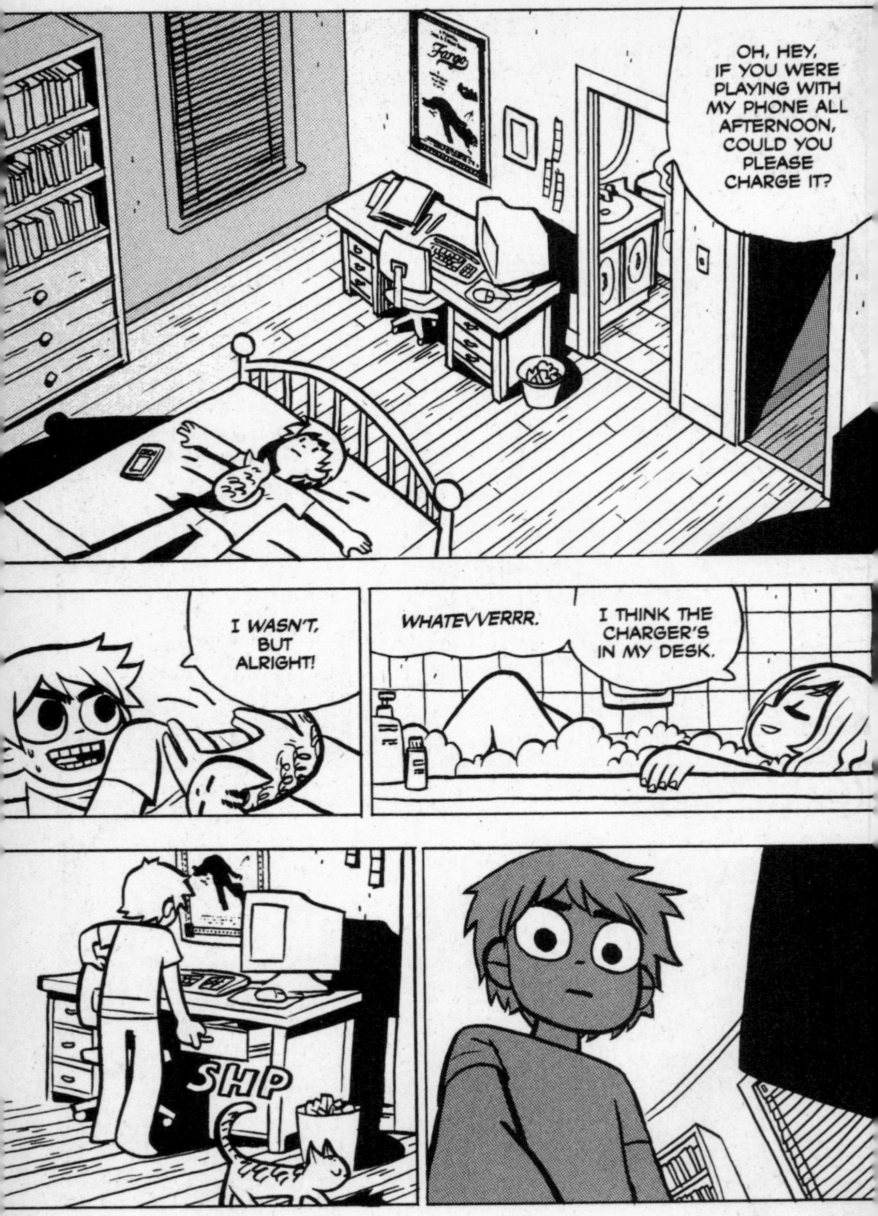
OH, HEY, IF YOU WERE PLAYING WITH MY PHONE ALL AFTERNOON, COULD YOU PLEASE CHARGE IT?
I *WASN'T*, BUT ALRIGHT!
WHATEVVERRR.
I THINK THE CHARGER'S IN MY DESK.
SHP

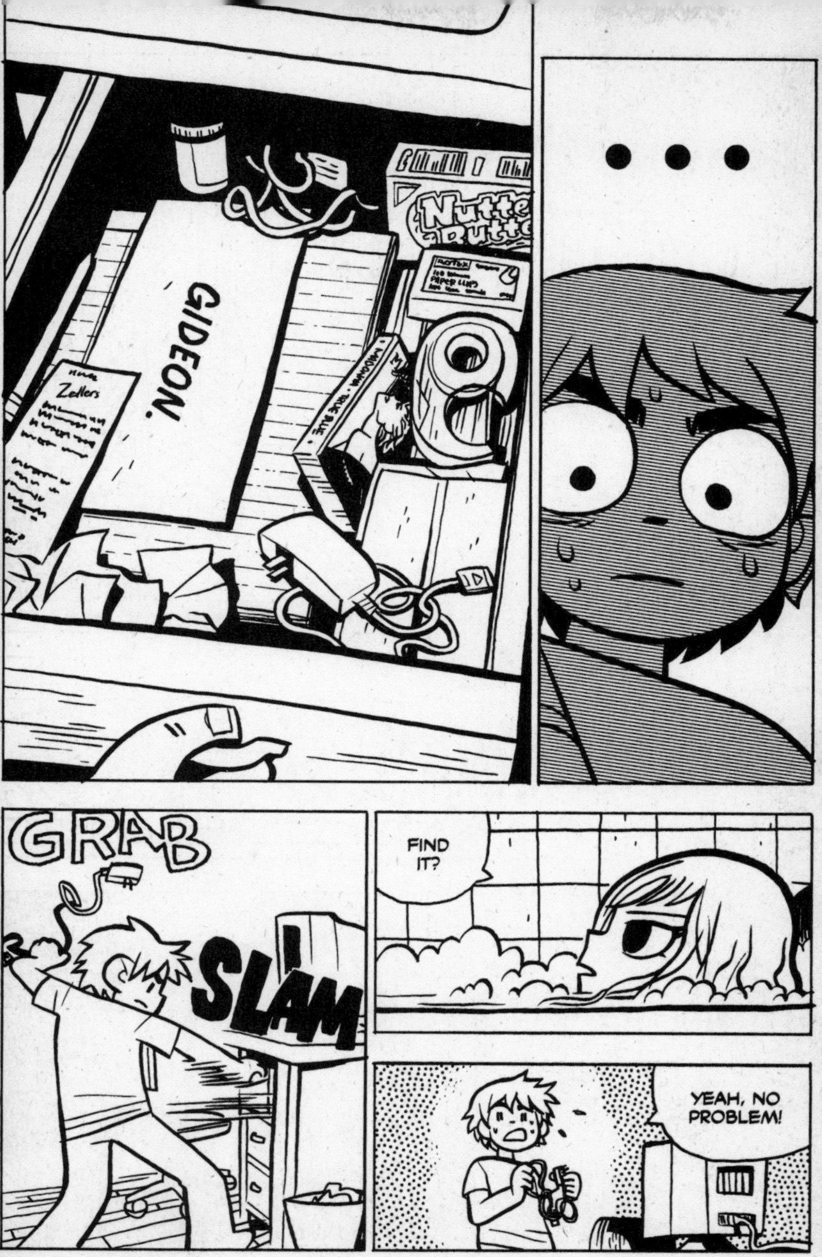

GIDEON.
Zellers
Nutter Butter
...
GRAB
SLAM
FIND IT?
YEAH, NO PROBLEM!

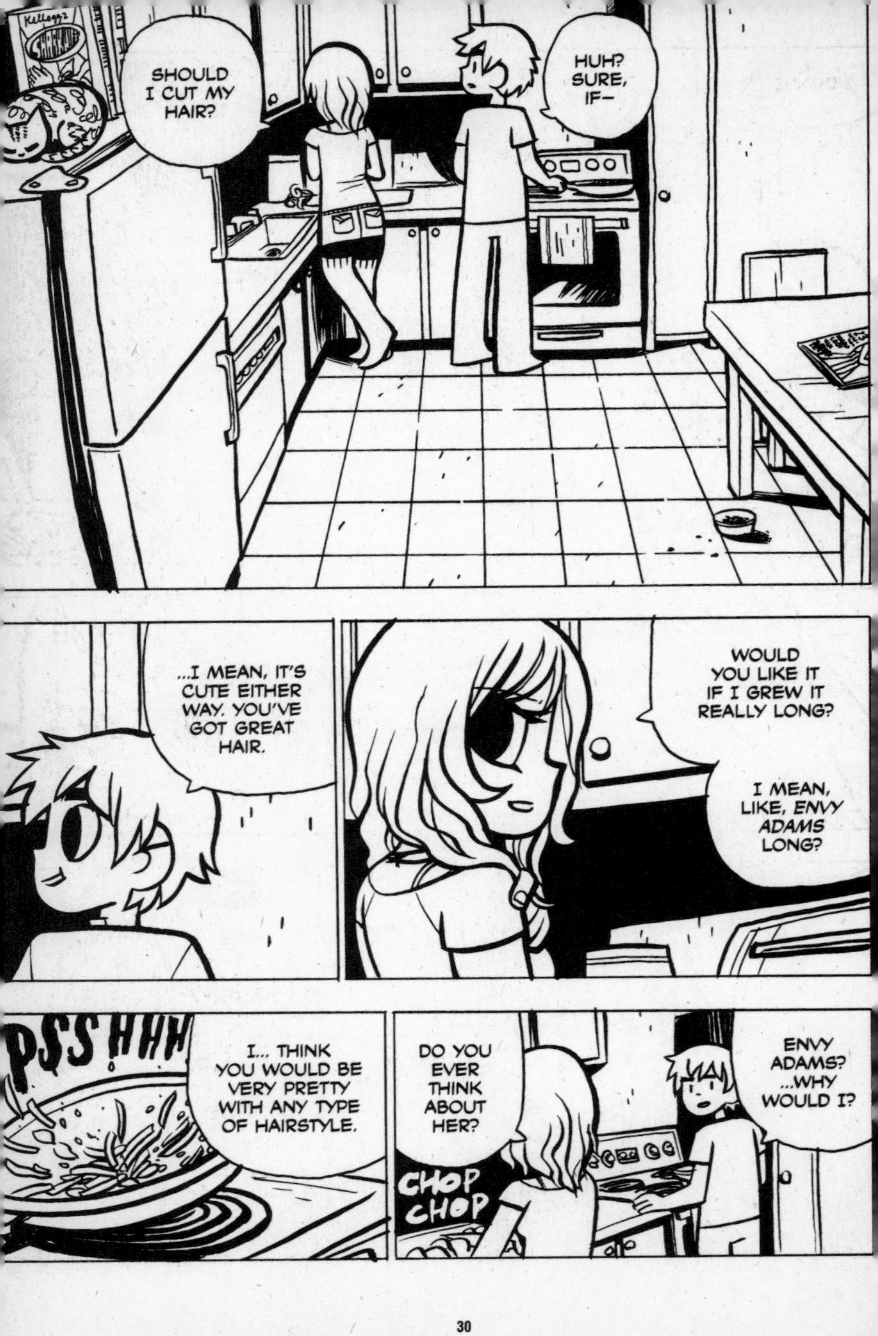
SHOULD I CUT MY HAIR?
HUH? SURE, IF—
...I MEAN, IT'S CUTE EITHER WAY. YOU'VE GOT GREAT HAIR.
WOULD YOU LIKE IT IF I GREW IT REALLY LONG?
I MEAN, LIKE, *ENVY ADAMS* LONG?
PSSHHH
I... THINK YOU WOULD BE VERY PRETTY WITH ANY TYPE OF HAIRSTYLE.
DO YOU EVER THINK ABOUT HER?
CHOP CHOP
ENVY ADAMS? ...WHY WOULD I?

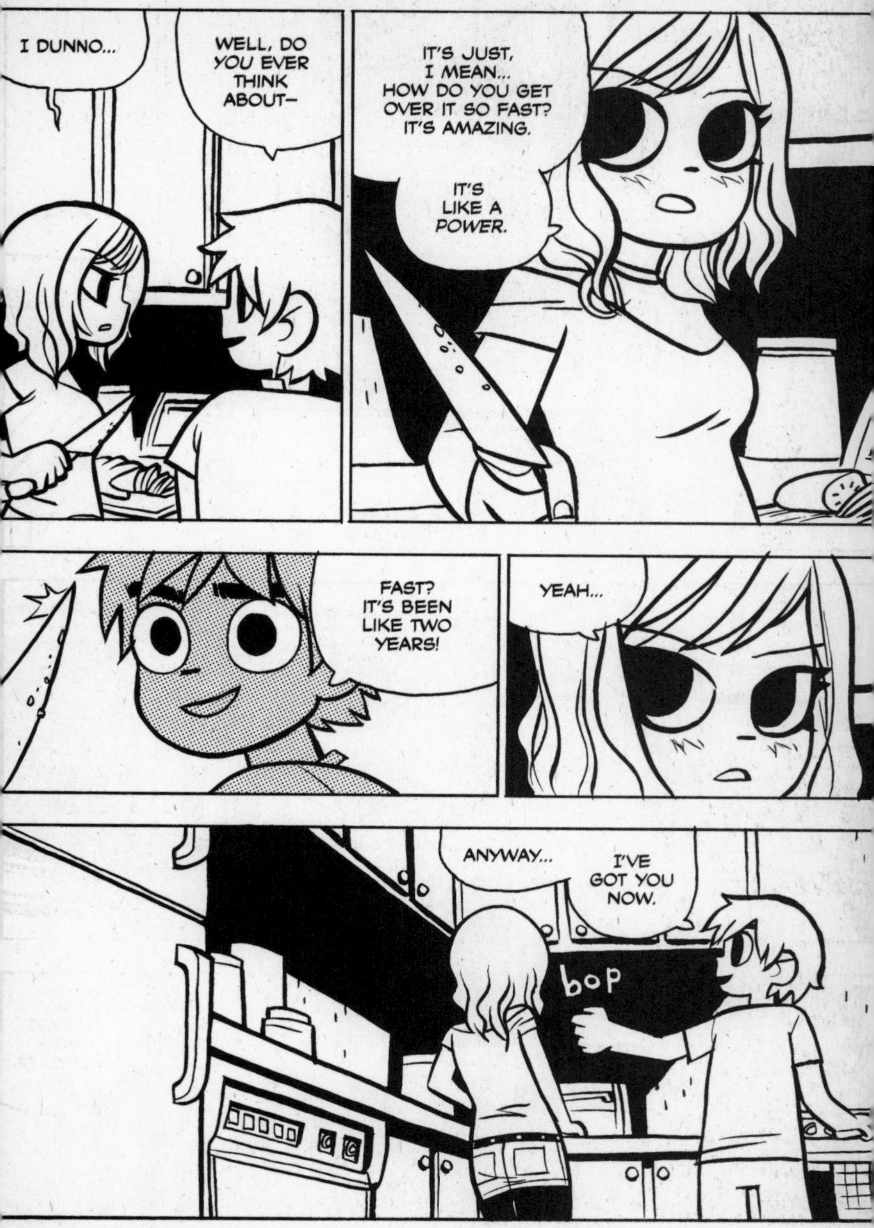
I DUNNO...
WELL, DO YOU EVER THINK ABOUT—
IT'S JUST, I MEAN... HOW DO YOU GET OVER IT SO FAST? IT'S AMAZING.
IT'S LIKE A POWER.
FAST? IT'S BEEN LIKE TWO YEARS!
YEAH...
ANYWAY...
I'VE GOT YOU NOW.
bop

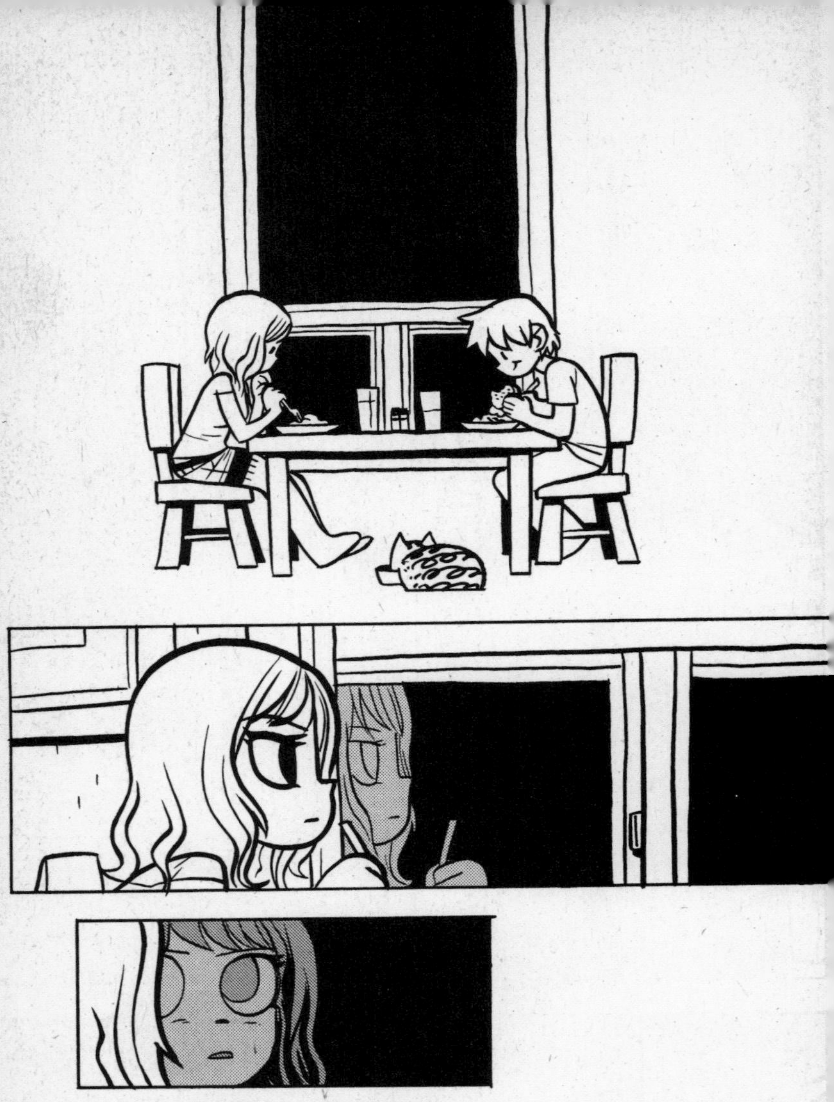

27

CAN'T FACE UP

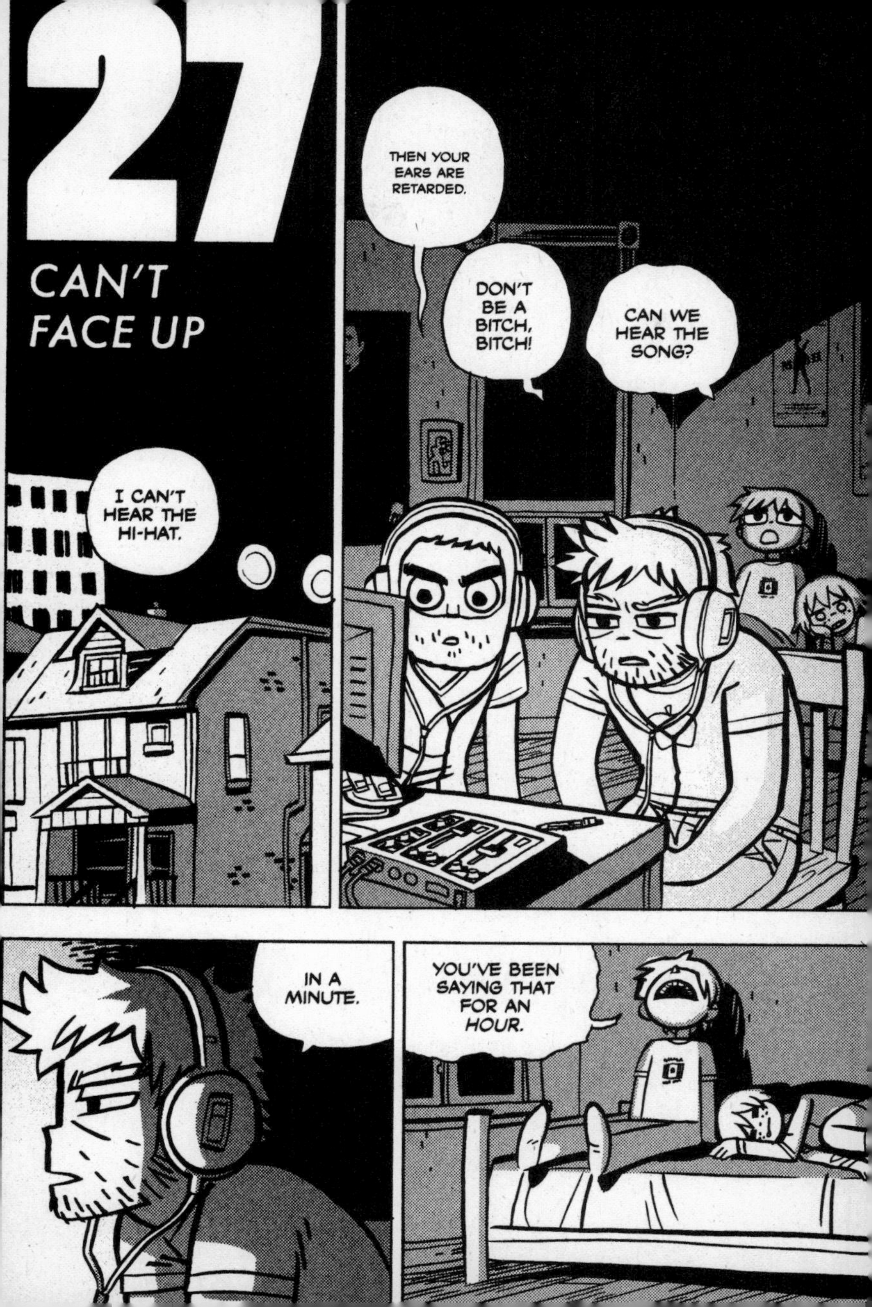
I CAN'T HEAR THE HI-HAT.
THEN YOUR EARS ARE RETARDED.
DON'T BE A BITCH, BITCH!
CAN WE HEAR THE SONG?
IN A MINUTE.
YOU'VE BEEN SAYING THAT FOR AN *HOUR*.

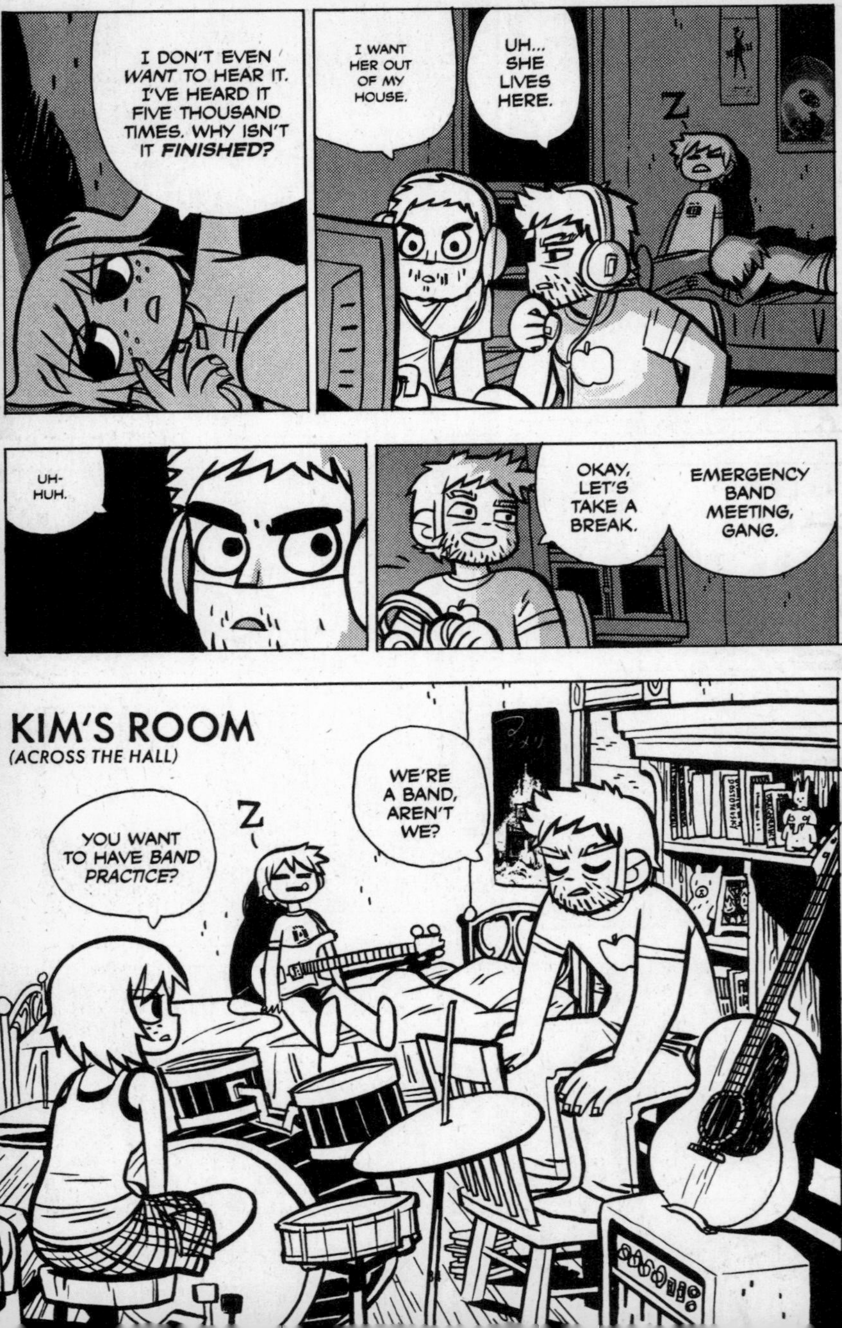
I DON'T EVEN *WANT* TO HEAR IT. I'VE HEARD IT FIVE THOUSAND TIMES. WHY ISN'T IT ***FINISHED?***
I WANT HER OUT OF MY HOUSE.
UH... SHE LIVES HERE.
Z
UH-HUH.
OKAY, LET'S TAKE A BREAK.
EMERGENCY BAND MEETING, GANG.
KIM'S ROOM
(ACROSS THE HALL)
YOU WANT TO HAVE BAND *PRACTICE?*
Z
WE'RE A BAND, AREN'T WE?

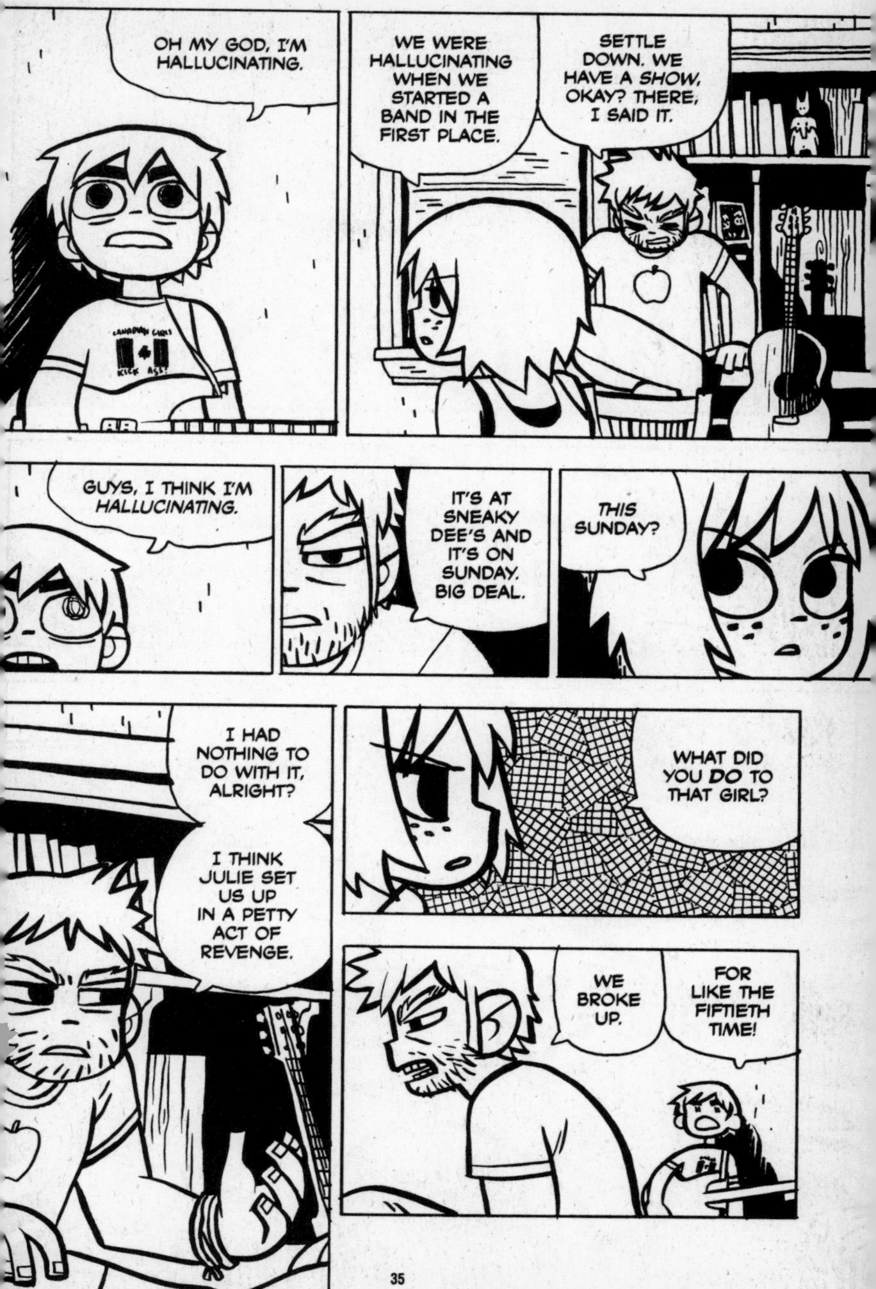
OH MY GOD, I'M HALLUCINATING.
WE WERE HALLUCINATING WHEN WE STARTED A BAND IN THE FIRST PLACE.
SETTLE DOWN. WE HAVE A *SHOW*, OKAY? THERE, I SAID IT.
CANADIAN GIRLS KICK ASS!
GUYS, I THINK I'M *HALLUCINATING.*
IT'S AT SNEAKY DEE'S AND IT'S ON SUNDAY. BIG DEAL.
THIS SUNDAY?
I HAD NOTHING TO DO WITH IT, ALRIGHT?
I THINK JULIE SET US UP IN A PETTY ACT OF REVENGE.
WHAT DID YOU ***DO*** TO THAT GIRL?
WE BROKE UP.
FOR LIKE THE FIFTIETH TIME!

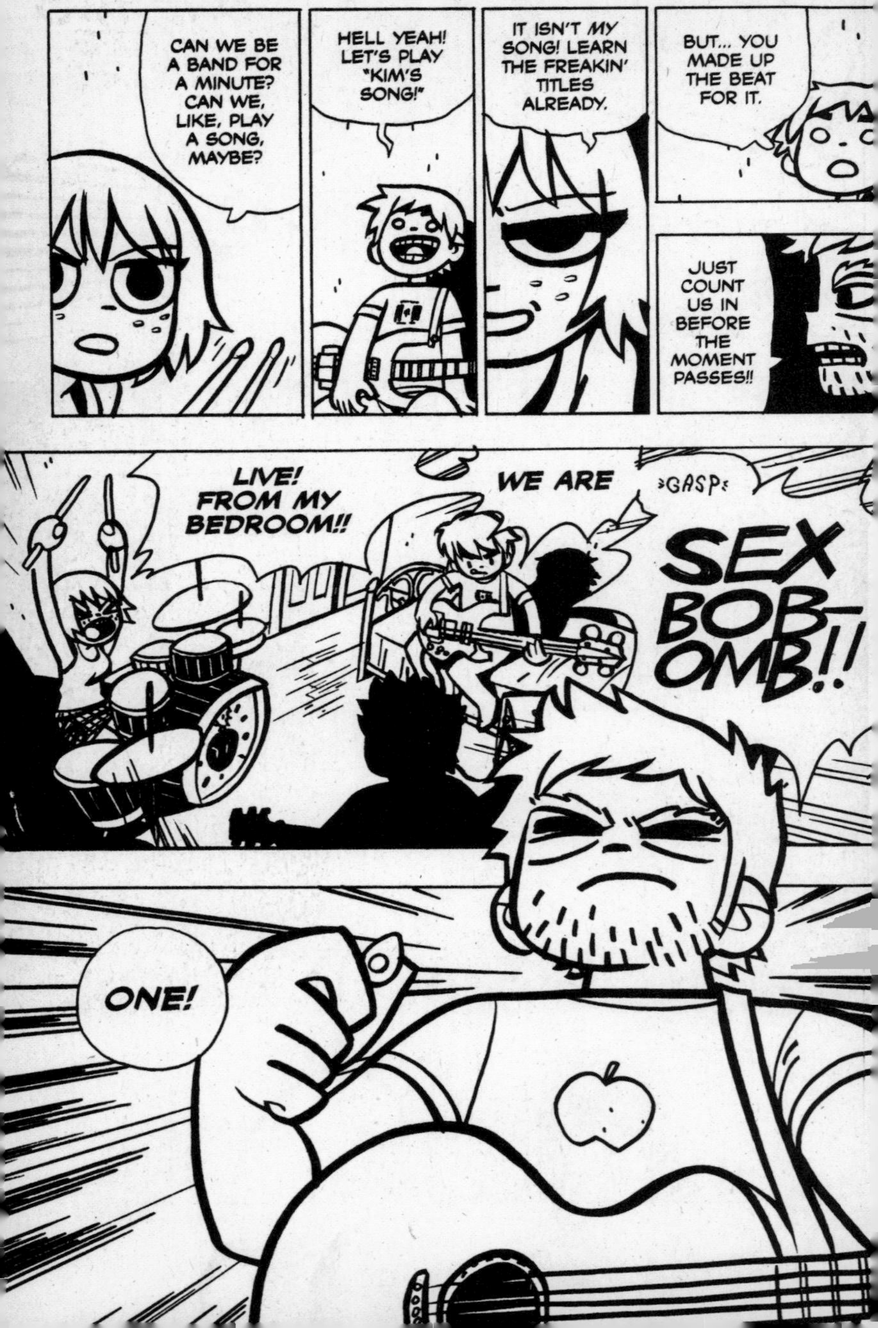

CAN WE BE A BAND FOR A MINUTE? CAN WE, LIKE, PLAY A SONG, MAYBE?
HELL YEAH! LET'S PLAY "KIM'S SONG!"
IT ISN'T *MY* SONG! LEARN THE FREAKIN' TITLES ALREADY.
BUT... YOU MADE UP THE BEAT FOR IT.
JUST COUNT US IN BEFORE THE MOMENT PASSES!!
LIVE! FROM MY BEDROOM!!
WE ARE
GASP
SEX BOB-OMB!!
ONE!

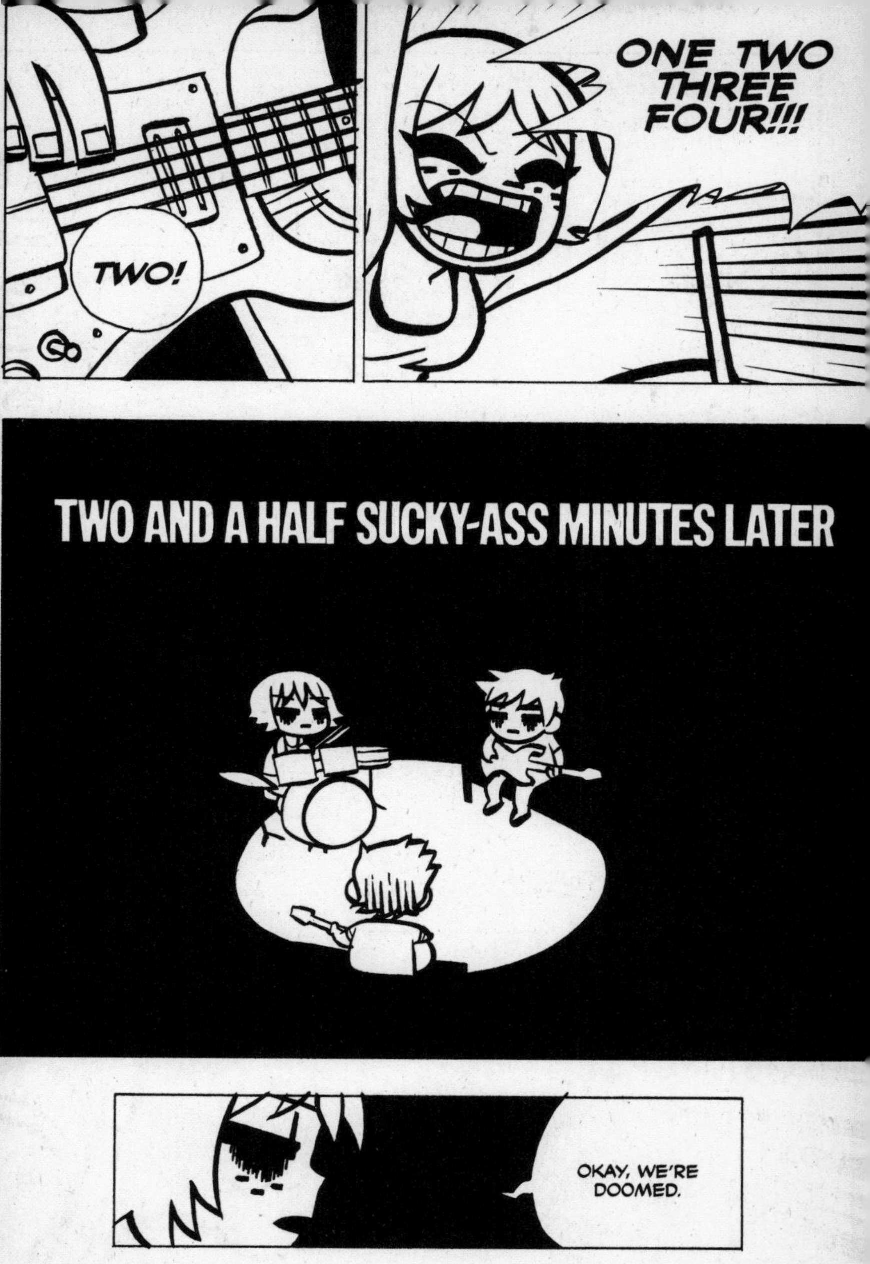
TWO!
ONE TWO THREE FOUR!!!
TWO AND A HALF SUCKY-ASS MINUTES LATER
OKAY, WE'RE DOOMED.

A SCHOOL DAY

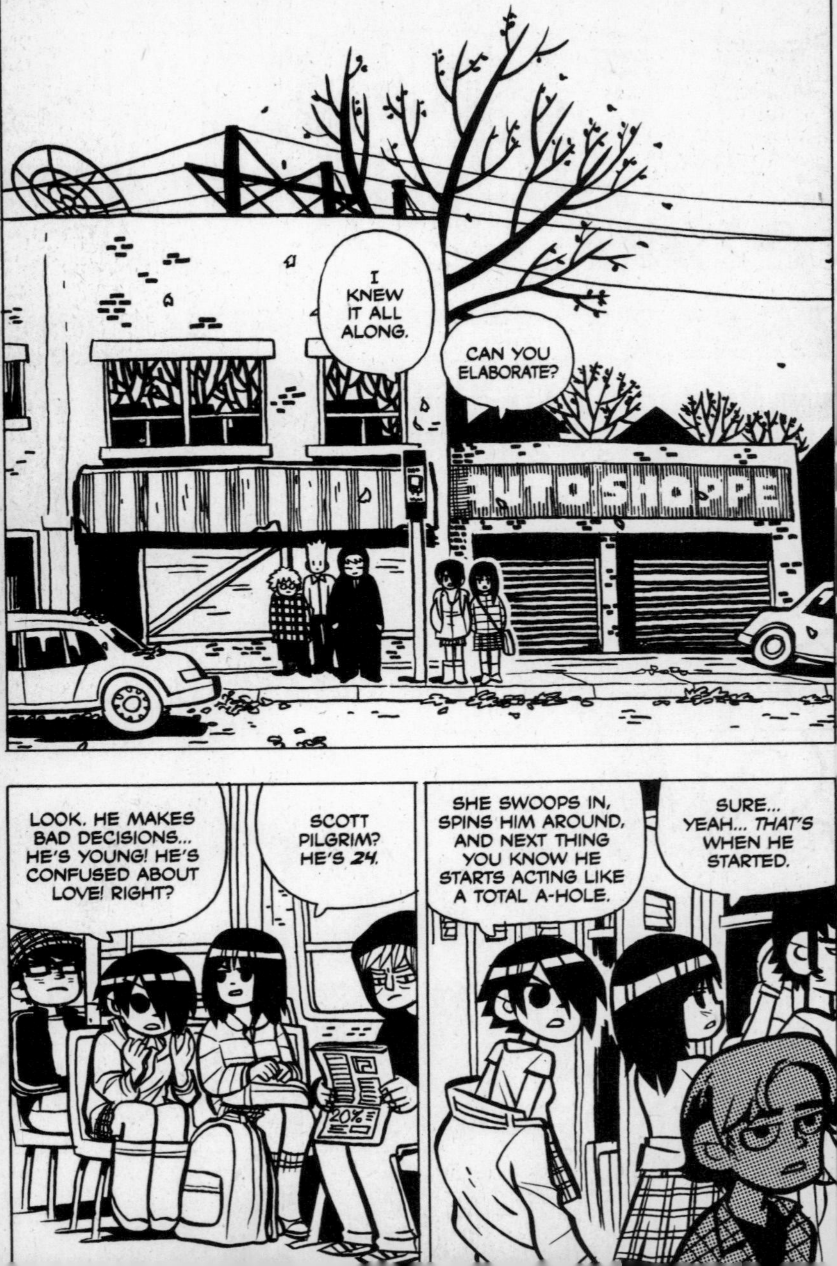
I KNEW IT ALL ALONG.
CAN YOU ELABORATE?
AUTO SHOPPE
LOOK. HE MAKES BAD DECISIONS... HE'S YOUNG! HE'S CONFUSED ABOUT LOVE! RIGHT?
SCOTT PILGRIM? HE'S *24*.
20%
SHE SWOOPS IN, SPINS HIM AROUND, AND NEXT THING YOU KNOW HE STARTS ACTING LIKE A TOTAL A-HOLE.
SURE... YEAH... *THAT'S* WHEN HE STARTED.

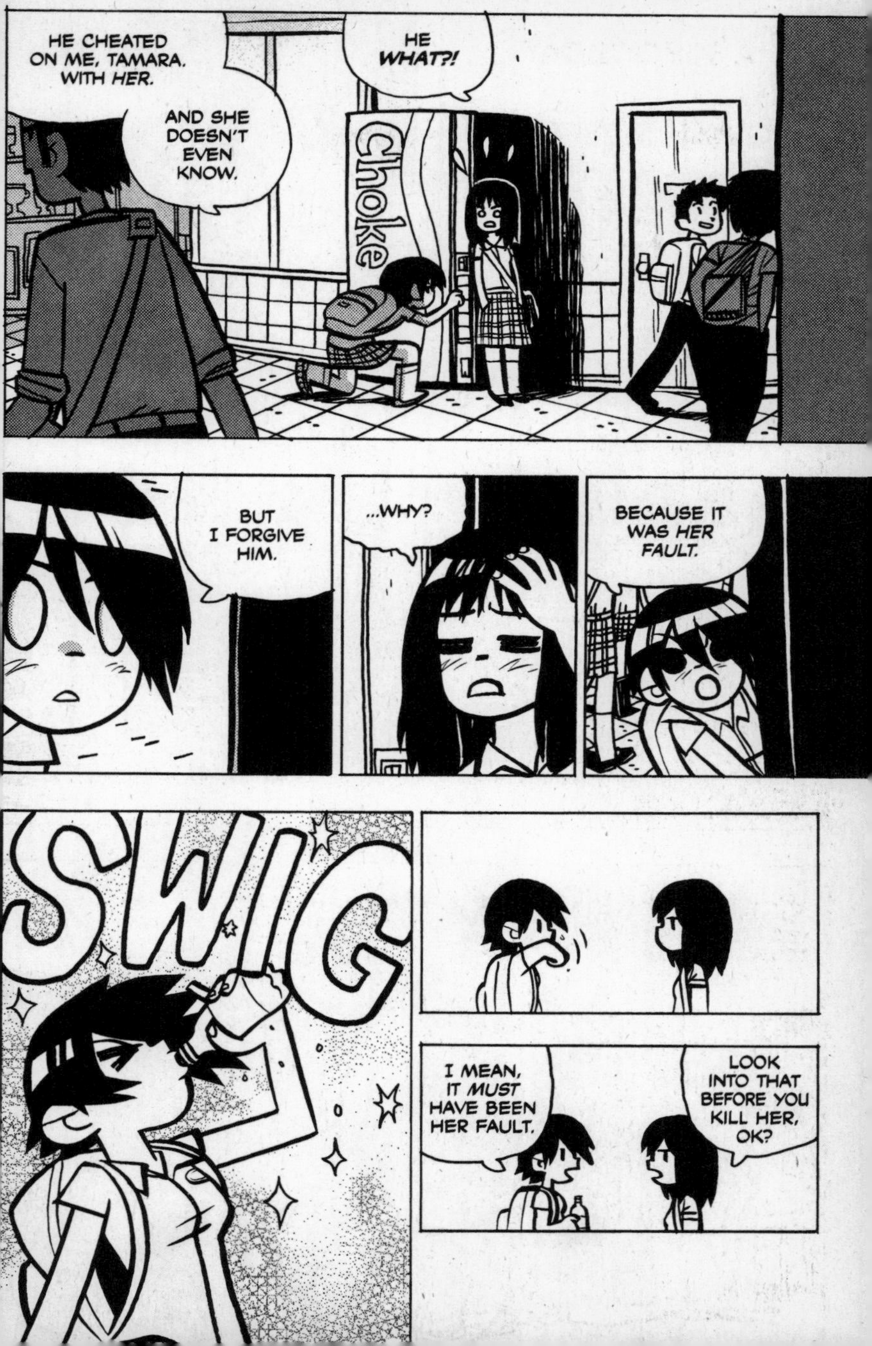
HE CHEATED ON ME, TAMARA. WITH HER.
HE WHAT?!
AND SHE DOESN'T EVEN KNOW.
Choke
BUT I FORGIVE HIM.
...WHY?
BECAUSE IT WAS HER FAULT.
SWIG
I MEAN, IT MUST HAVE BEEN HER FAULT.
LOOK INTO THAT BEFORE YOU KILL HER, OK?

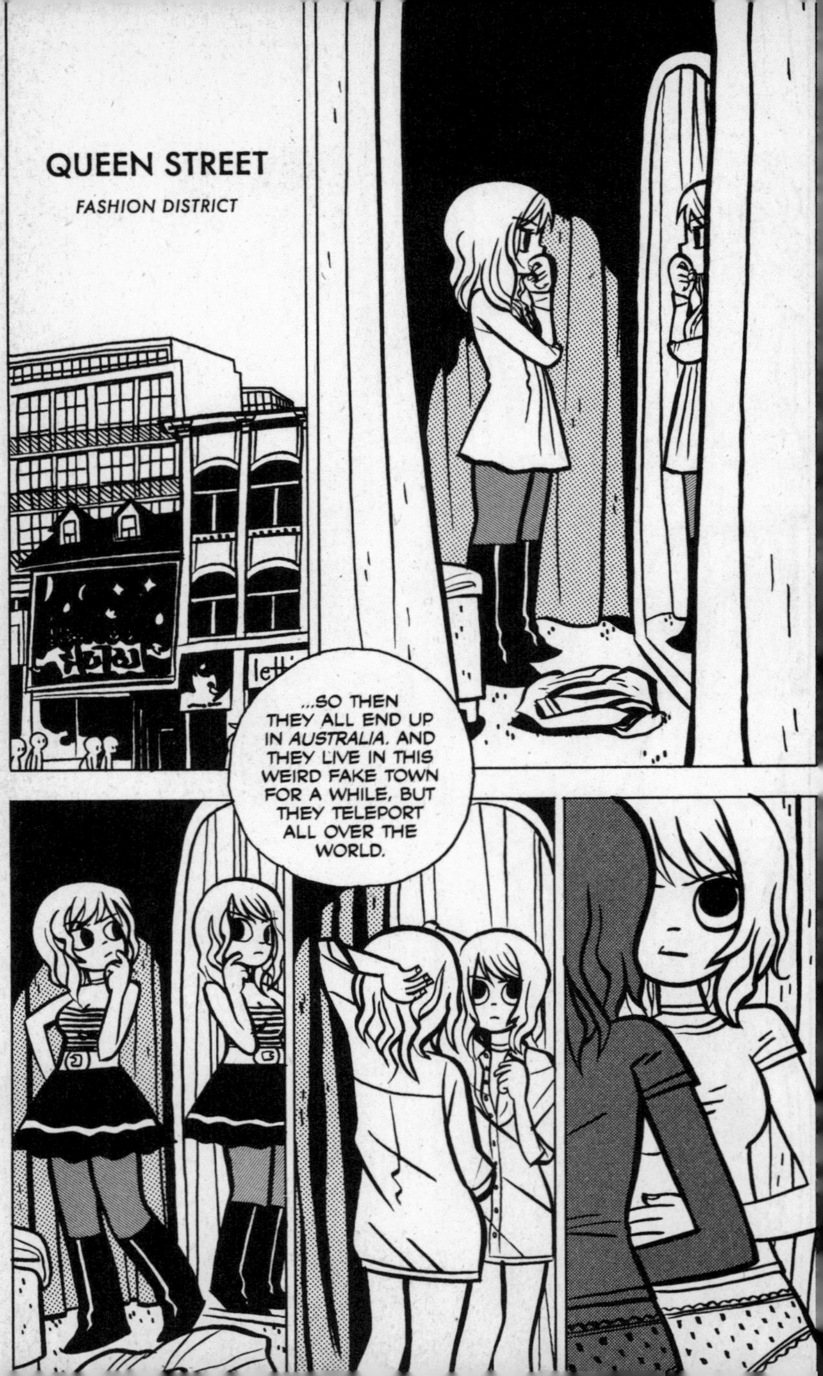
QUEEN STREET
FASHION DISTRICT
...SO THEN THEY ALL END UP IN *AUSTRALIA*, AND THEY LIVE IN THIS WEIRD FAKE TOWN FOR A WHILE, BUT THEY TELEPORT ALL OVER THE WORLD.

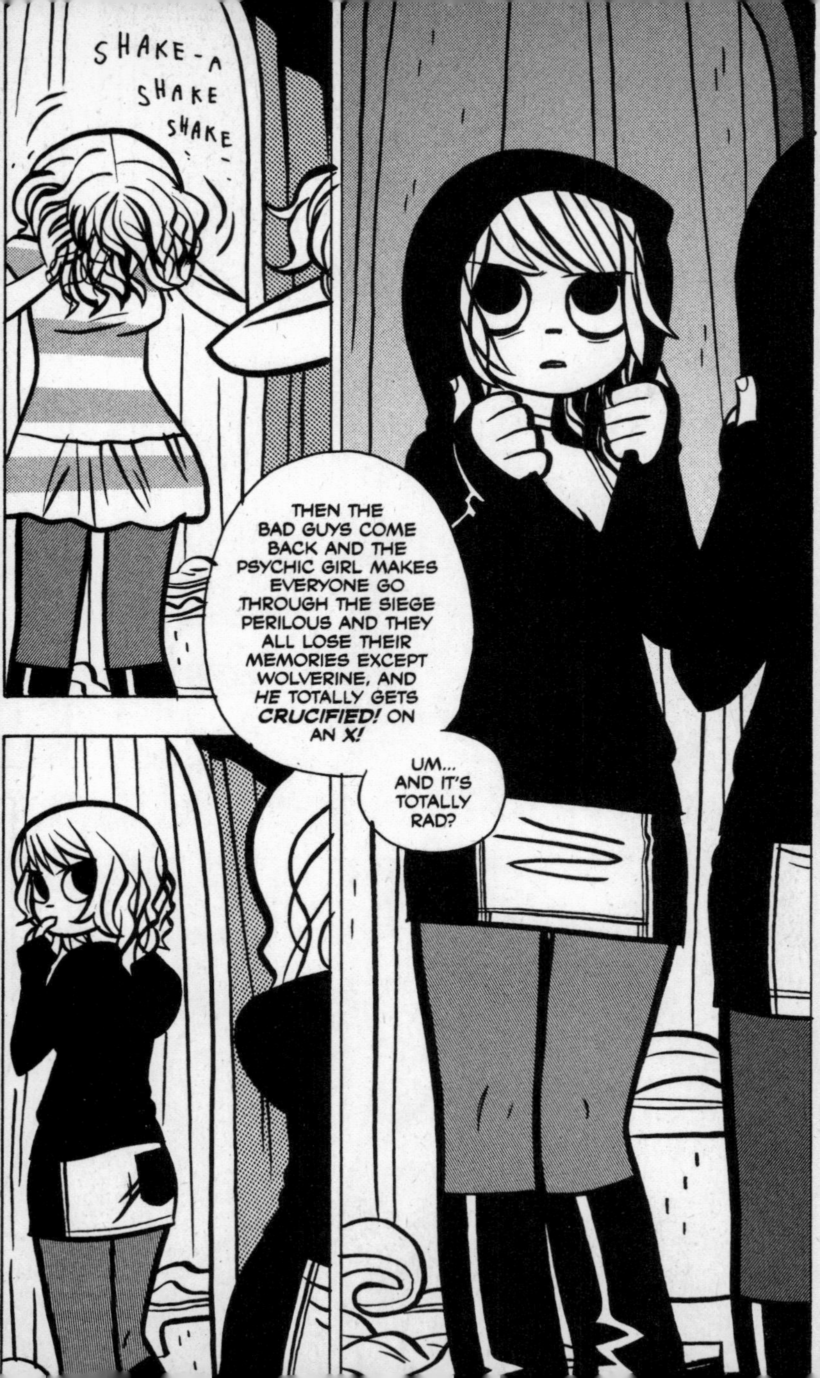
SHAKE-A SHAKE SHAKE
THEN THE BAD GUYS COME BACK AND THE PSYCHIC GIRL MAKES EVERYONE GO THROUGH THE SIEGE PERILOUS AND THEY ALL LOSE THEIR MEMORIES EXCEPT WOLVERINE, AND HE TOTALLY GETS CRUCIFIED! ON AN X!
UM... AND IT'S TOTALLY RAD?

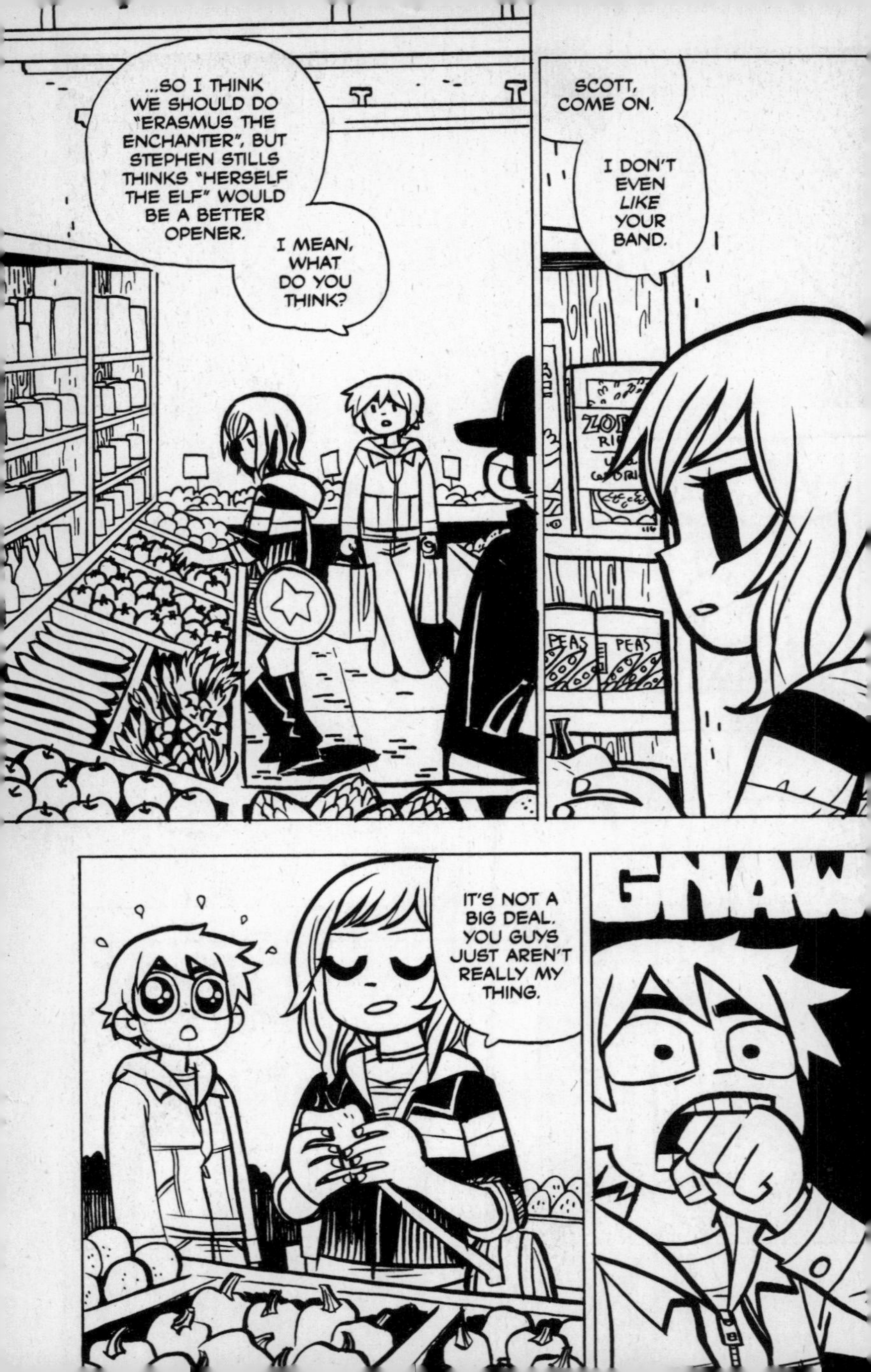
...SO I THINK WE SHOULD DO "ERASMUS THE ENCHANTER", BUT STEPHEN STILLS THINKS "HERSELF THE ELF" WOULD BE A BETTER OPENER.
I MEAN, WHAT DO YOU THINK?
SCOTT, COME ON.
I DON'T EVEN *LIKE* YOUR BAND.
PEAS
PEAS
IT'S NOT A BIG DEAL. YOU GUYS JUST AREN'T REALLY MY THING.
GNAW

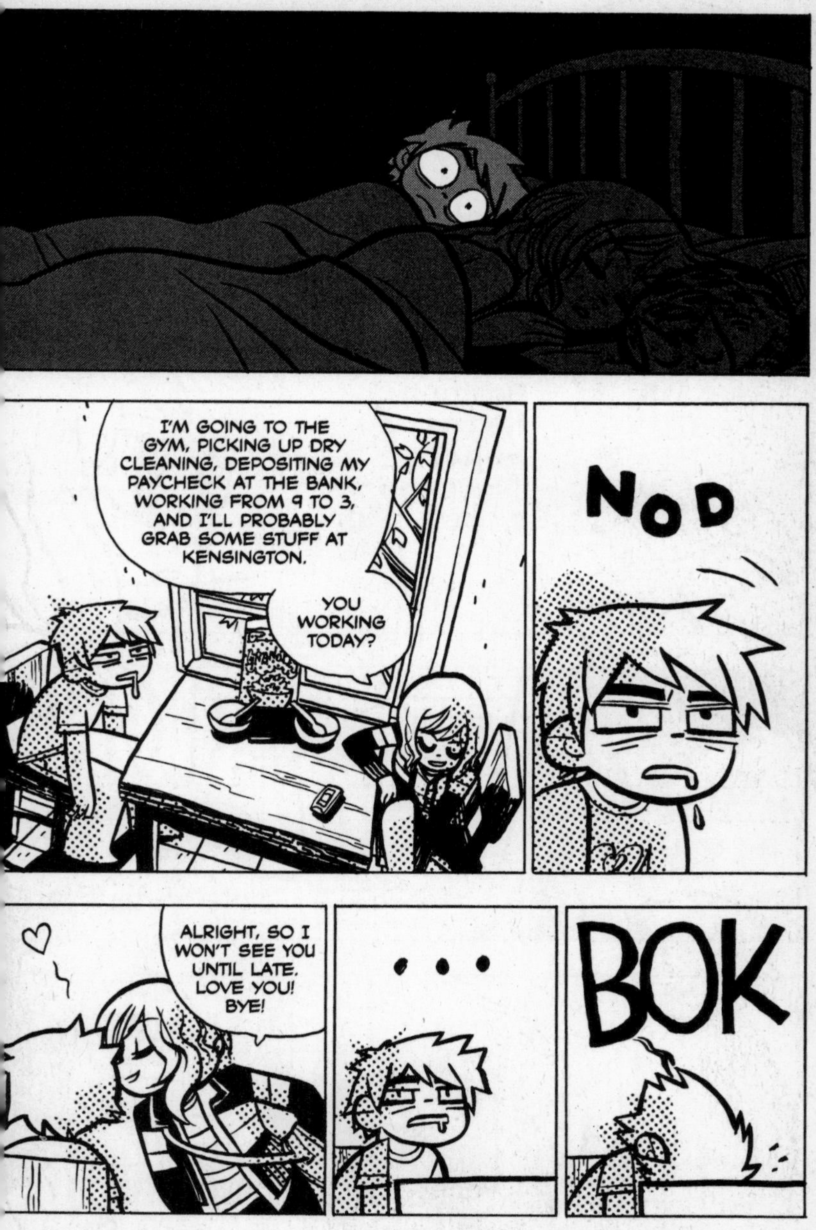
I'M GOING TO THE GYM, PICKING UP DRY CLEANING, DEPOSITING MY PAYCHECK AT THE BANK, WORKING FROM 9 TO 3, AND I'LL PROBABLY GRAB SOME STUFF AT KENSINGTON.
YOU WORKING TODAY?
NOD
ALRIGHT, SO I WON'T SEE YOU UNTIL LATE. LOVE YOU! BYE!
...
BOK

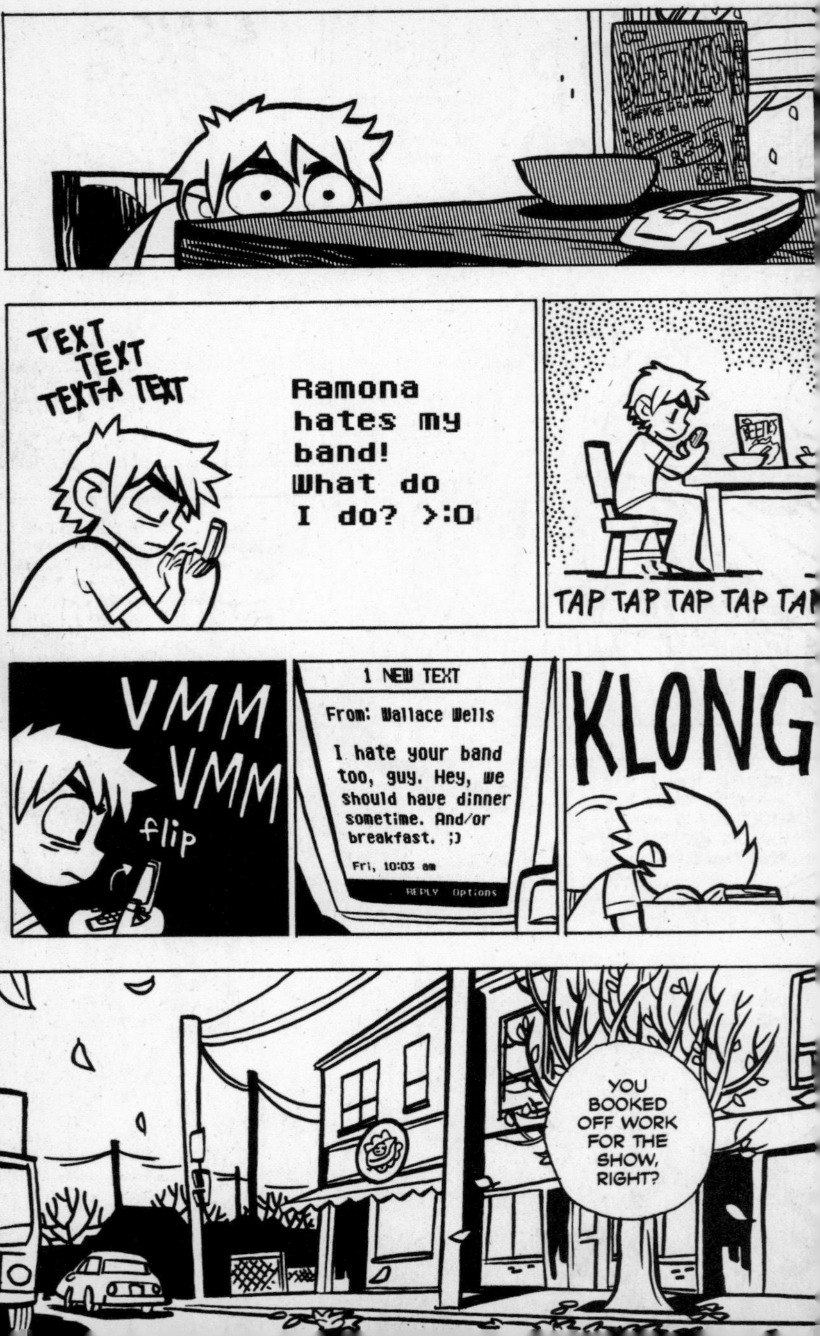

TEXT TEXT TEXT-A TEXT
Ramona hates my band! What do I do? >:O
TAP TAP TAP TAP TAP
VMM VMM
flip
1 NEW TEXT
From: Wallace Wells
I hate your band too, guy. Hey, we should have dinner sometime. And/or breakfast. ;)
Fri, 10:03 am
REPLY Options
KLONG
YOU BOOKED OFF WORK FOR THE SHOW, RIGHT?

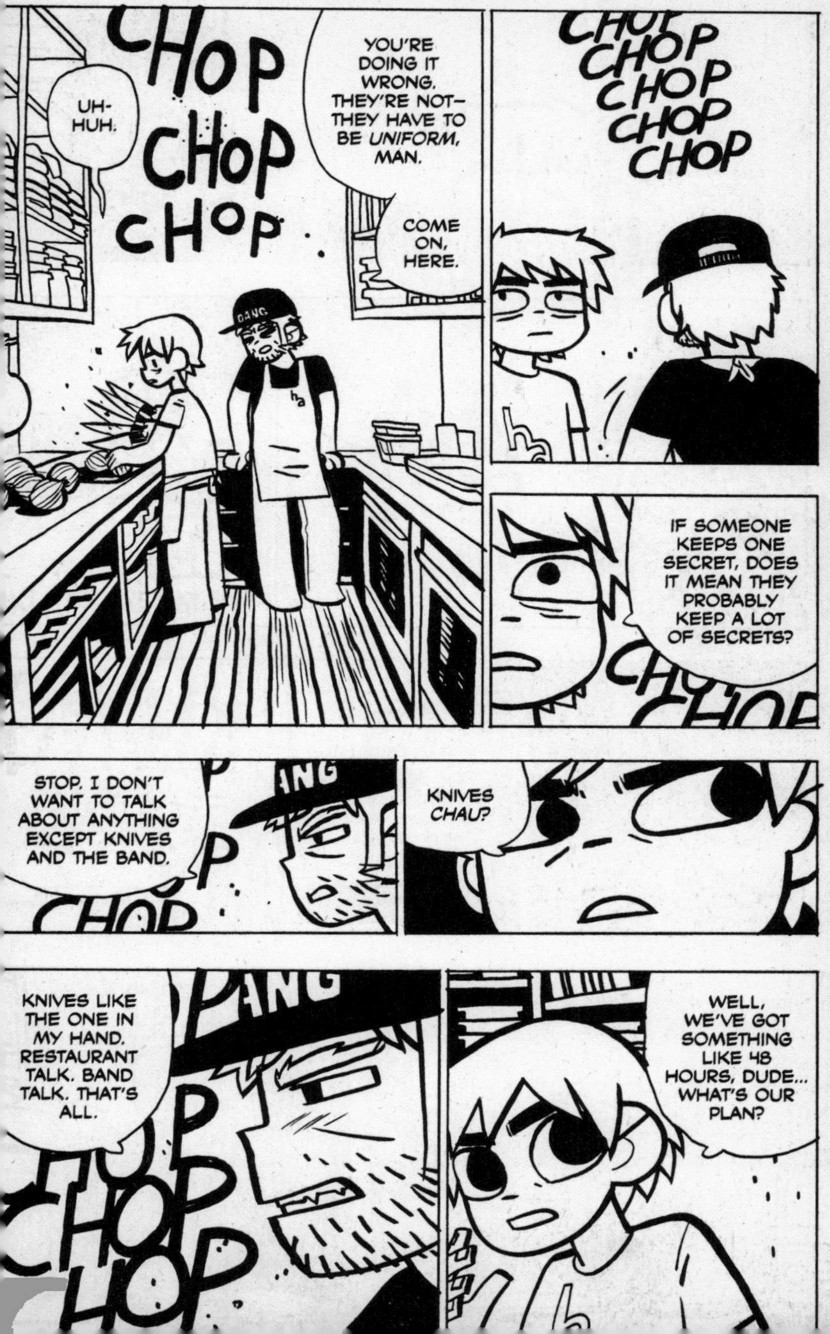
CHOP
CHOP
CHOP
UH-HUH.
YOU'RE DOING IT WRONG. THEY'RE NOT– THEY HAVE TO BE *UNIFORM*, MAN.
COME ON, HERE.
DANG
CHOP CHOP CHOP CHOP
IF SOMEONE KEEPS ONE SECRET, DOES IT MEAN THEY PROBABLY KEEP A LOT OF SECRETS?
STOP. I DON'T WANT TO TALK ABOUT ANYTHING EXCEPT KNIVES AND THE BAND.
KNIVES *CHAU?*
KNIVES LIKE THE ONE IN MY HAND. RESTAURANT TALK. BAND TALK. THAT'S ALL.
CHOP
CHOP
WELL, WE'VE GOT SOMETHING LIKE 48 HOURS, DUDE... WHAT'S OUR PLAN?

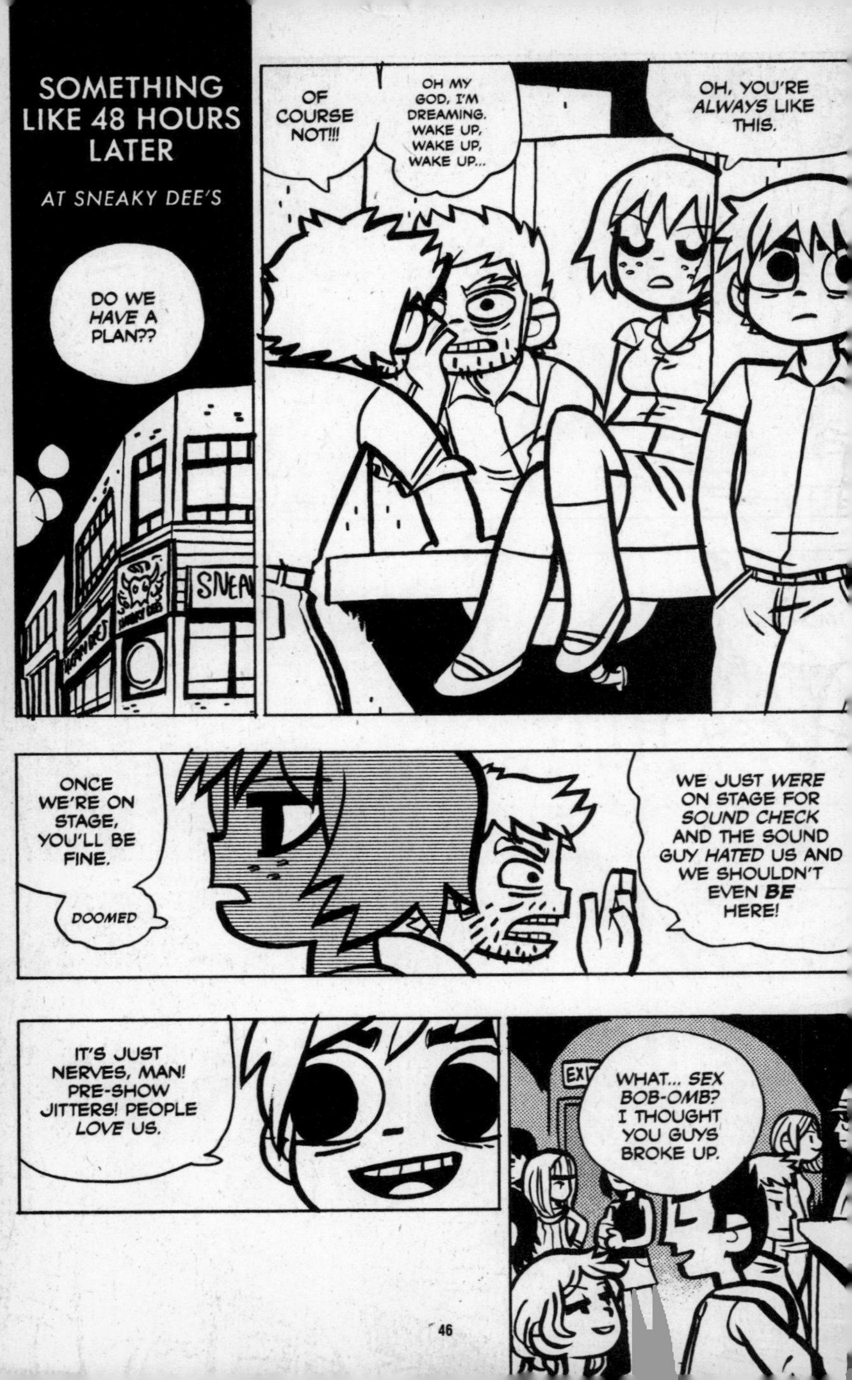
SOMETHING LIKE 48 HOURS LATER
AT SNEAKY DEE'S
DO WE HAVE A PLAN??
OF COURSE NOT!!!
OH MY GOD, I'M DREAMING. WAKE UP, WAKE UP, WAKE UP...
OH, YOU'RE ALWAYS LIKE THIS.
ONCE WE'RE ON STAGE, YOU'LL BE FINE.
DOOMED
WE JUST WERE ON STAGE FOR SOUND CHECK AND THE SOUND GUY HATED US AND WE SHOULDN'T EVEN BE HERE!
IT'S JUST NERVES, MAN! PRE-SHOW JITTERS! PEOPLE LOVE US.
WHAT... SEX BOB-OMB? I THOUGHT YOU GUYS BROKE UP.

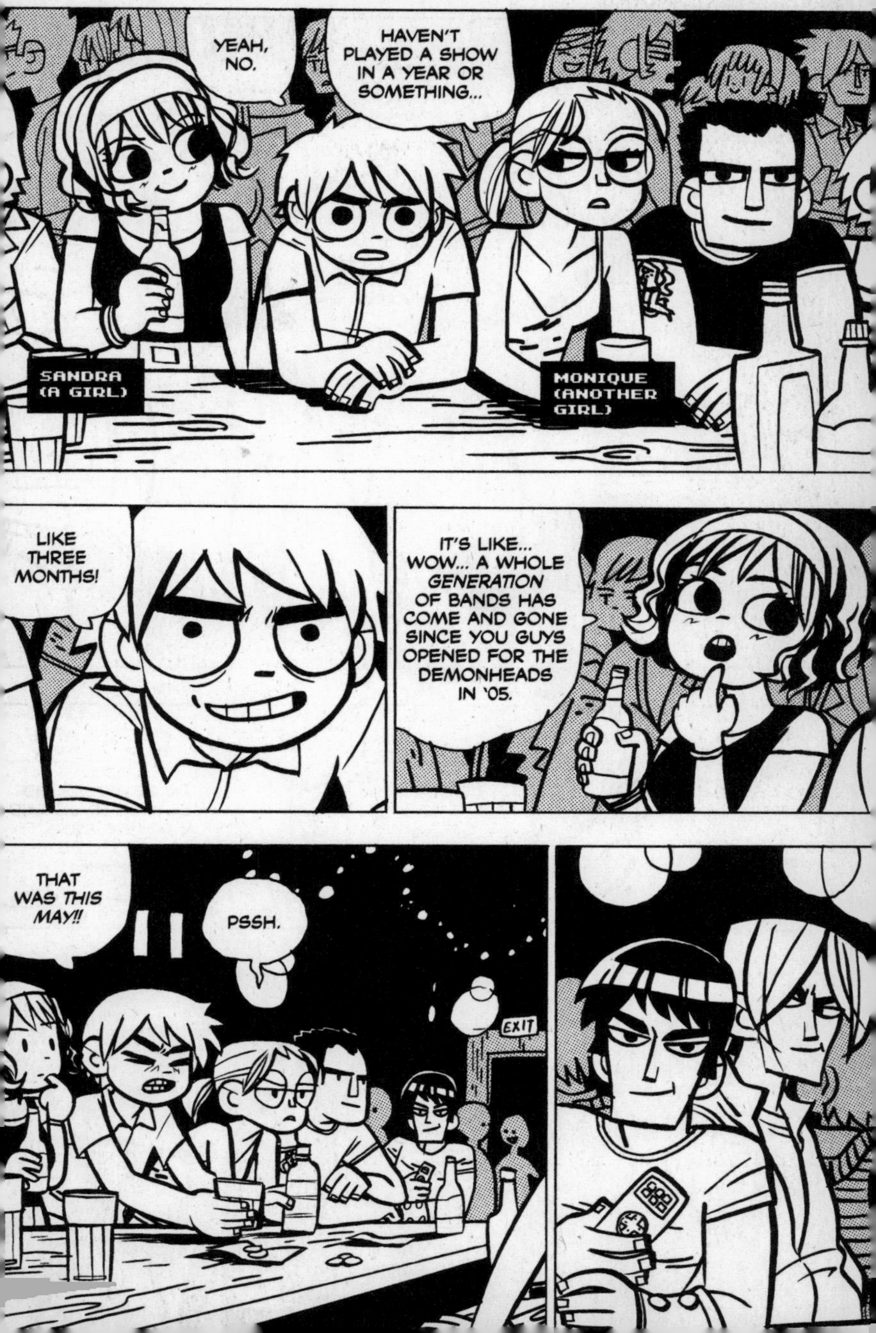
YEAH, NO.
HAVEN'T PLAYED A SHOW IN A YEAR OR SOMETHING...
SANDRA (A GIRL)
MONIQUE (ANOTHER GIRL)
LIKE THREE MONTHS!
IT'S LIKE... WOW... A WHOLE *GENERATION* OF BANDS HAS COME AND GONE SINCE YOU GUYS OPENED FOR THE DEMONHEADS IN '05.
THAT WAS *THIS MAY!!*
PSSH.
EXIT

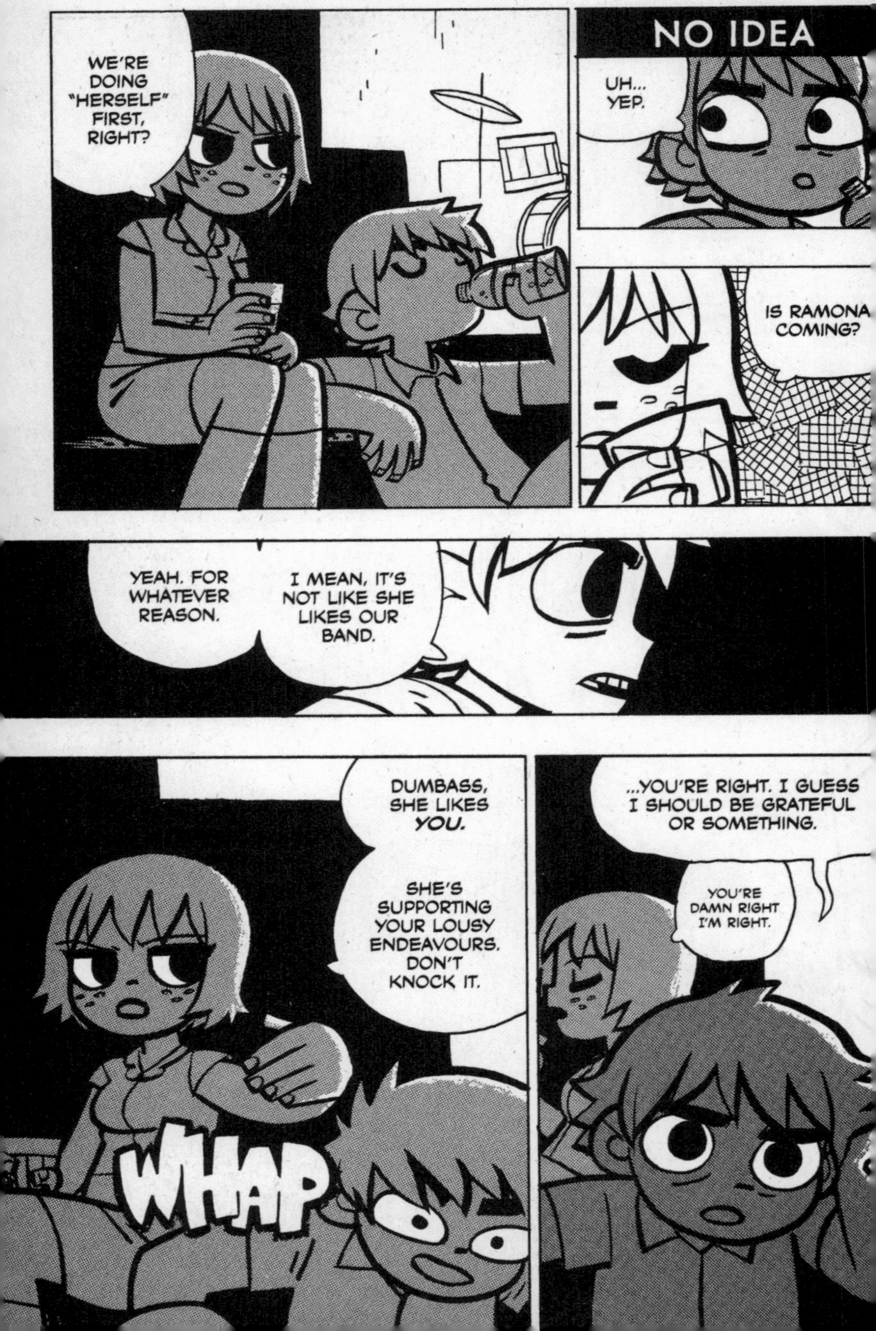
WE'RE DOING "HERSELF" FIRST, RIGHT?
NO IDEA
UH... YEP.
IS RAMONA COMING?
YEAH. FOR WHATEVER REASON.
I MEAN, IT'S NOT LIKE SHE LIKES OUR BAND.
DUMBASS, SHE LIKES *YOU.*
SHE'S SUPPORTING YOUR LOUSY ENDEAVOURS. DON'T KNOCK IT.
WHAP
...YOU'RE RIGHT. I GUESS I SHOULD BE GRATEFUL OR SOMETHING.
YOU'RE DAMN RIGHT I'M RIGHT.

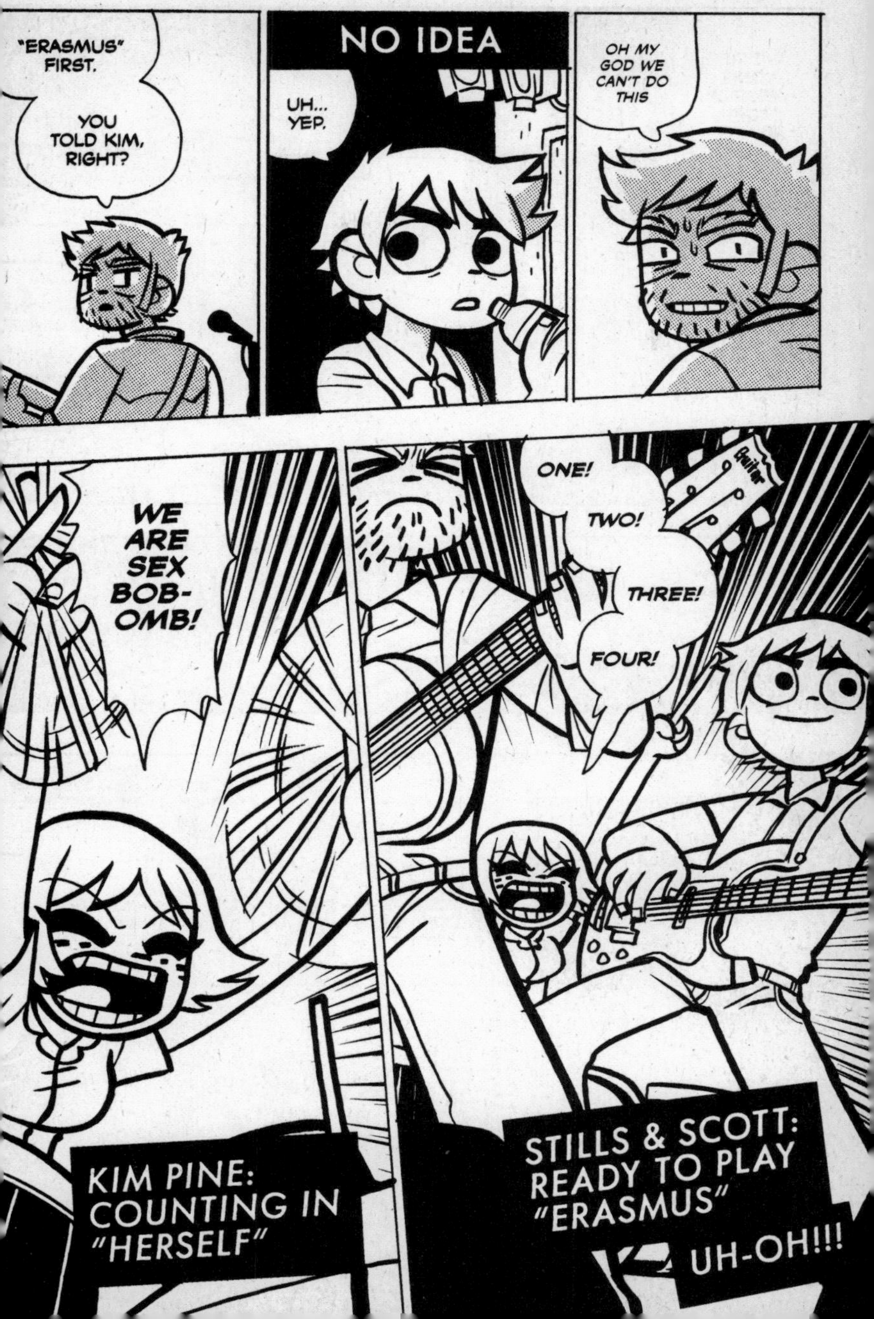

"ERASMUS" FIRST.
YOU TOLD KIM, RIGHT?
NO IDEA
UH... YEP.
OH MY GOD WE CAN'T DO THIS
WE ARE SEX BOB-OMB!
ONE!
TWO!
THREE!
FOUR!
KIM PINE: COUNTING IN "HERSELF"
STILLS & SCOTT: READY TO PLAY "ERASMUS"
UH-OH!!!

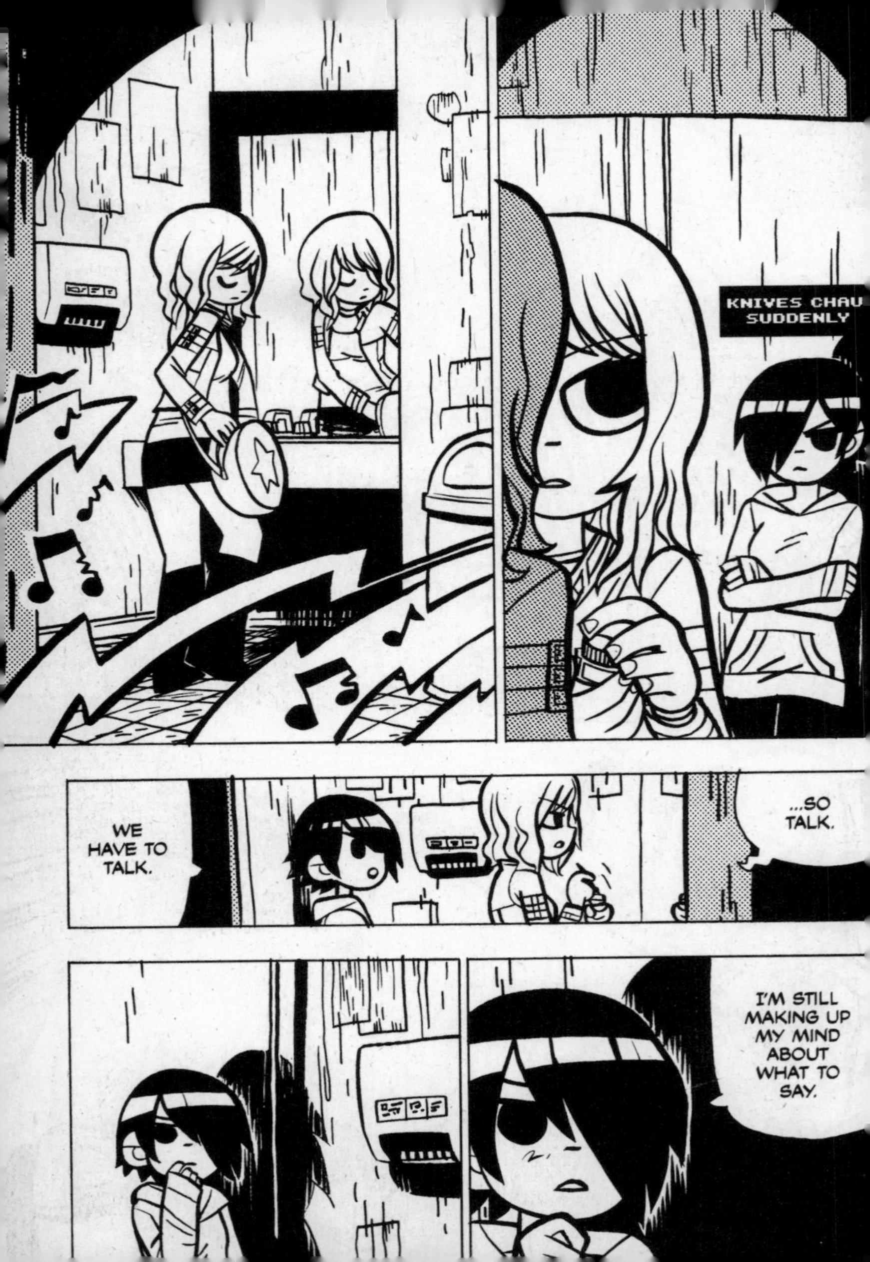
KNIVES CHAU SUDDENLY
WE HAVE TO TALK.
...SO TALK.
I'M STILL MAKING UP MY MIND ABOUT WHAT TO SAY.

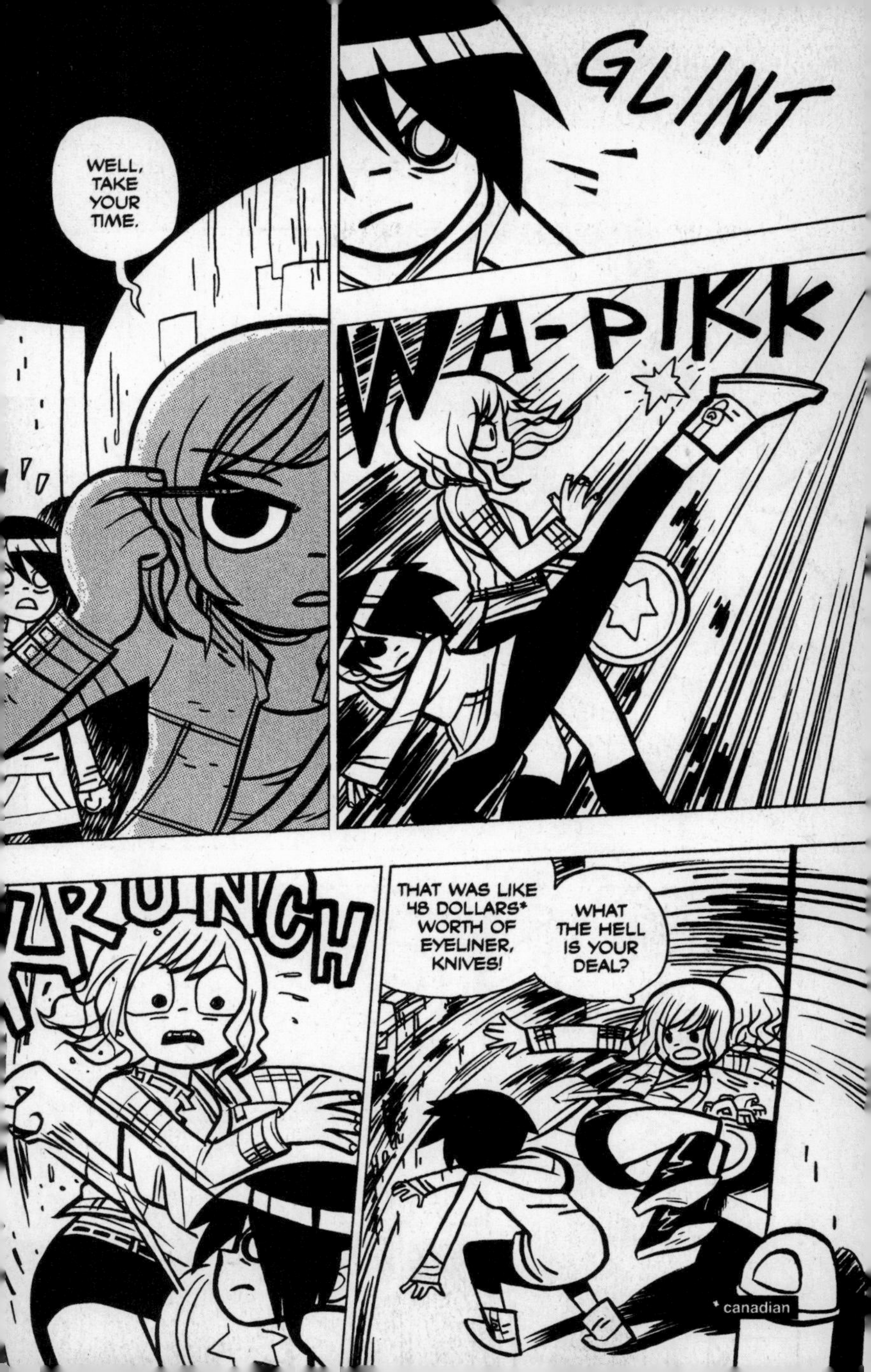
WELL, TAKE YOUR TIME.
GLINT
WA-PIKK
KRUNCH
THAT WAS LIKE 48 DOLLARS* WORTH OF EYELINER, KNIVES!
WHAT THE HELL IS YOUR DEAL?
* canadian

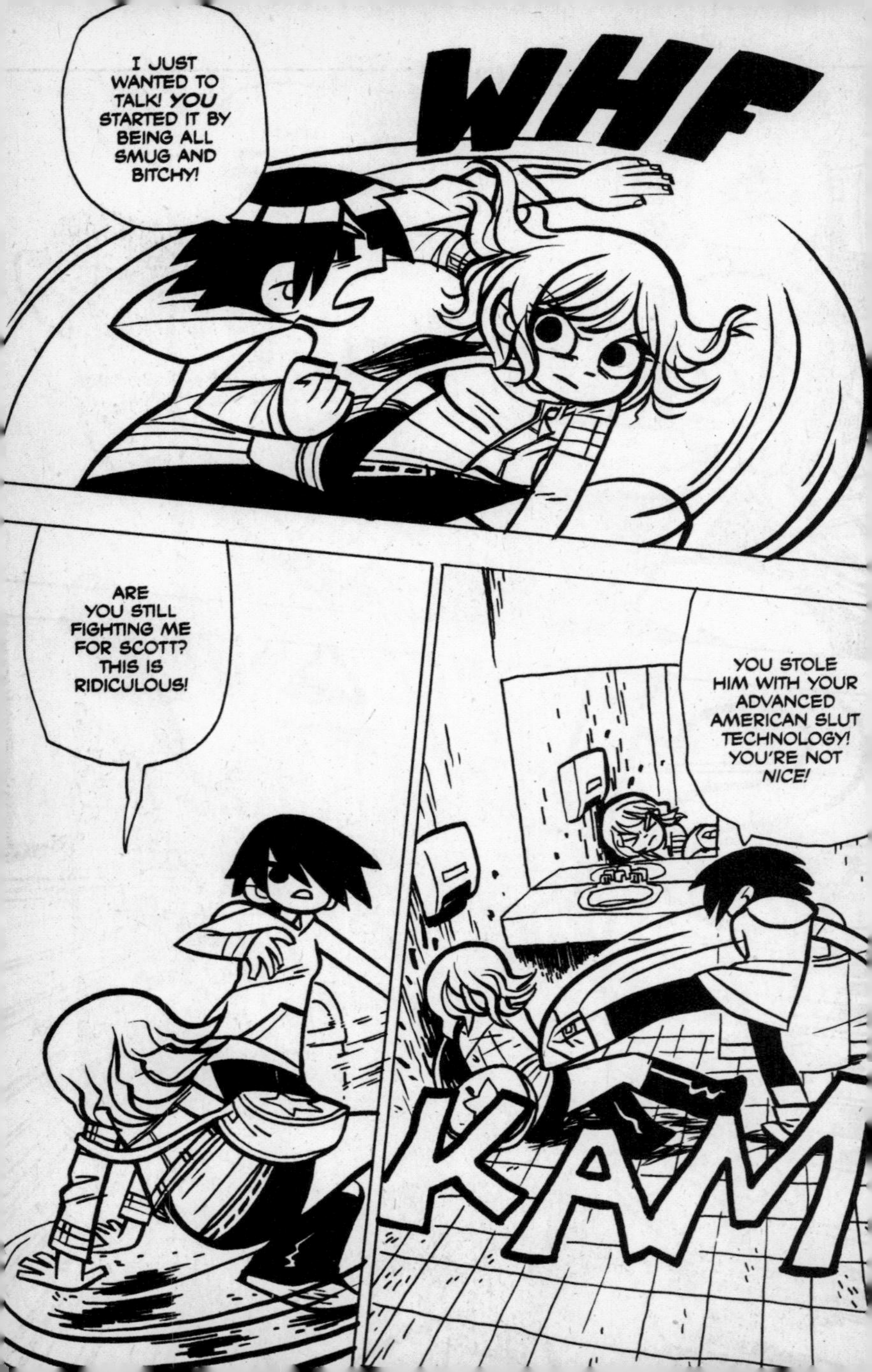
I JUST WANTED TO TALK! *YOU* STARTED IT BY BEING ALL SMUG AND BITCHY!
WHF
ARE YOU STILL FIGHTING ME FOR SCOTT? THIS IS RIDICULOUS!
YOU STOLE HIM WITH YOUR ADVANCED AMERICAN SLUT TECHNOLOGY! YOU'RE NOT *NICE!*
KAM

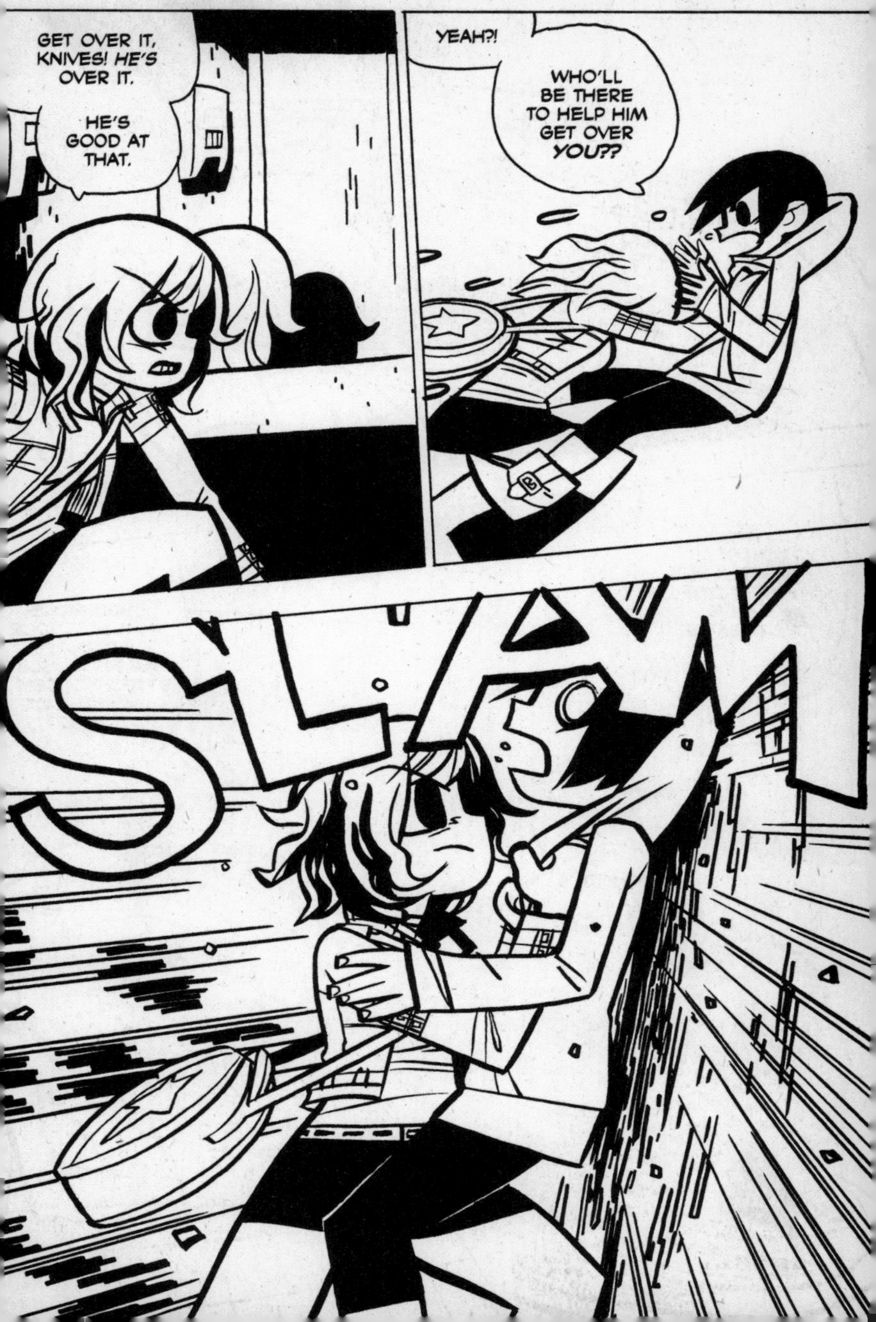
GET OVER IT, KNIVES! HE'S OVER IT.
HE'S GOOD AT THAT.
YEAH?!
WHO'LL BE THERE TO HELP HIM GET OVER YOU??
SLAM

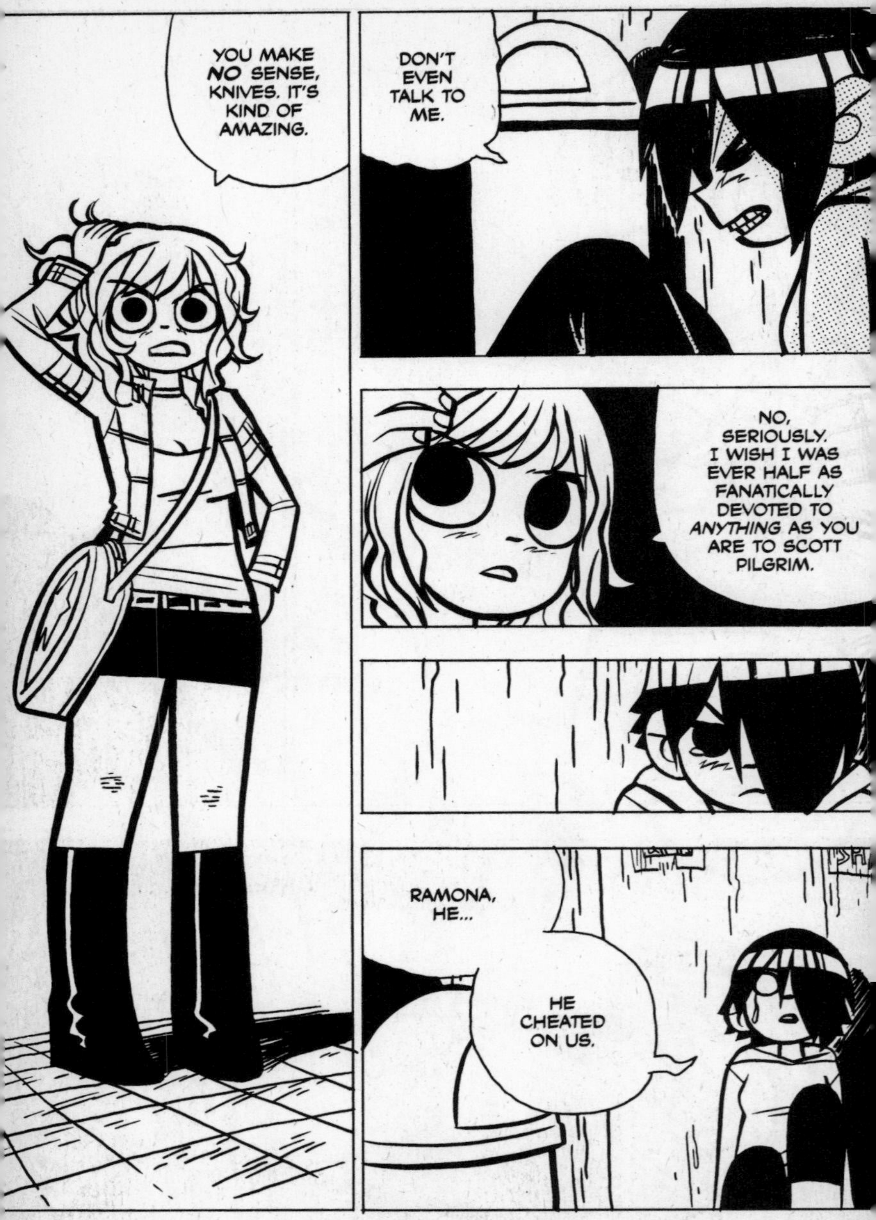
YOU MAKE NO SENSE, KNIVES. IT'S KIND OF AMAZING.
DON'T EVEN TALK TO ME.
NO, SERIOUSLY. I WISH I WAS EVER HALF AS FANATICALLY DEVOTED TO ANYTHING AS YOU ARE TO SCOTT PILGRIM.
RAMONA, HE...
HE CHEATED ON US.

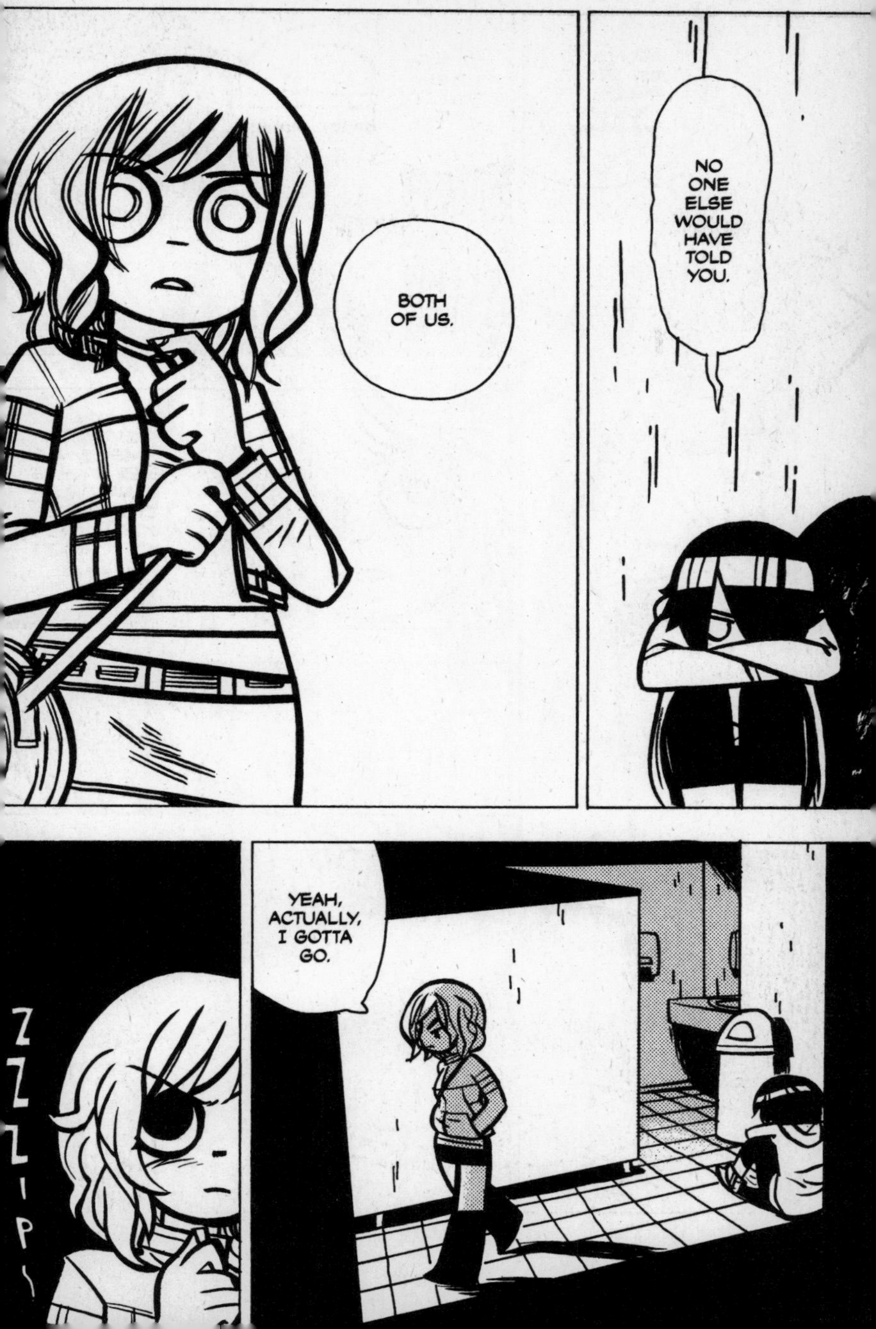
BOTH OF US.
NO ONE ELSE WOULD HAVE TOLD YOU.
YEAH, ACTUALLY, I GOTTA GO.
ZZZIP

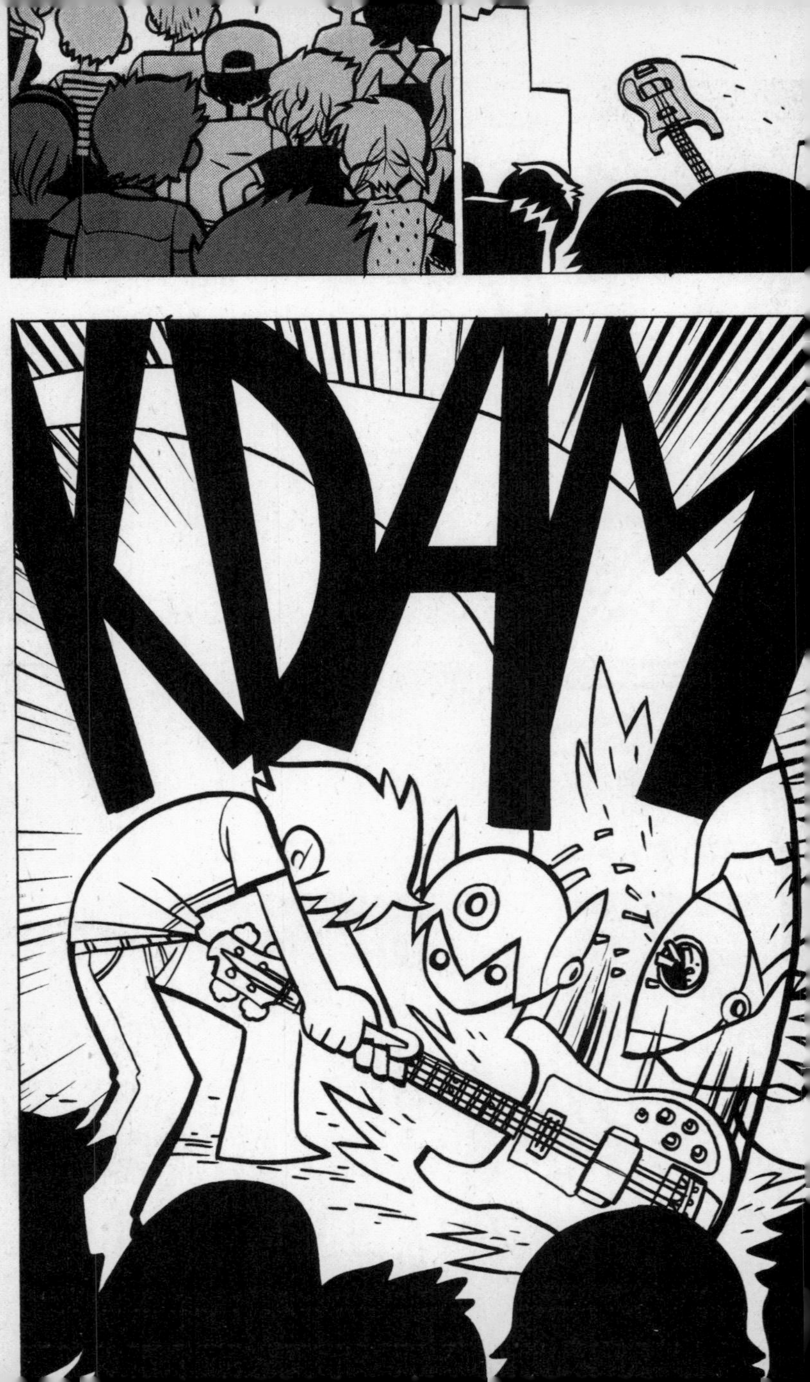
KDAM

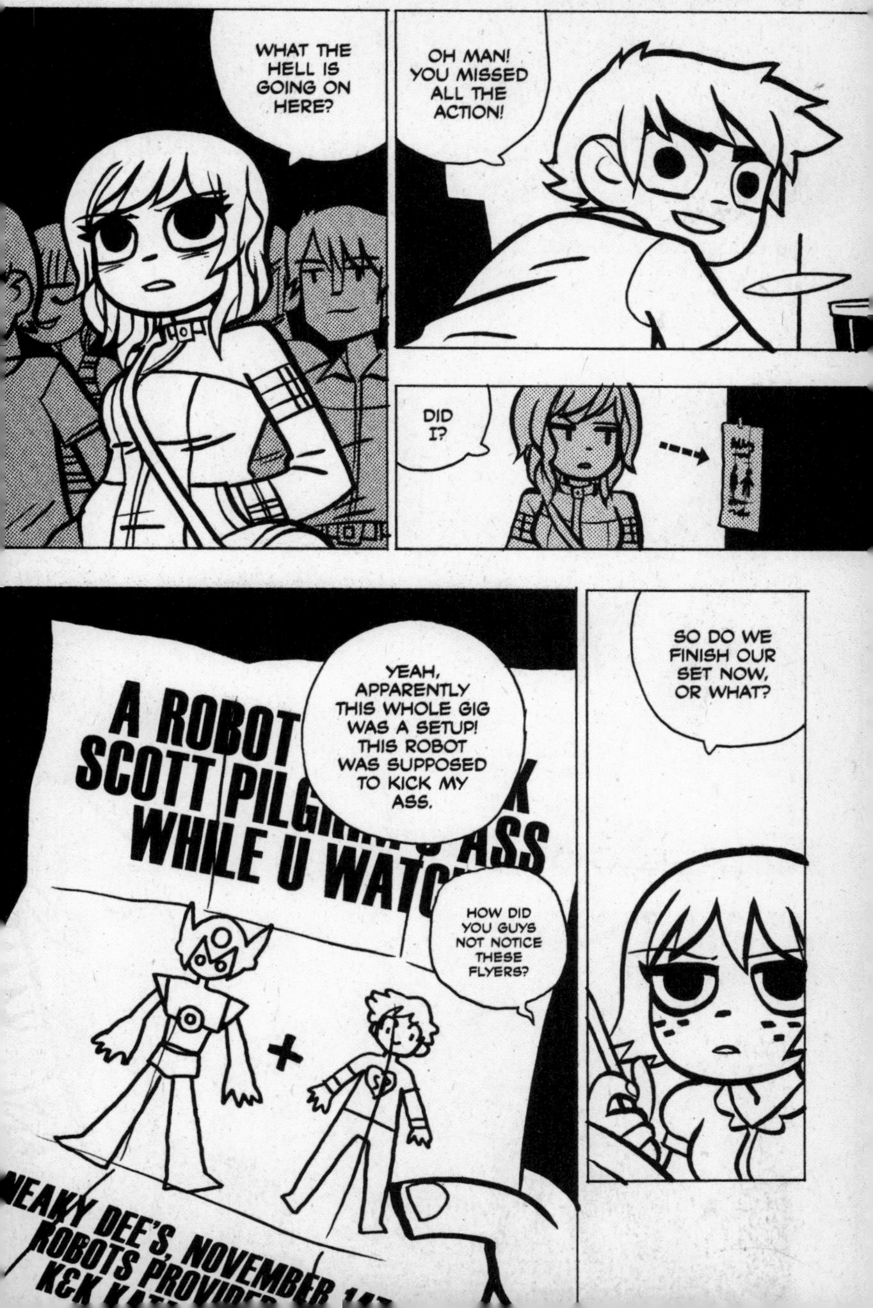
WHAT THE HELL IS GOING ON HERE?
OH MAN! YOU MISSED ALL THE ACTION!
DID I?
YEAH, APPARENTLY THIS WHOLE GIG WAS A SETUP! THIS ROBOT WAS SUPPOSED TO KICK MY ASS.
A ROBOT
SCOTT PILG
WHILE U WATC
HOW DID YOU GUYS NOT NOTICE THESE FLYERS?
NEAKY DEE'S, NOVEMBER
ROBOTS PROVIDE
K&K
SO DO WE FINISH OUR SET NOW, OR WHAT?

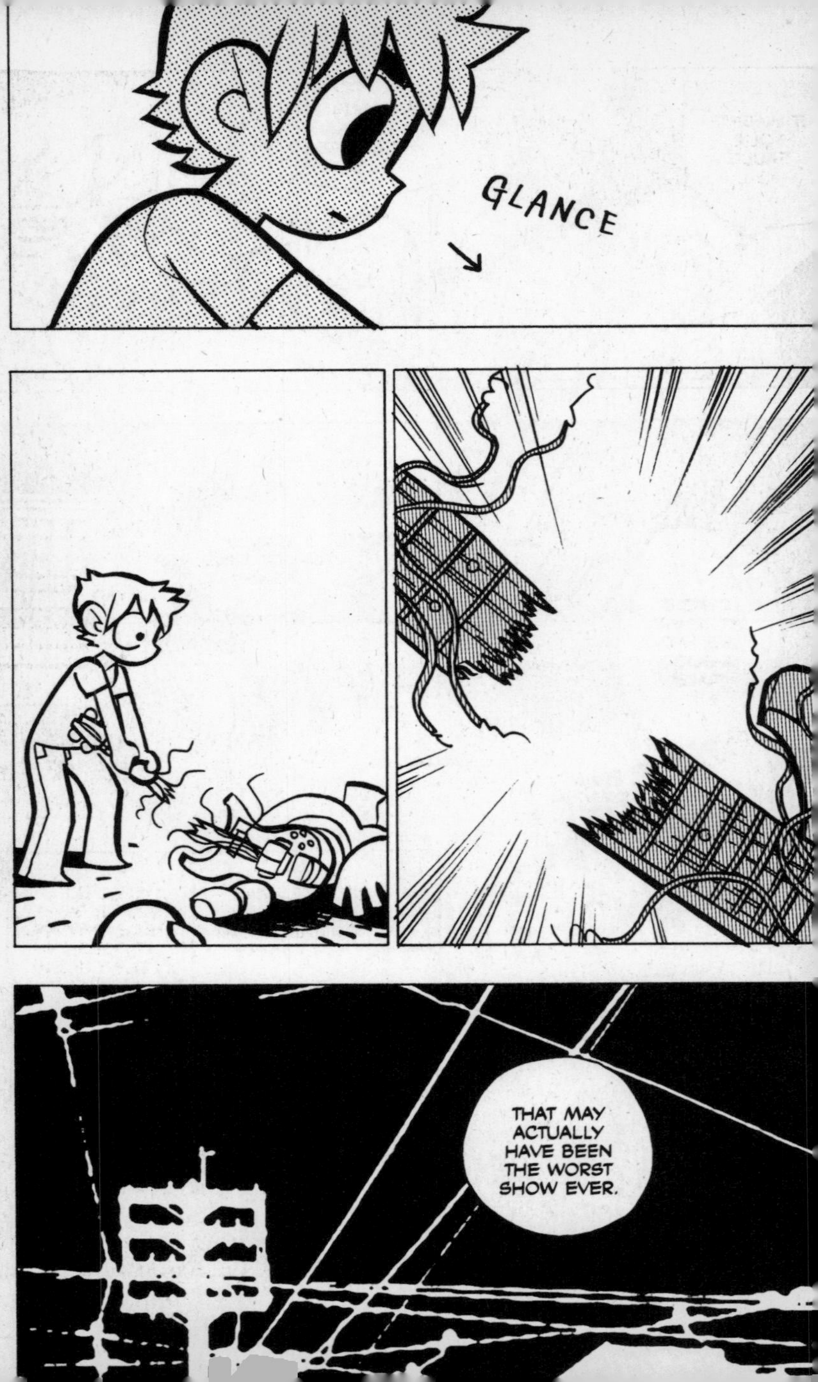
GLANCE
THAT MAY ACTUALLY HAVE BEEN THE WORST SHOW EVER.

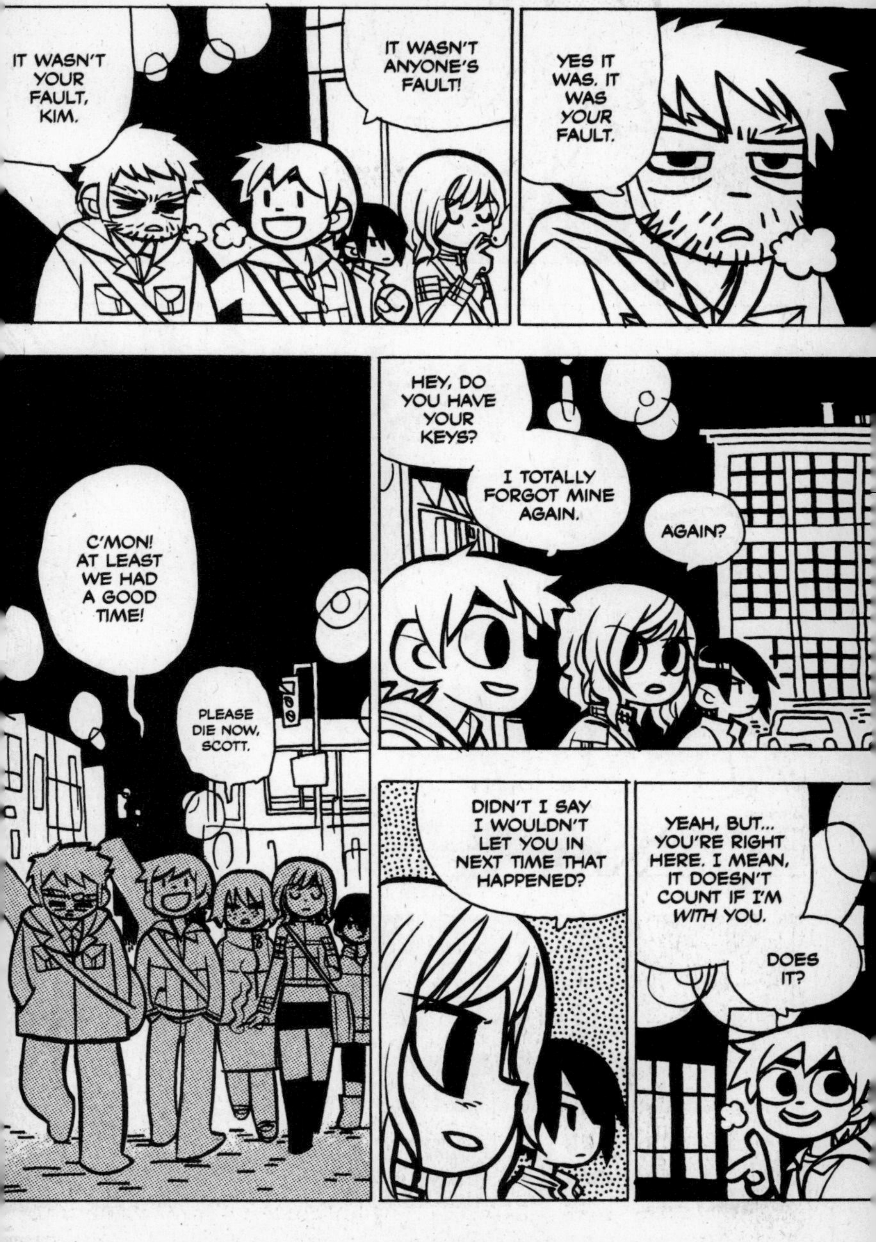
IT WASN'T YOUR FAULT, KIM.
IT WASN'T ANYONE'S FAULT!
YES IT WAS. IT WAS *YOUR* FAULT.
C'MON! AT LEAST WE HAD A GOOD TIME!
PLEASE DIE NOW, SCOTT.
HEY, DO YOU HAVE YOUR KEYS?
I TOTALLY FORGOT MINE AGAIN.
AGAIN?
DIDN'T I SAY I WOULDN'T LET YOU IN NEXT TIME THAT HAPPENED?
YEAH, BUT... YOU'RE RIGHT HERE. I MEAN, IT DOESN'T COUNT IF I'M *WITH* YOU.
DOES IT?

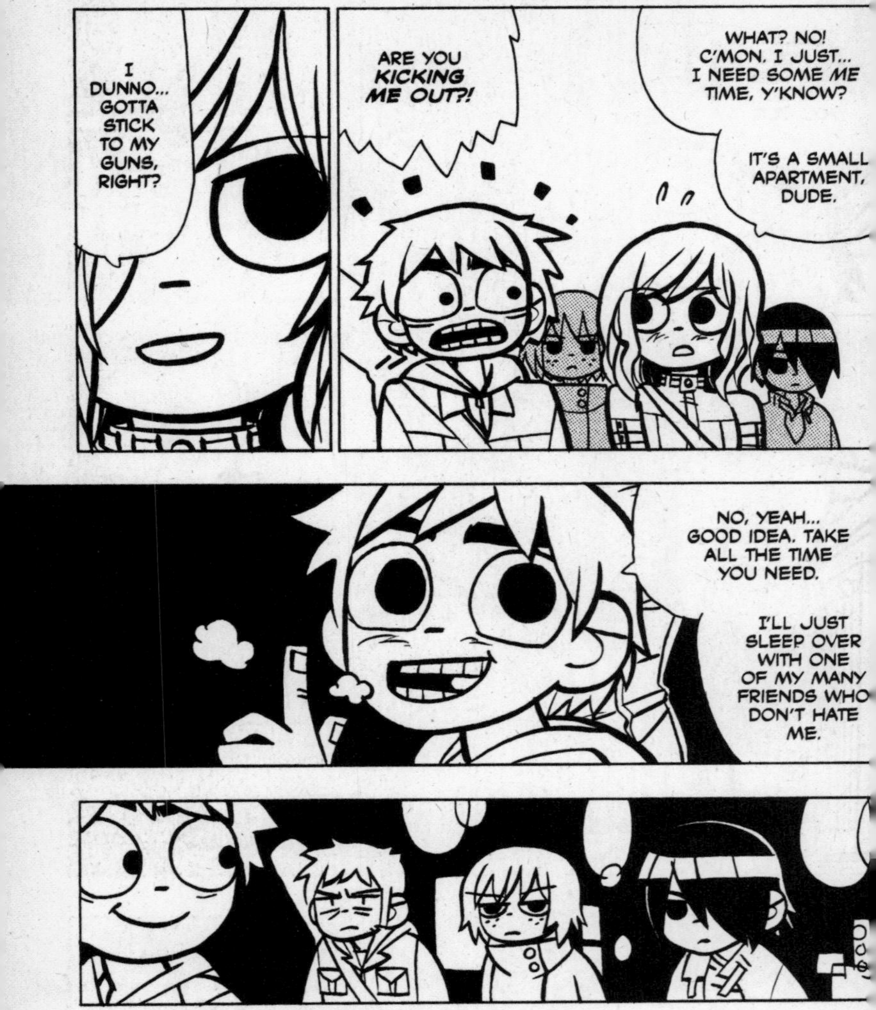
I DUNNO... GOTTA STICK TO MY GUNS, RIGHT?
ARE YOU *KICKING ME OUT?!*
WHAT? NO! C'MON. I JUST... I NEED SOME *ME* TIME, Y'KNOW?
IT'S A SMALL APARTMENT, DUDE.
NO, YEAH... GOOD IDEA. TAKE ALL THE TIME YOU NEED.
I'LL JUST SLEEP OVER WITH ONE OF MY MANY FRIENDS WHO DON'T HATE ME.

[redacted]

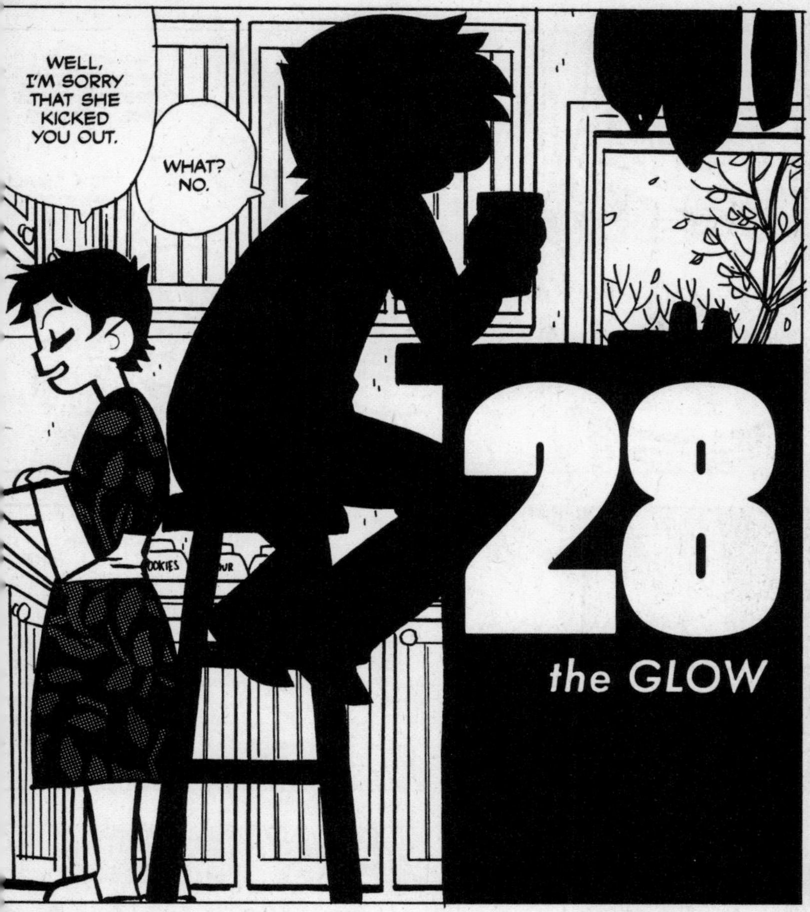
WELL, I'M SORRY THAT SHE KICKED YOU OUT.
WHAT? NO.
COOKIES
28
the GLOW

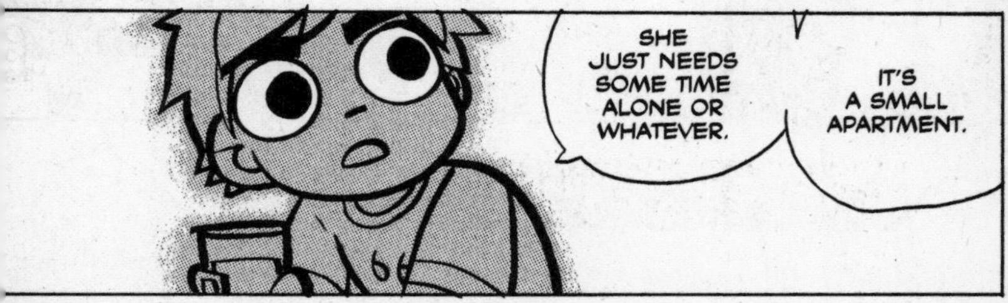
SHE JUST NEEDS SOME TIME ALONE OR WHATEVER.
IT'S A SMALL APARTMENT.

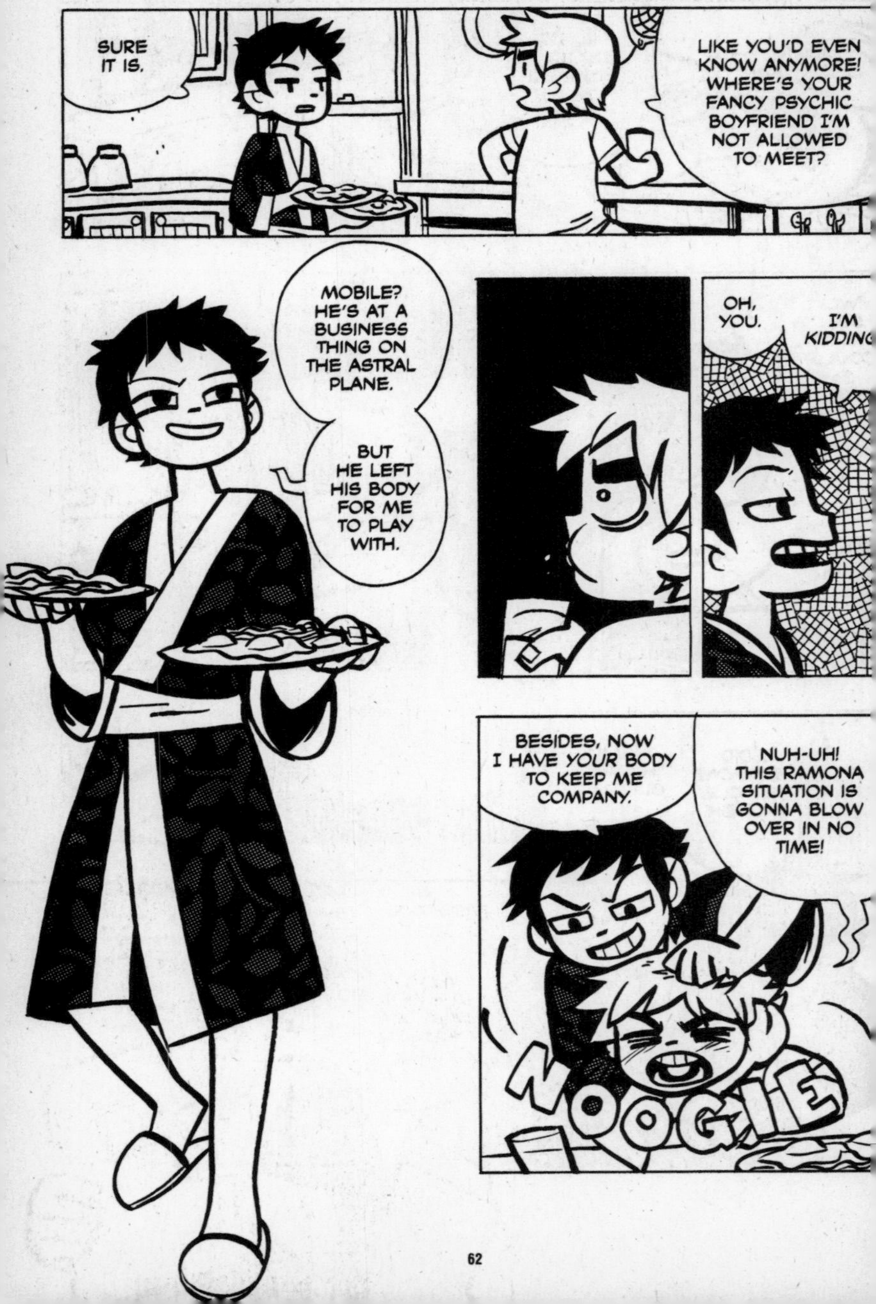
SURE IT IS.
LIKE YOU'D EVEN KNOW ANYMORE! WHERE'S YOUR FANCY PSYCHIC BOYFRIEND I'M NOT ALLOWED TO MEET?
MOBILE? HE'S AT A BUSINESS THING ON THE ASTRAL PLANE.
BUT HE LEFT HIS BODY FOR ME TO PLAY WITH.
OH, YOU.
I'M KIDDING
BESIDES, NOW I HAVE *YOUR* BODY TO KEEP ME COMPANY.
NUH-UH! THIS RAMONA SITUATION IS GONNA BLOW OVER IN NO TIME!
NOOGIE

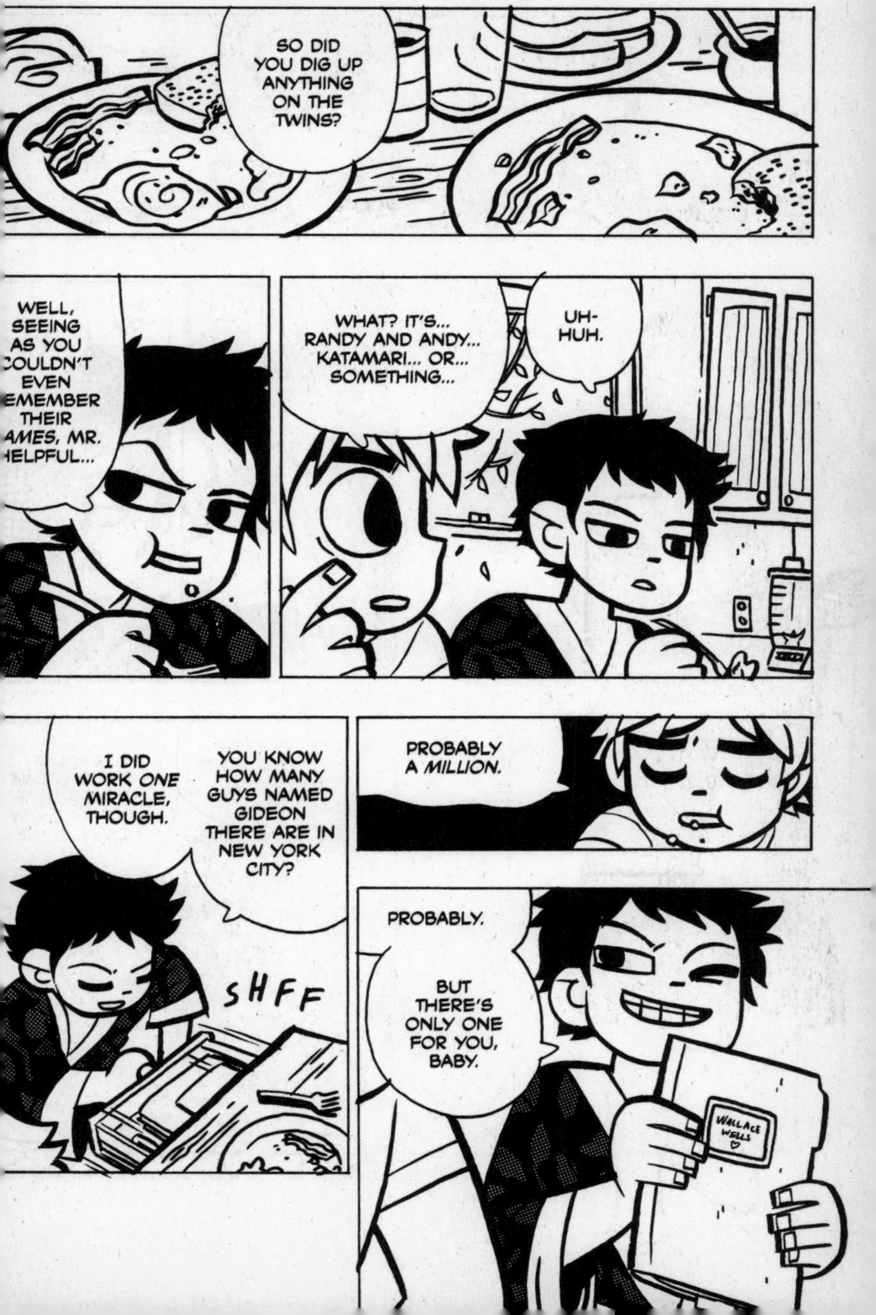
SO DID YOU DIG UP ANYTHING ON THE TWINS?
WELL, SEEING AS YOU COULDN'T EVEN REMEMBER THEIR NAMES, MR. HELPFUL...
WHAT? IT'S... RANDY AND ANDY... KATAMARI... OR... SOMETHING...
UH-HUH.
I DID WORK *ONE* MIRACLE, THOUGH.
YOU KNOW HOW MANY GUYS NAMED GIDEON THERE ARE IN NEW YORK CITY?
PROBABLY A *MILLION*.
SHFF
PROBABLY.
BUT THERE'S ONLY ONE FOR YOU, BABY.
WALLACE WELLS

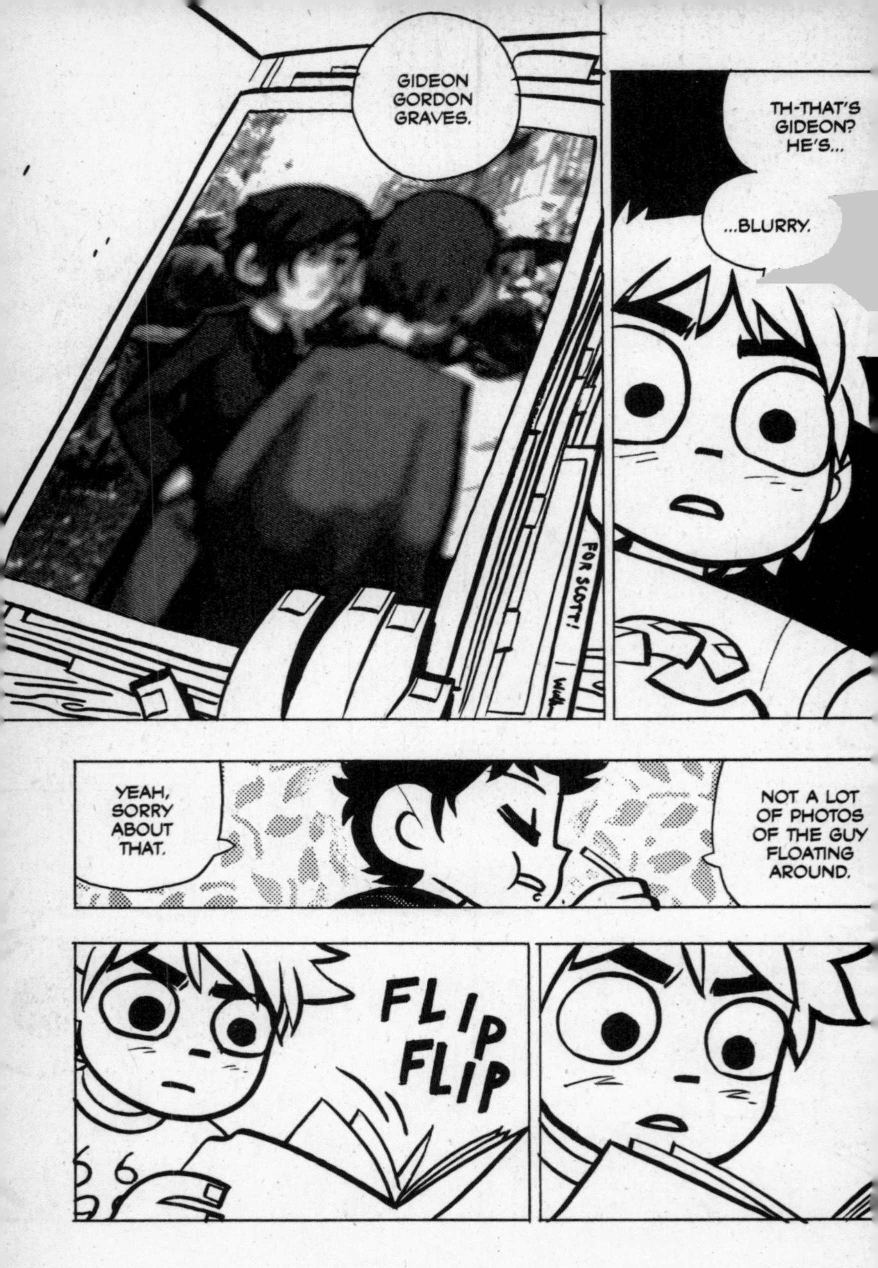
GIDEON GORDON GRAVES.
TH-THAT'S GIDEON? HE'S...
...BLURRY.
FOR SCOTT!
YEAH, SORRY ABOUT THAT.
NOT A LOT OF PHOTOS OF THE GUY FLOATING AROUND.
FLIP FLIP

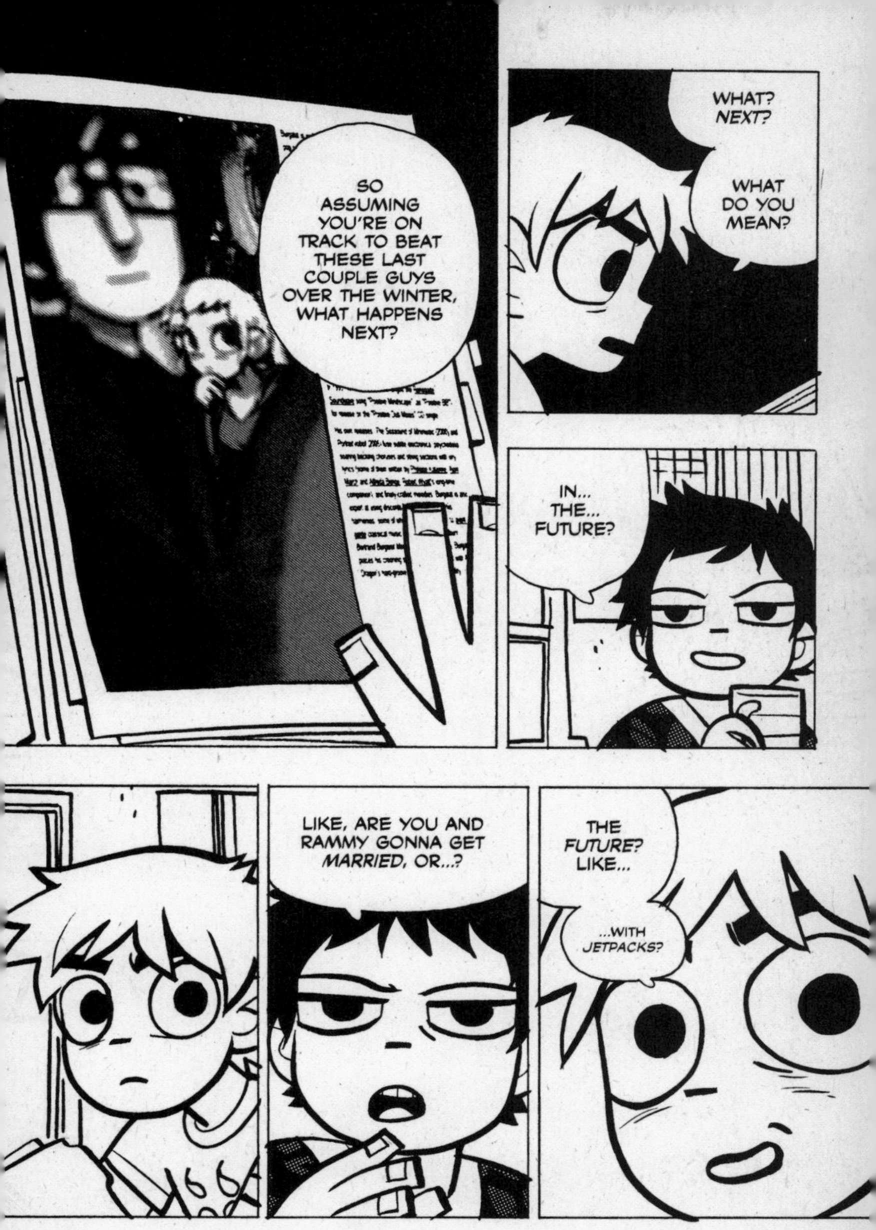
SO ASSUMING YOU'RE ON TRACK TO BEAT THESE LAST COUPLE GUYS OVER THE WINTER, WHAT HAPPENS NEXT?
WHAT? NEXT?
WHAT DO YOU MEAN?
IN... THE... FUTURE?
LIKE, ARE YOU AND RAMMY GONNA GET MARRIED, OR...?
THE FUTURE? LIKE...
...WITH JETPACKS?

THE VIDEO STORE

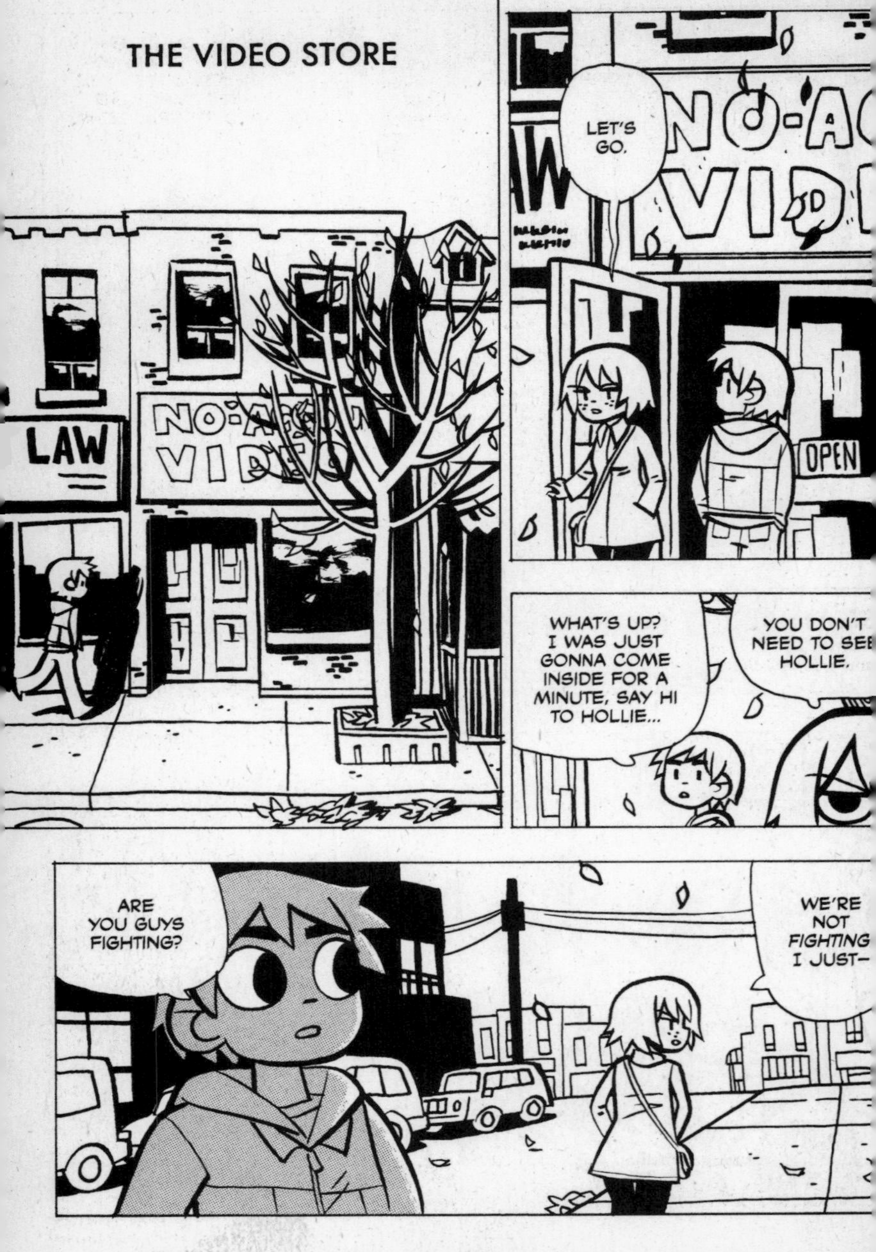
LAW
LET'S GO.
OPEN
WHAT'S UP? I WAS JUST GONNA COME INSIDE FOR A MINUTE, SAY HI TO HOLLIE...
YOU DON'T NEED TO SEE HOLLIE.
ARE YOU GUYS FIGHTING?
WE'RE NOT FIGHTING I JUST–

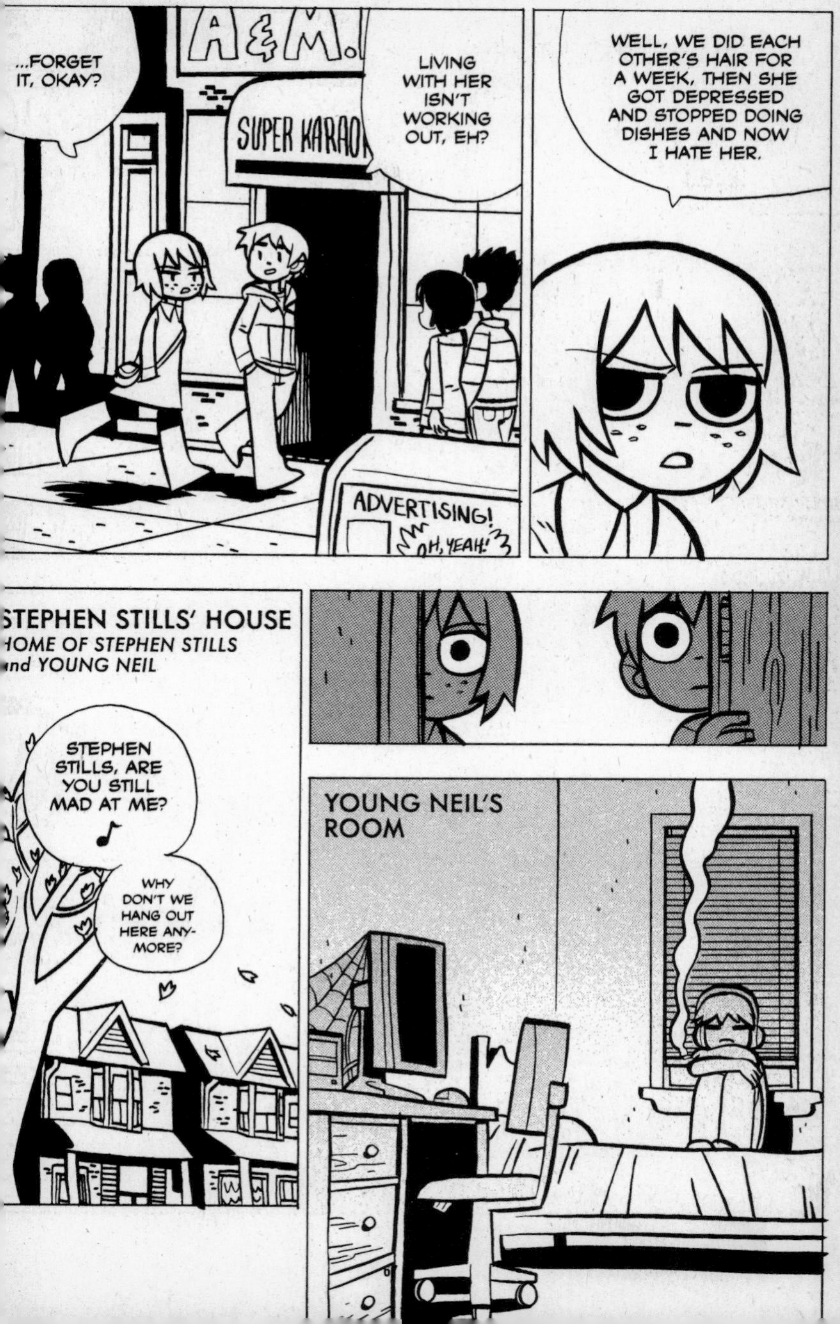

...FORGET IT, OKAY?
A&M.
SUPER KARAO
LIVING WITH HER ISN'T WORKING OUT, EH?
ADVERTISING!
OH, YEAH!
WELL, WE DID EACH OTHER'S HAIR FOR A WEEK, THEN SHE GOT DEPRESSED AND STOPPED DOING DISHES AND NOW I HATE HER.
STEPHEN STILLS' HOUSE
HOME OF STEPHEN STILLS and YOUNG NEIL
STEPHEN STILLS, ARE YOU STILL MAD AT ME?
WHY DON'T WE HANG OUT HERE ANY-MORE?
YOUNG NEIL'S ROOM

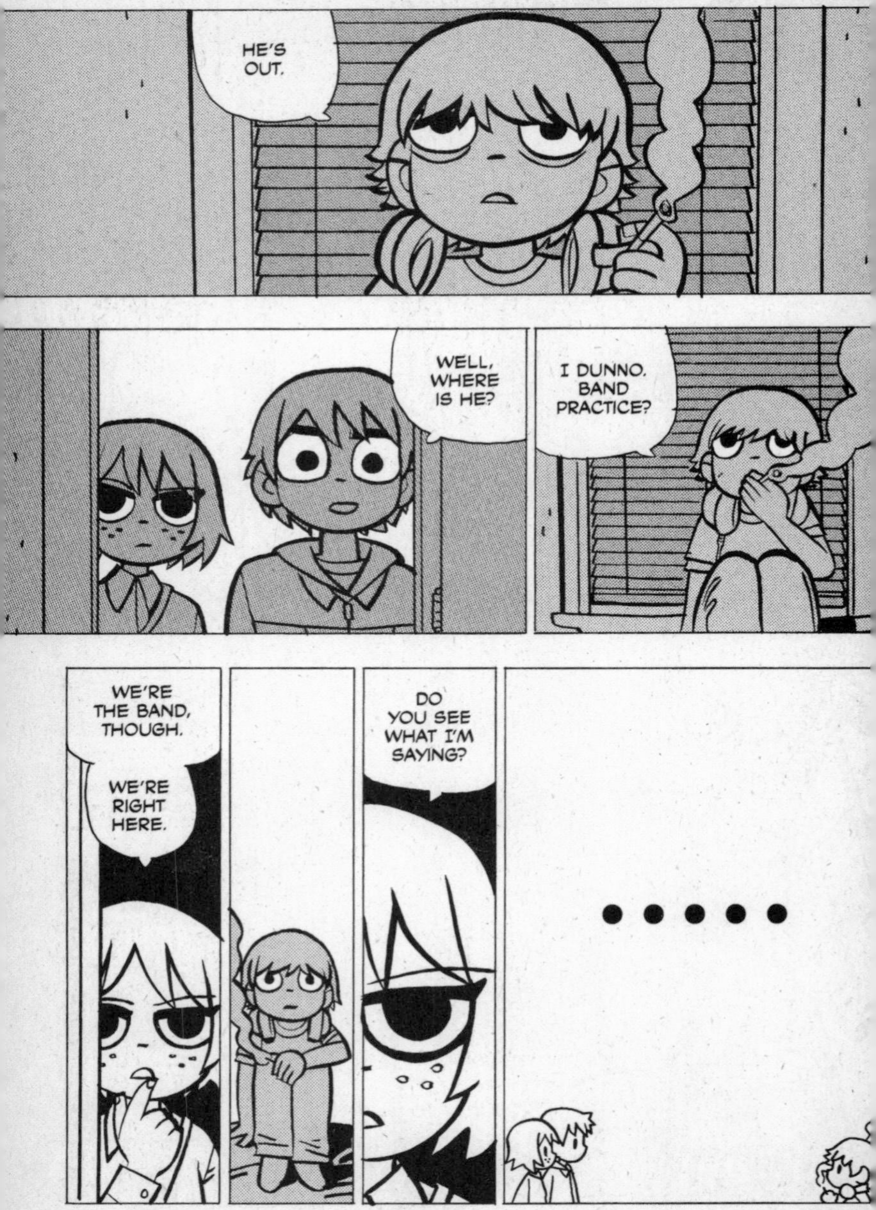
HE'S OUT.
WELL, WHERE IS HE?
I DUNNO. BAND PRACTICE?
WE'RE THE BAND, THOUGH.
WE'RE RIGHT HERE.
DO YOU SEE WHAT I'M SAYING?
.....

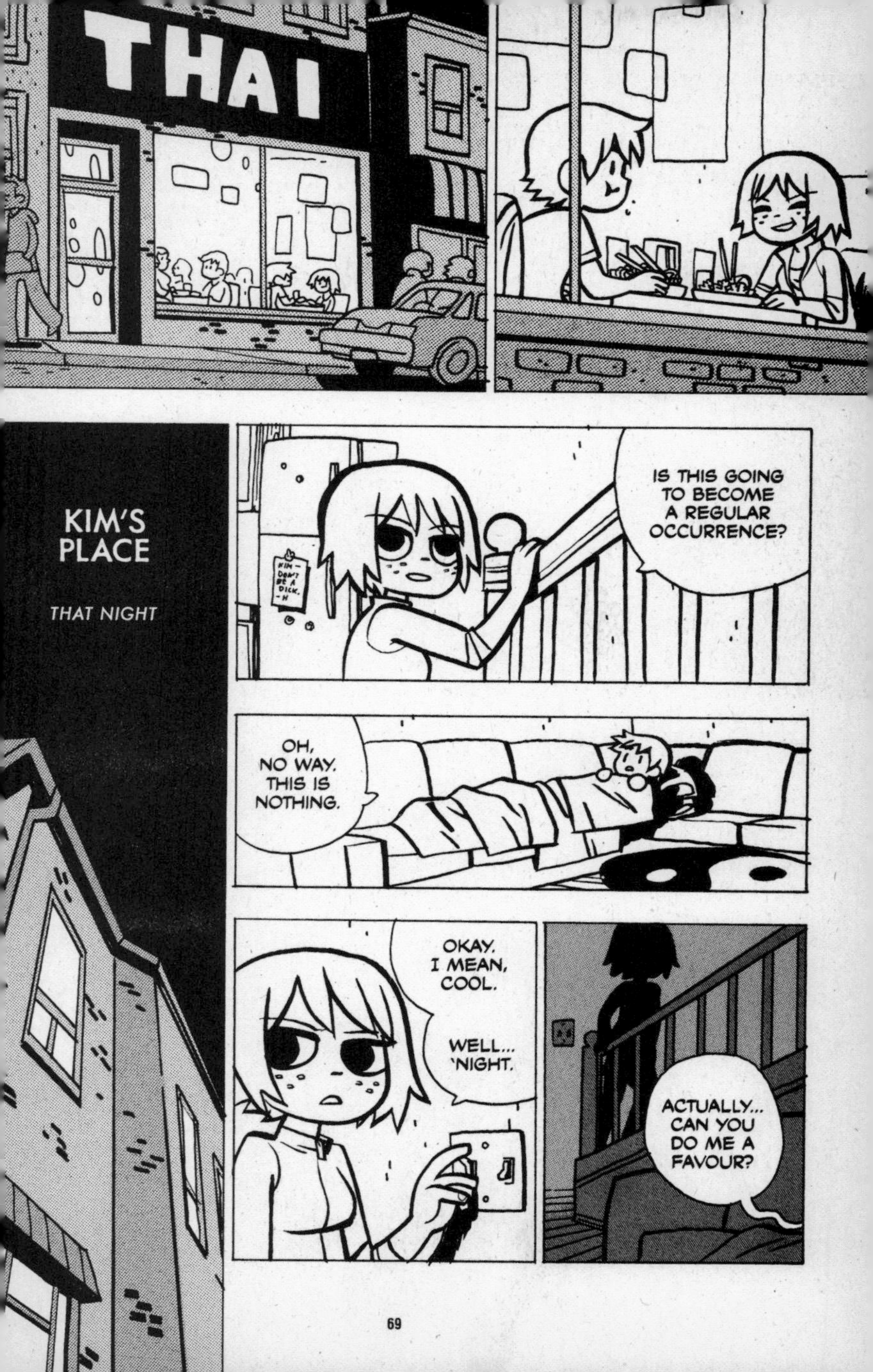
THAI
KIM'S PLACE
THAT NIGHT
IS THIS GOING TO BECOME A REGULAR OCCURRENCE?
KIM - DON'T BE A DICK. -H
OH, NO WAY. THIS IS NOTHING.
OKAY. I MEAN, COOL.
WELL... 'NIGHT.
ACTUALLY... CAN YOU DO ME A FAVOUR?

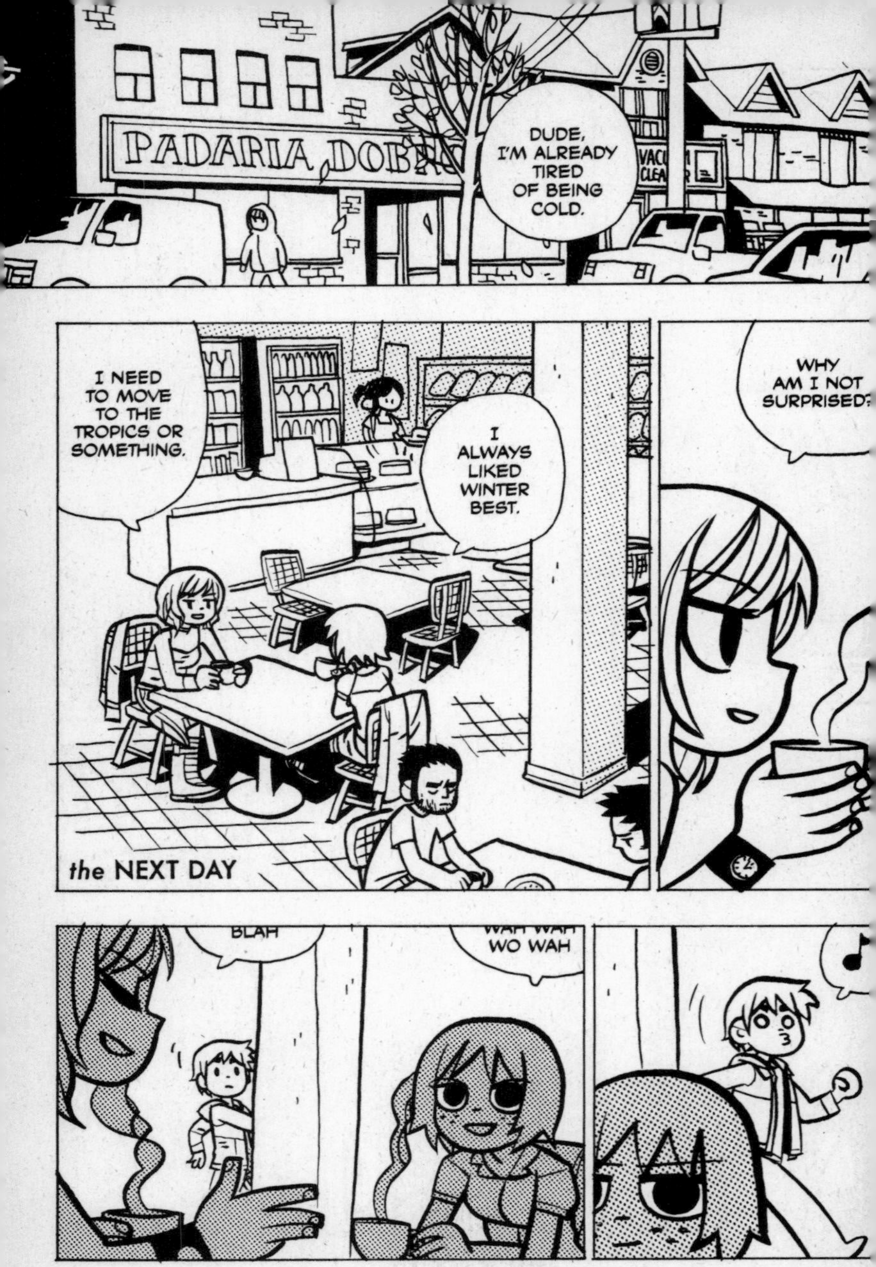
PADARIA DOBR
DUDE, I'M ALREADY TIRED OF BEING COLD.
VACU CLEA
I NEED TO MOVE TO THE TROPICS OR SOMETHING.
I ALWAYS LIKED WINTER BEST.
the NEXT DAY
WHY AM I NOT SURPRISED?
BLAH
WAH WAH WO WAH

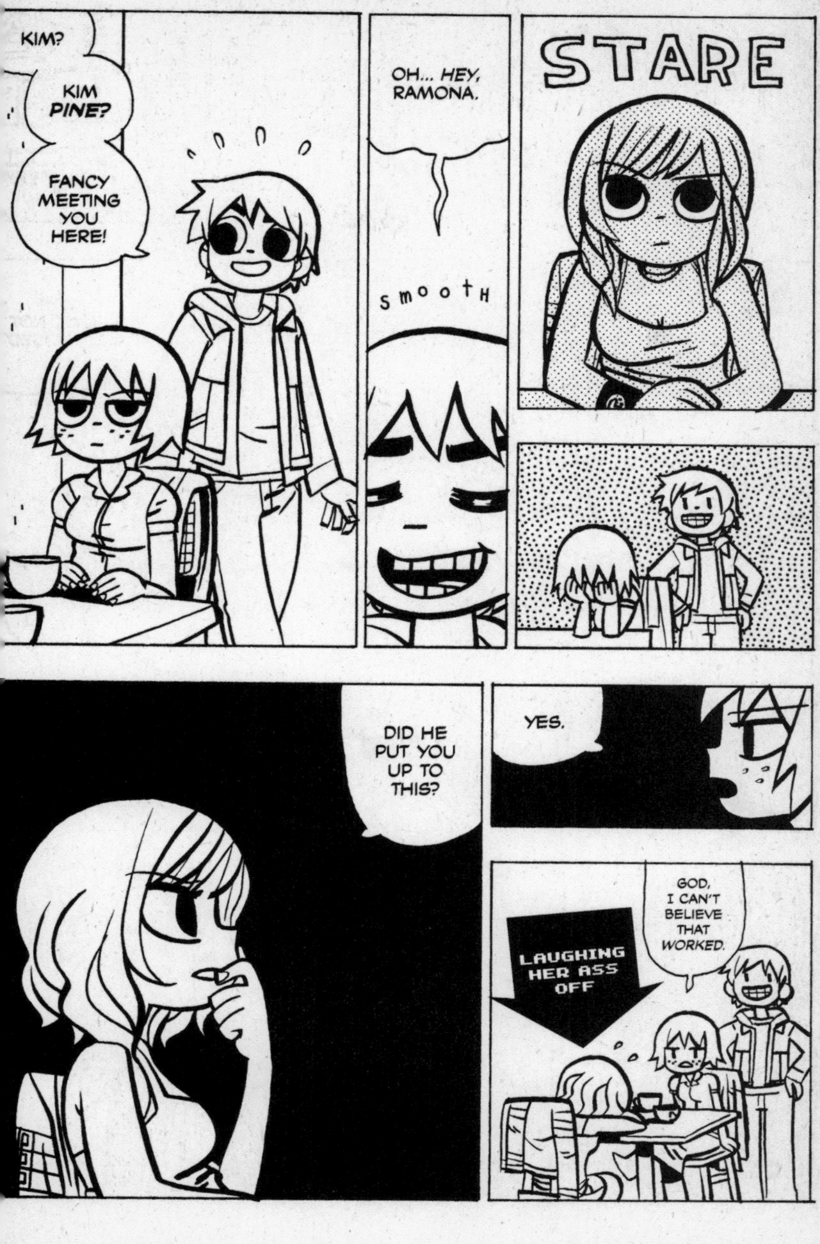
KIM?
KIM PINE?
FANCY MEETING YOU HERE!
OH... HEY, RAMONA.
SMOOTH
STARE
DID HE PUT YOU UP TO THIS?
YES.
LAUGHING HER ASS OFF
GOD, I CAN'T BELIEVE THAT WORKED.

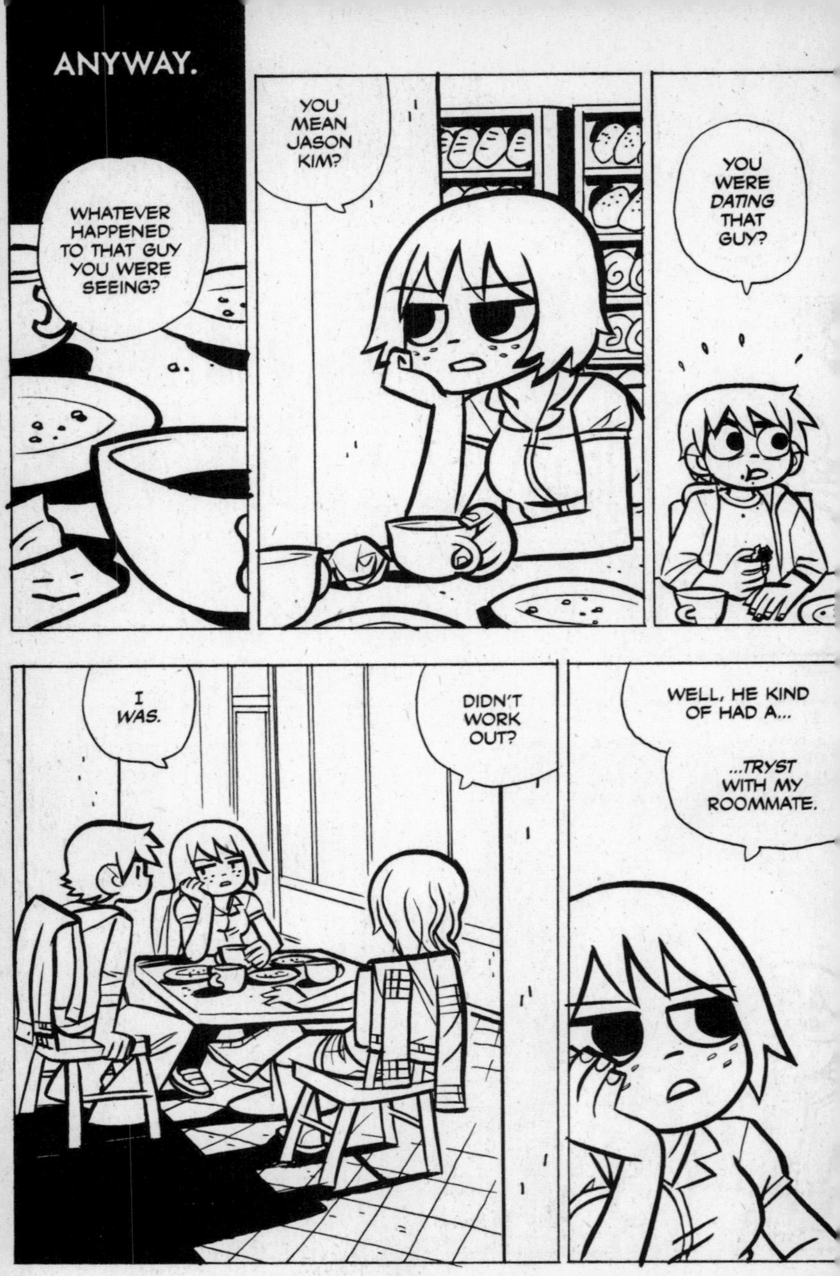
ANYWAY.
WHATEVER HAPPENED TO THAT GUY YOU WERE SEEING?
YOU MEAN JASON KIM?
YOU WERE *DATING* THAT GUY?
I *WAS.*
DIDN'T WORK OUT?
WELL, HE KIND OF HAD A...
...*TRYST* WITH MY ROOMMATE.

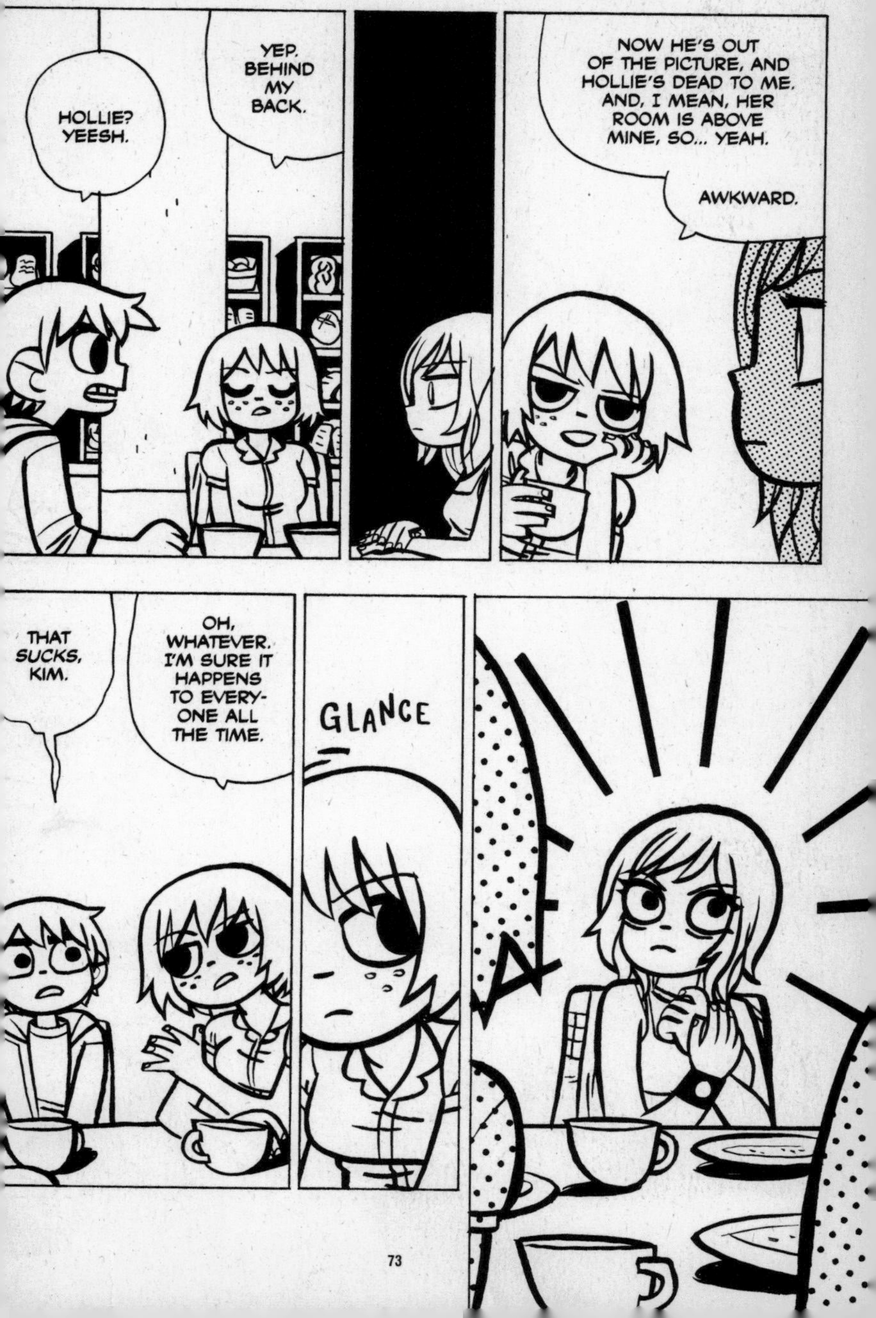
HOLLIE? YEESH.
YEP. BEHIND MY BACK.
NOW HE'S OUT OF THE PICTURE, AND HOLLIE'S DEAD TO ME. AND, I MEAN, HER ROOM IS ABOVE MINE, SO... YEAH.
AWKWARD.
THAT SUCKS, KIM.
OH, WHATEVER. I'M SURE IT HAPPENS TO EVERY-ONE ALL THE TIME.
GLANCE

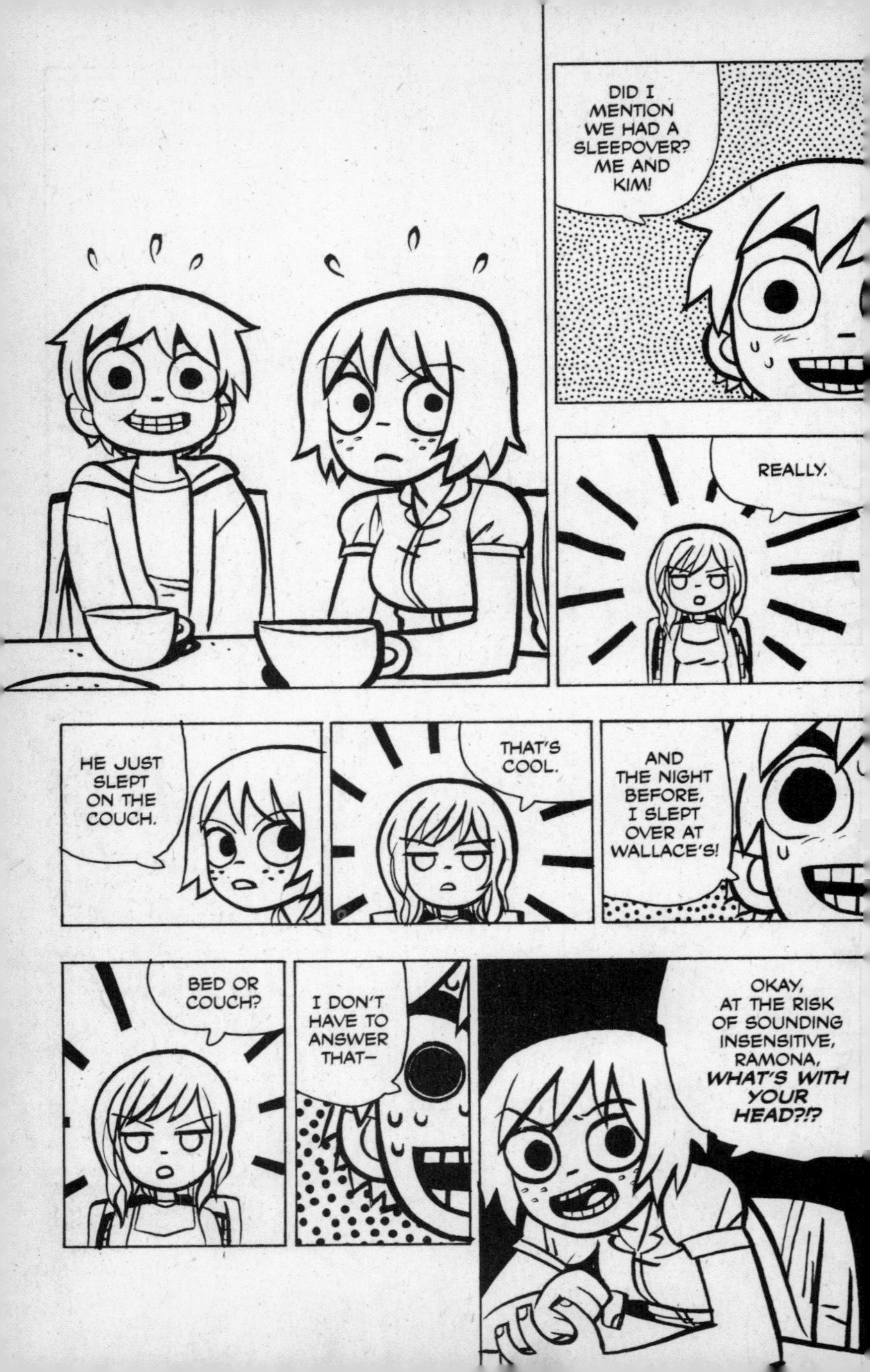
DID I MENTION WE HAD A SLEEPOVER? ME AND KIM!
REALLY.
HE JUST SLEPT ON THE COUCH.
THAT'S COOL.
AND THE NIGHT BEFORE, I SLEPT OVER AT WALLACE'S!
BED OR COUCH?
I DON'T HAVE TO ANSWER THAT—
OKAY, AT THE RISK OF SOUNDING INSENSITIVE, RAMONA, *WHAT'S WITH YOUR HEAD?!?*

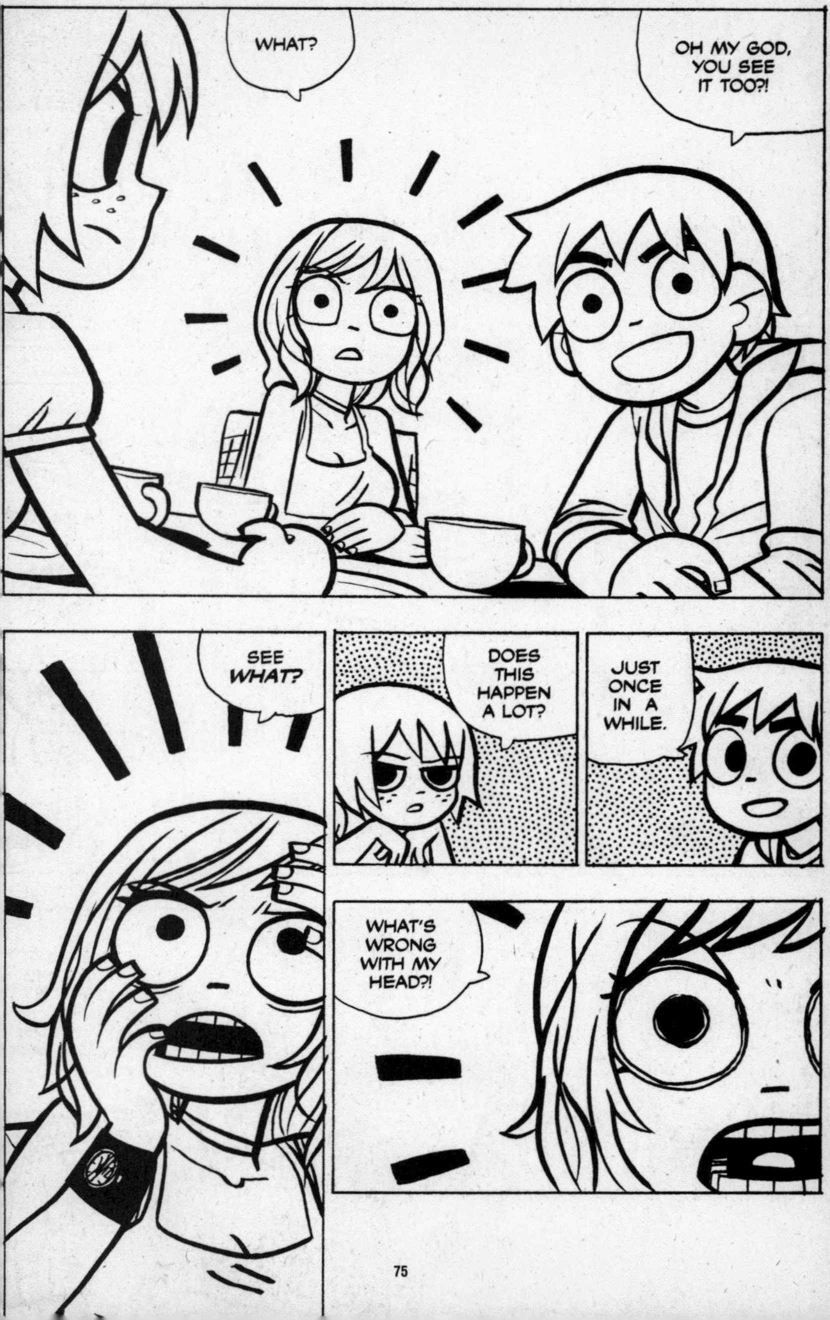
WHAT?
OH MY GOD, YOU SEE IT TOO?!
SEE *WHAT?*
DOES THIS HAPPEN A LOT?
JUST ONCE IN A WHILE.
WHAT'S WRONG WITH MY HEAD?!

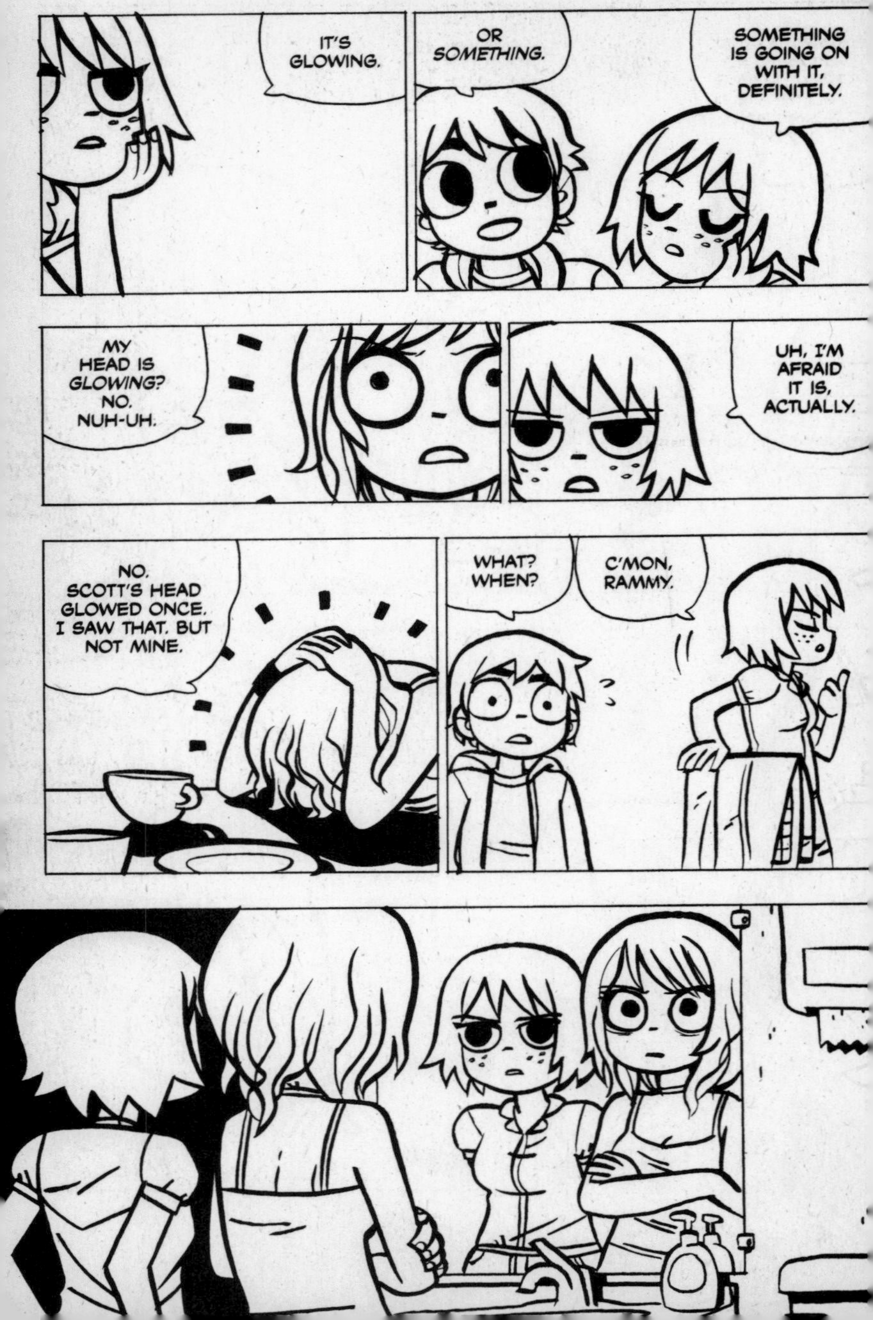
IT'S GLOWING.
OR SOMETHING.
SOMETHING IS GOING ON WITH IT, DEFINITELY.
MY HEAD IS GLOWING? NO. NUH-UH.
UH, I'M AFRAID IT IS, ACTUALLY.
NO. SCOTT'S HEAD GLOWED ONCE. I SAW THAT. BUT NOT MINE.
WHAT? WHEN?
C'MON, RAMMY.

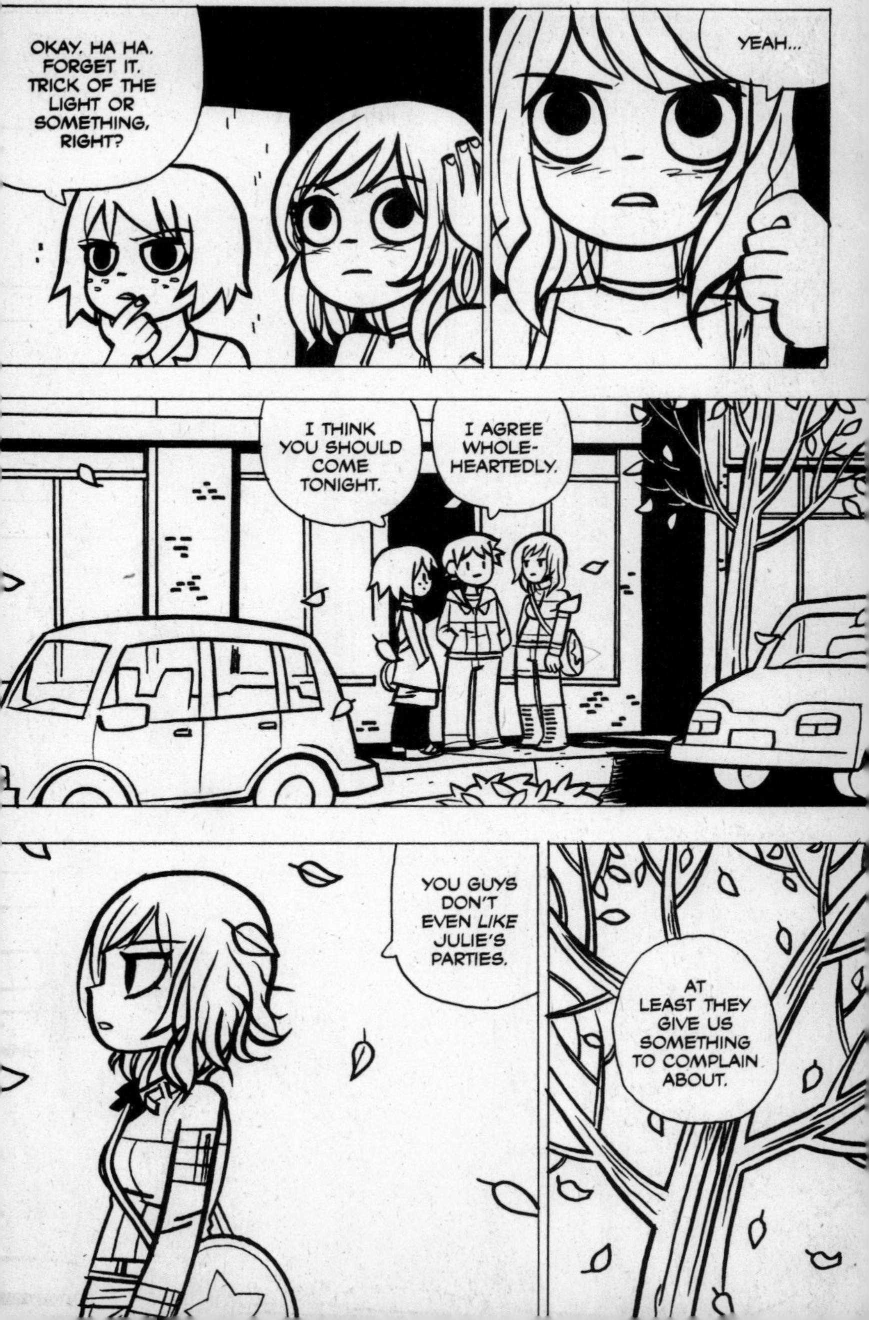
OKAY. HA HA. FORGET IT. TRICK OF THE LIGHT OR SOMETHING, RIGHT?
YEAH...
I THINK YOU SHOULD COME TONIGHT.
I AGREE WHOLE-HEARTEDLY.
YOU GUYS DON'T EVEN *LIKE* JULIE'S PARTIES.
AT LEAST THEY GIVE US SOMETHING TO COMPLAIN ABOUT.

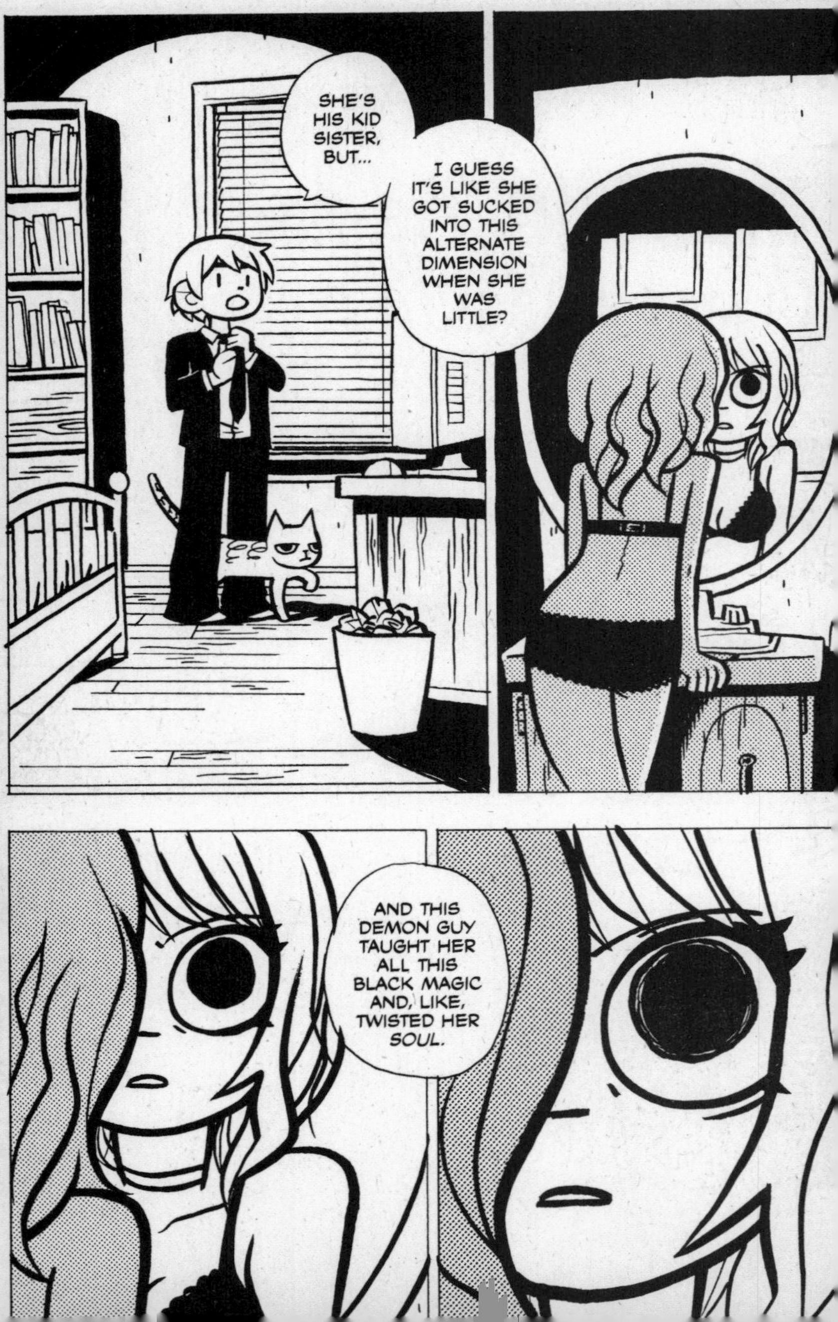
SHE'S HIS KID SISTER, BUT...
I GUESS IT'S LIKE SHE GOT SUCKED INTO THIS ALTERNATE DIMENSION WHEN SHE WAS LITTLE?
AND THIS DEMON GUY TAUGHT HER ALL THIS BLACK MAGIC AND, LIKE, TWISTED HER *SOUL*.

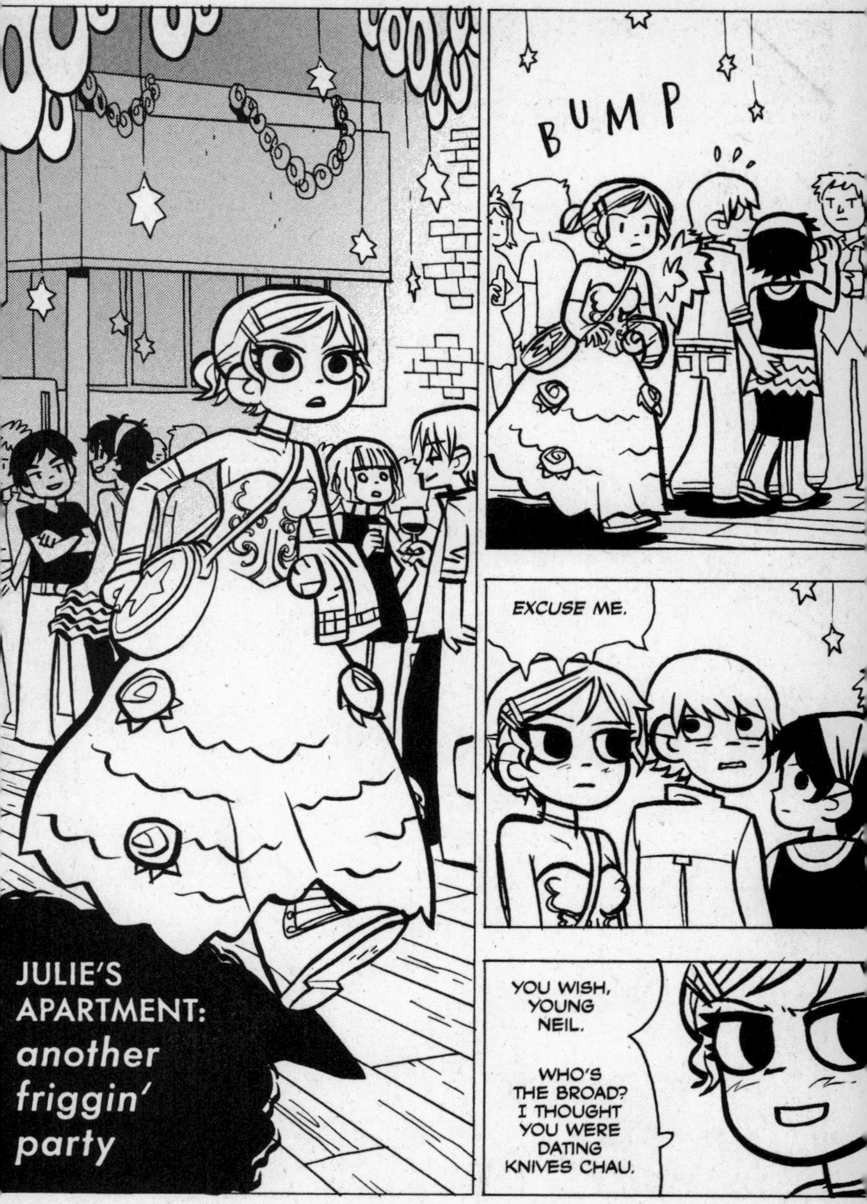
JULIE'S APARTMENT: another friggin' party
BUMP
EXCUSE ME.
YOU WISH, YOUNG NEIL.
WHO'S THE BROAD? I THOUGHT YOU WERE DATING KNIVES CHAU.

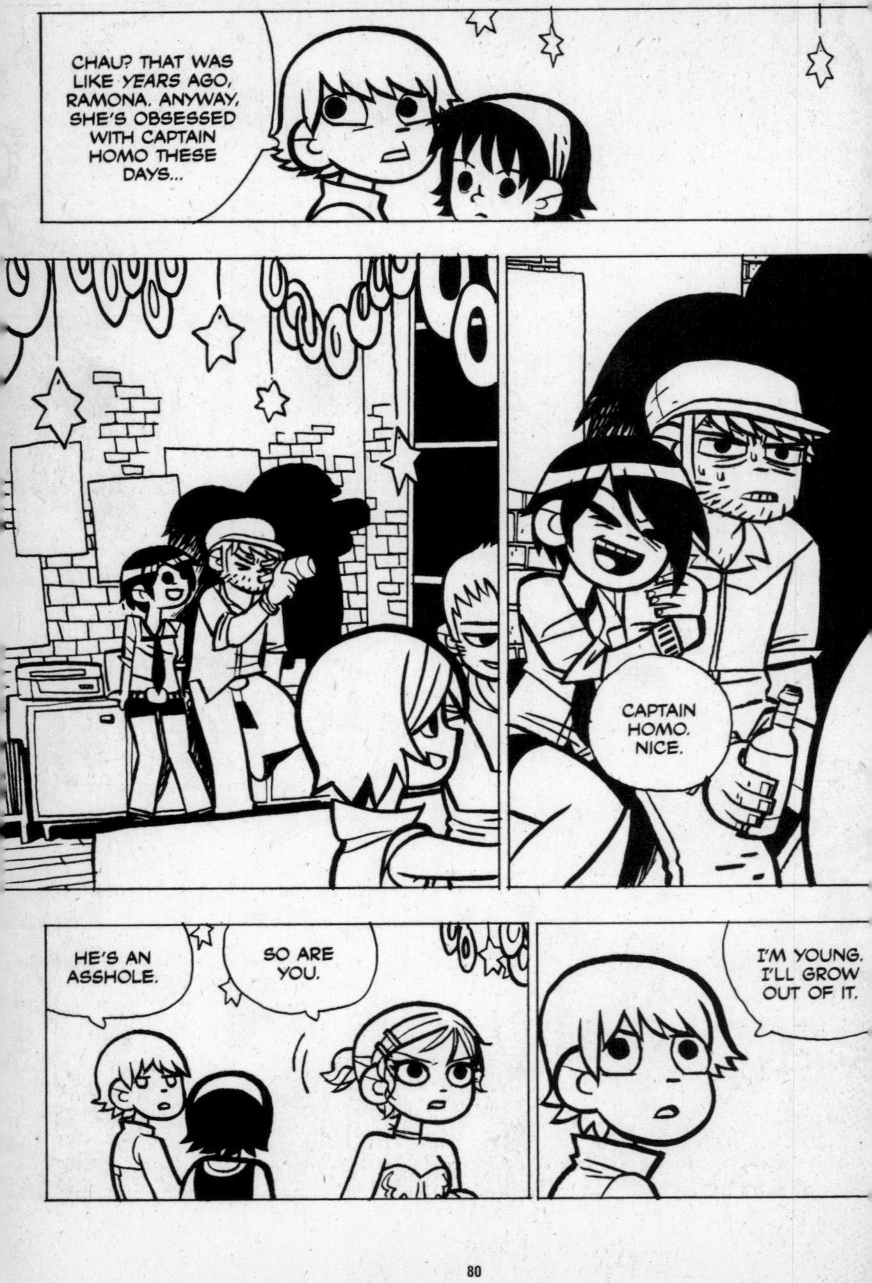

CHAU? THAT WAS LIKE *YEARS* AGO, RAMONA. ANYWAY, SHE'S OBSESSED WITH CAPTAIN HOMO THESE DAYS...
CAPTAIN HOMO. NICE.
HE'S AN ASSHOLE.
SO ARE YOU.
I'M YOUNG. I'LL GROW OUT OF IT.

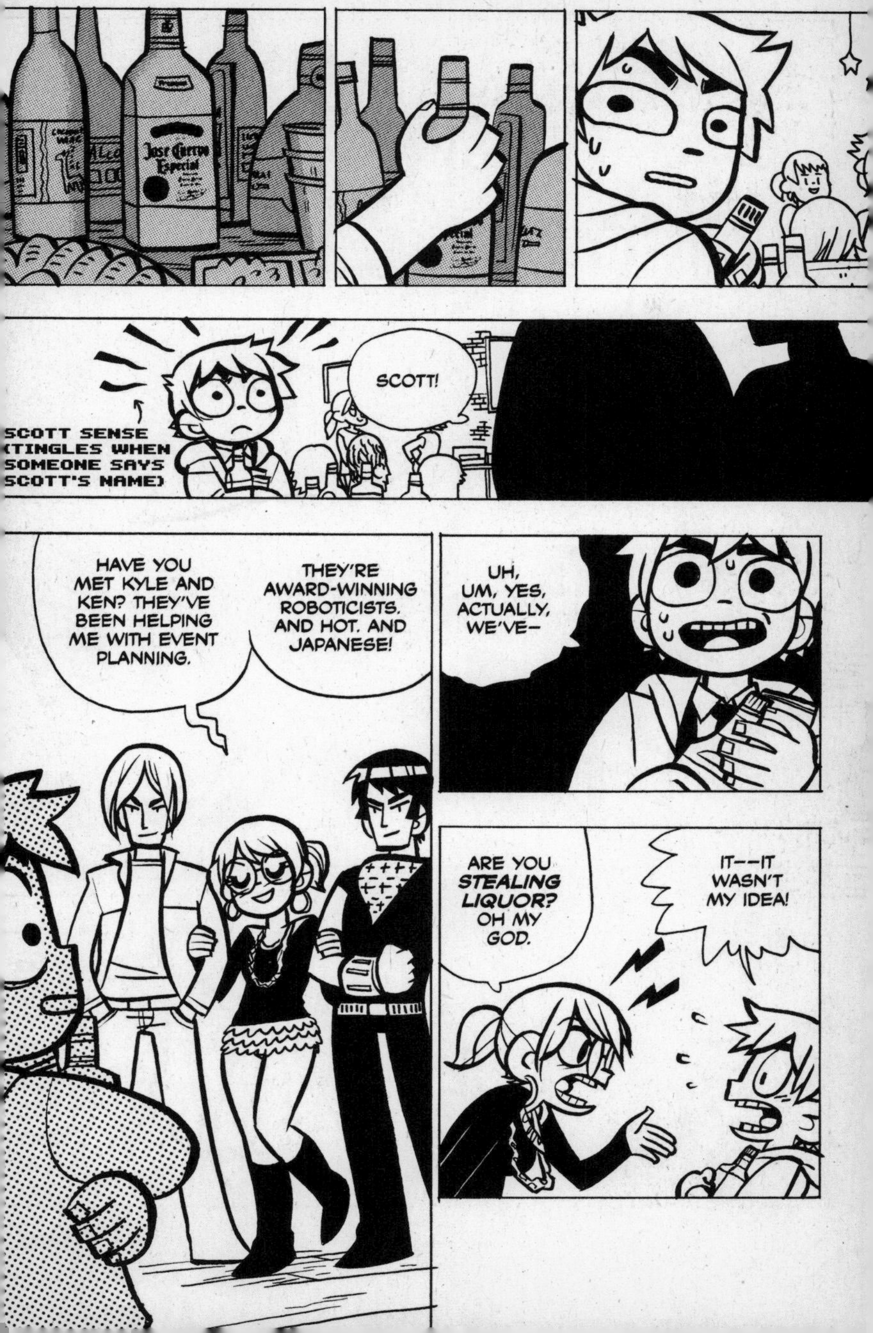

SCOTT!
SCOTT SENSE (TINGLES WHEN SOMEONE SAYS SCOTT'S NAME)
HAVE YOU MET KYLE AND KEN? THEY'VE BEEN HELPING ME WITH EVENT PLANNING.
THEY'RE AWARD-WINNING ROBOTICISTS. AND HOT. AND JAPANESE!
UH, UM, YES, ACTUALLY, WE'VE–
ARE YOU *STEALING LIQUOR?* OH MY GOD.
IT--IT WASN'T MY IDEA!

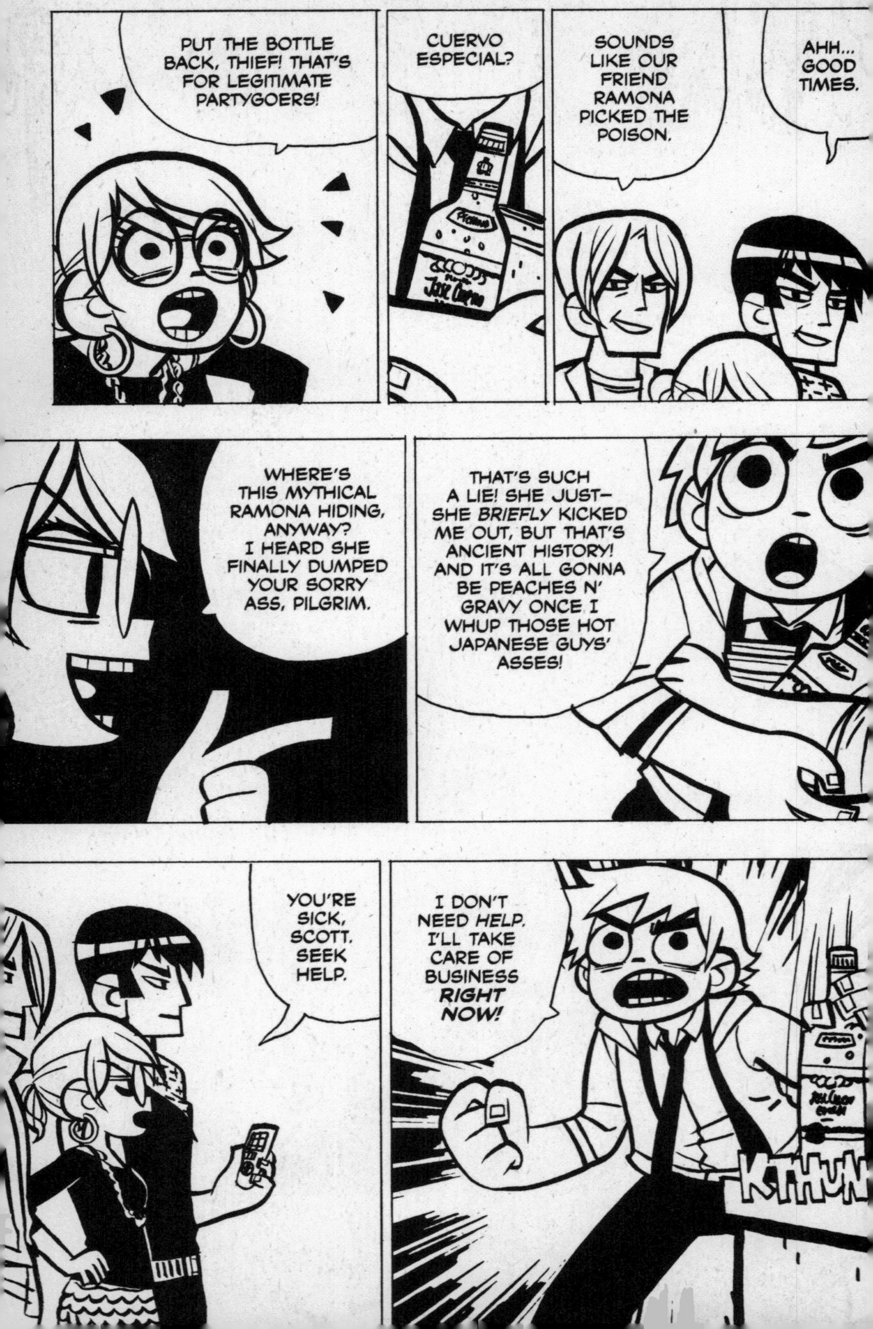

PUT THE BOTTLE BACK, THIEF! THAT'S FOR LEGITIMATE PARTYGOERS!
CUERVO ESPECIAL?
SOUNDS LIKE OUR FRIEND RAMONA PICKED THE POISON.
AHH... GOOD TIMES.
WHERE'S THIS MYTHICAL RAMONA HIDING, ANYWAY? I HEARD SHE FINALLY DUMPED YOUR SORRY ASS, PILGRIM.
THAT'S SUCH A LIE! SHE JUST— SHE *BRIEFLY* KICKED ME OUT, BUT THAT'S ANCIENT HISTORY! AND IT'S ALL GONNA BE PEACHES N' GRAVY ONCE I WHUP THOSE HOT JAPANESE GUYS' ASSES!
YOU'RE SICK, SCOTT. SEEK HELP.
I DON'T NEED *HELP*. I'LL TAKE CARE OF BUSINESS ***RIGHT NOW!***
KTHUN

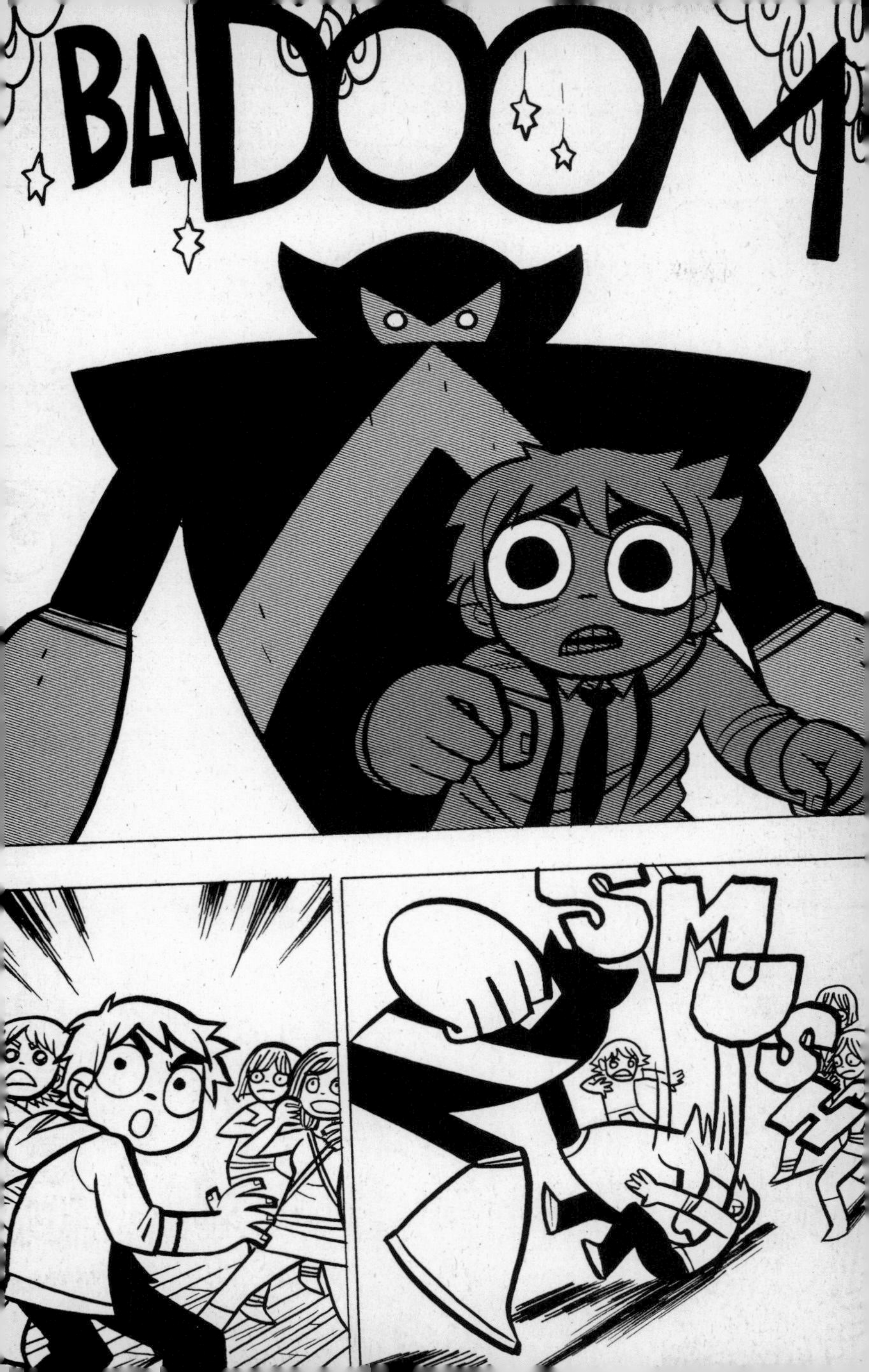
BADOOM
SMUSH

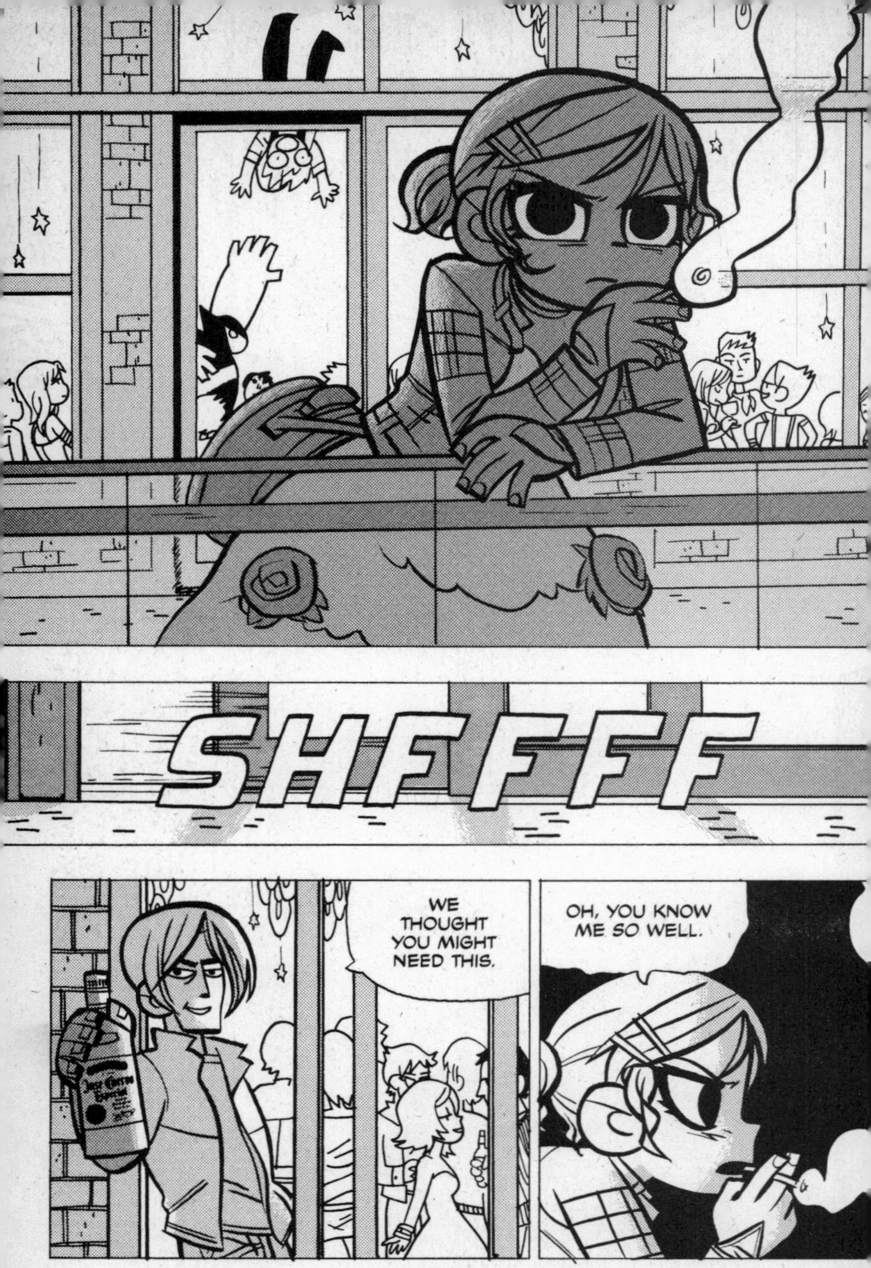
SHFFFF
WE THOUGHT YOU MIGHT NEED THIS.
OH, YOU KNOW ME SO WELL.

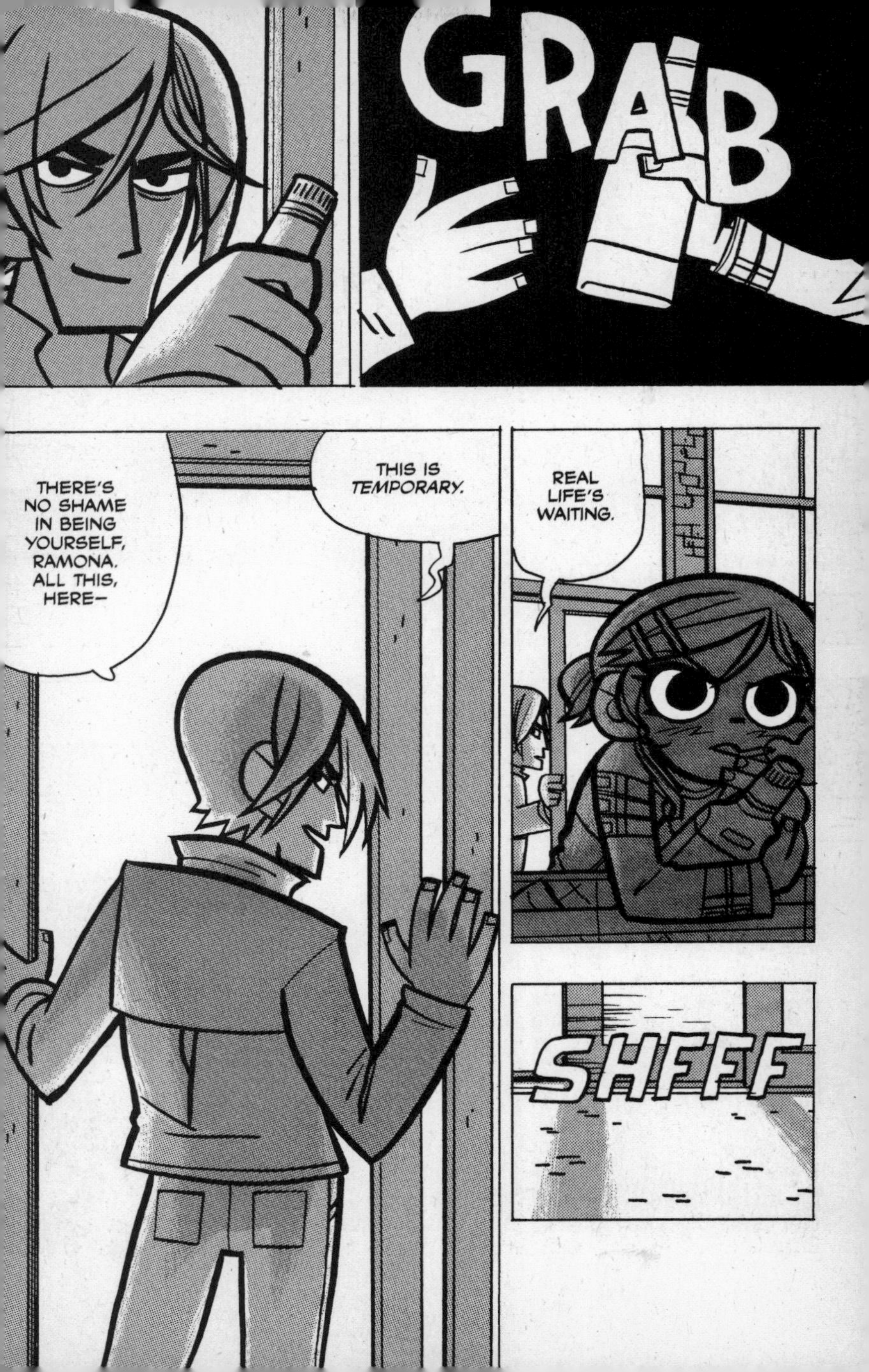
GRAB
THERE'S NO SHAME IN BEING YOURSELF, RAMONA. ALL THIS, HERE—
THIS IS *TEMPORARY.*
REAL LIFE'S WAITING.
SHFFF

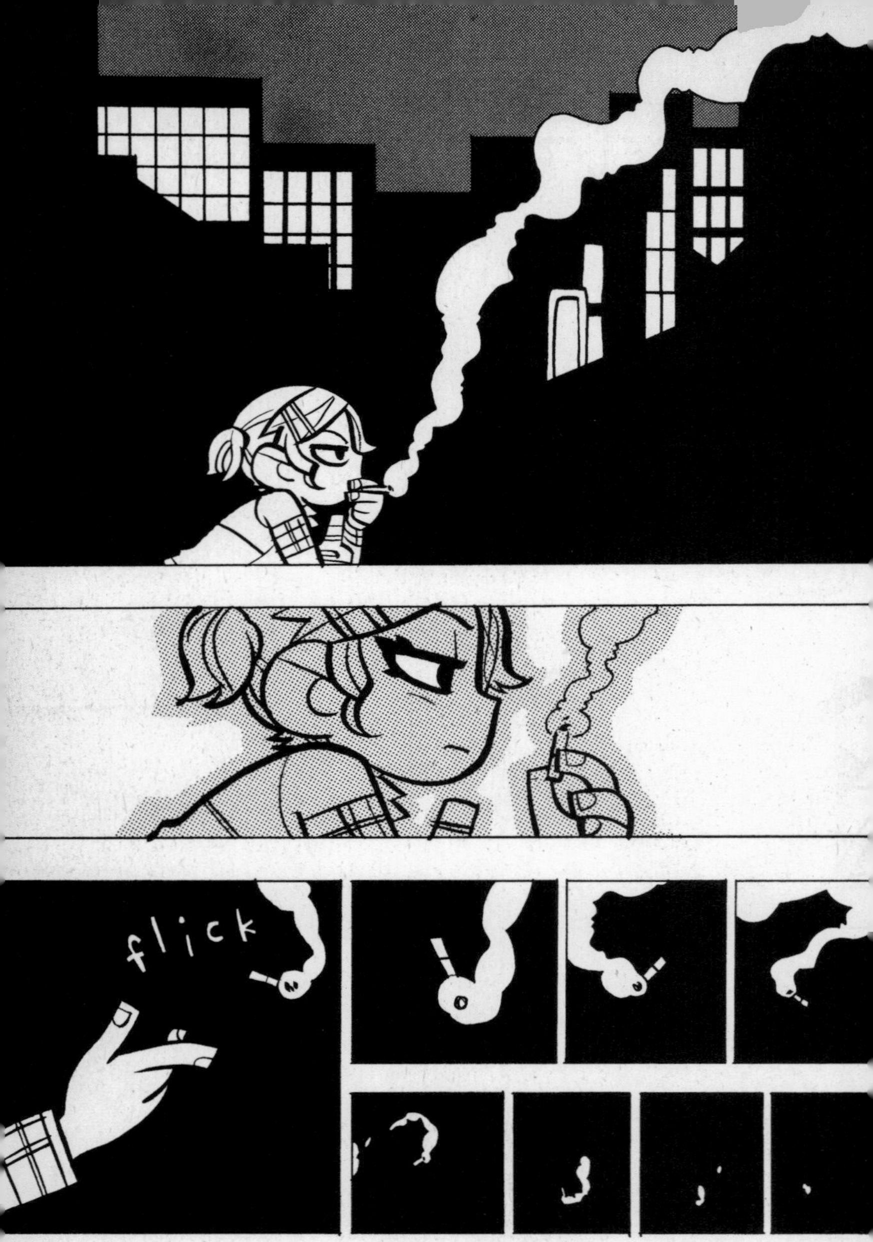
flick

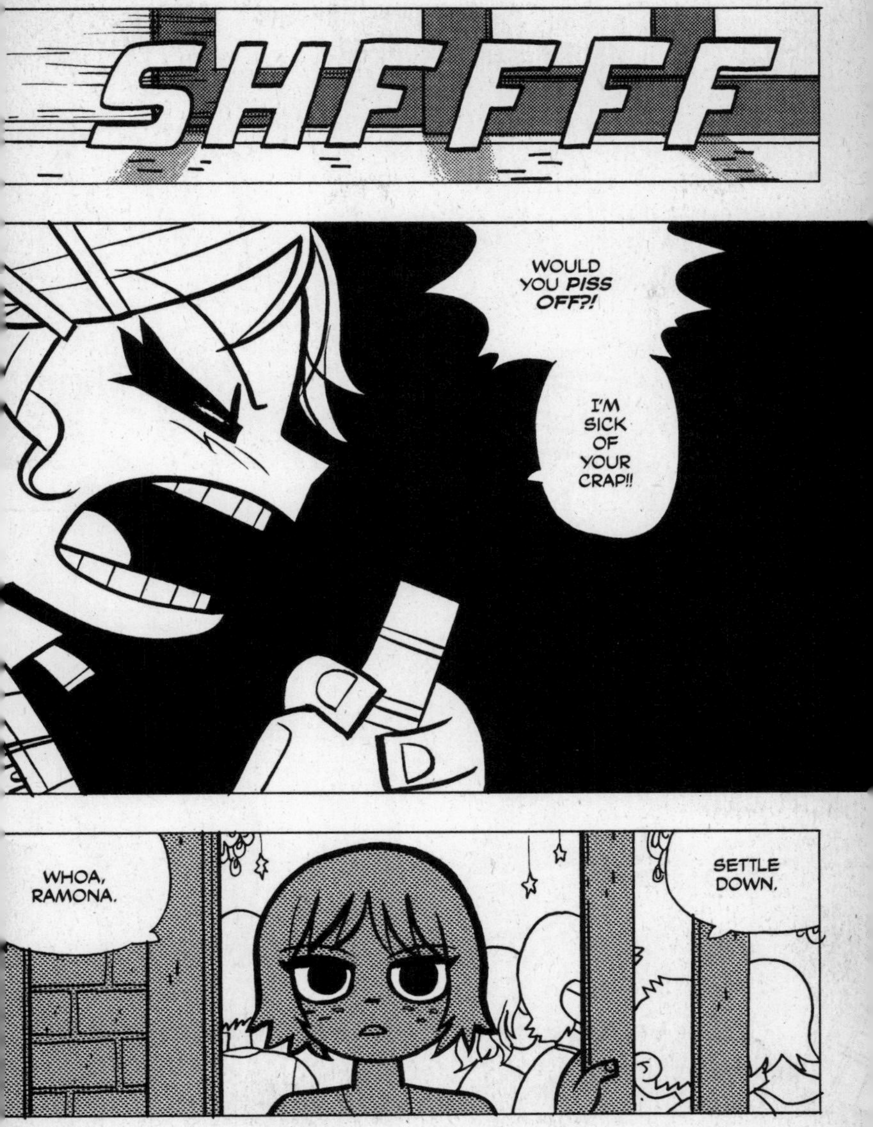
SHFFFF
WOULD YOU PISS OFF?!
I'M SICK OF YOUR CRAP!!
WHOA, RAMONA.
SETTLE DOWN.

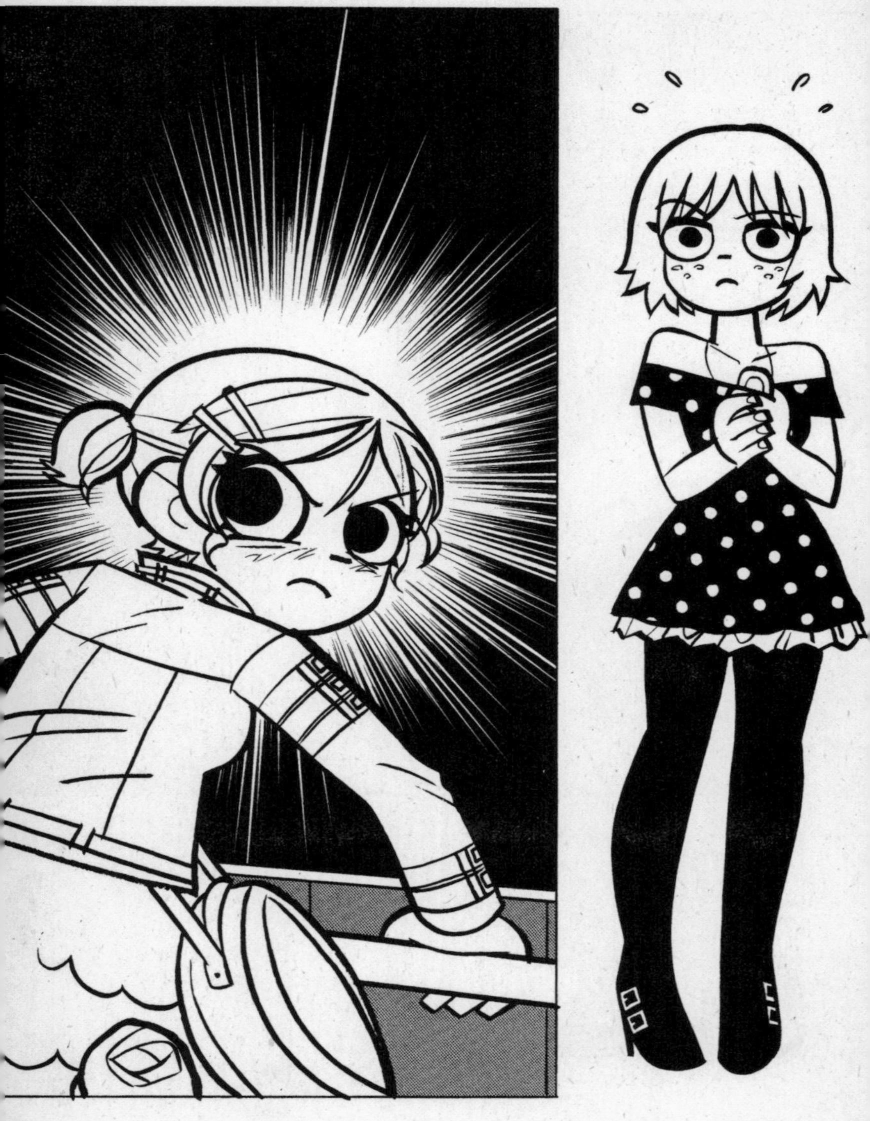

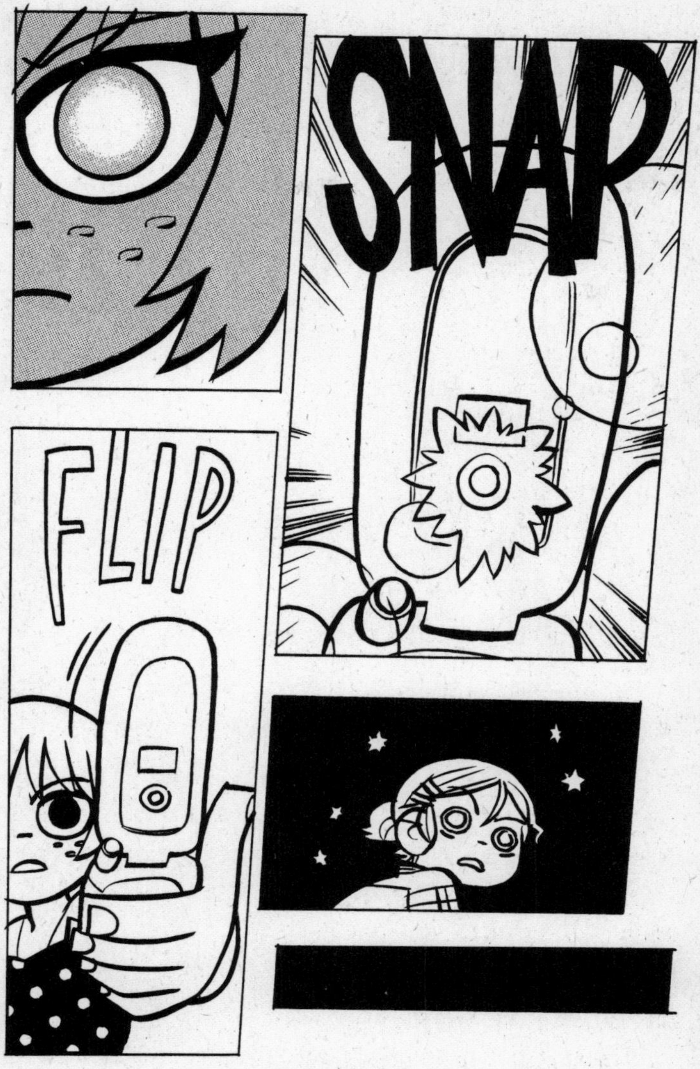
FLIP
SNAP

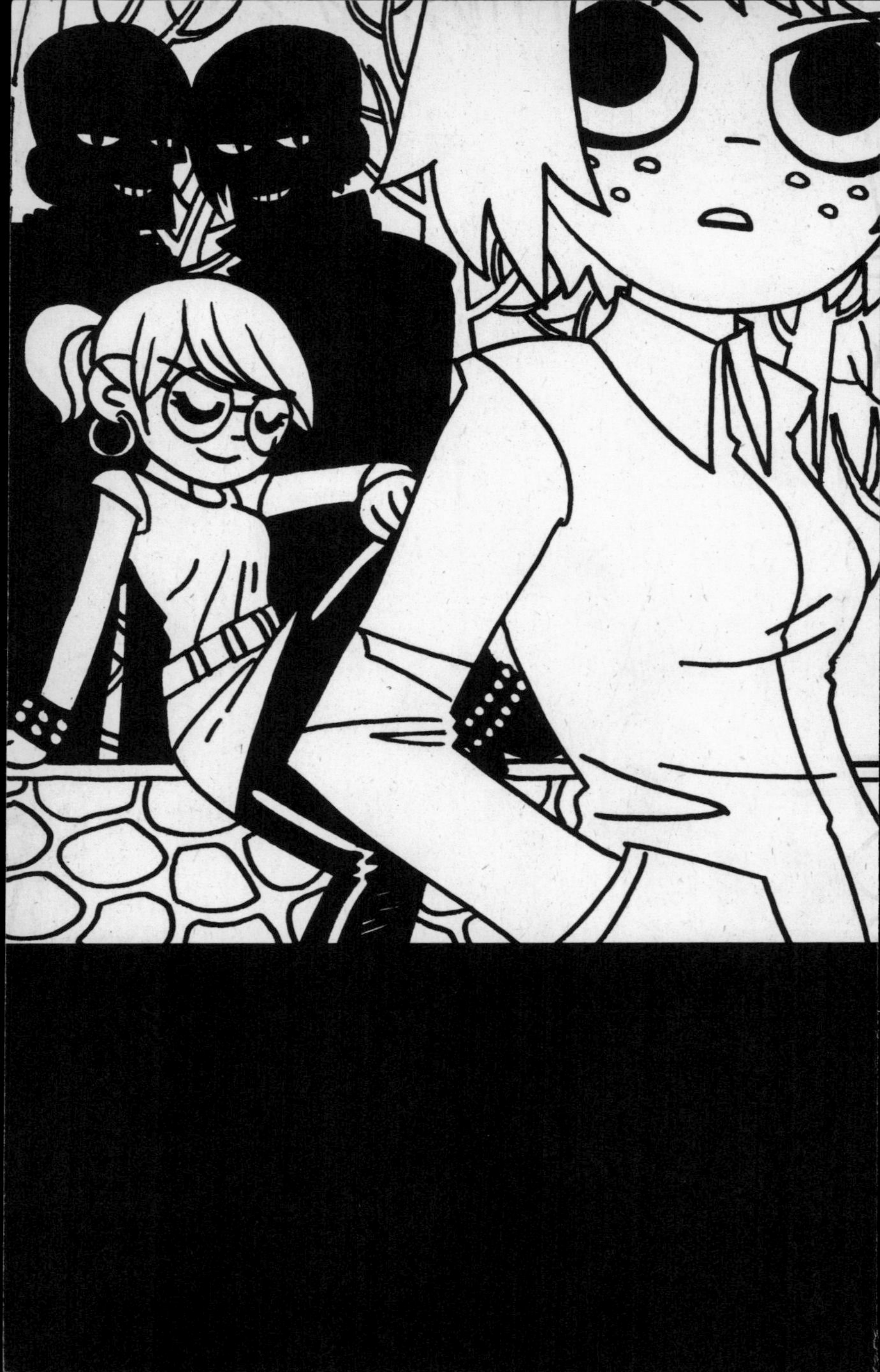

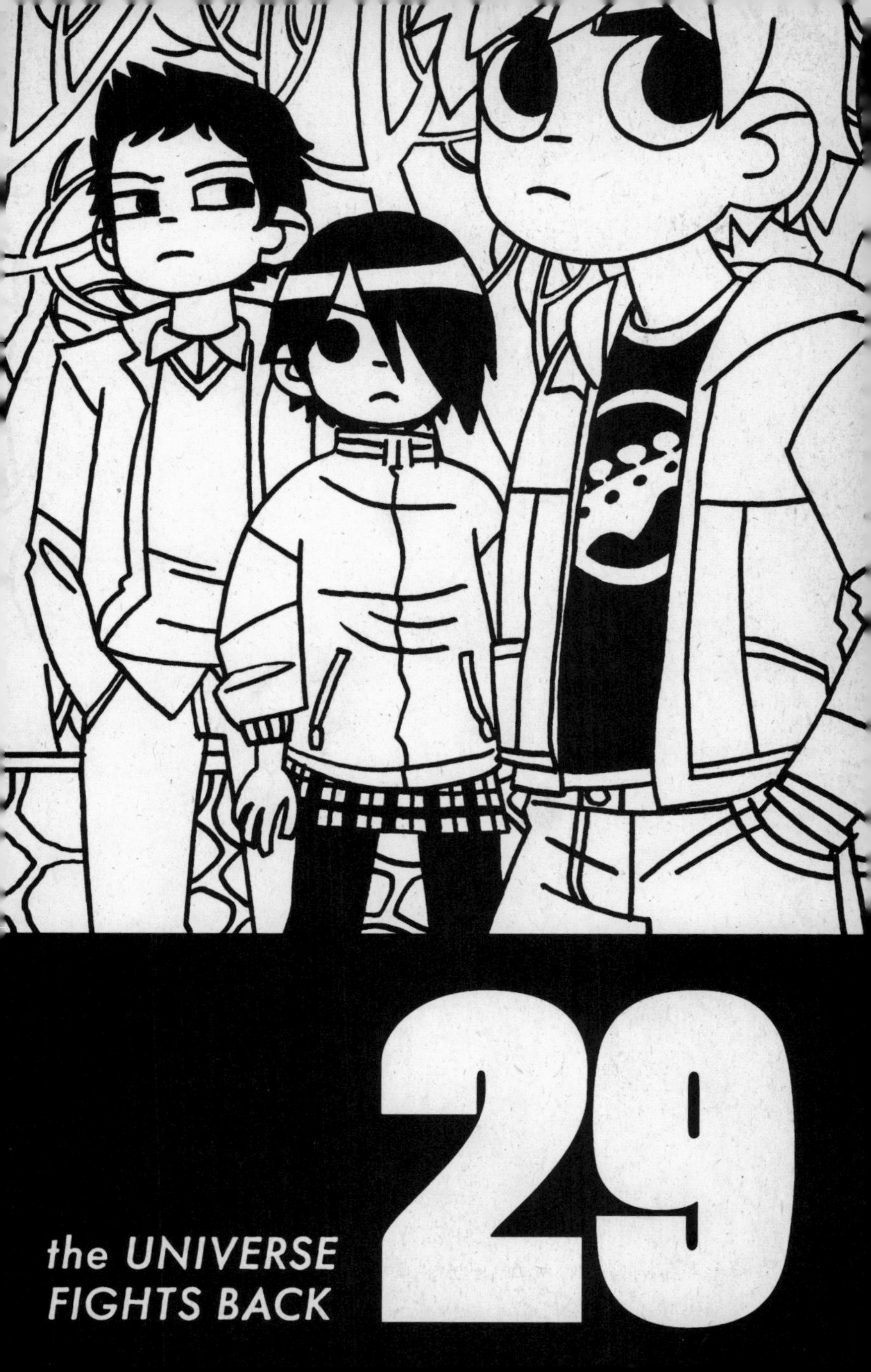

29

the UNIVERSE FIGHTS BACK

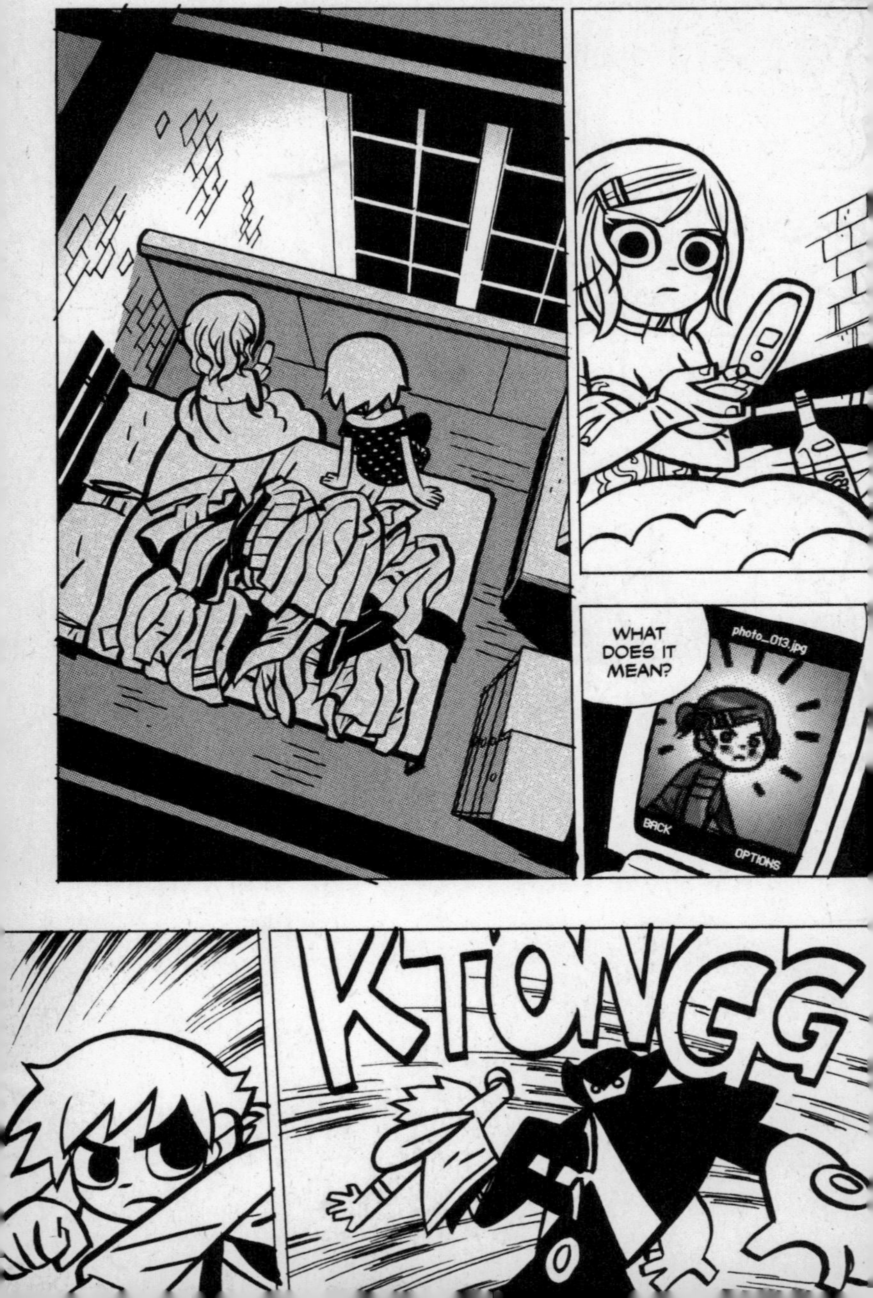
WHAT DOES IT MEAN?
photo_013.jpg
BACK
OPTIONS
KTONGG

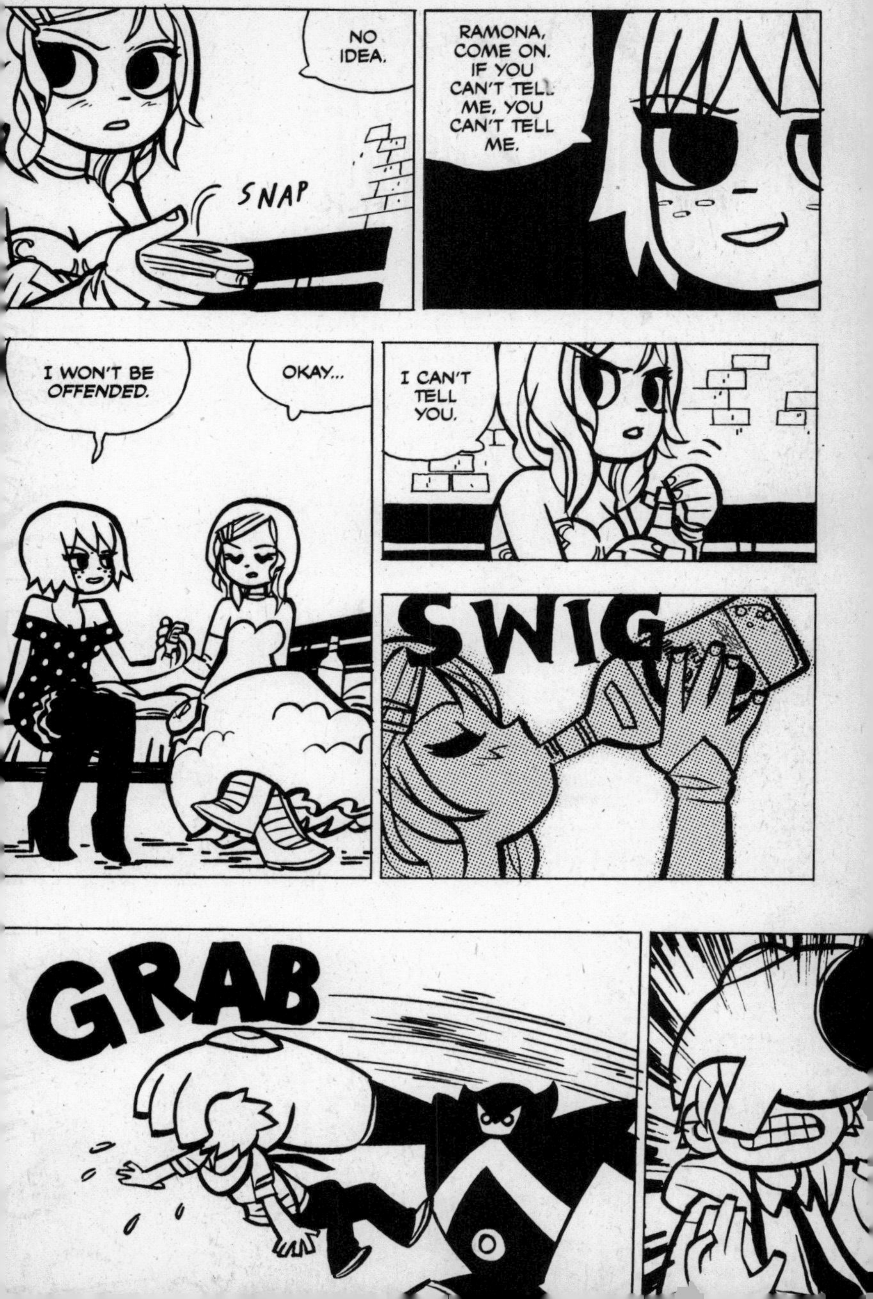
NO IDEA.
SNAP
RAMONA, COME ON. IF YOU CAN'T TELL ME, YOU CAN'T TELL ME.
I WON'T BE OFFENDED.
OKAY...
I CAN'T TELL YOU.
SWIG
GRAB

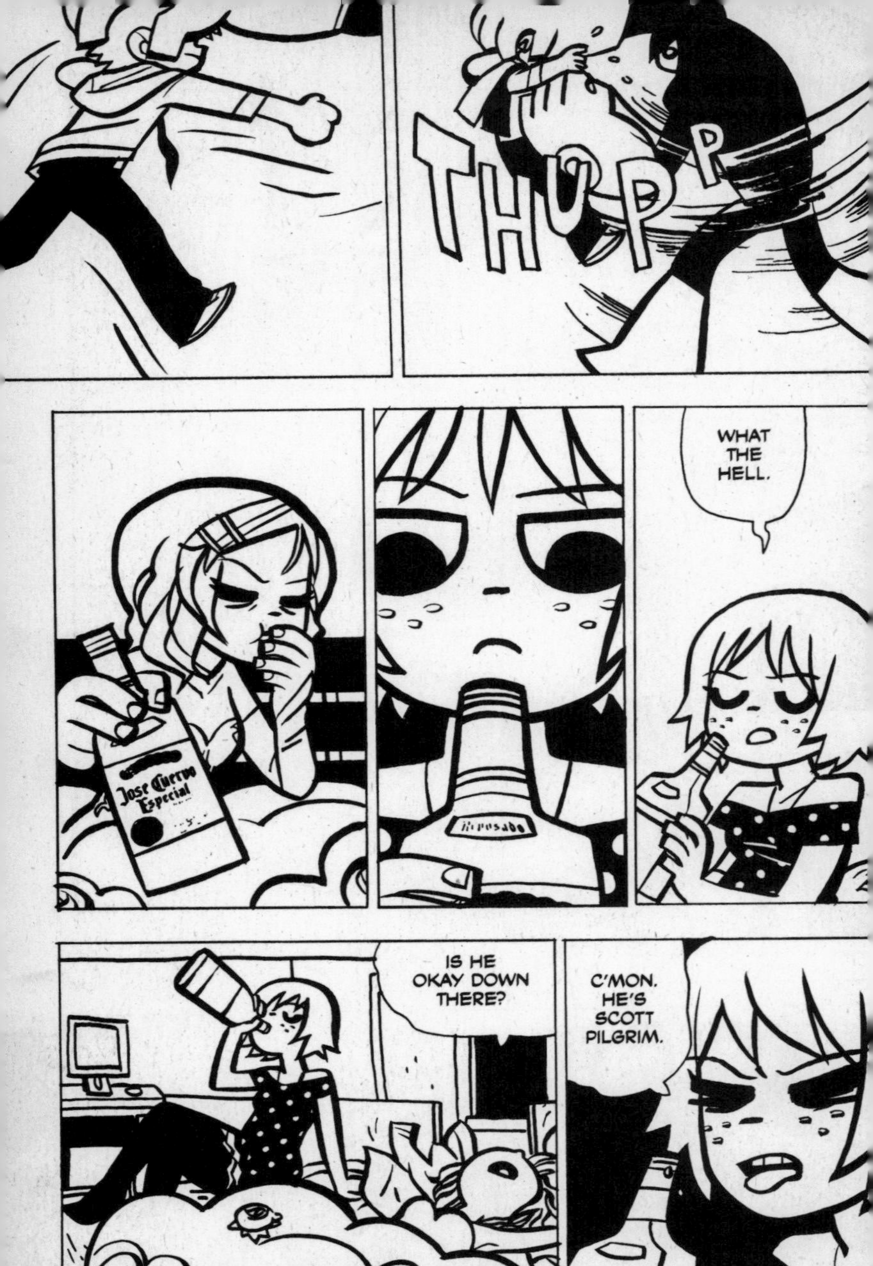
THUPP
Jose Cuervo
Especial
Reposado
WHAT THE HELL.
IS HE OKAY DOWN THERE?
C'MON. HE'S SCOTT PILGRIM.

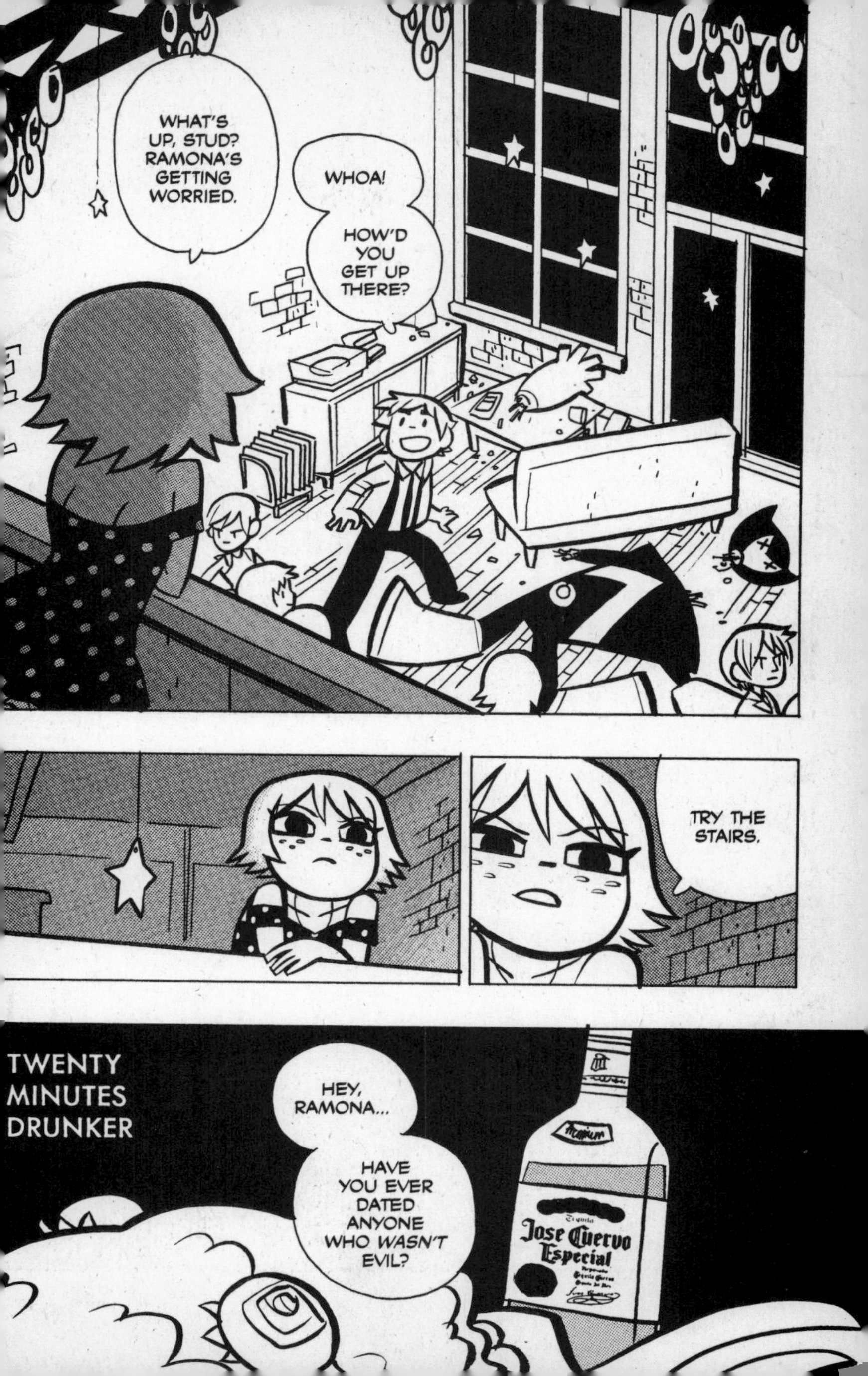
WHAT'S UP, STUD? RAMONA'S GETTING WORRIED.
WHOA!
HOW'D YOU GET UP THERE?
TRY THE STAIRS.
TWENTY MINUTES DRUNKER
HEY, RAMONA...
HAVE YOU EVER DATED ANYONE WHO *WASN'T* EVIL?
Jose Cuervo Especial

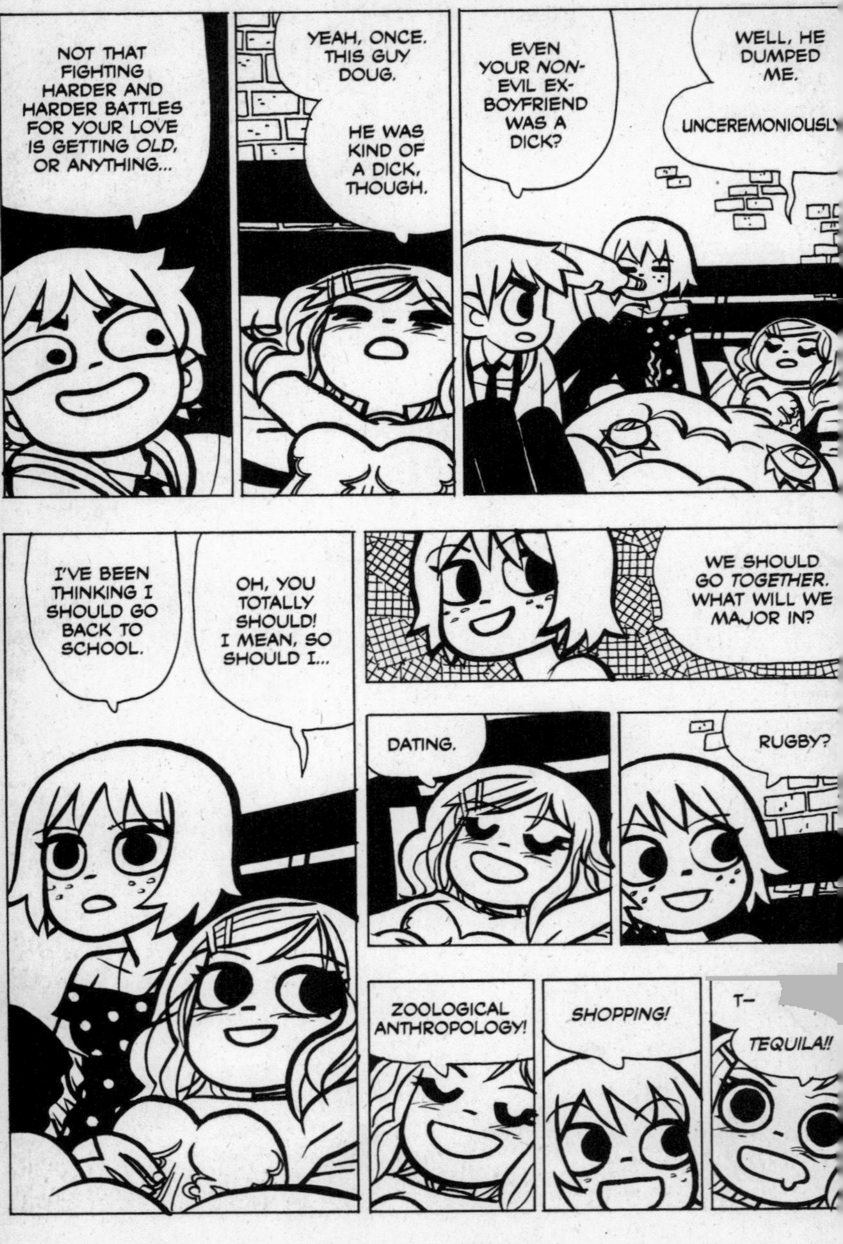
NOT THAT FIGHTING HARDER AND HARDER BATTLES FOR YOUR LOVE IS GETTING *OLD*, OR ANYTHING...
YEAH, ONCE. THIS GUY DOUG.
HE WAS KIND OF A DICK, THOUGH.
EVEN YOUR *NON*-EVIL EX-BOYFRIEND WAS A DICK?
WELL, HE DUMPED ME.
UNCEREMONIOUSLY
I'VE BEEN THINKING I SHOULD GO BACK TO SCHOOL.
OH, YOU TOTALLY SHOULD! I MEAN, SO SHOULD I...
WE SHOULD GO *TOGETHER*. WHAT WILL WE MAJOR IN?
DATING.
RUGBY?
ZOOLOGICAL ANTHROPOLOGY!
SHOPPING!
T—
TEQUILA!!

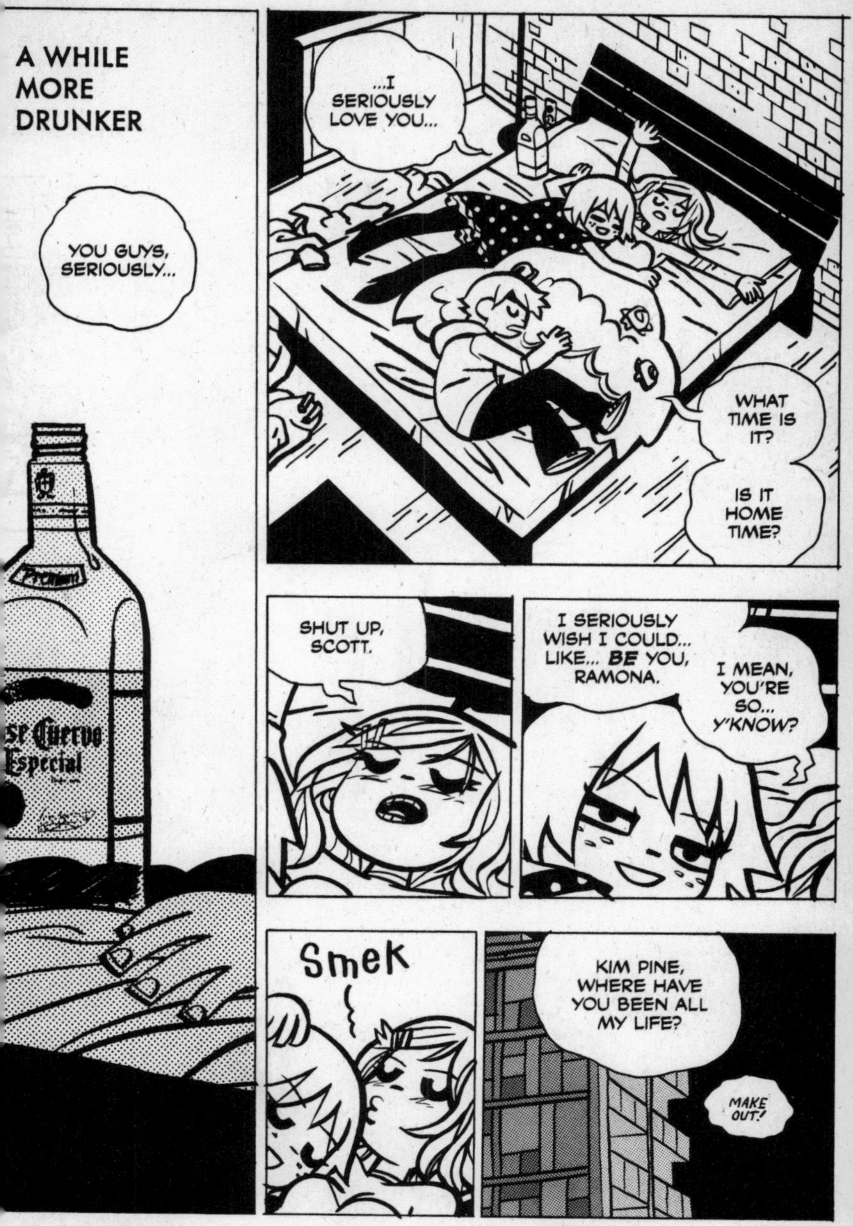
A WHILE MORE DRUNKER
YOU GUYS, SERIOUSLY...
...I SERIOUSLY LOVE YOU...
WHAT TIME IS IT?
IS IT HOME TIME?
SHUT UP, SCOTT.
I SERIOUSLY WISH I COULD... LIKE... *BE* YOU, RAMONA.
I MEAN, YOU'RE SO... Y'KNOW?
Smek
KIM PINE, WHERE HAVE YOU BEEN ALL MY LIFE?
MAKE OUT!

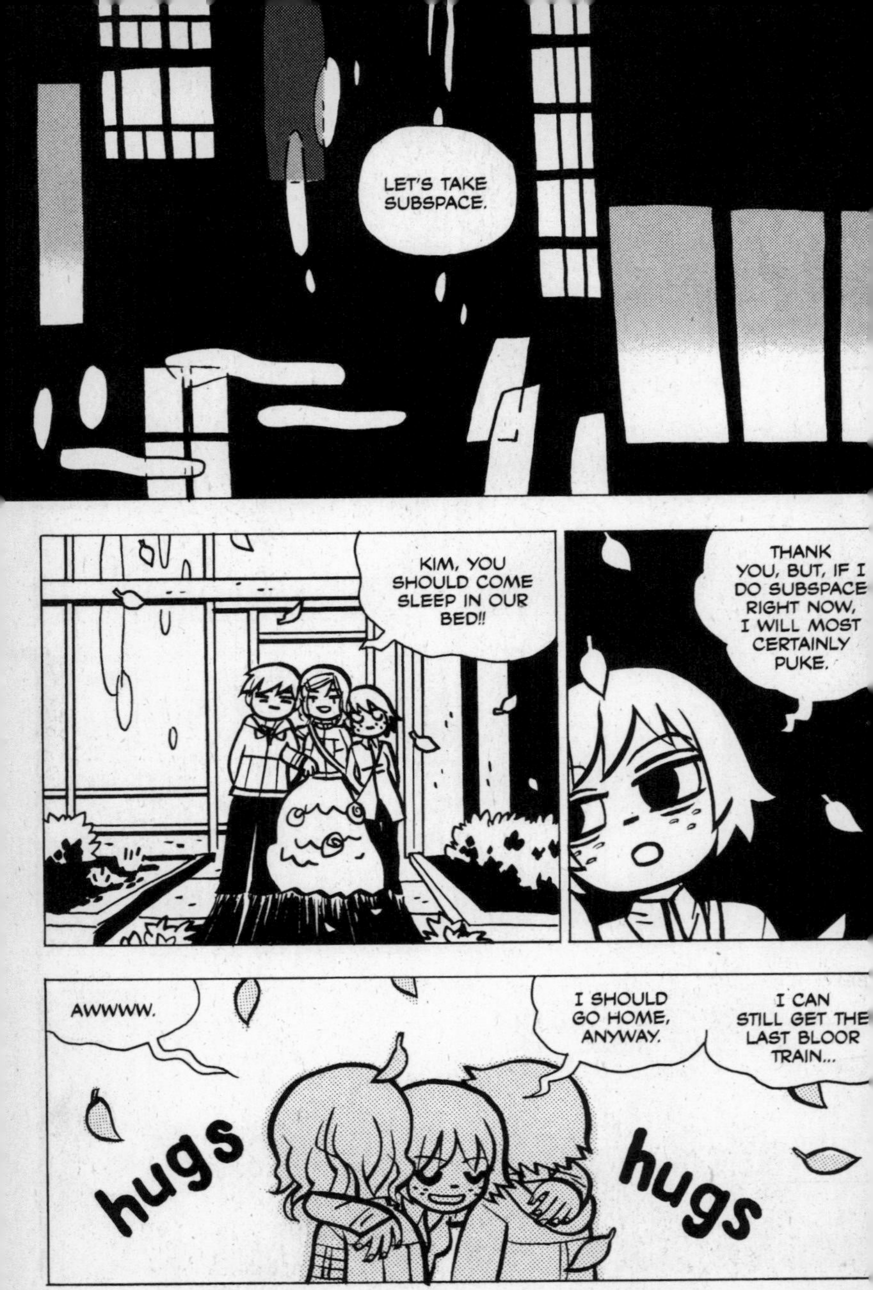
LET'S TAKE SUBSPACE.
KIM, YOU SHOULD COME SLEEP IN OUR BED!!
THANK YOU, BUT, IF I DO SUBSPACE RIGHT NOW, I WILL MOST CERTAINLY PUKE.
AWWWW.
I SHOULD GO HOME, ANYWAY.
I CAN STILL GET THE LAST BLOOR TRAIN...
hugs
hugs

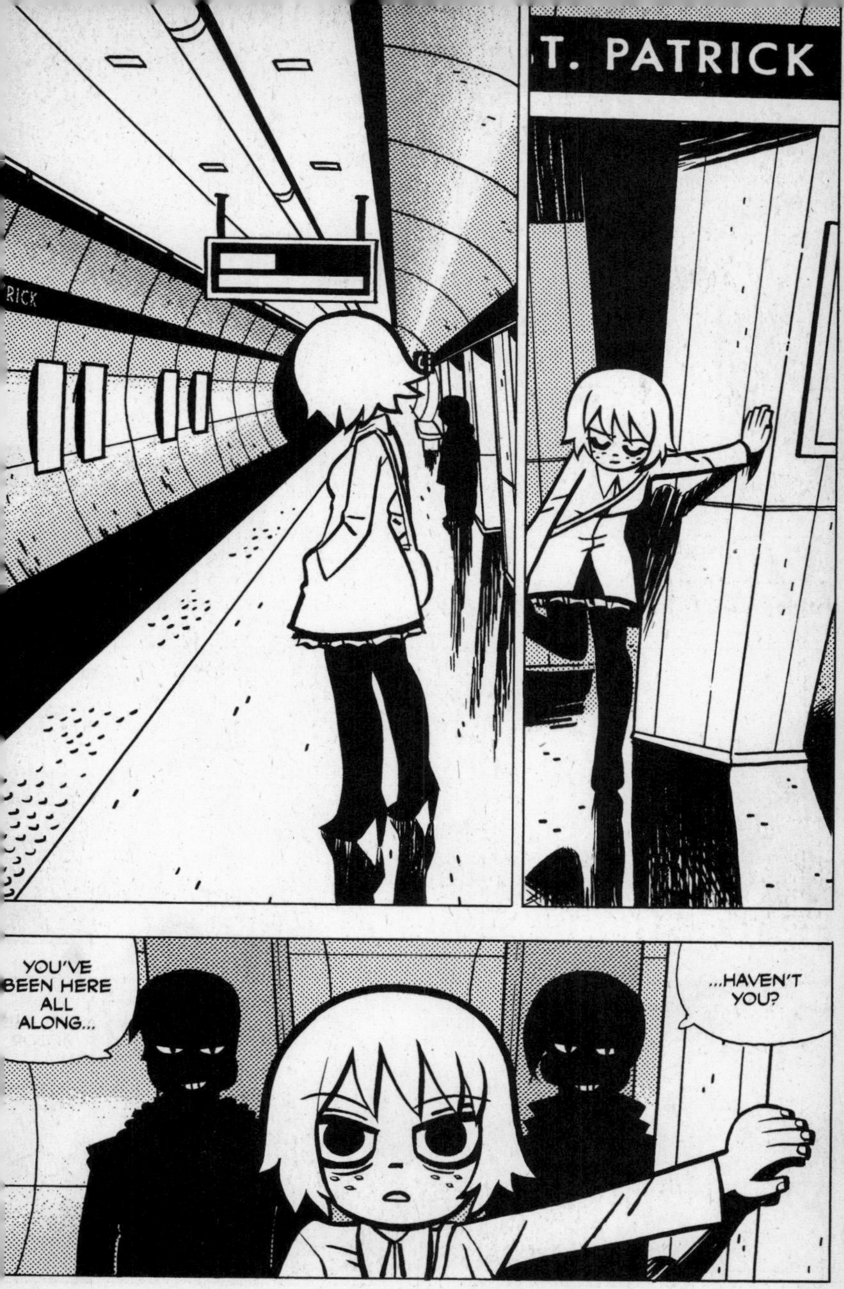
RICK
T. PATRICK
YOU'VE BEEN HERE ALL ALONG...
...HAVEN'T YOU?

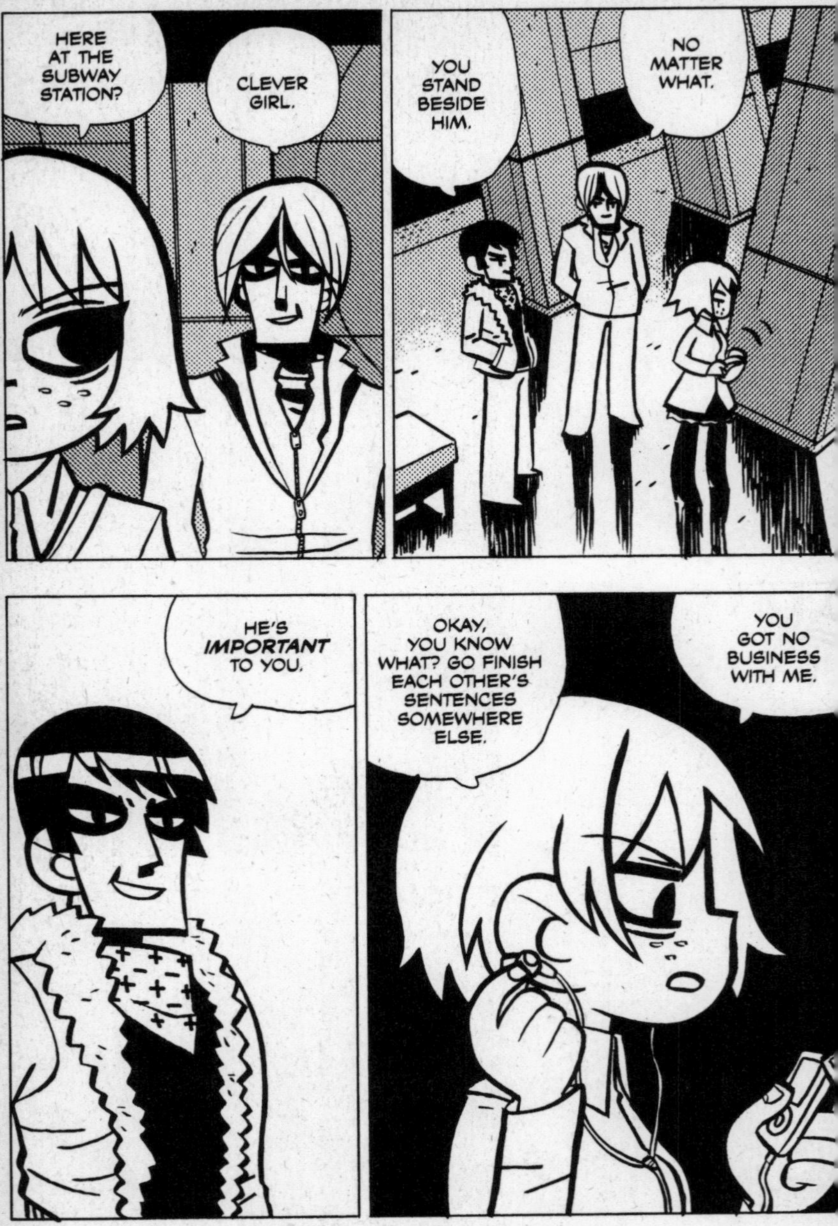
HERE AT THE SUBWAY STATION?
CLEVER GIRL.
YOU STAND BESIDE HIM.
NO MATTER WHAT.
HE'S *IMPORTANT* TO YOU.
OKAY, YOU KNOW WHAT? GO FINISH EACH OTHER'S SENTENCES SOMEWHERE ELSE.
YOU GOT NO BUSINESS WITH ME.

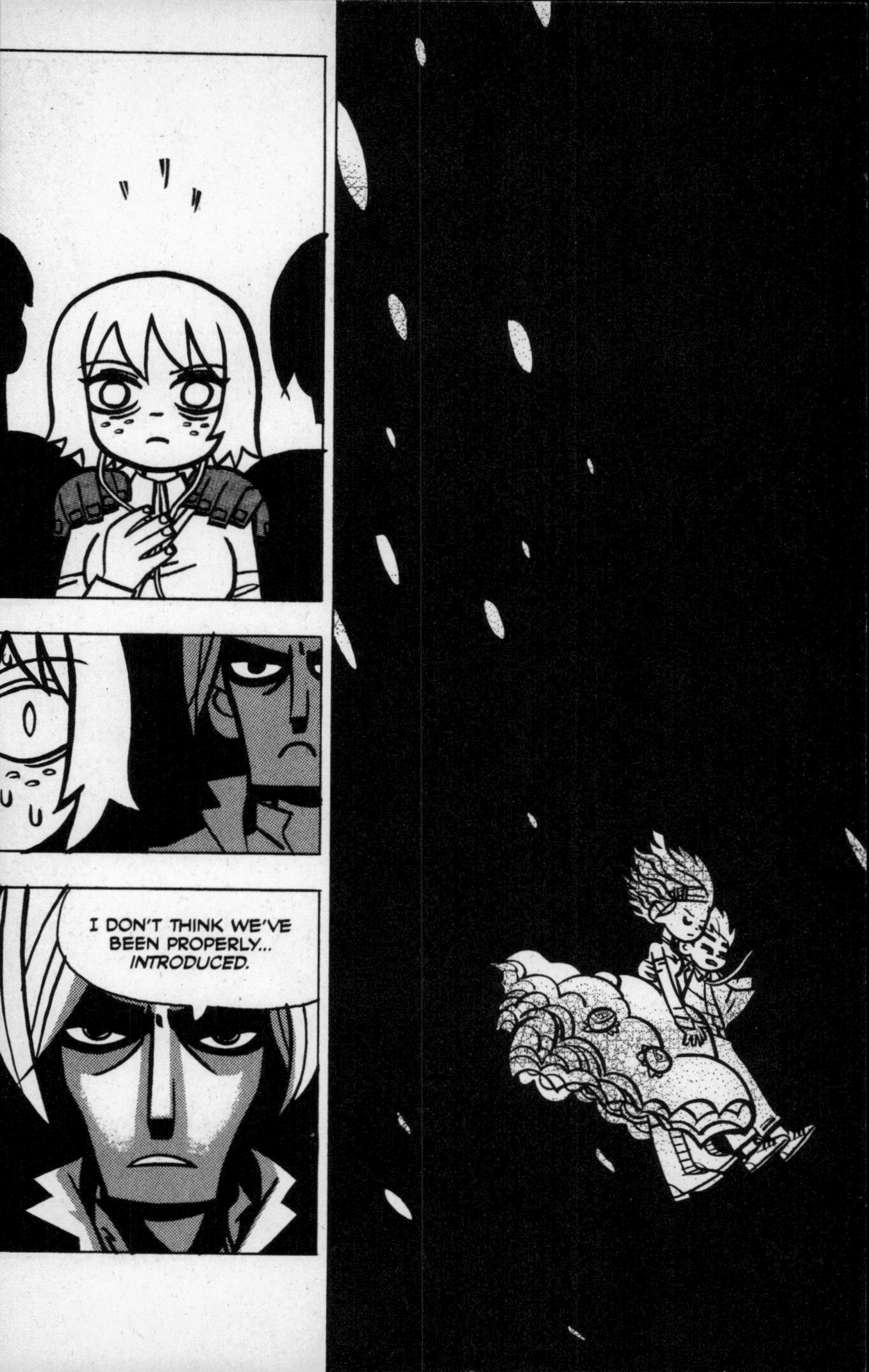
I DON'T THINK WE'VE BEEN PROPERLY... *INTRODUCED.*

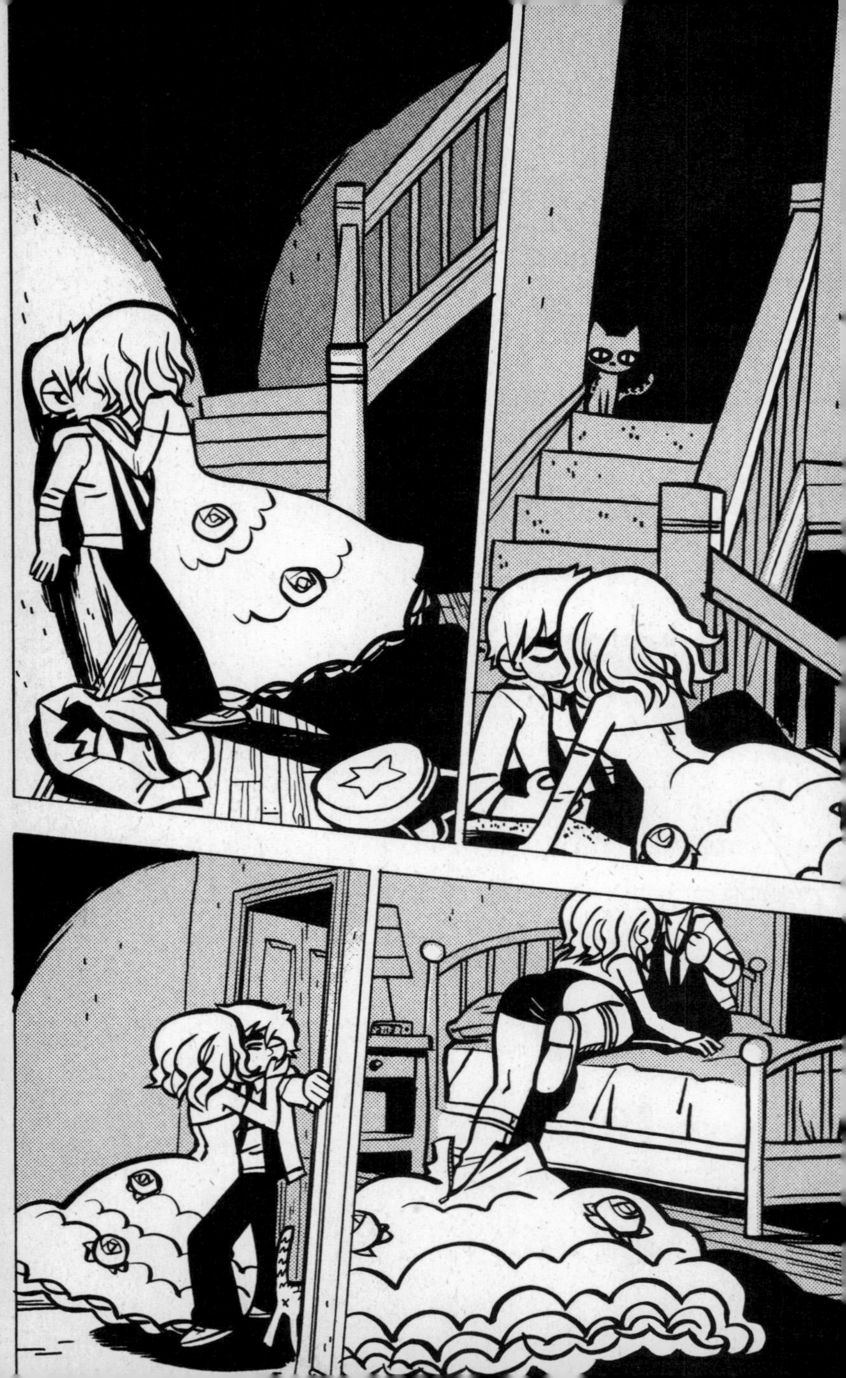

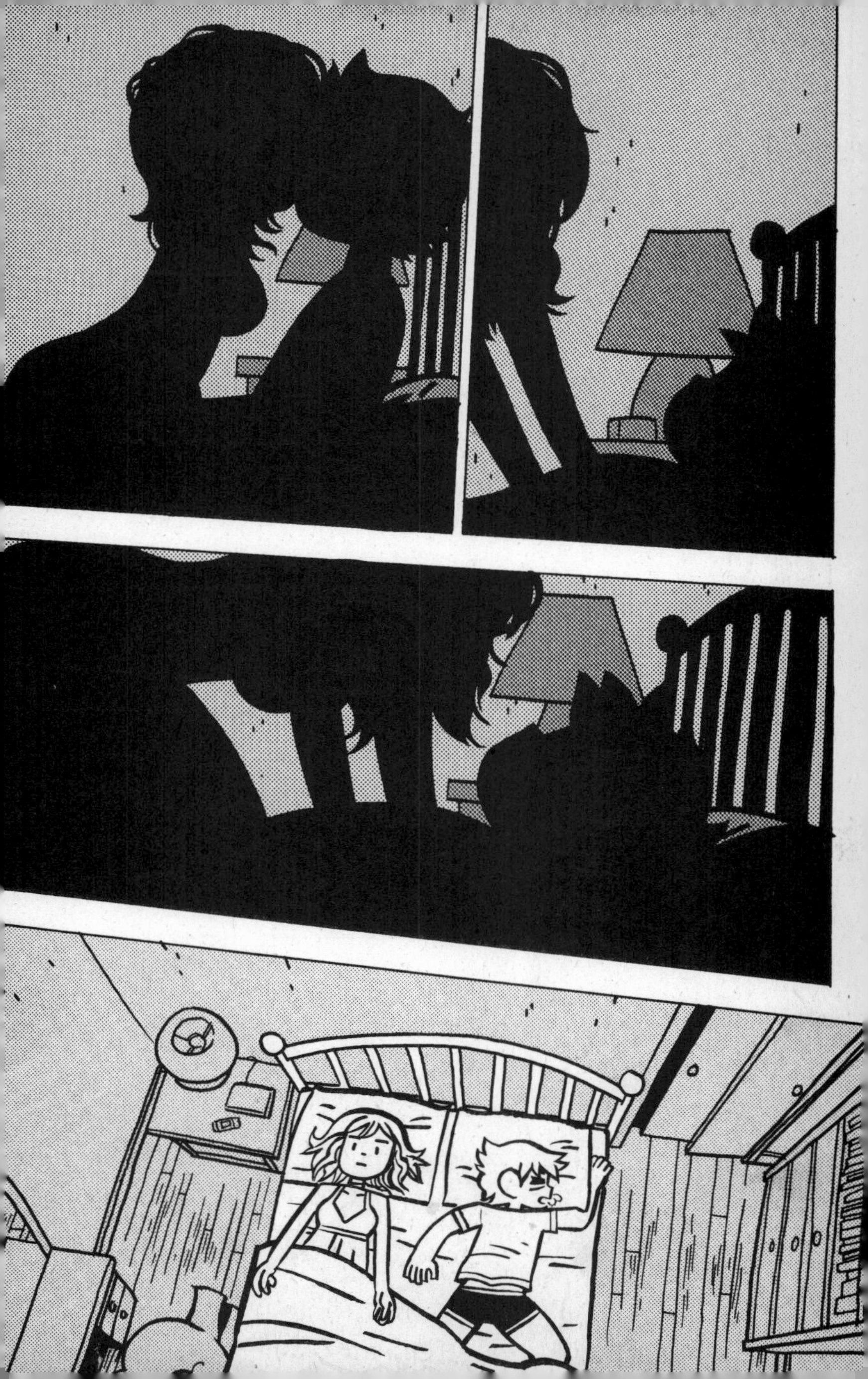

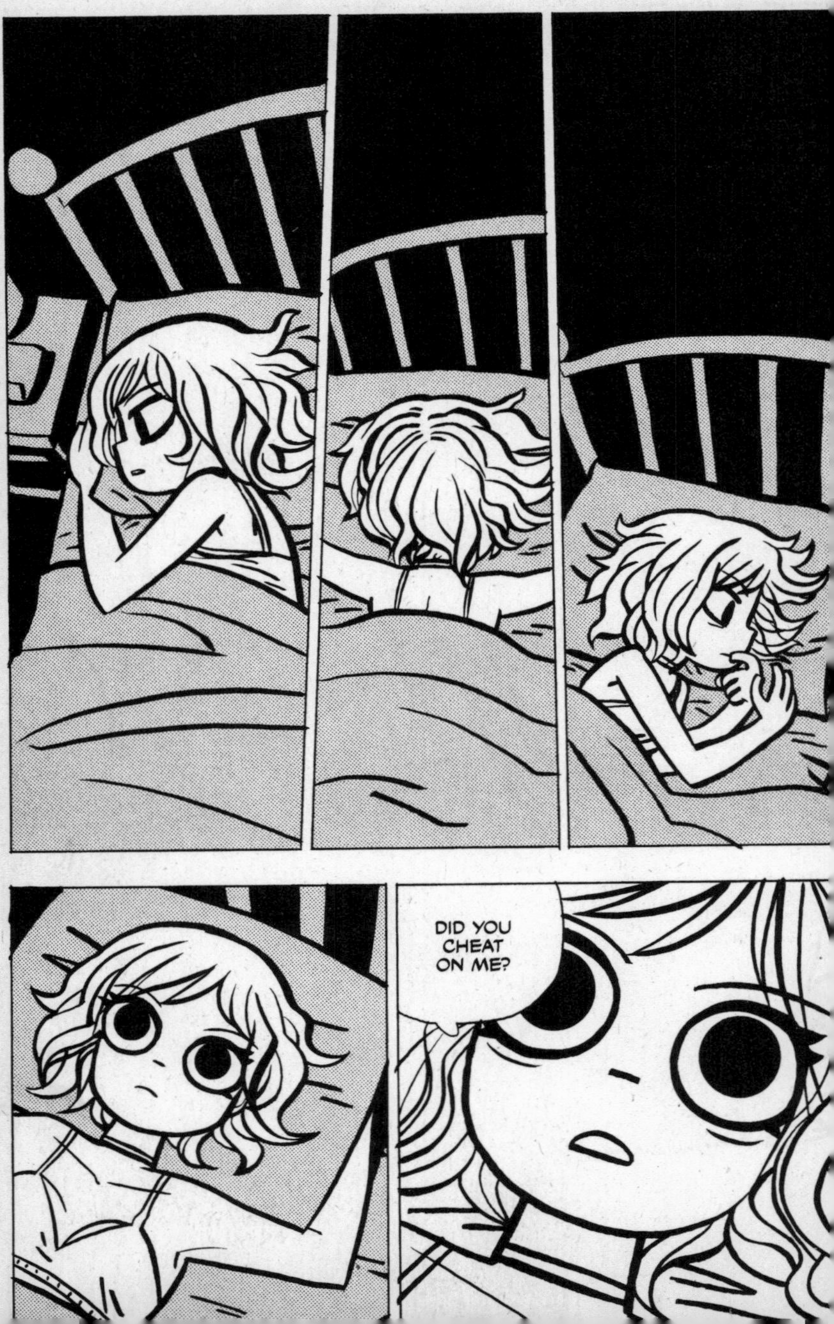
DID YOU CHEAT ON ME?

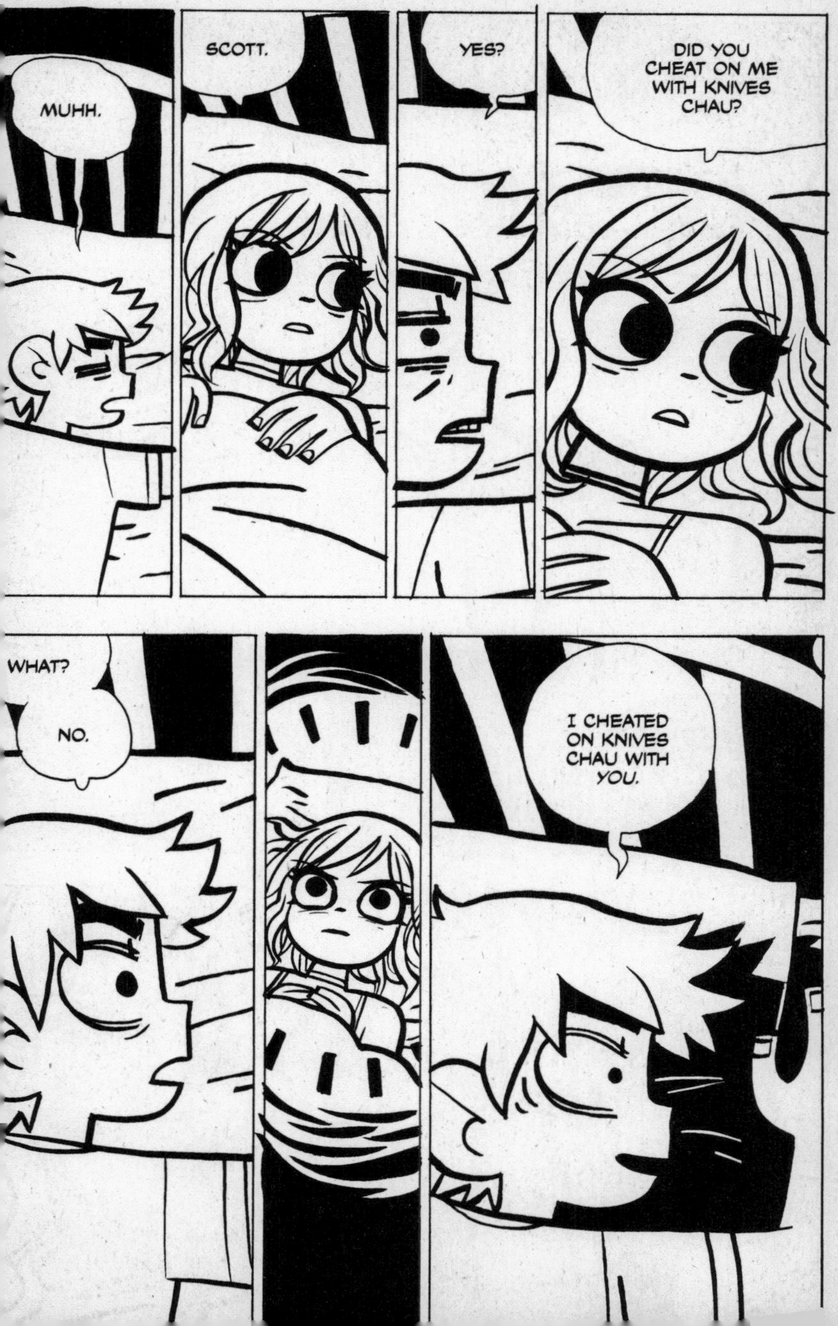
MUHH.
SCOTT.
YES?
DID YOU CHEAT ON ME WITH KNIVES CHAU?
WHAT?
NO.
I CHEATED ON KNIVES CHAU WITH *YOU.*

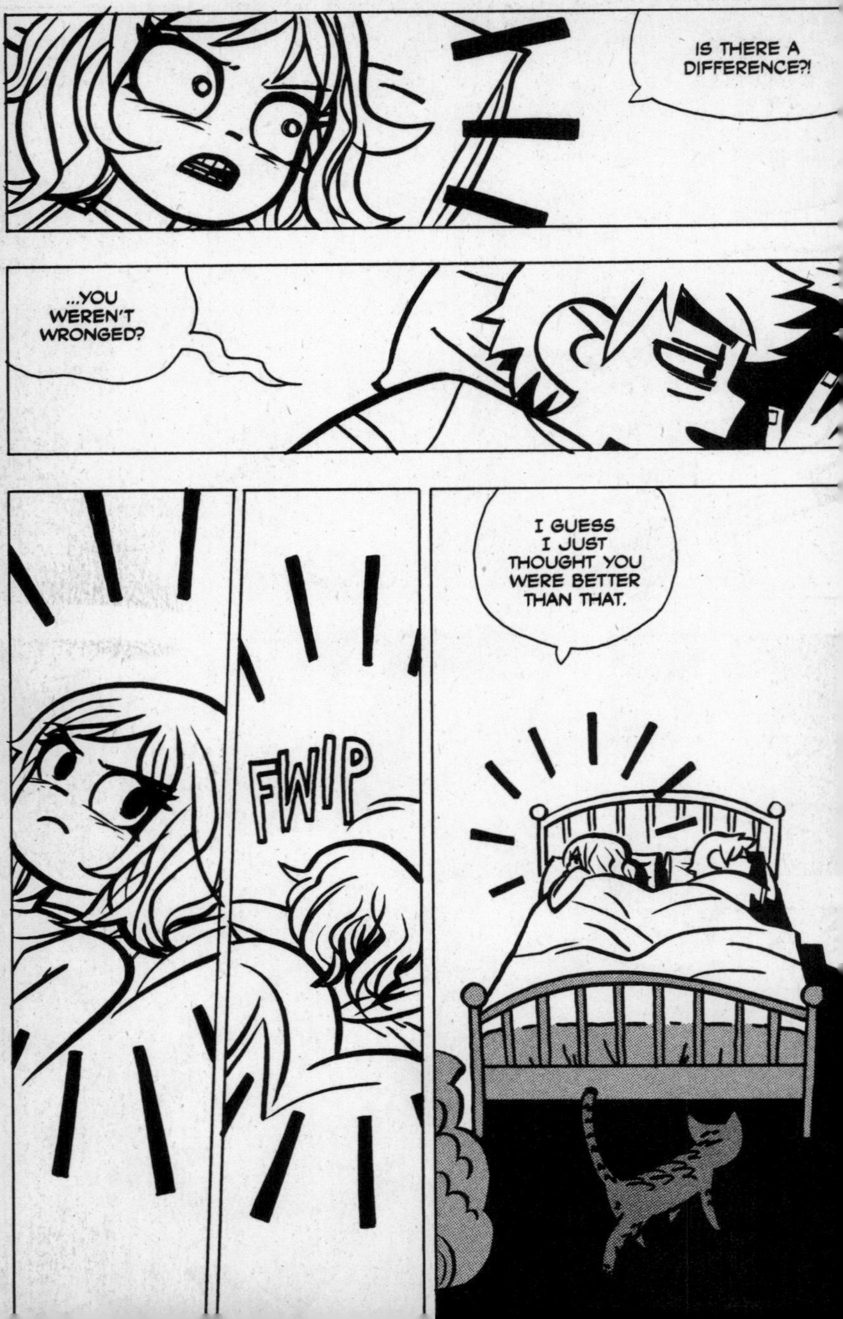
IS THERE A DIFFERENCE?!
...YOU WEREN'T WRONGED?
FWIP
I GUESS I JUST THOUGHT YOU WERE BETTER THAN THAT.

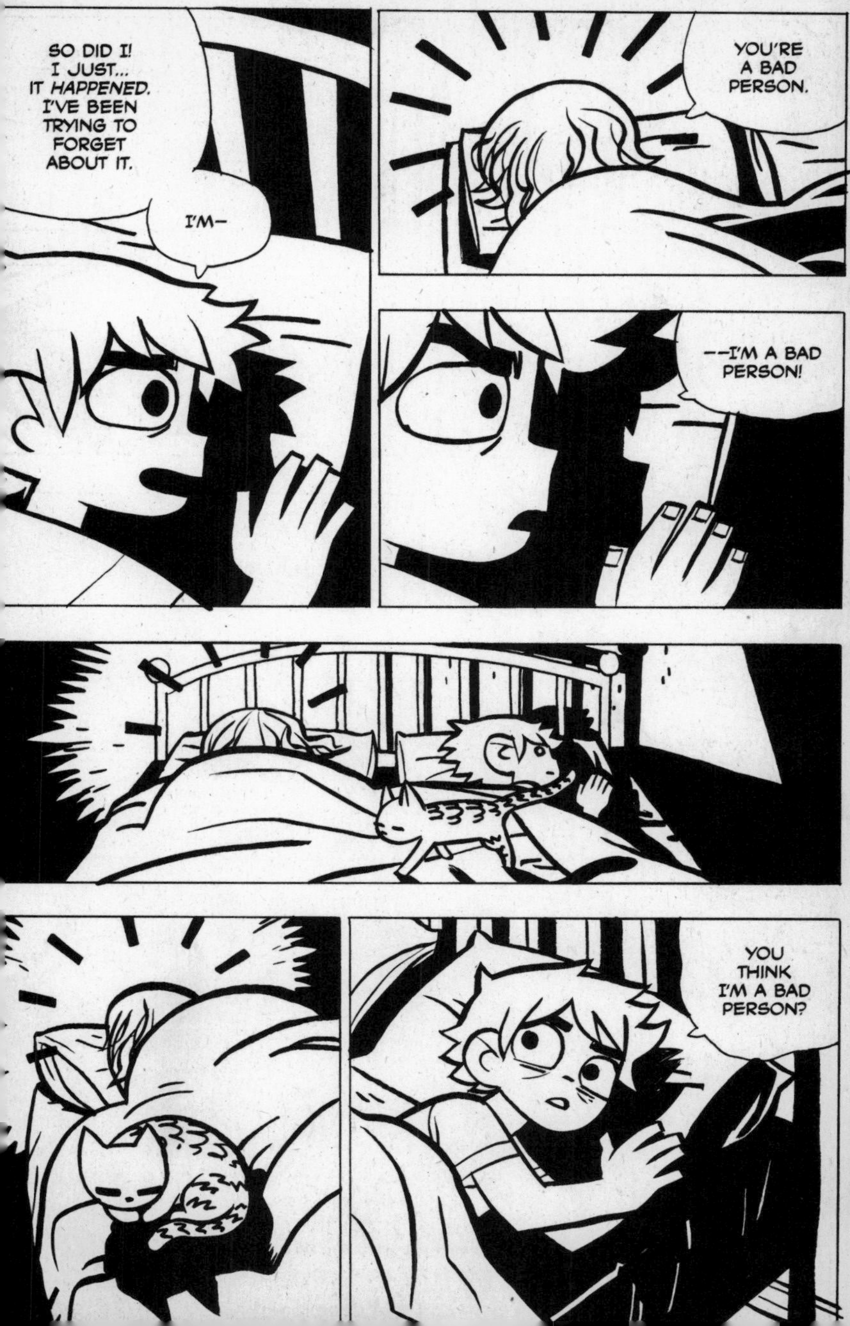
SO DID I! I JUST... IT *HAPPENED.* I'VE BEEN TRYING TO FORGET ABOUT IT.
I'M–
YOU'RE A BAD PERSON.
--I'M A BAD PERSON!
YOU THINK I'M A BAD PERSON?

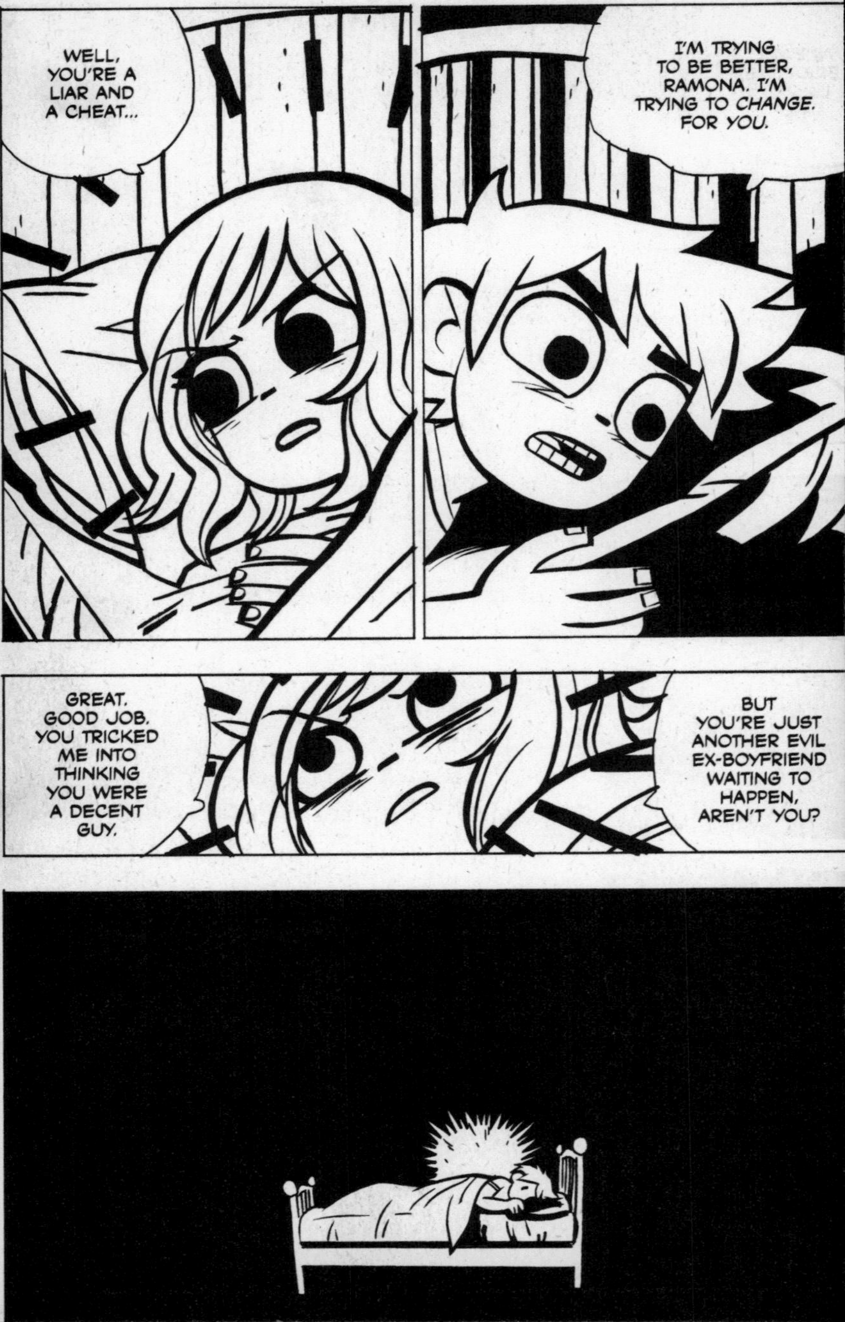
WELL, YOU'RE A LIAR AND A CHEAT...
I'M TRYING TO BE BETTER, RAMONA. I'M TRYING TO *CHANGE*. FOR *YOU*.
GREAT. GOOD JOB. YOU TRICKED ME INTO THINKING YOU WERE A DECENT GUY.
BUT YOU'RE JUST ANOTHER EVIL EX-BOYFRIEND WAITING TO HAPPEN, AREN'T YOU?

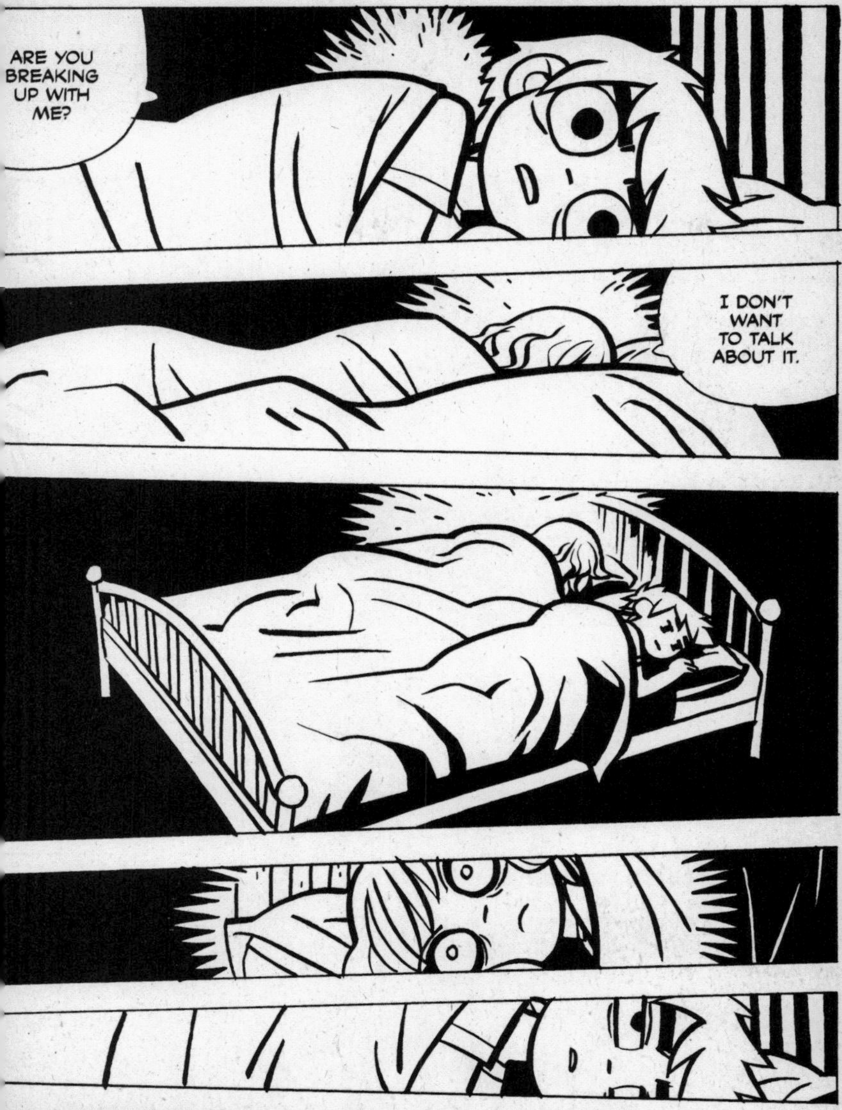
ARE YOU BREAKING UP WITH ME?
I DON'T WANT TO TALK ABOUT IT.

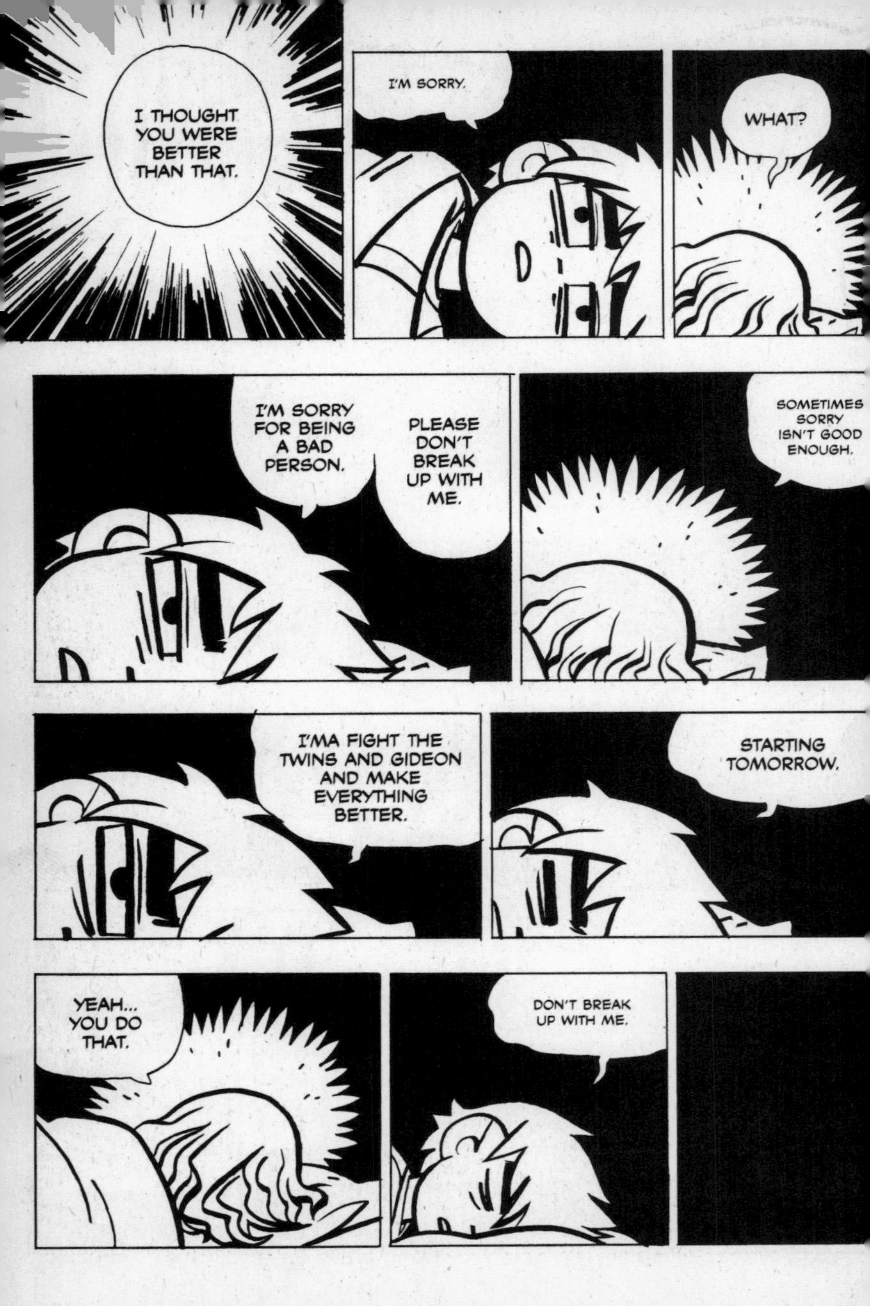
I THOUGHT YOU WERE BETTER THAN THAT.
I'M SORRY.
WHAT?
I'M SORRY FOR BEING A BAD PERSON.
PLEASE DON'T BREAK UP WITH ME.
SOMETIMES SORRY ISN'T GOOD ENOUGH.
I'MA FIGHT THE TWINS AND GIDEON AND MAKE EVERYTHING BETTER.
STARTING TOMORROW.
YEAH... YOU DO THAT.
DON'T BREAK UP WITH ME.

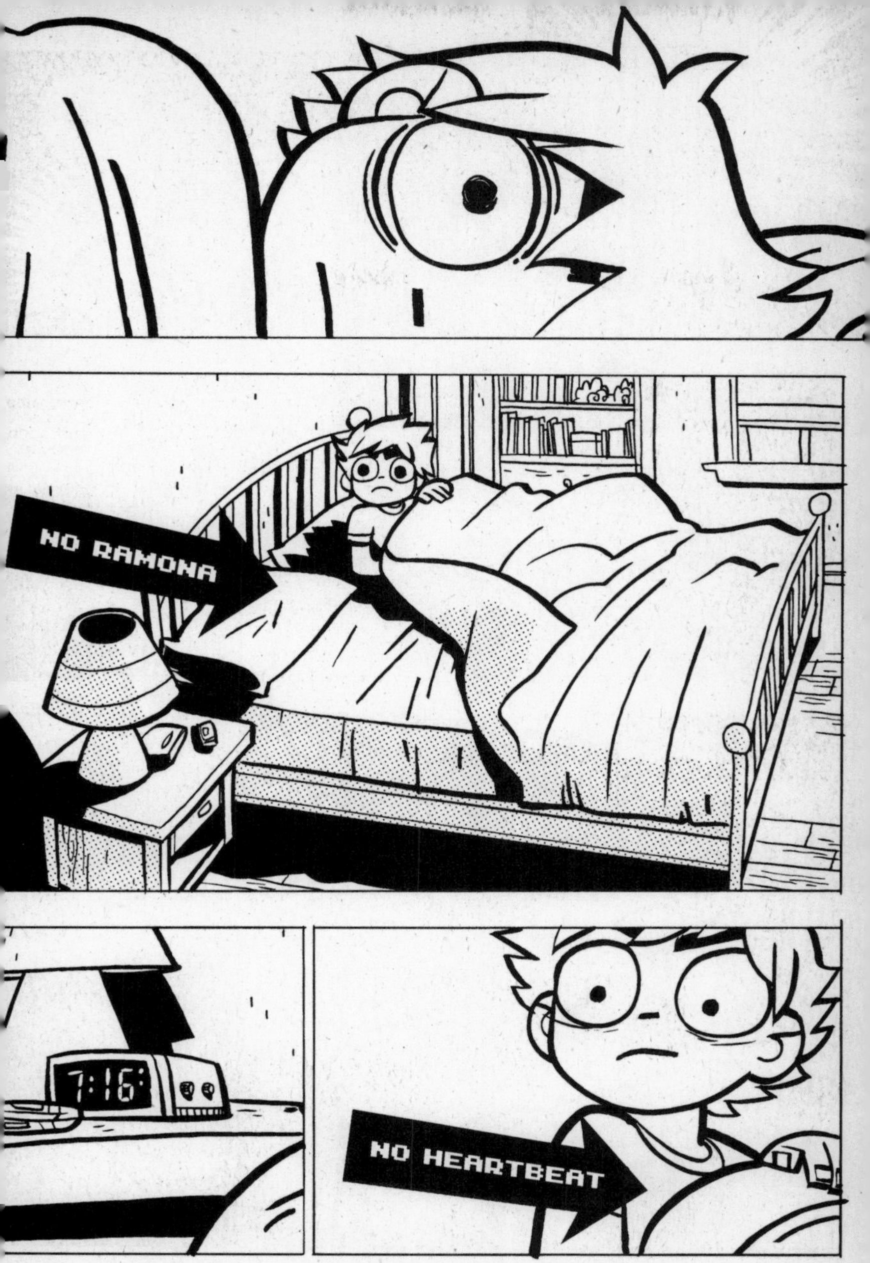
NO RAMONA
7:16
NO HEARTBEAT

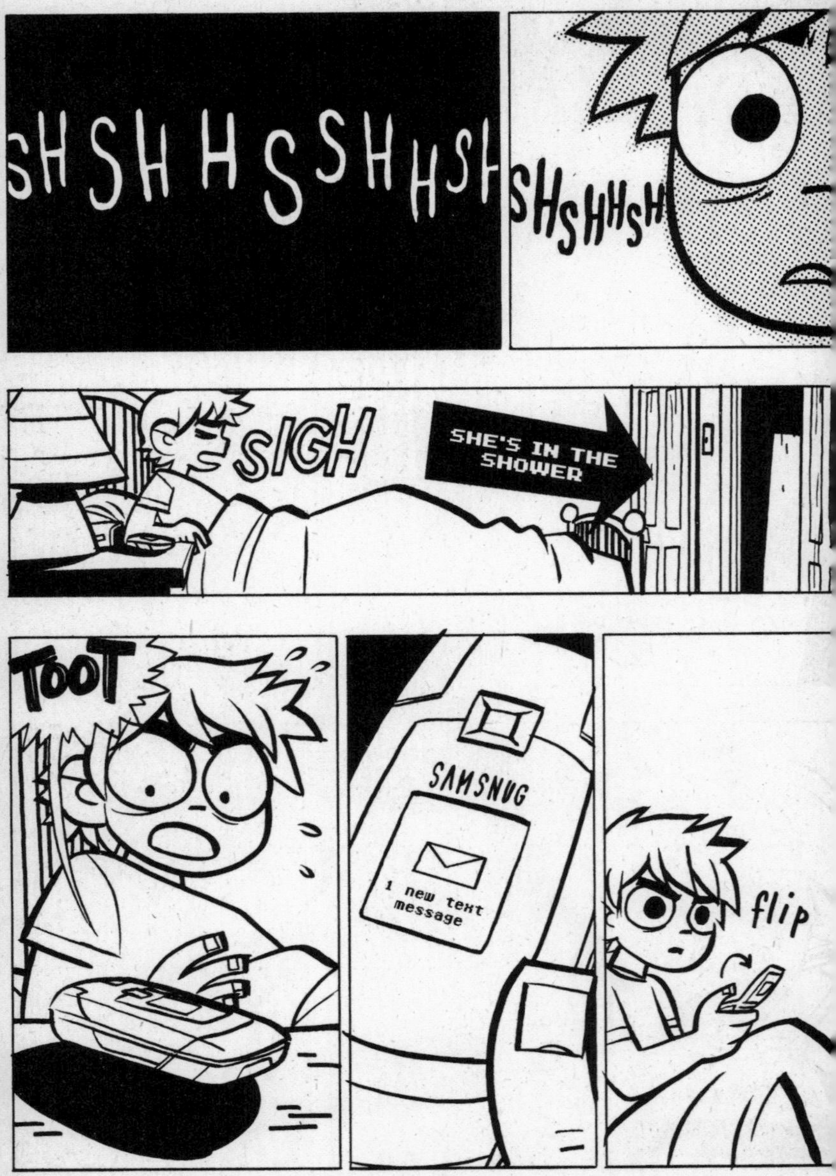

SHSHHSSHHSH
SHSHHSH
SIGH
SHE'S IN THE SHOWER
TOOT
SAMSNUG
1 new text message
flip

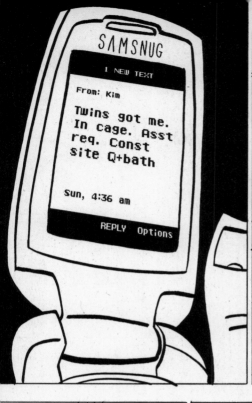

SAMSNUG

1 NEW TEXT

From: Kim

Twins got me. In cage. Asst req. Const site Q+bath

Sun, 4:36 am

REPLY Options

UH-OH.

I HAVE TO GO RESCUE KIM, BUT I'LL BE BACK!!

DON'T BREAK UP WITH ME WHILE I'M OUT, OKAY?!

CLOMP CLOMP CLOM CLO

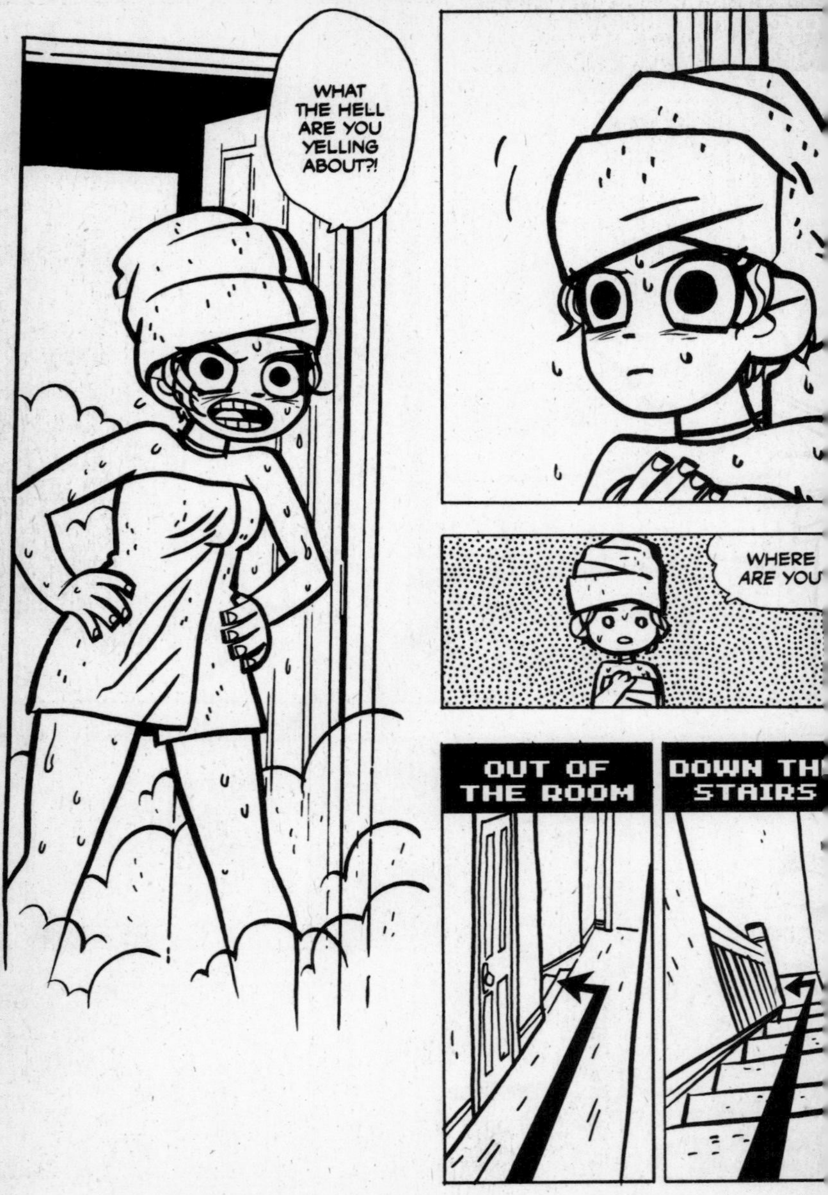
WHAT THE HELL ARE YOU YELLING ABOUT?!
WHERE ARE YOU
OUT OF THE ROOM
DOWN THE STAIRS

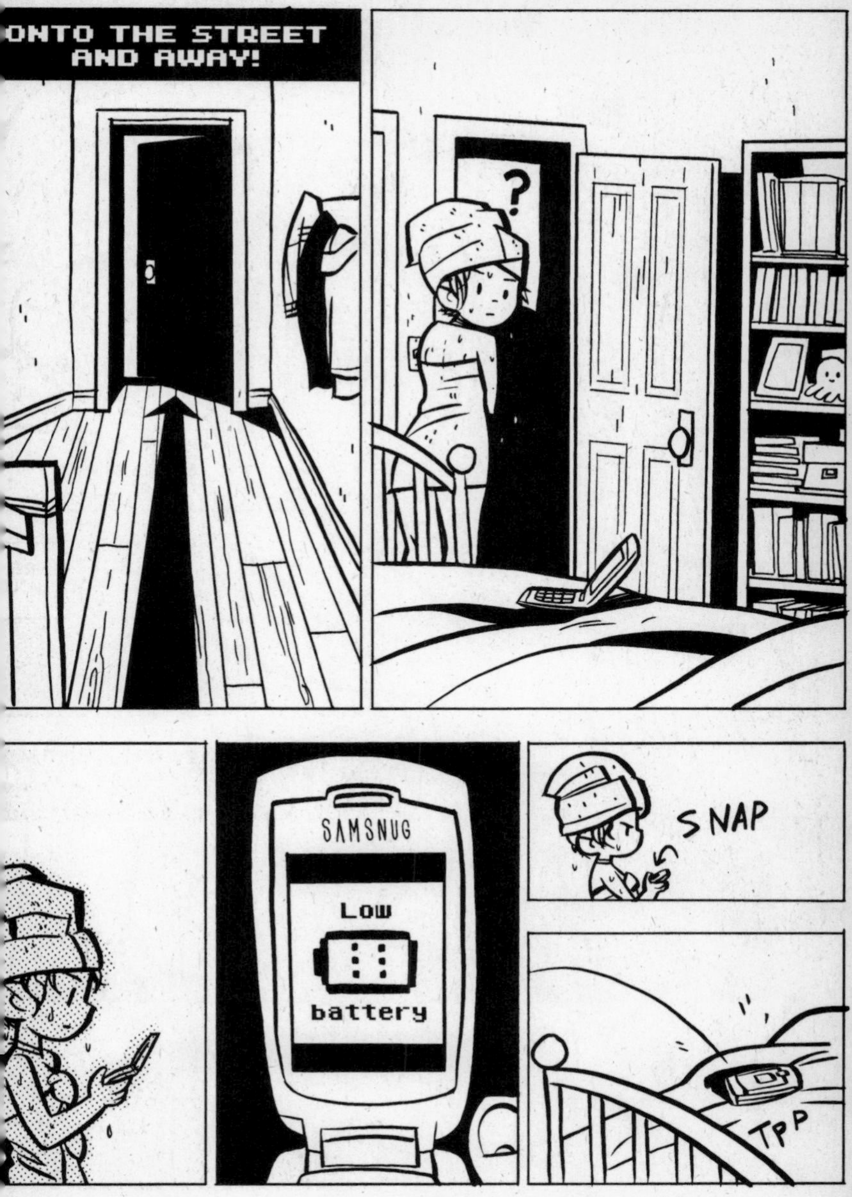
ONTO THE STREET AND AWAY!
?
SAMSNUG
Low
battery
SNAP
TPP

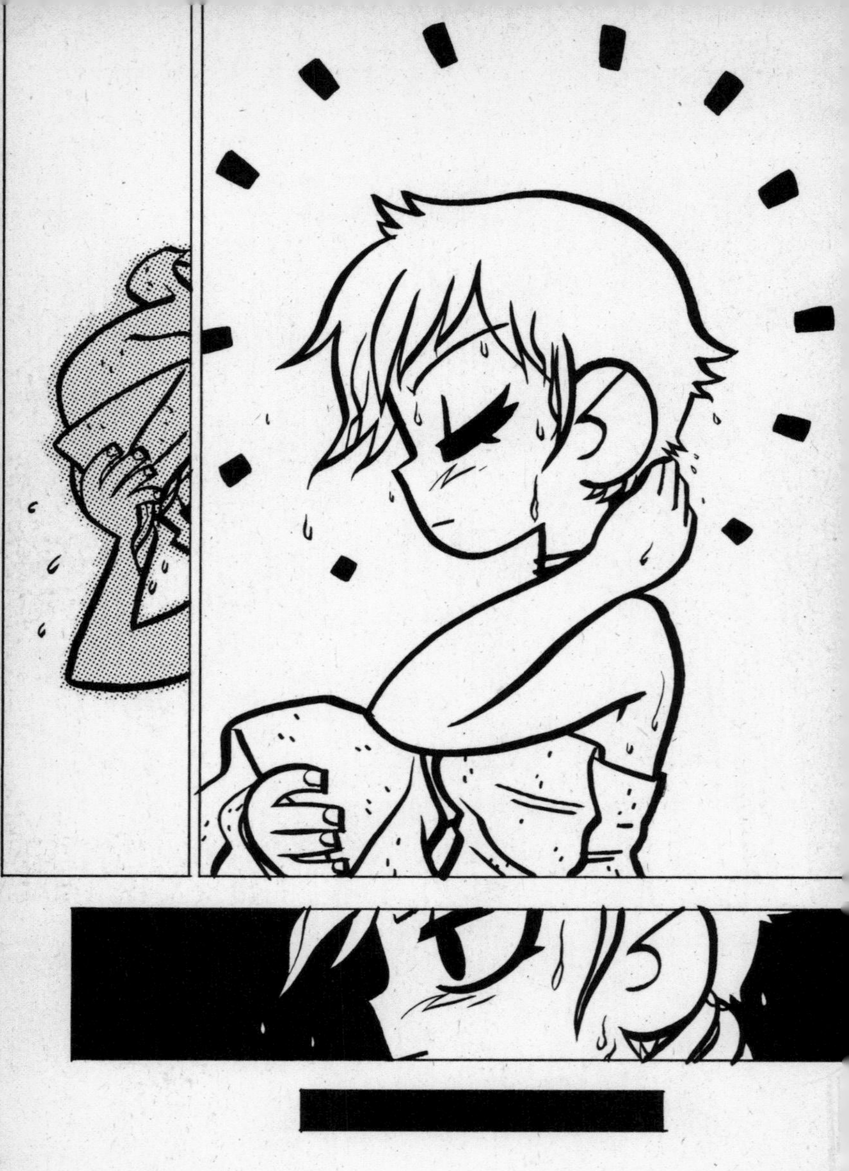

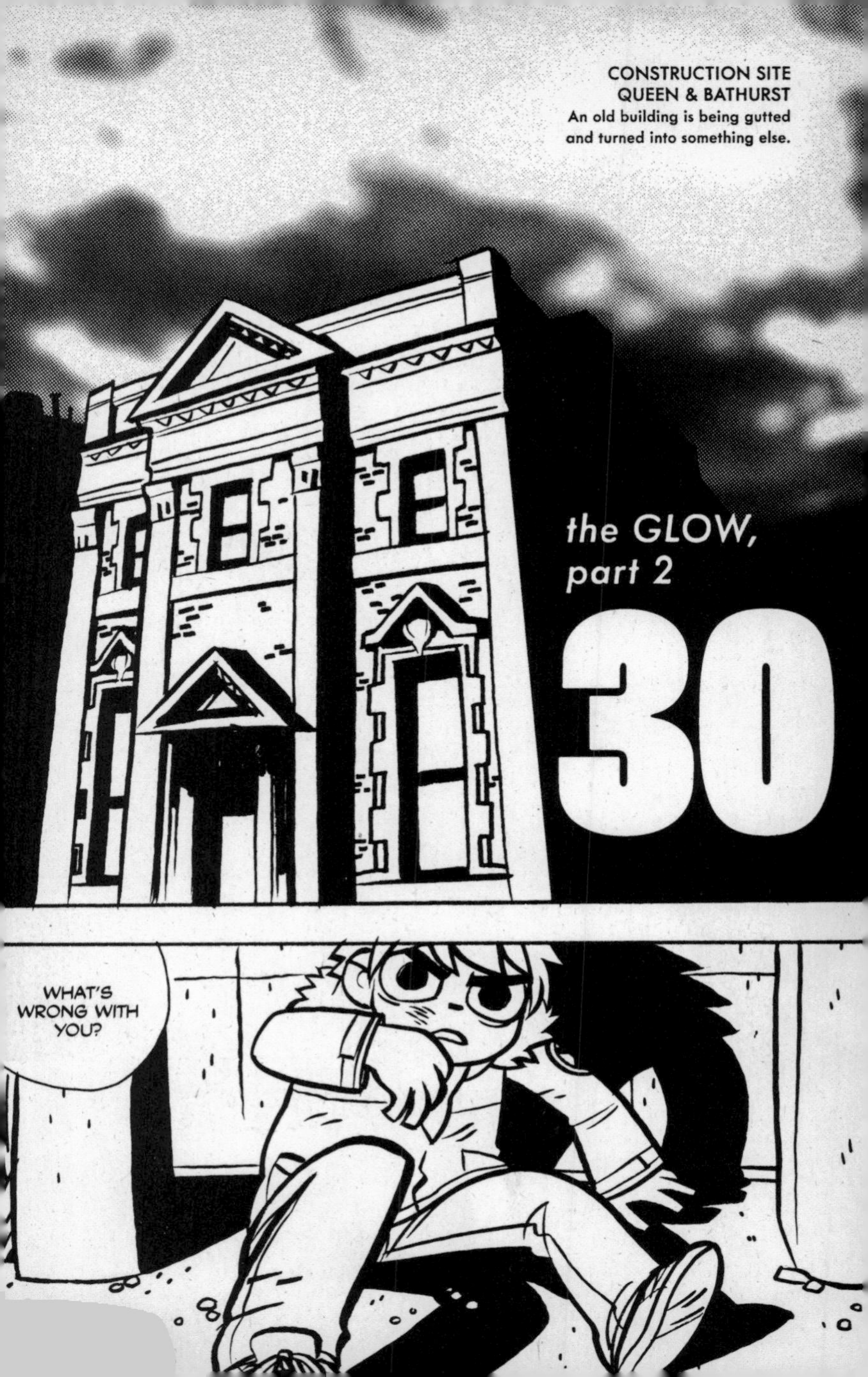
CONSTRUCTION SITE
QUEEN & BATHURST
An old building is being gutted and turned into something else.
the GLOW, part 2
30
WHAT'S WRONG WITH YOU?

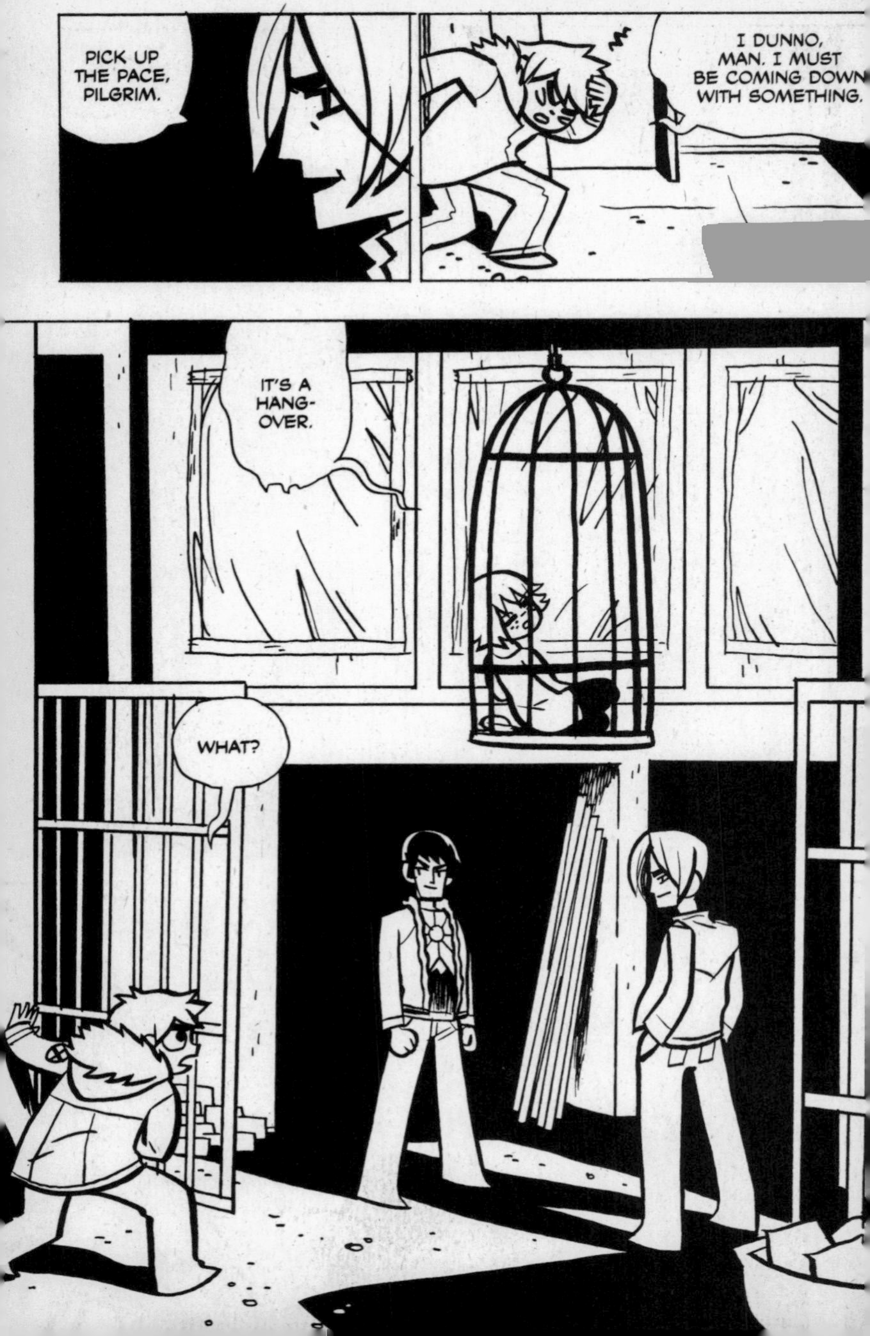
PICK UP THE PACE, PILGRIM.
I DUNNO, MAN. I MUST BE COMING DOWN WITH SOMETHING.
IT'S A HANG-OVER.
WHAT?

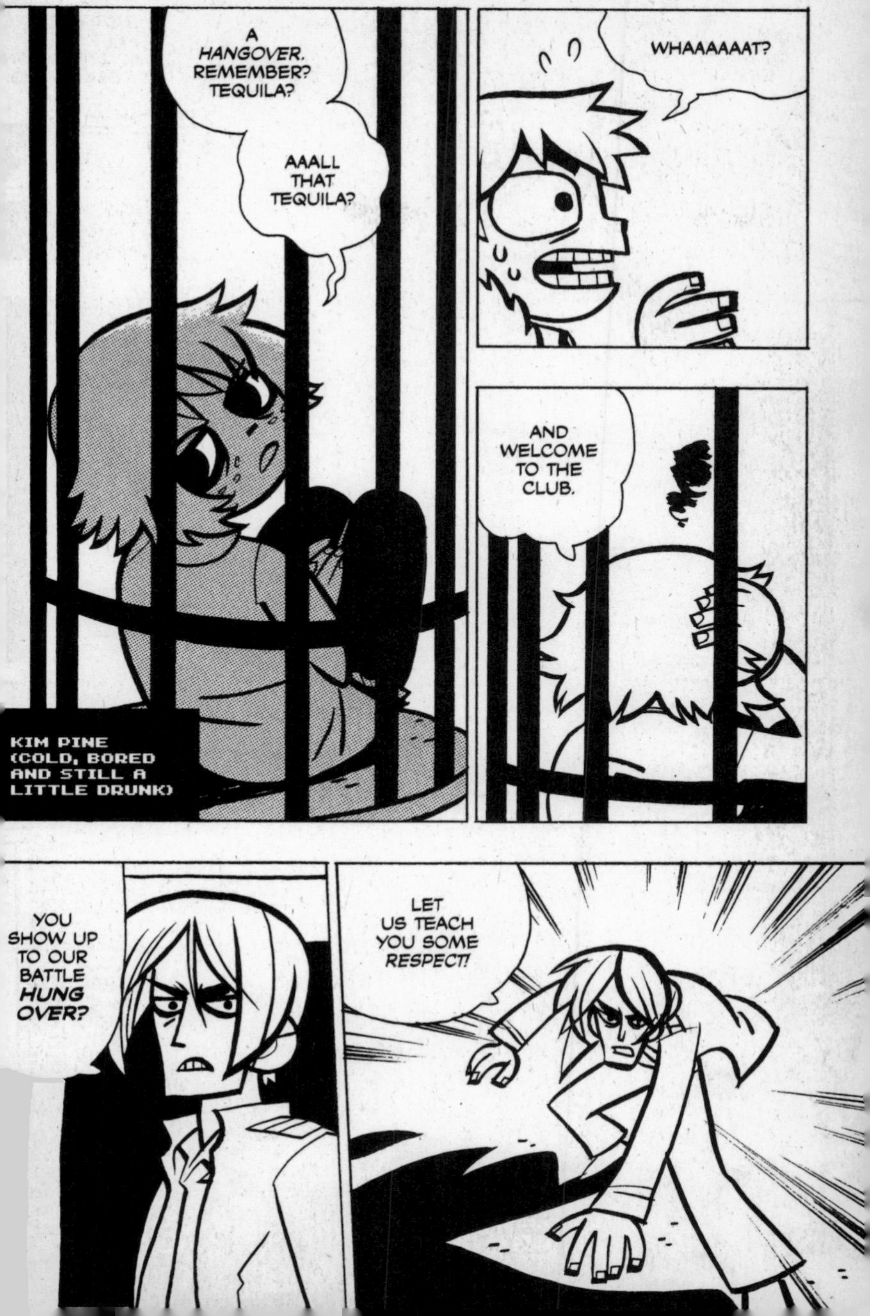
A HANGOVER. REMEMBER? TEQUILA?
AAALL THAT TEQUILA?
KIM PINE (COLD, BORED AND STILL A LITTLE DRUNK)
WHAAAAAAT?
AND WELCOME TO THE CLUB.
YOU SHOW UP TO OUR BATTLE HUNG OVER?
LET US TEACH YOU SOME RESPECT!

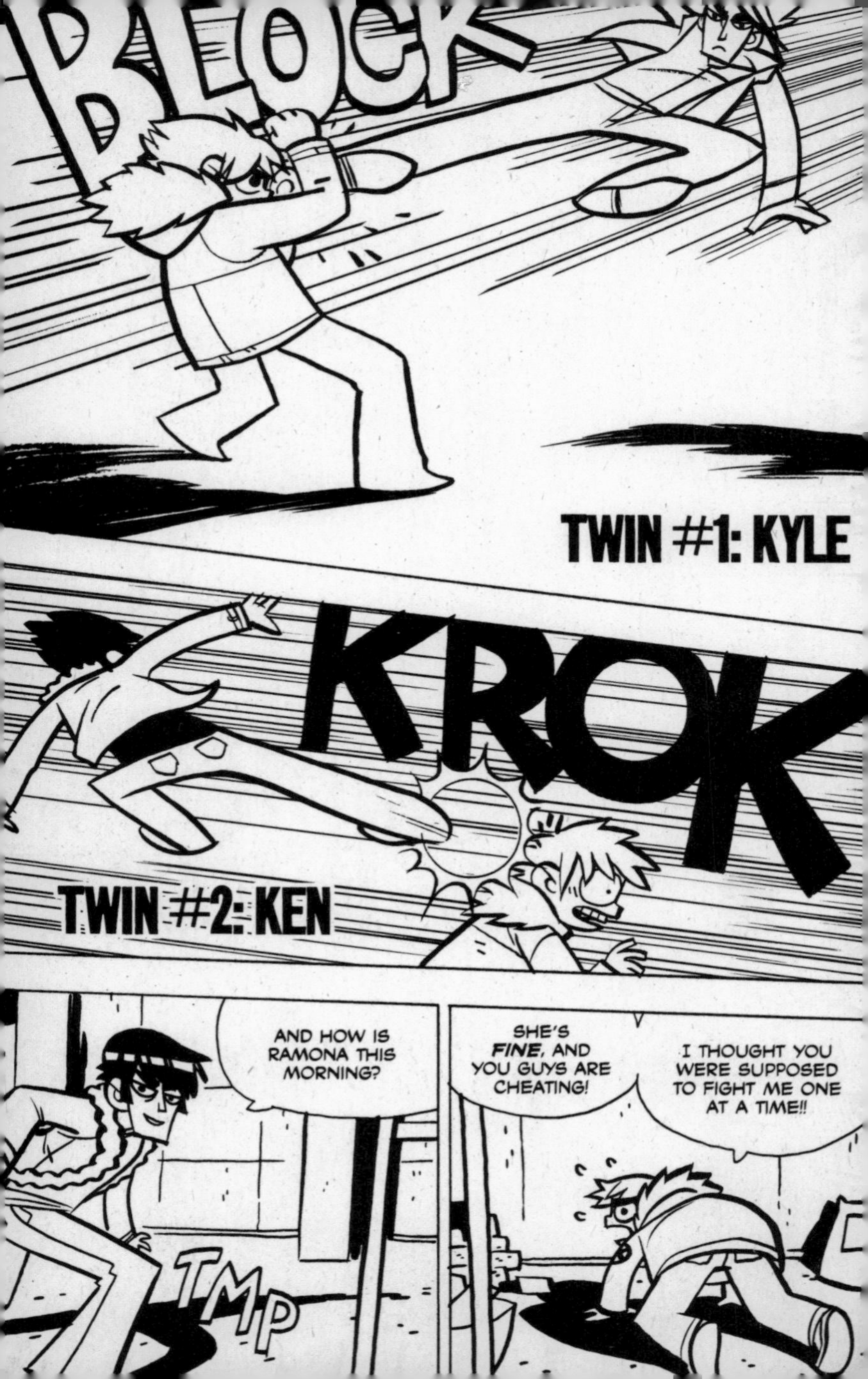
BLOCK
TWIN #1: KYLE
KROK
TWIN #2: KEN
AND HOW IS RAMONA THIS MORNING?
TMP
SHE'S *FINE*, AND YOU GUYS ARE CHEATING!
I THOUGHT YOU WERE SUPPOSED TO FIGHT ME ONE AT A TIME!!

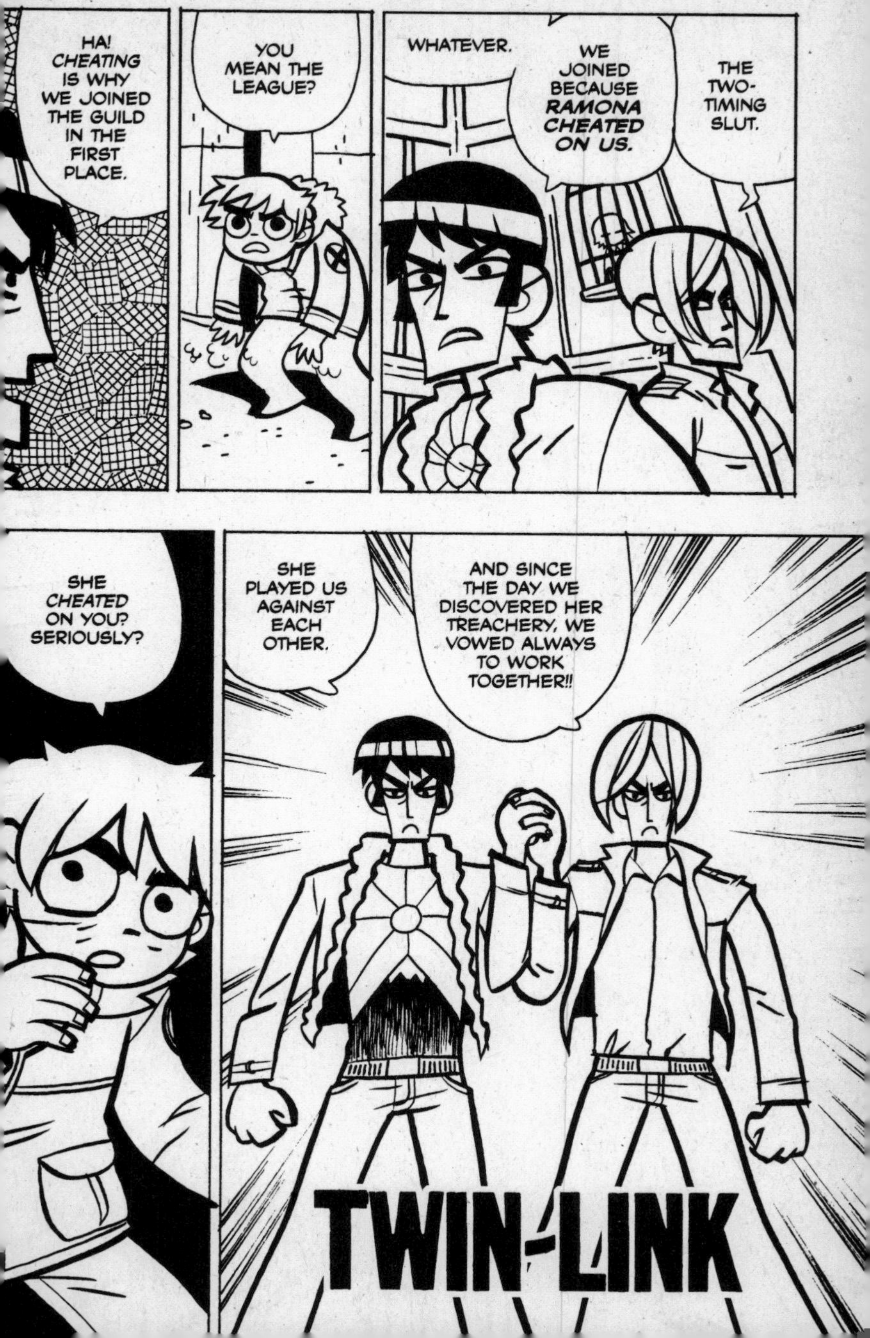
HA! CHEATING IS WHY WE JOINED THE GUILD IN THE FIRST PLACE.
YOU MEAN THE LEAGUE?
WHATEVER.
WE JOINED BECAUSE RAMONA CHEATED ON US.
THE TWO-TIMING SLUT.
SHE CHEATED ON YOU? SERIOUSLY?
SHE PLAYED US AGAINST EACH OTHER.
AND SINCE THE DAY WE DISCOVERED HER TREACHERY, WE VOWED ALWAYS TO WORK TOGETHER!!
TWIN-LINK

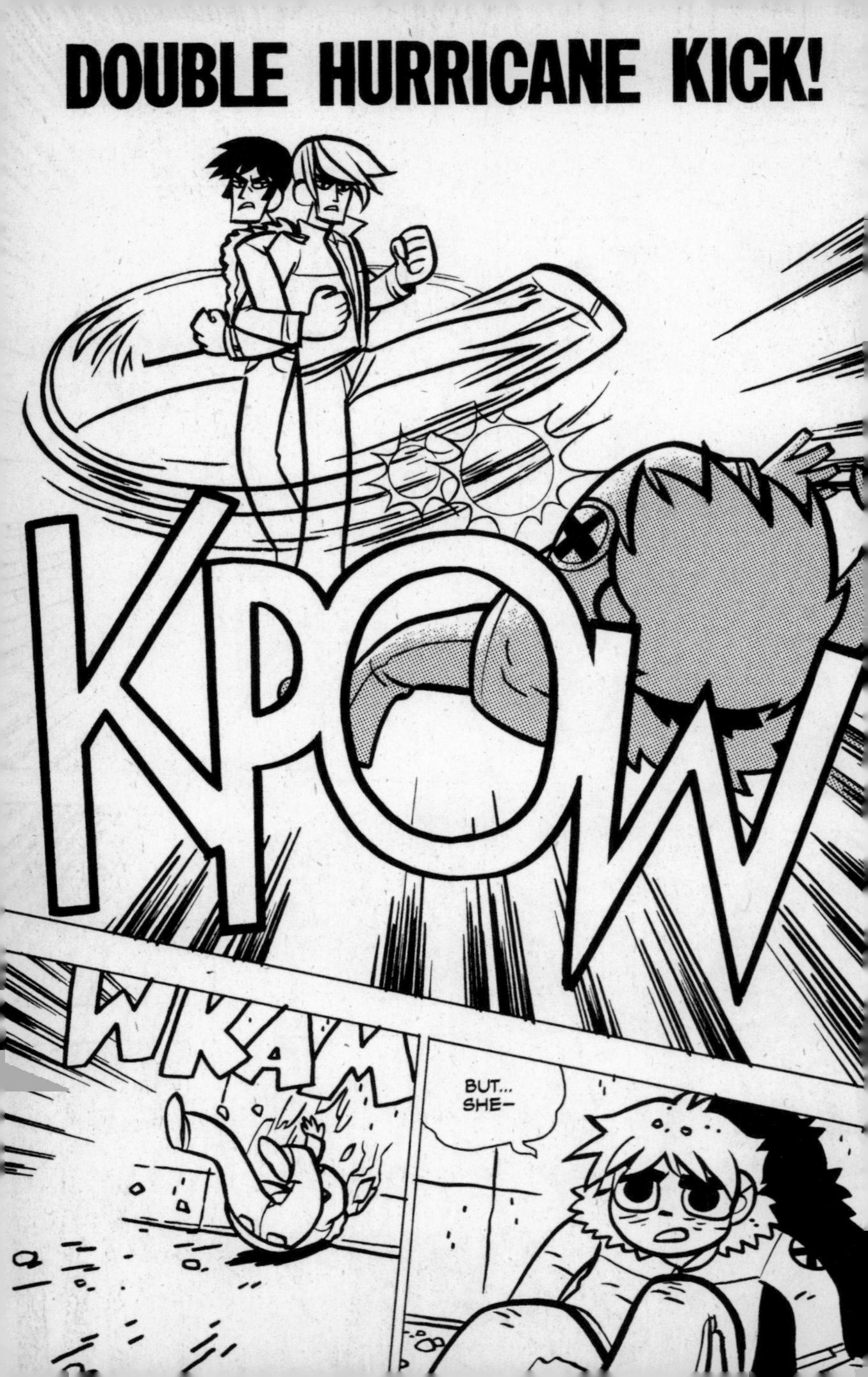
DOUBLE HURRICANE KICK!
KPOW
WKA
BUT... SHE—

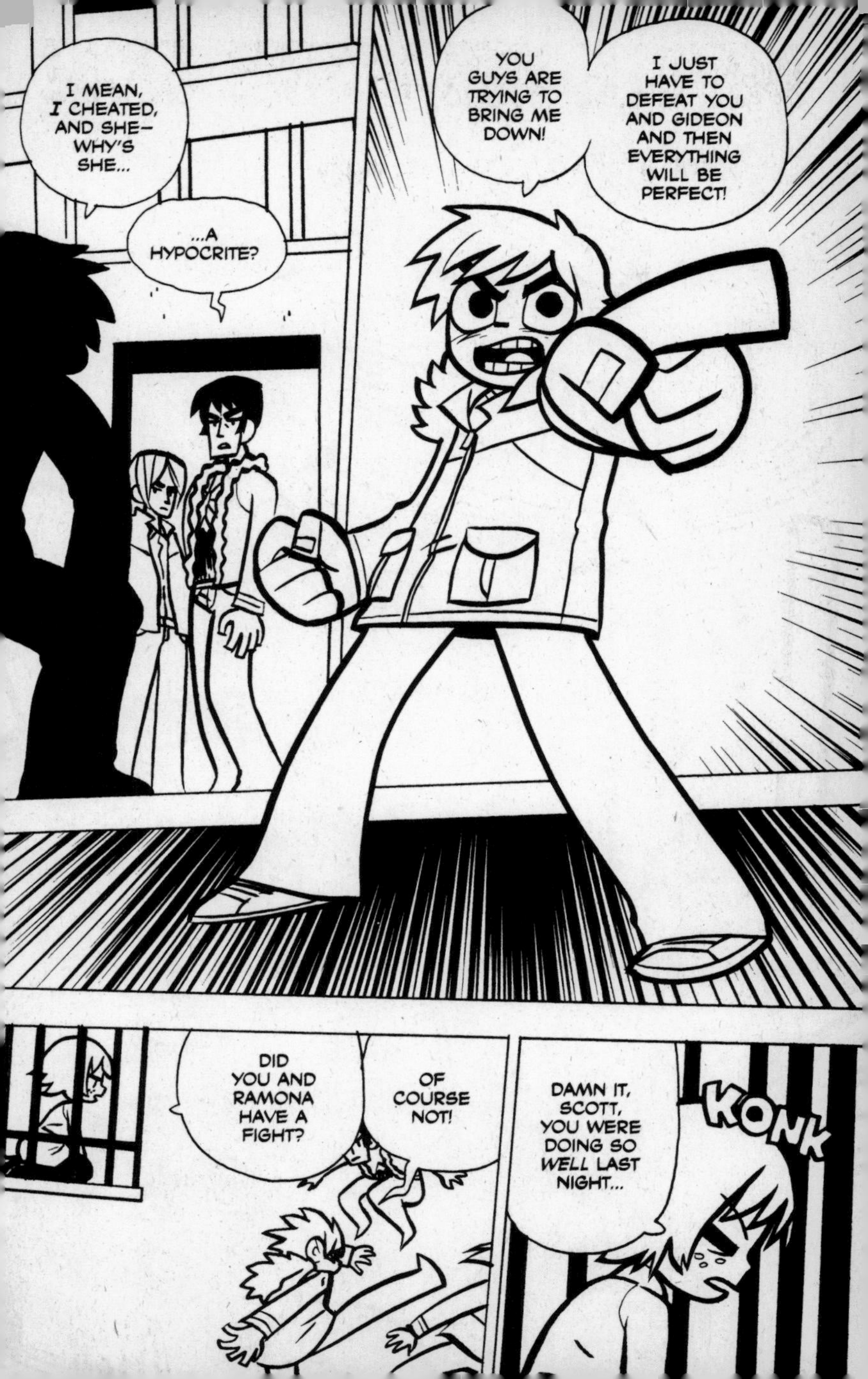
I MEAN, *I* CHEATED, AND SHE— WHY'S SHE...
...A HYPOCRITE?
YOU GUYS ARE TRYING TO BRING ME DOWN!
I JUST HAVE TO DEFEAT YOU AND GIDEON AND THEN EVERYTHING WILL BE PERFECT!
DID YOU AND RAMONA HAVE A FIGHT?
OF COURSE NOT!
DAMN IT, SCOTT, YOU WERE DOING SO *WELL* LAST NIGHT...
KONK

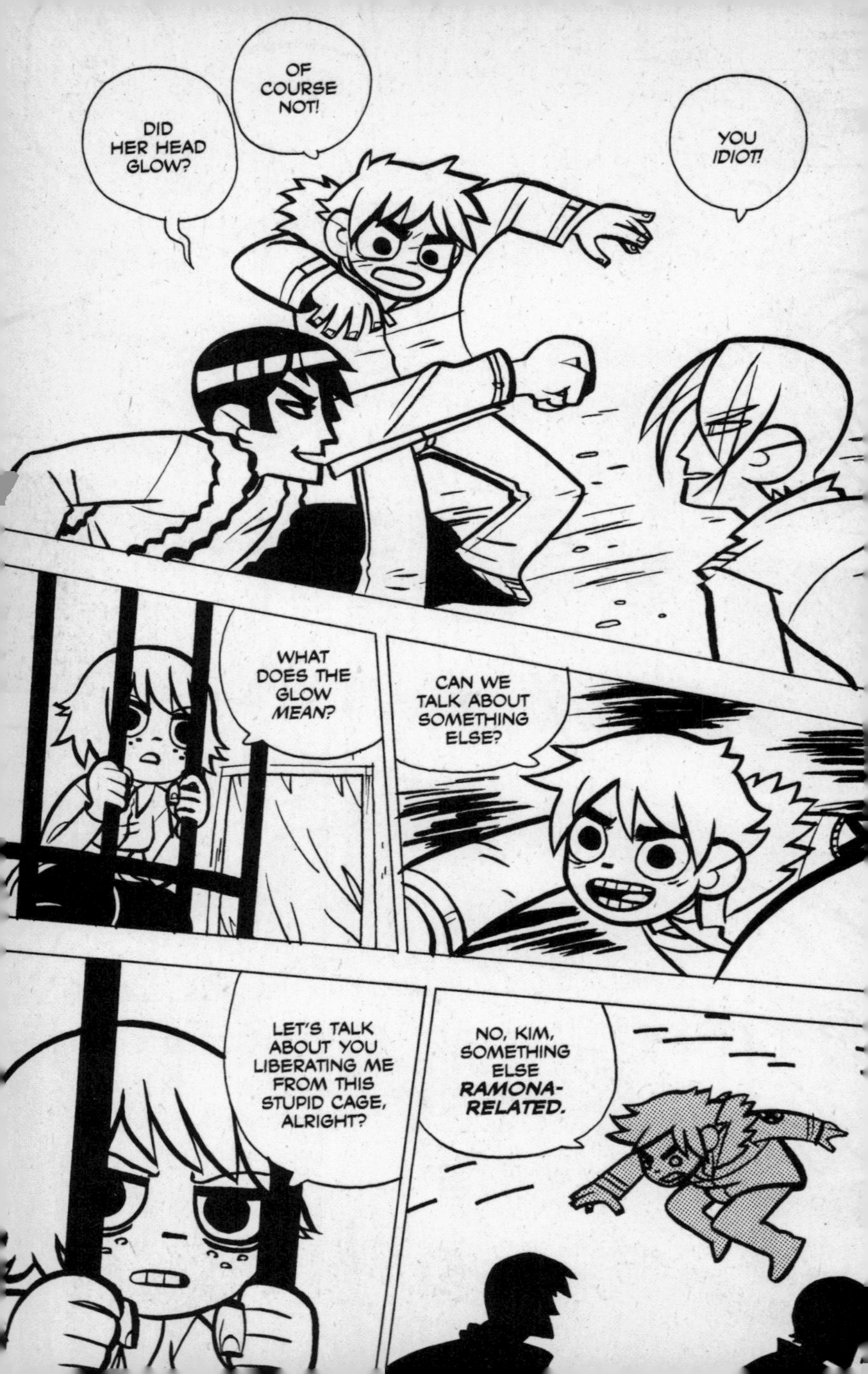
DID HER HEAD GLOW?
OF COURSE NOT!
YOU IDIOT!
WHAT DOES THE GLOW MEAN?
CAN WE TALK ABOUT SOMETHING ELSE?
LET'S TALK ABOUT YOU LIBERATING ME FROM THIS STUPID CAGE, ALRIGHT?
NO, KIM, SOMETHING ELSE RAMONA-RELATED.

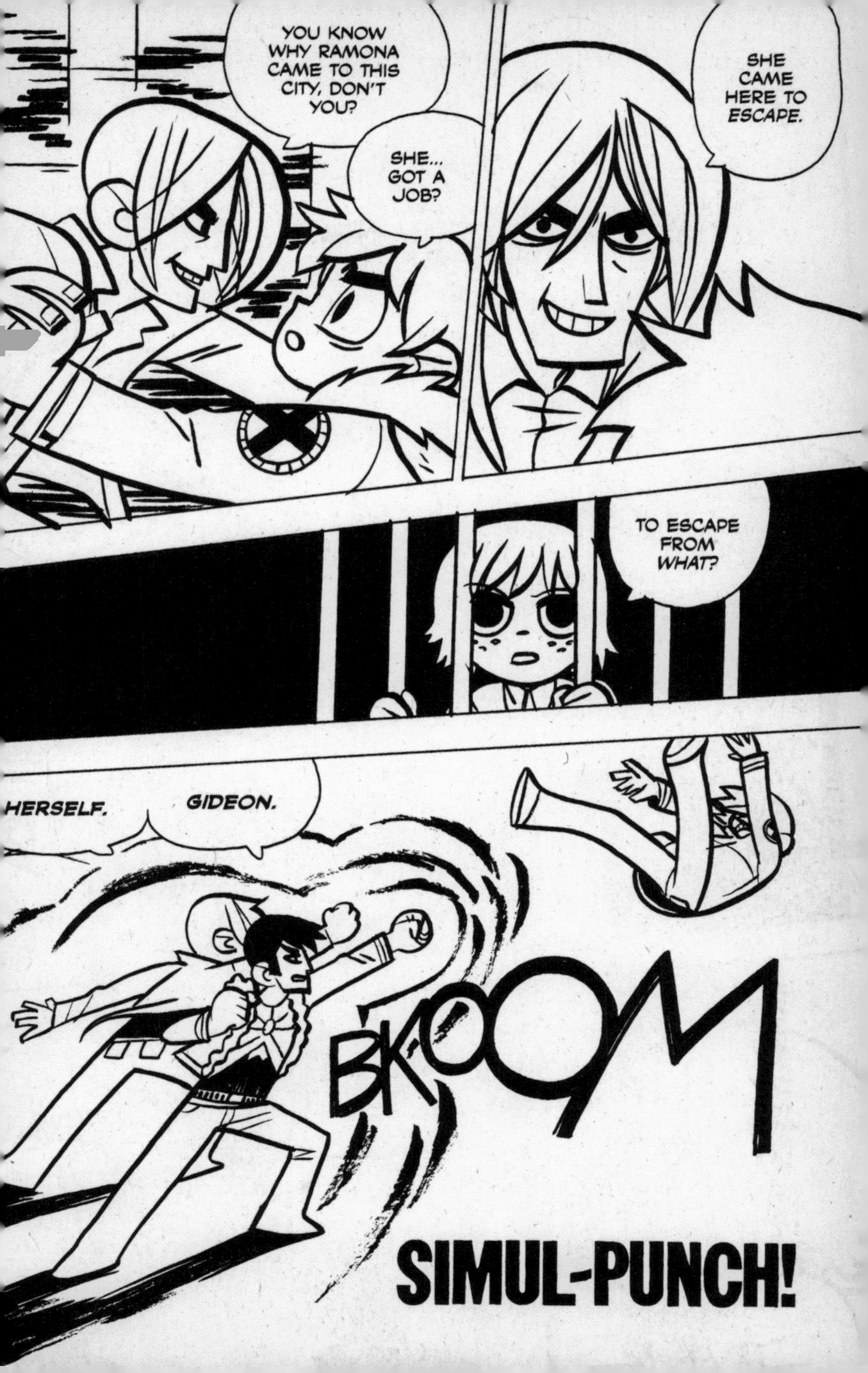
YOU KNOW WHY RAMONA CAME TO THIS CITY, DON'T YOU?
SHE... GOT A JOB?
SHE CAME HERE TO ESCAPE.
TO ESCAPE FROM WHAT?
HERSELF.
GIDEON.
BKOOM
SIMUL-PUNCH!

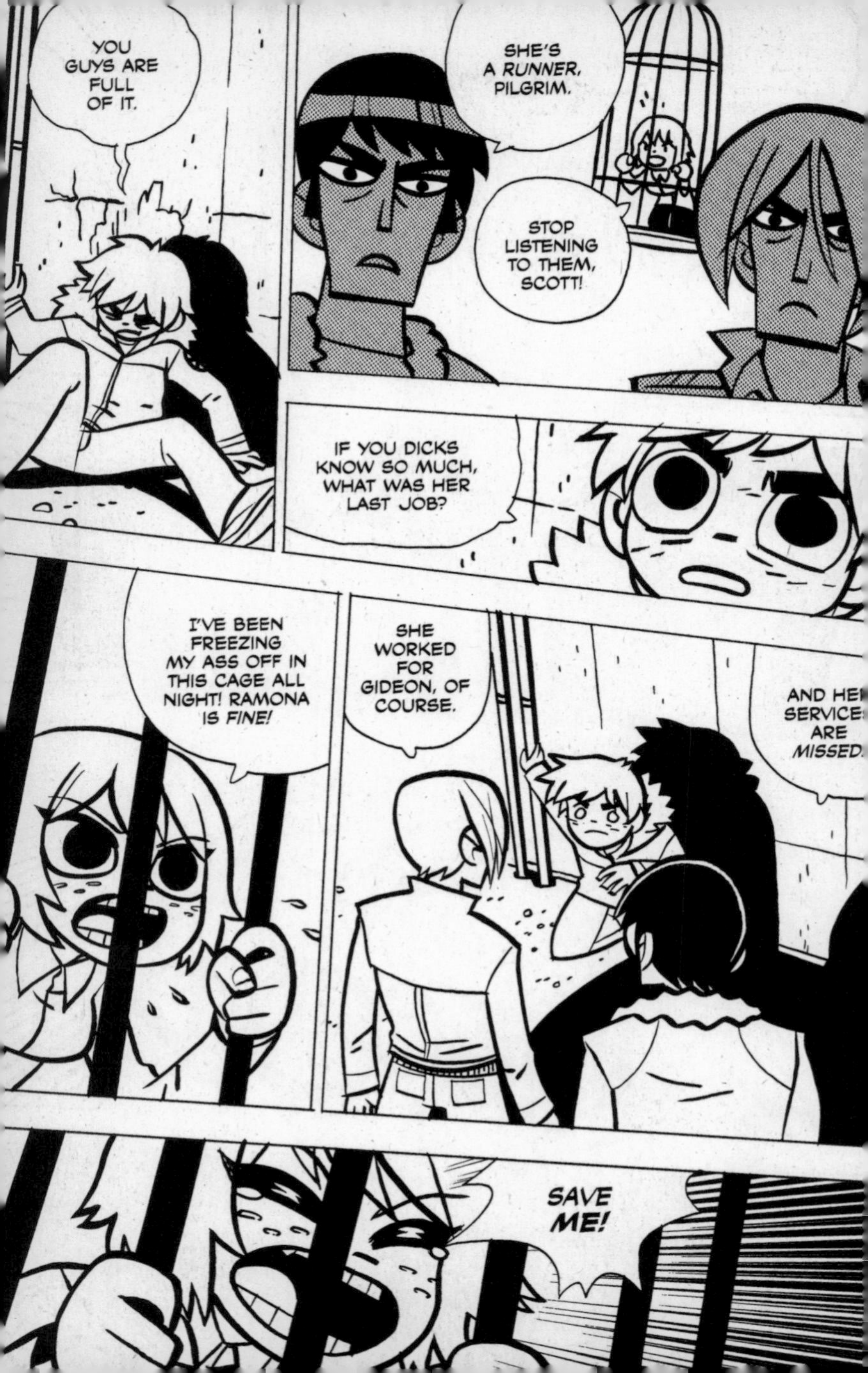
YOU GUYS ARE FULL OF IT.
SHE'S A *RUNNER,* PILGRIM.
STOP LISTENING TO THEM, SCOTT!
IF YOU DICKS KNOW SO MUCH, WHAT WAS HER LAST JOB?
I'VE BEEN FREEZING MY ASS OFF IN THIS CAGE ALL NIGHT! RAMONA IS *FINE!*
SHE WORKED FOR GIDEON, OF COURSE.
AND HE SERVICE ARE *MISSED.*
SAVE ME!

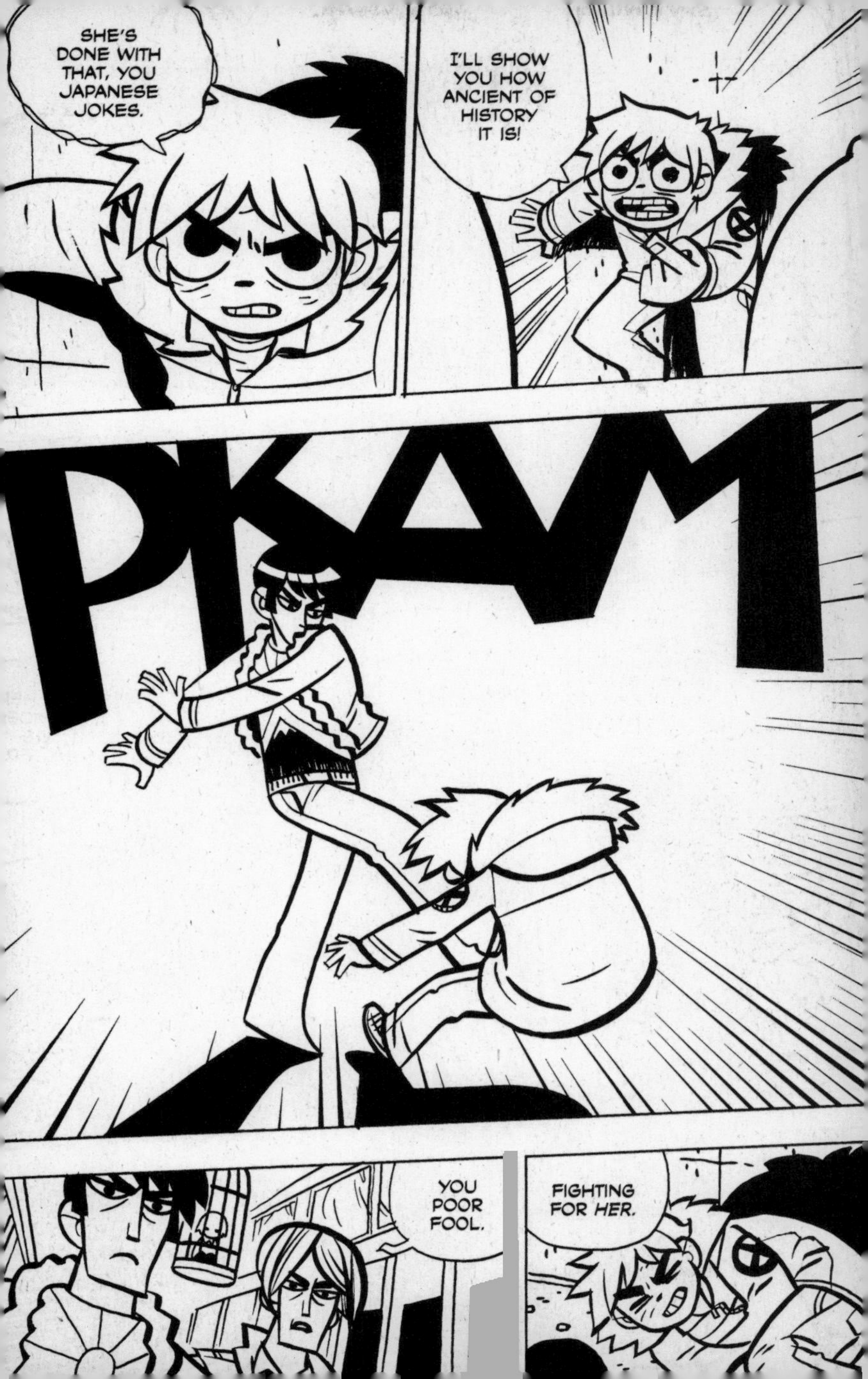
SHE'S DONE WITH THAT, YOU JAPANESE JOKES.
I'LL SHOW YOU HOW ANCIENT OF HISTORY IT IS!
PKAM
YOU POOR FOOL.
FIGHTING FOR *HER*.

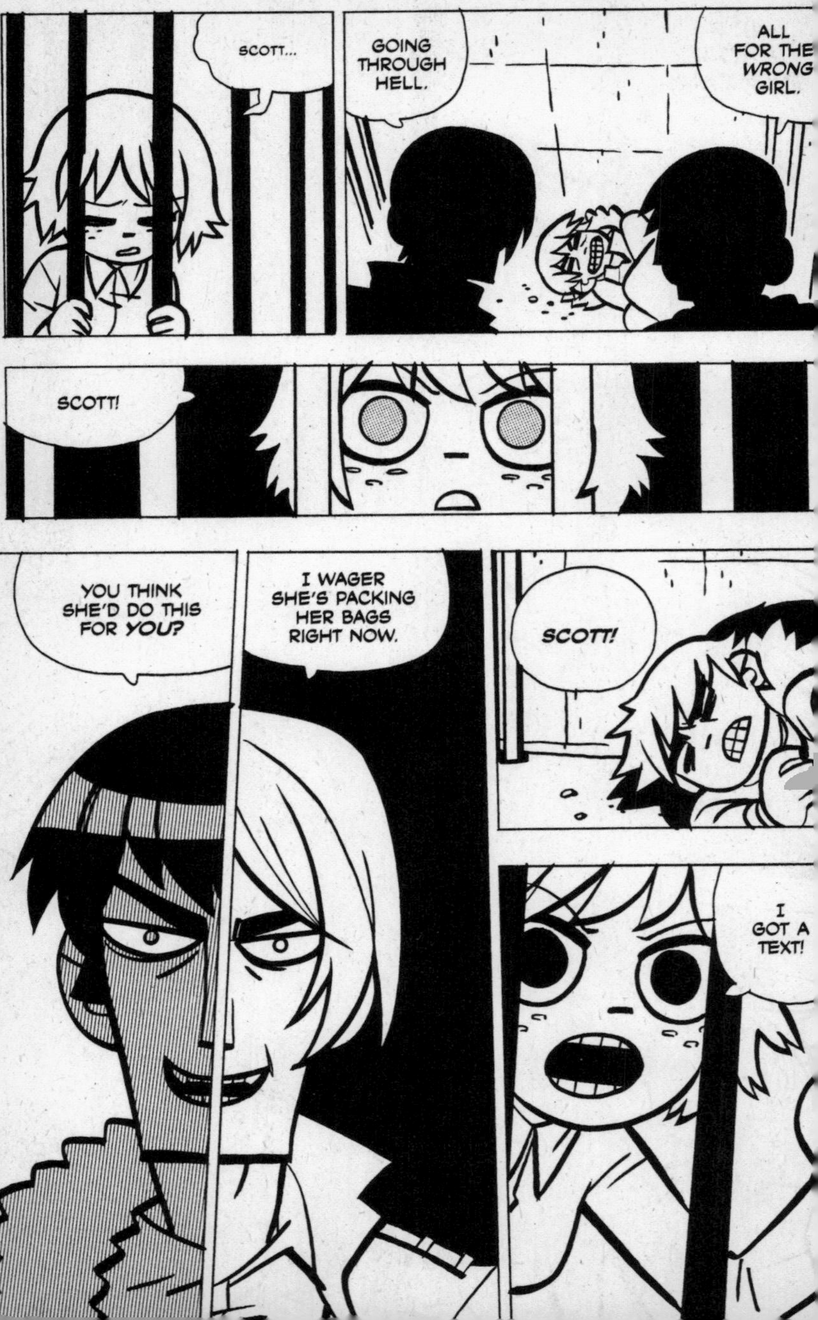
SCOTT...
GOING THROUGH HELL.
ALL FOR THE *WRONG* GIRL.
SCOTT!
YOU THINK SHE'D DO THIS FOR *YOU?*
I WAGER SHE'S PACKING HER BAGS RIGHT NOW.
SCOTT!
I GOT A TEXT!

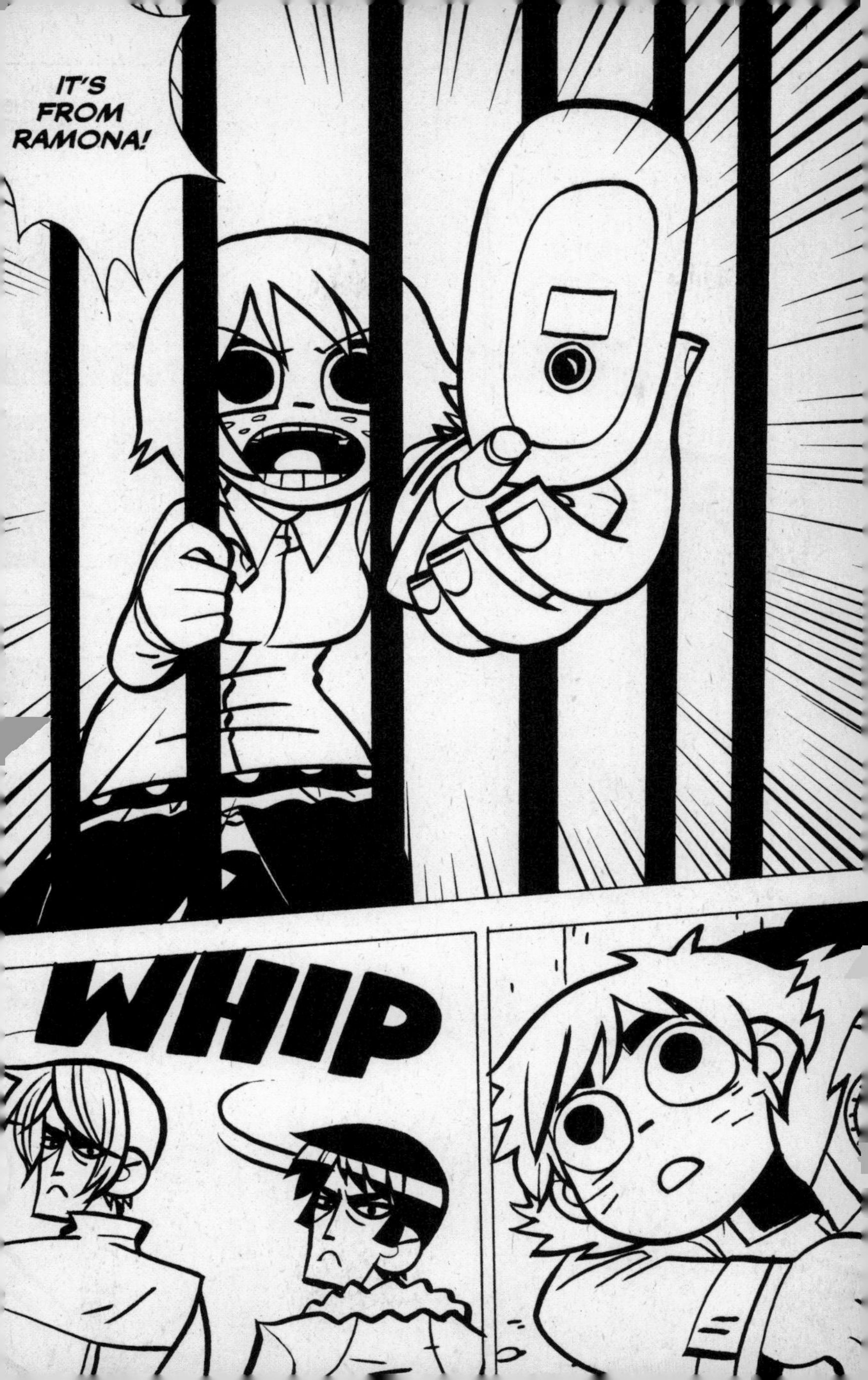
IT'S FROM RAMONA!
WHIP

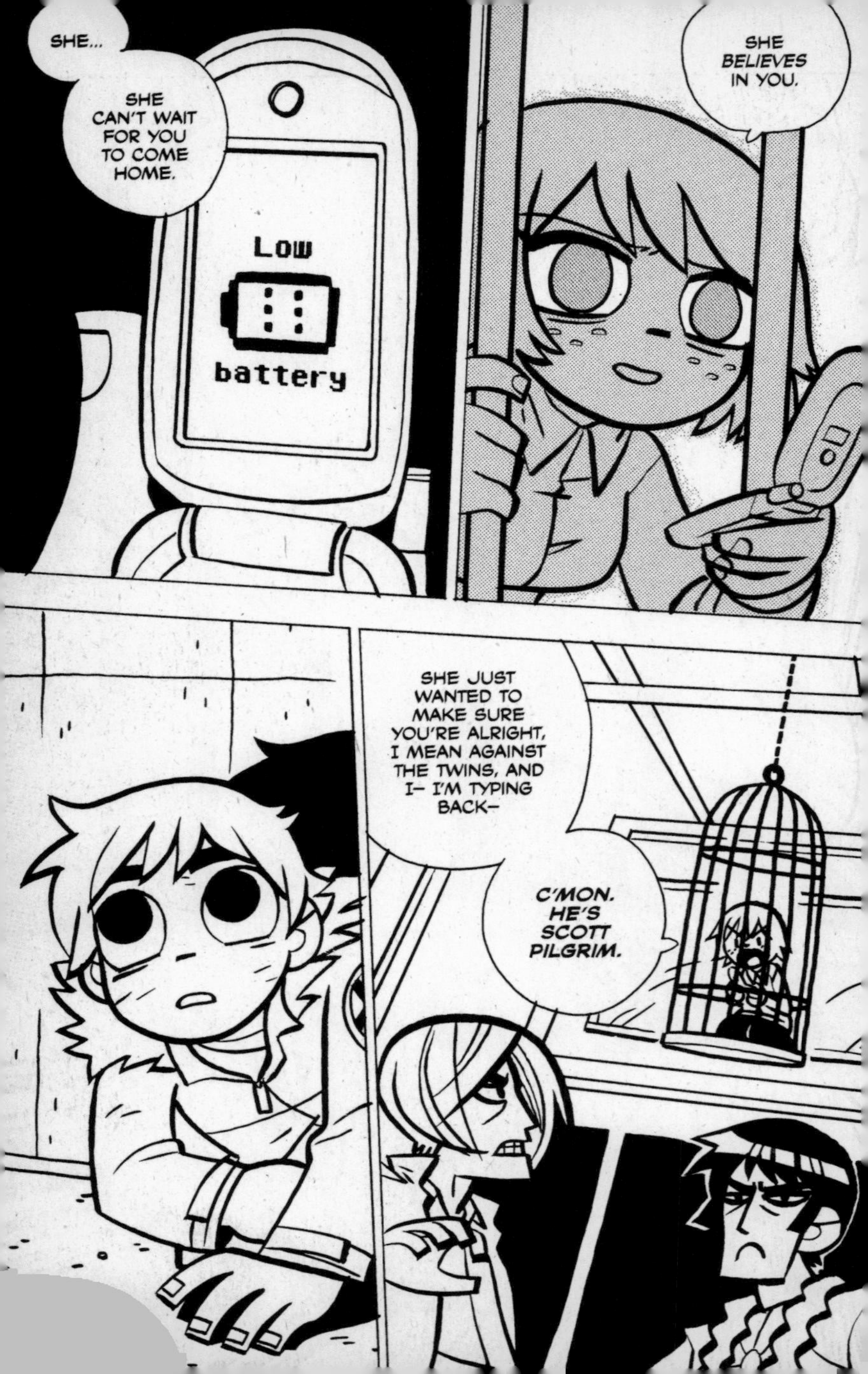
SHE...
SHE CAN'T WAIT FOR YOU TO COME HOME.
Low
battery
SHE BELIEVES IN YOU.
SHE JUST WANTED TO MAKE SURE YOU'RE ALRIGHT, I MEAN AGAINST THE TWINS, AND I– I'M TYPING BACK–
C'MON. HE'S SCOTT PILGRIM.

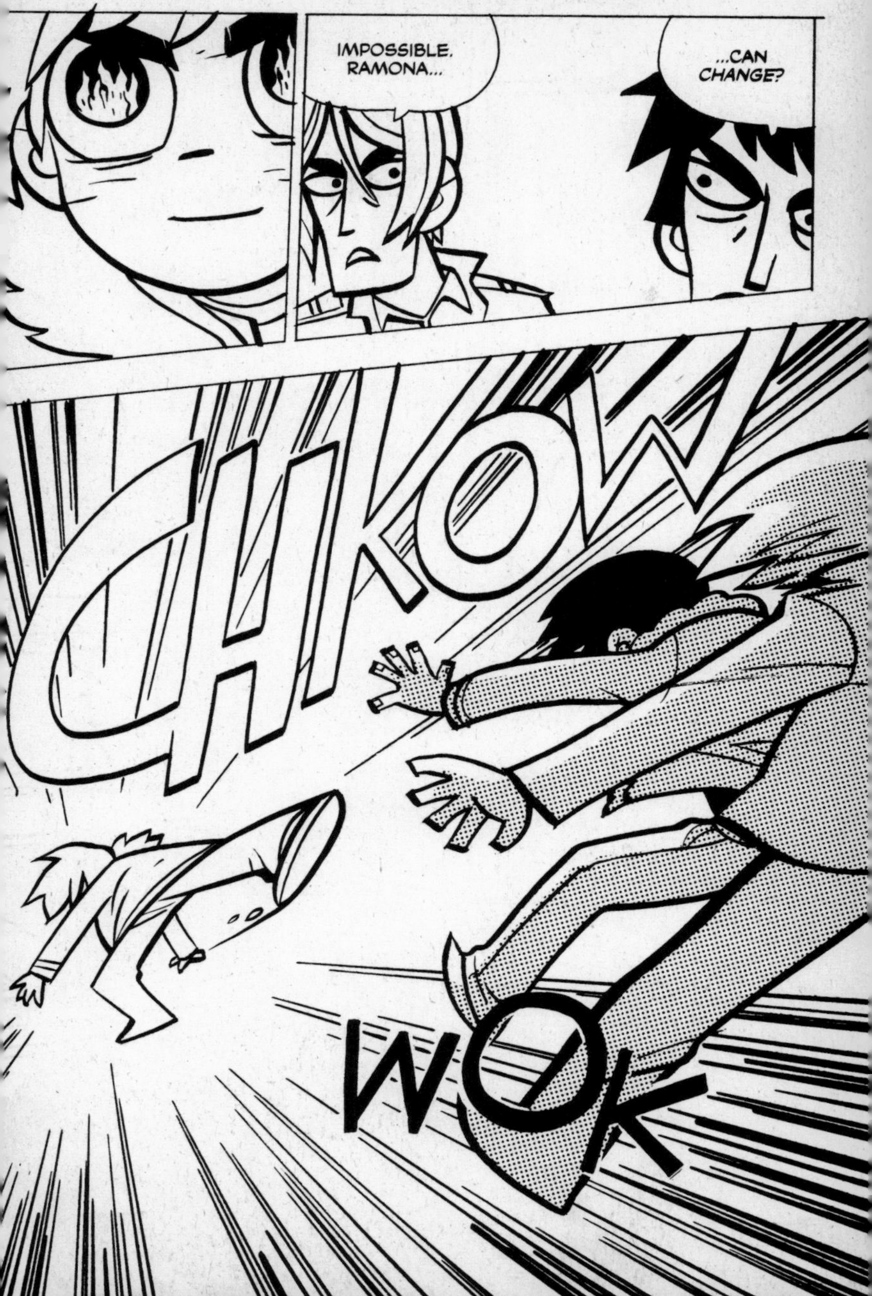
IMPOSSIBLE. RAMONA...
...CAN CHANGE?
CHKOW
WOK

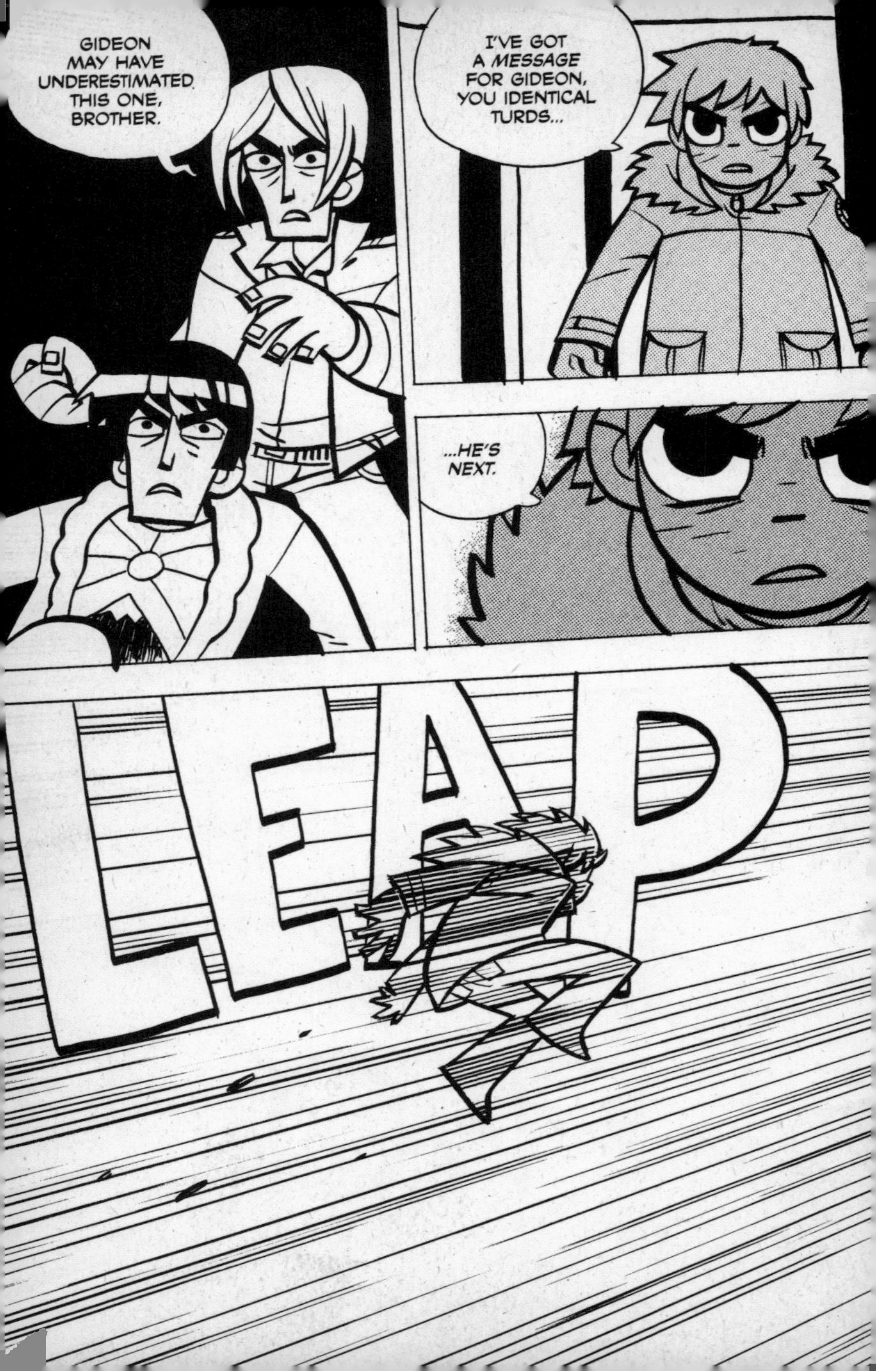
GIDEON MAY HAVE UNDERESTIMATED THIS ONE, BROTHER.
I'VE GOT A *MESSAGE* FOR GIDEON, YOU IDENTICAL TURDS...
...HE'S NEXT.
LEAP

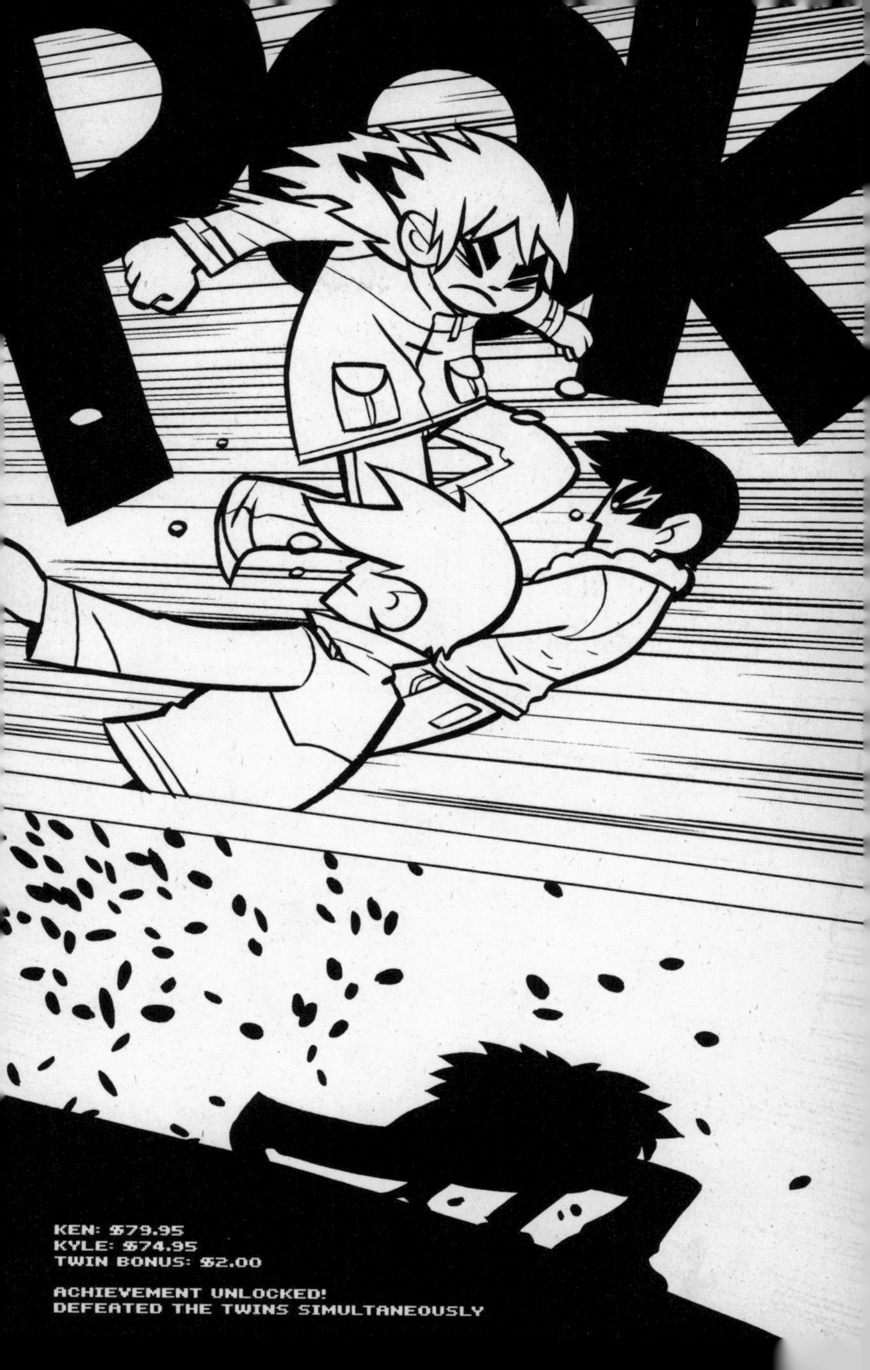
KEN: $79.95
KYLE: $74.95
TWIN BONUS: $2.00
ACHIEVEMENT UNLOCKED!
DEFEATED THE TWINS SIMULTANEOUSLY

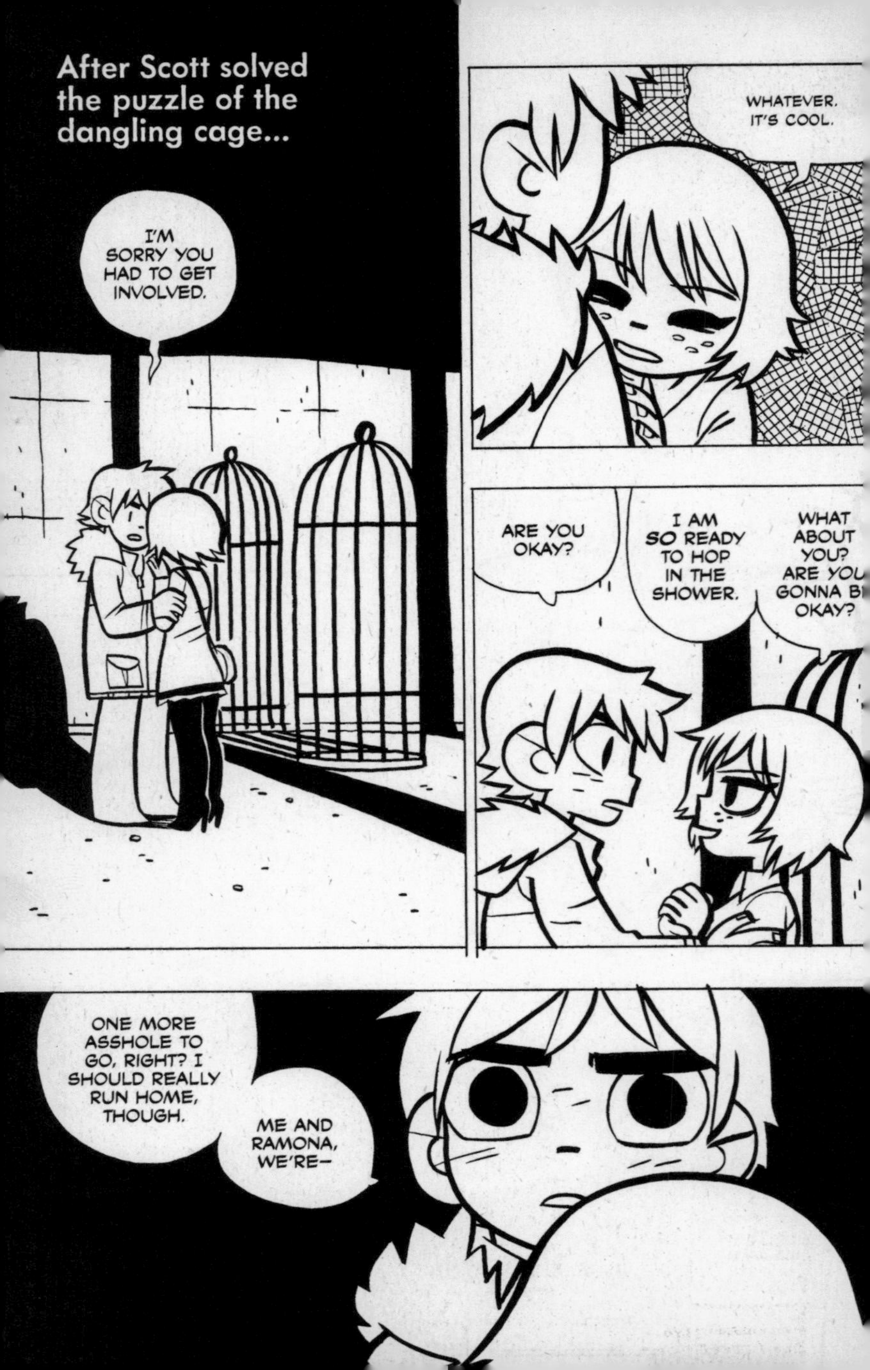
After Scott solved the puzzle of the dangling cage...
I'M SORRY YOU HAD TO GET INVOLVED.
WHATEVER. IT'S COOL.
ARE YOU OKAY?
I AM SO READY TO HOP IN THE SHOWER.
WHAT ABOUT YOU? ARE YOU GONNA BE OKAY?
ONE MORE ASSHOLE TO GO, RIGHT? I SHOULD REALLY RUN HOME, THOUGH.
ME AND RAMONA, WE'RE—

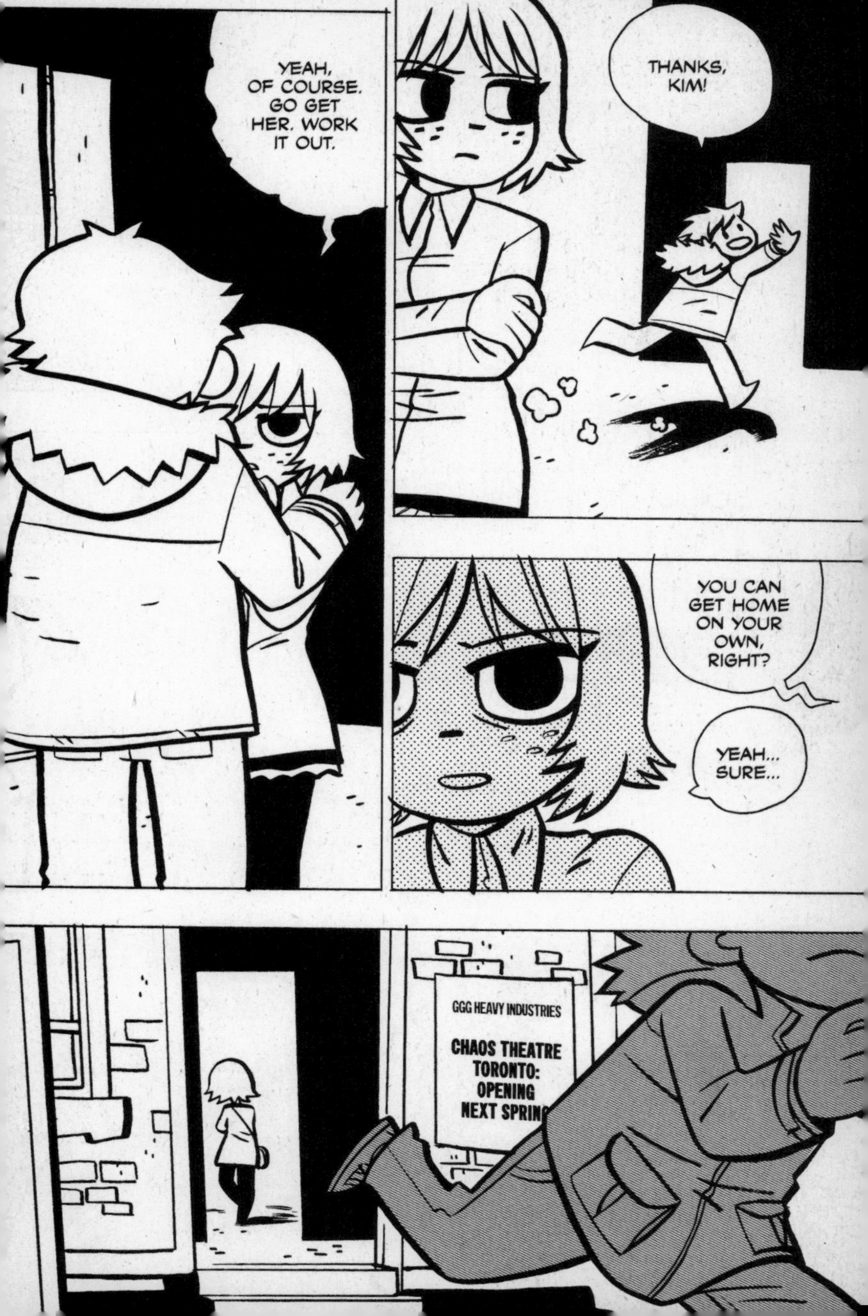
YEAH, OF COURSE. GO GET HER. WORK IT OUT.
THANKS, KIM!
YOU CAN GET HOME ON YOUR OWN, RIGHT?
YEAH... SURE...
GGG HEAVY INDUSTRIES
CHAOS THEATRE TORONTO: OPENING NEXT SPRIN

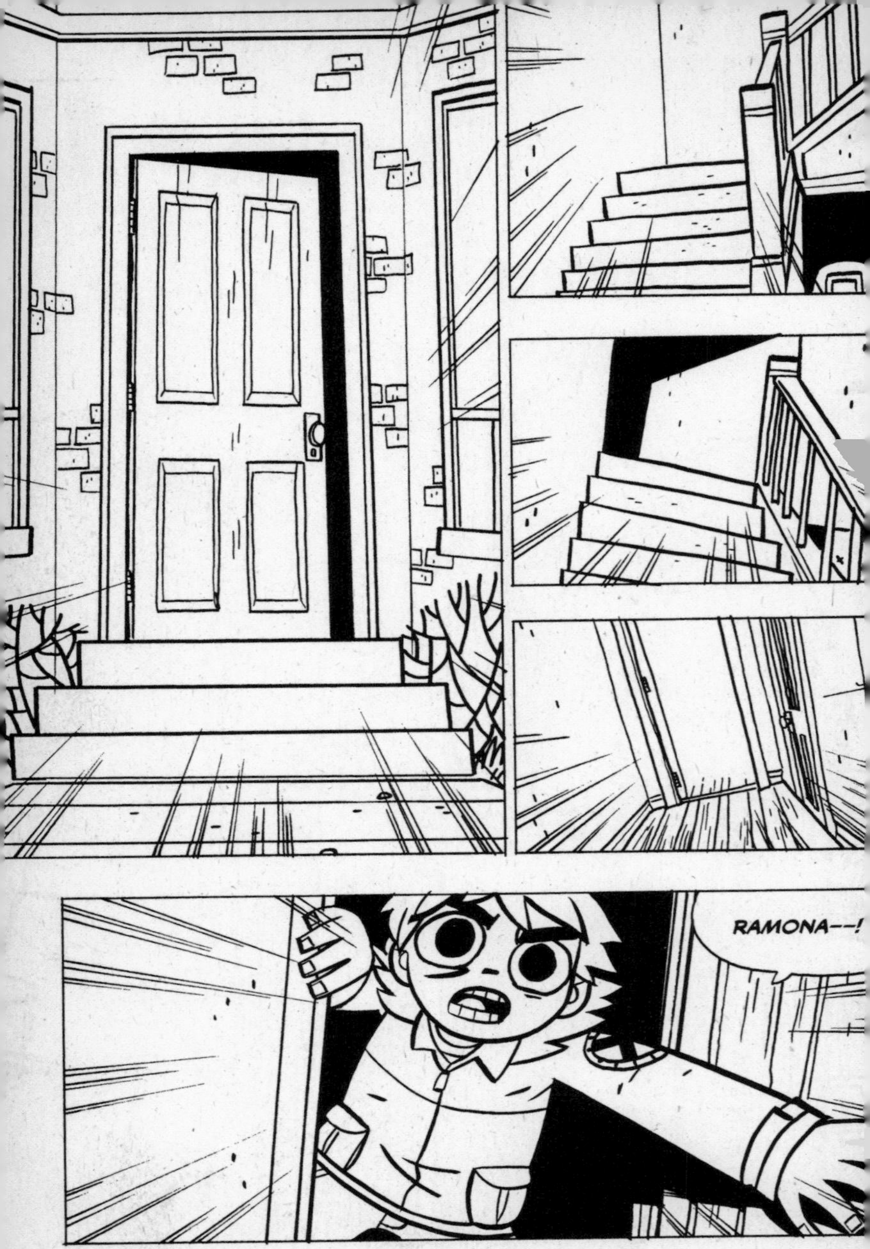
RAMONA--!

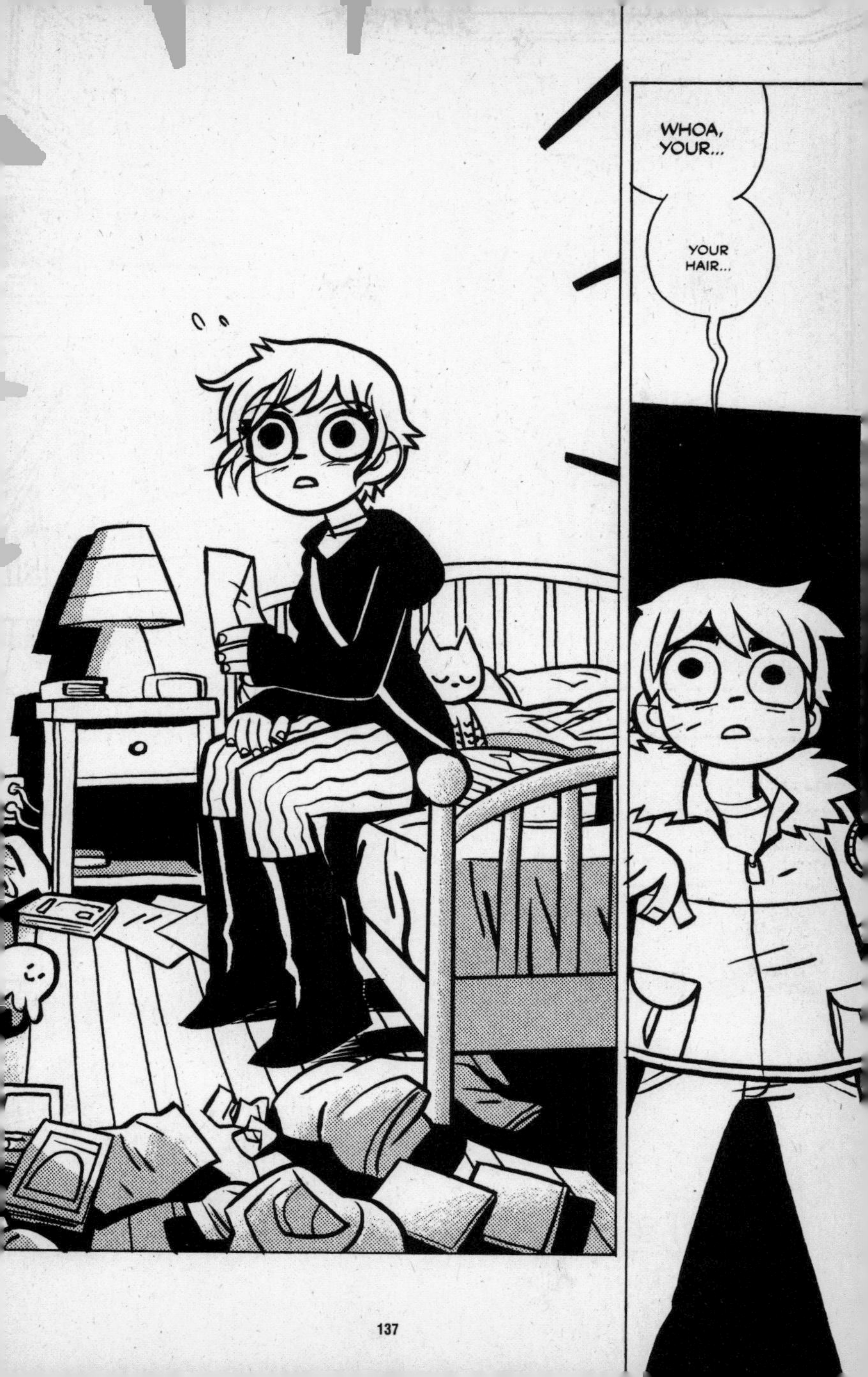
WHOA, YOUR...
YOUR HAIR...

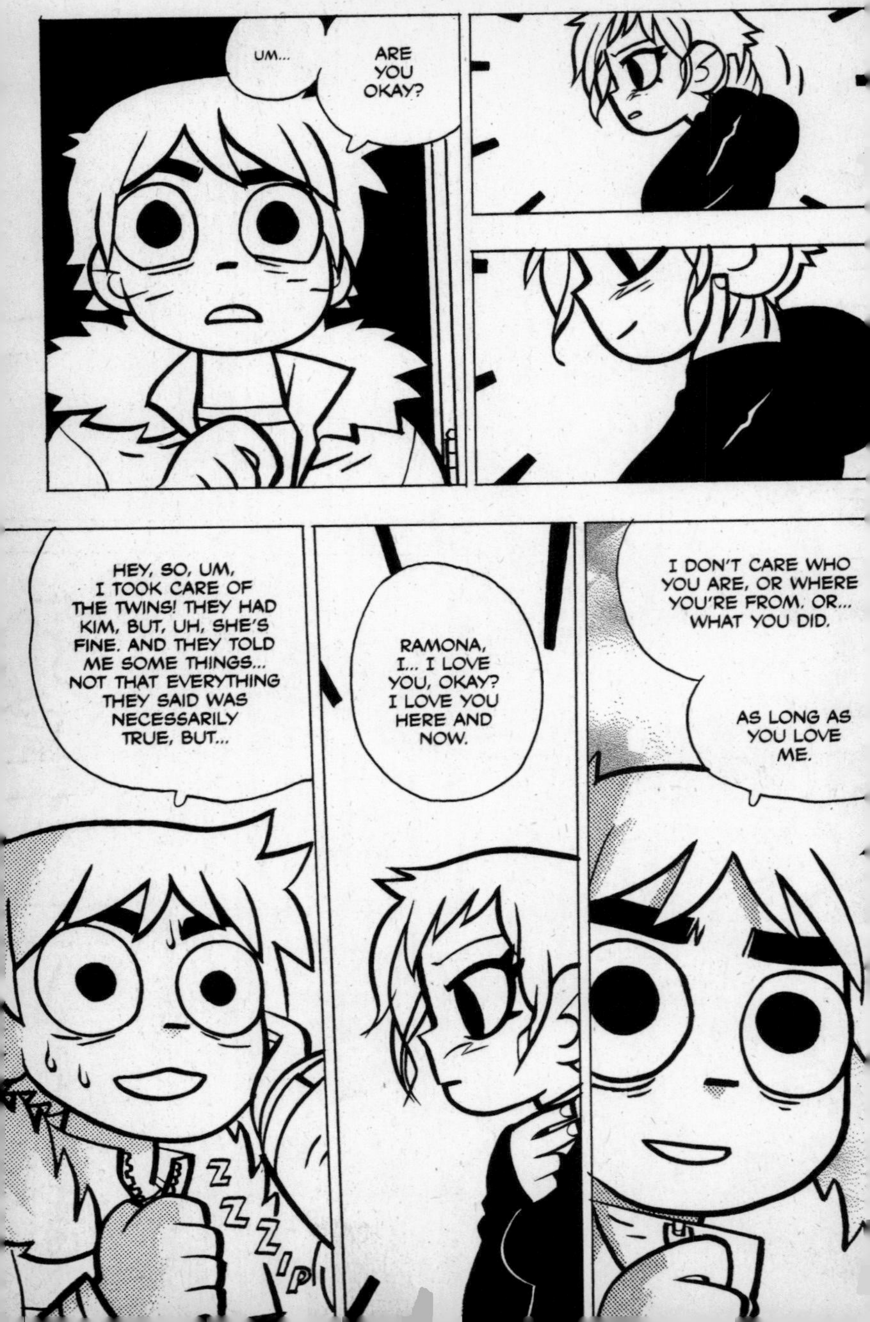
UM...
ARE YOU OKAY?
HEY, SO, UM, I TOOK CARE OF THE TWINS! THEY HAD KIM, BUT, UH, SHE'S FINE. AND THEY TOLD ME SOME THINGS... NOT THAT EVERYTHING THEY SAID WAS NECESSARILY TRUE, BUT...
ZZZIP
RAMONA, I... I LOVE YOU, OKAY? I LOVE YOU HERE AND NOW.
I DON'T CARE WHO YOU ARE, OR WHERE YOU'RE FROM. OR... WHAT YOU DID.
AS LONG AS YOU LOVE ME.

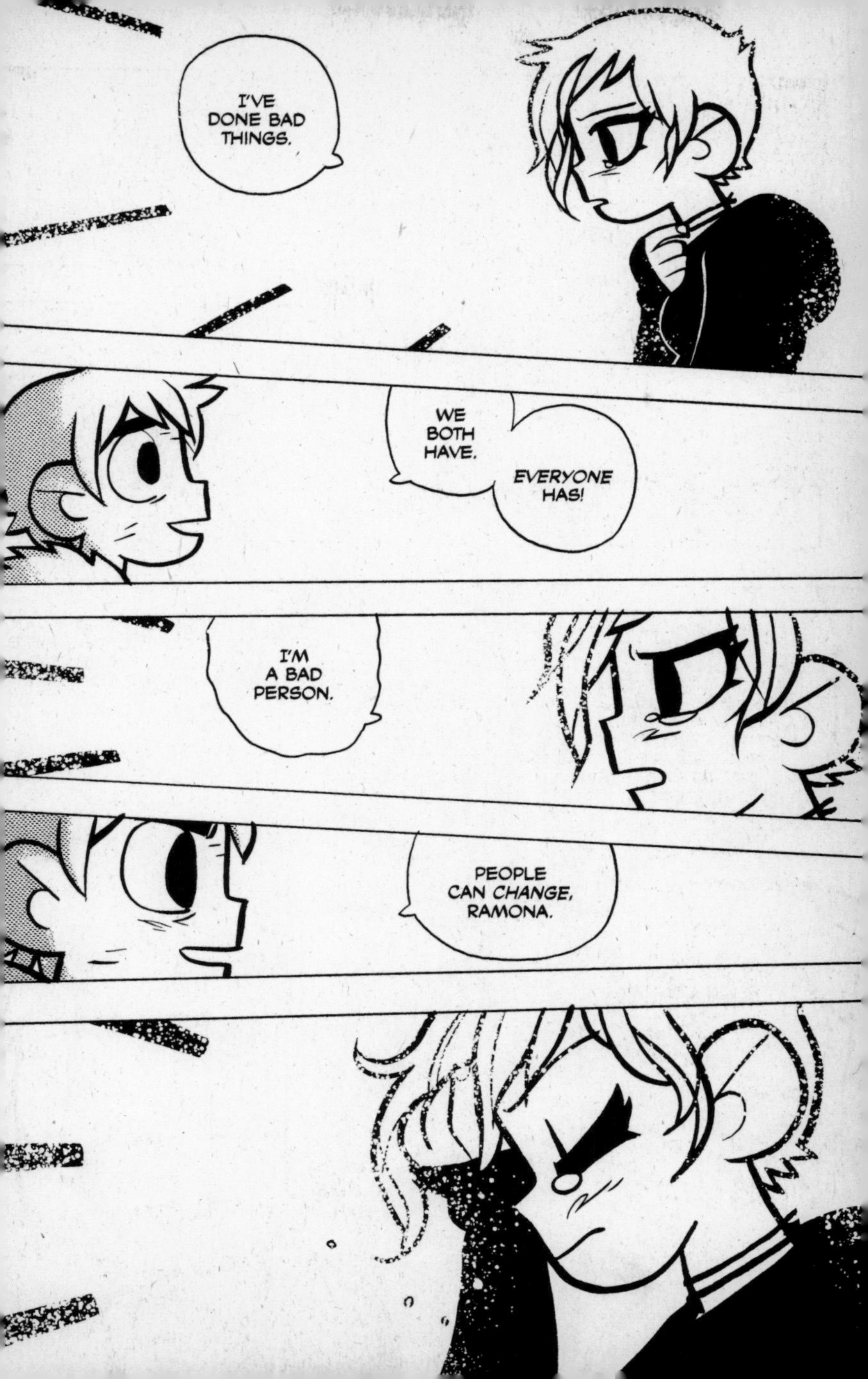
I'VE DONE BAD THINGS.
WE BOTH HAVE.
EVERYONE HAS!
I'M A BAD PERSON.
PEOPLE CAN *CHANGE*, RAMONA.

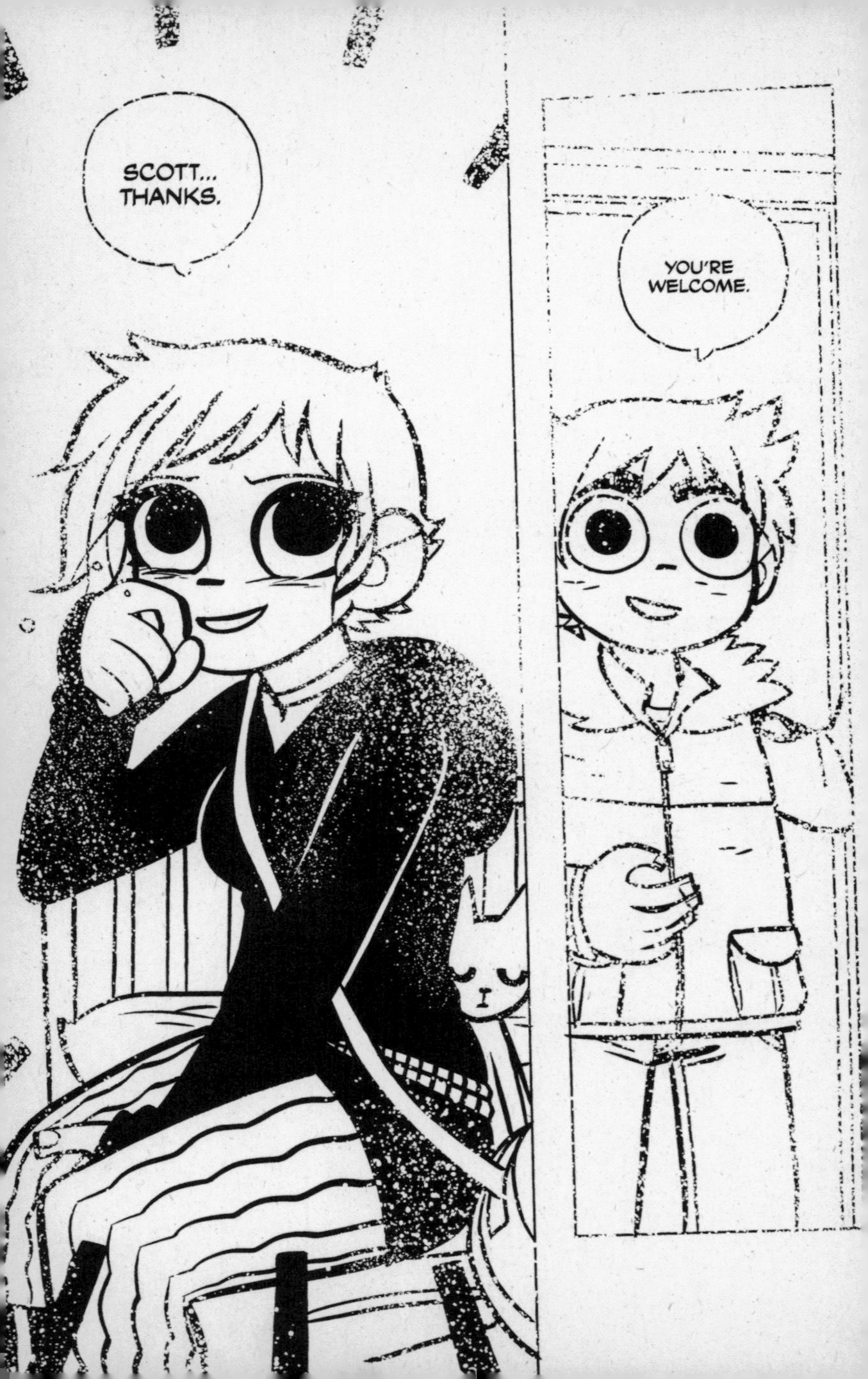
SCOTT... THANKS.
YOU'RE WELCOME.

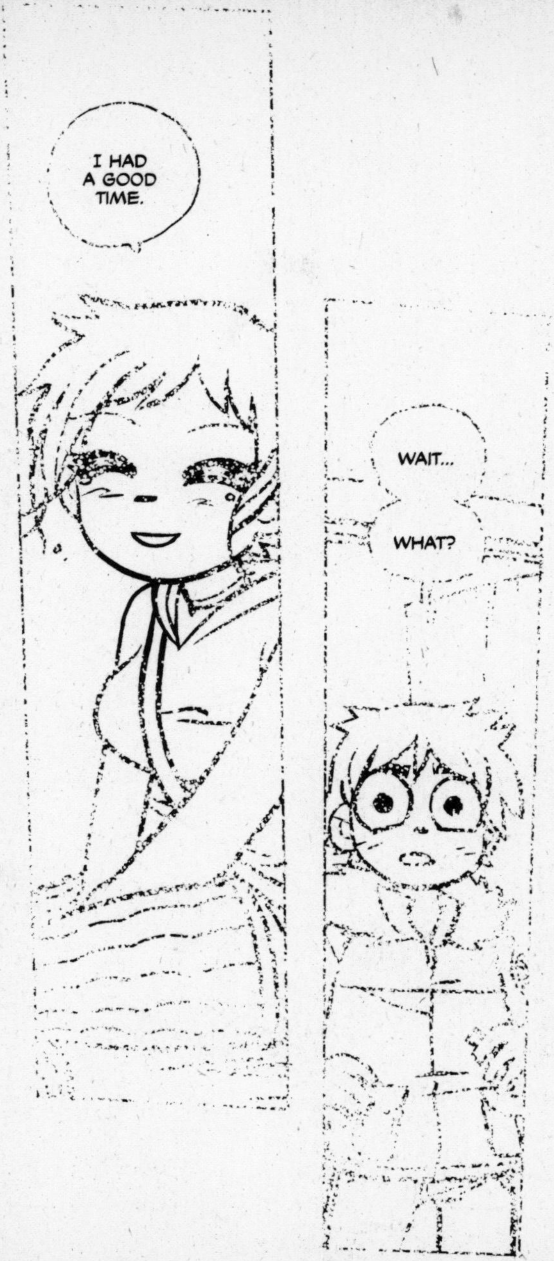
I HAD A GOOD TIME.
WAIT...
WHAT?

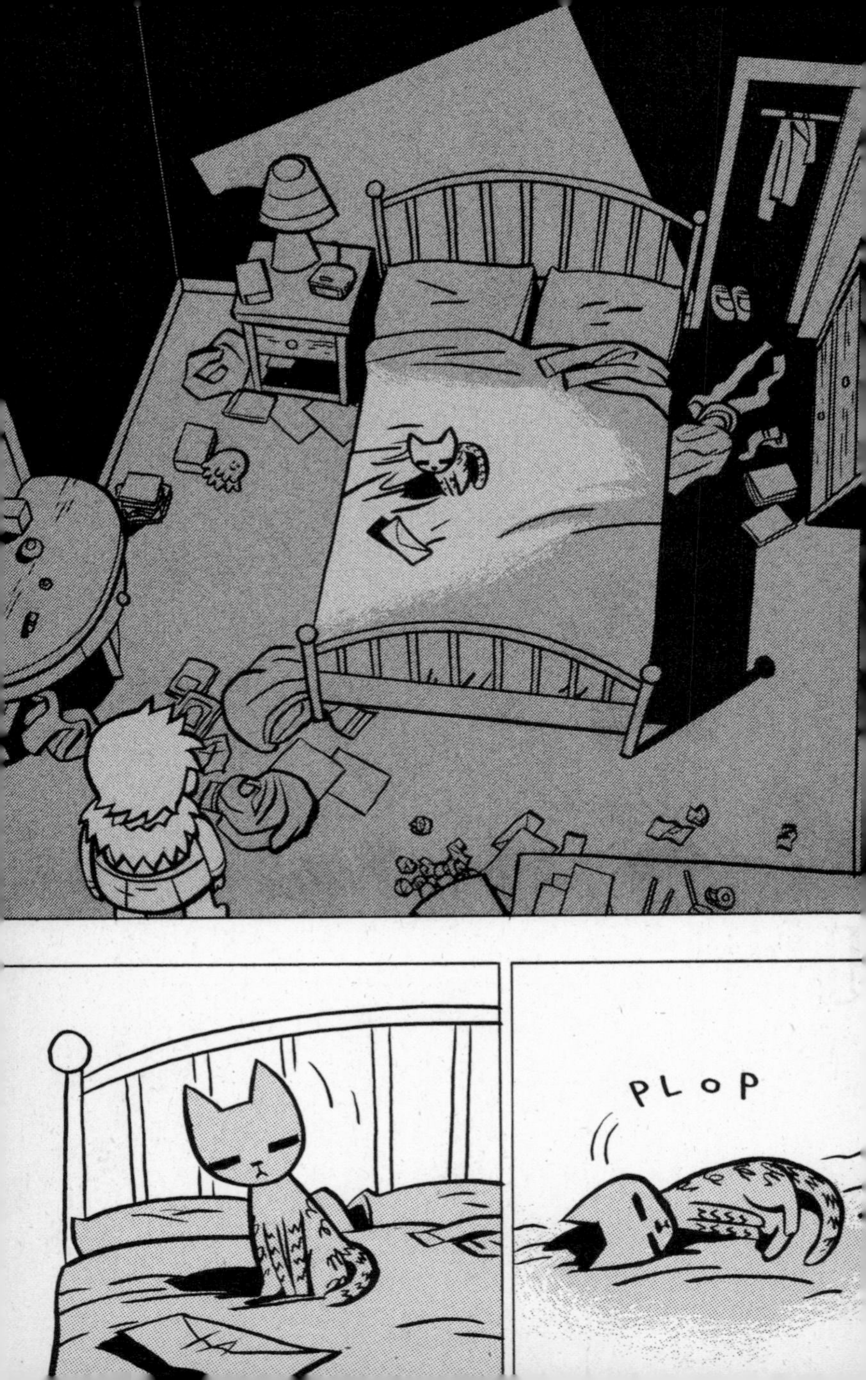
PLOP

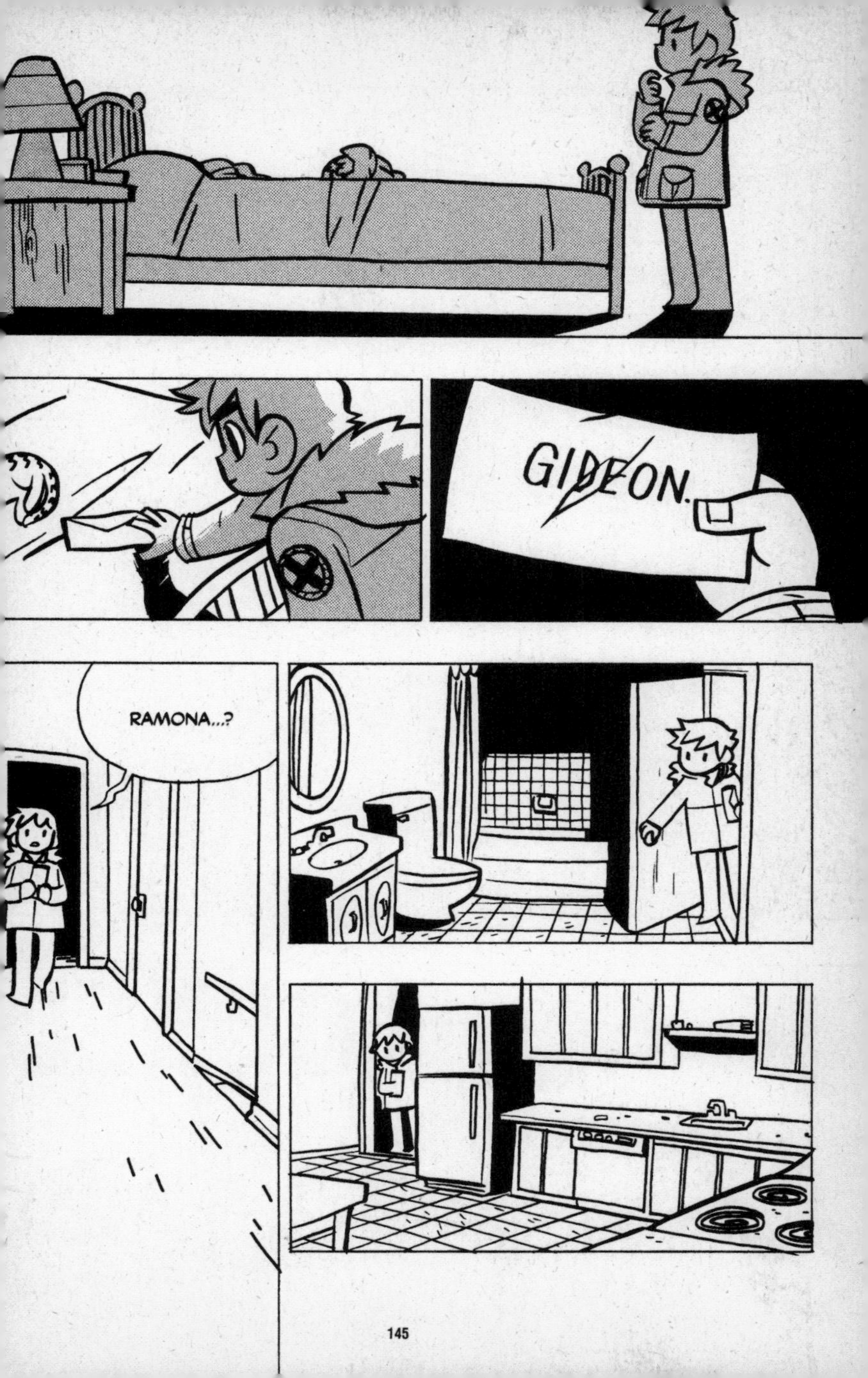
GIDEON.
RAMONA...?

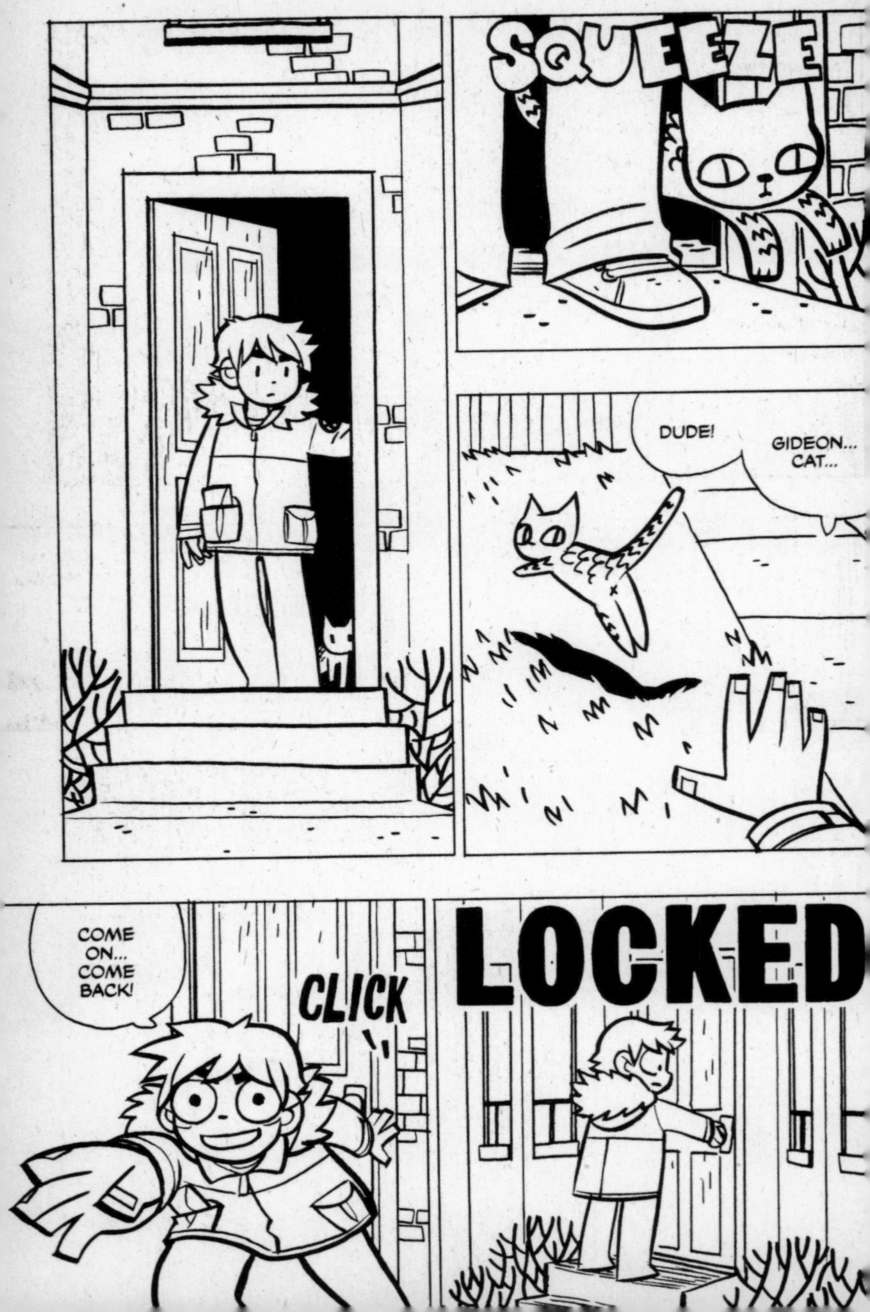
SQUEEZE
DUDE!
GIDEON... CAT...
COME ON... COME BACK!
CLICK
LOCKED

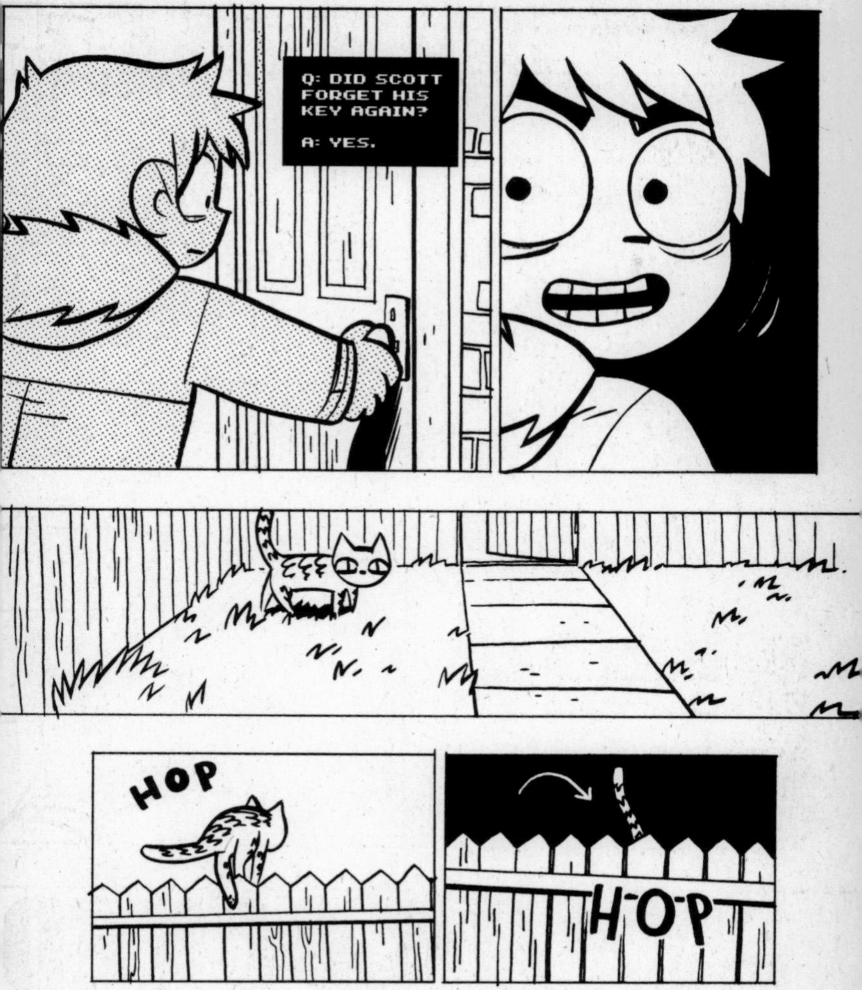
Q: DID SCOTT FORGET HIS KEY AGAIN?
A: YES.
HOP
H-O-P

[redacted]

31
WORLD of RUIN

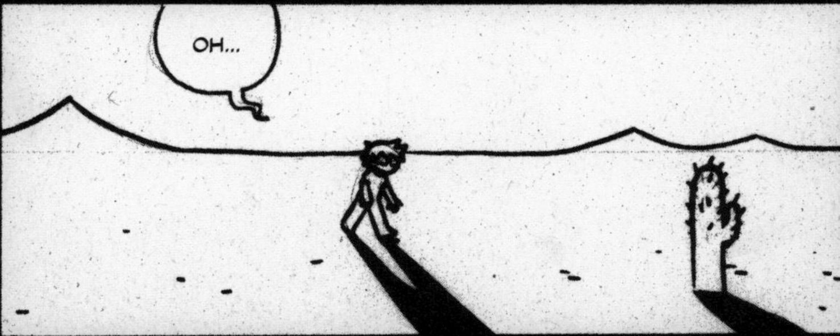

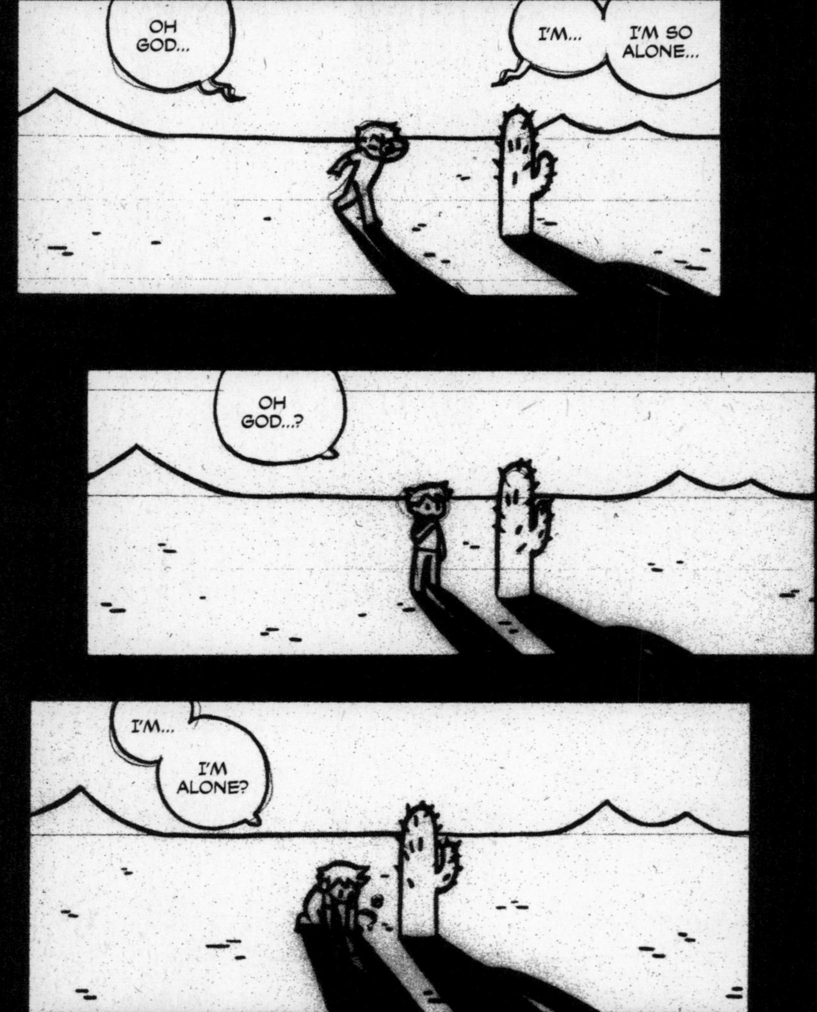
OH GOD...
I'M...
I'M SO ALONE...
OH GOD...?
I'M...
I'M ALONE?

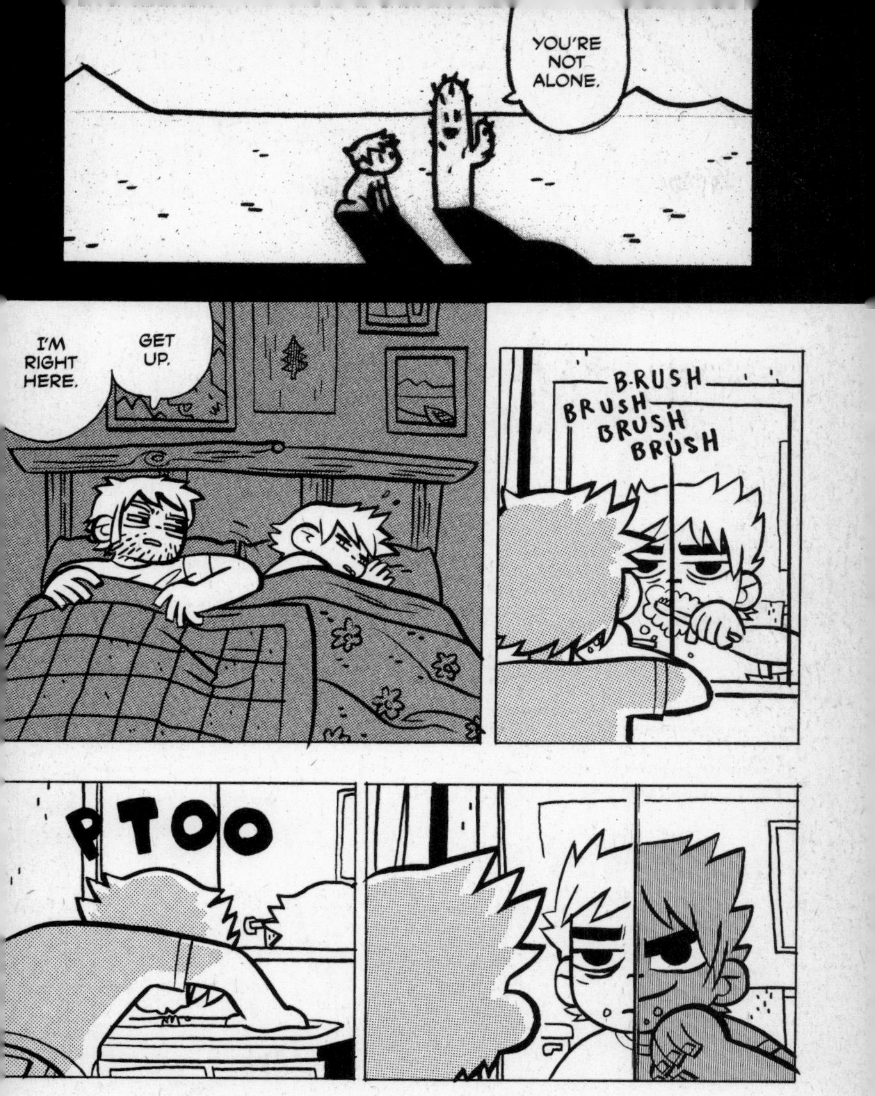

YOU'RE NOT ALONE.
I'M RIGHT HERE.
GET UP.
B-RUSH
BRUSH
BRUSH
BRUSH
PTOO

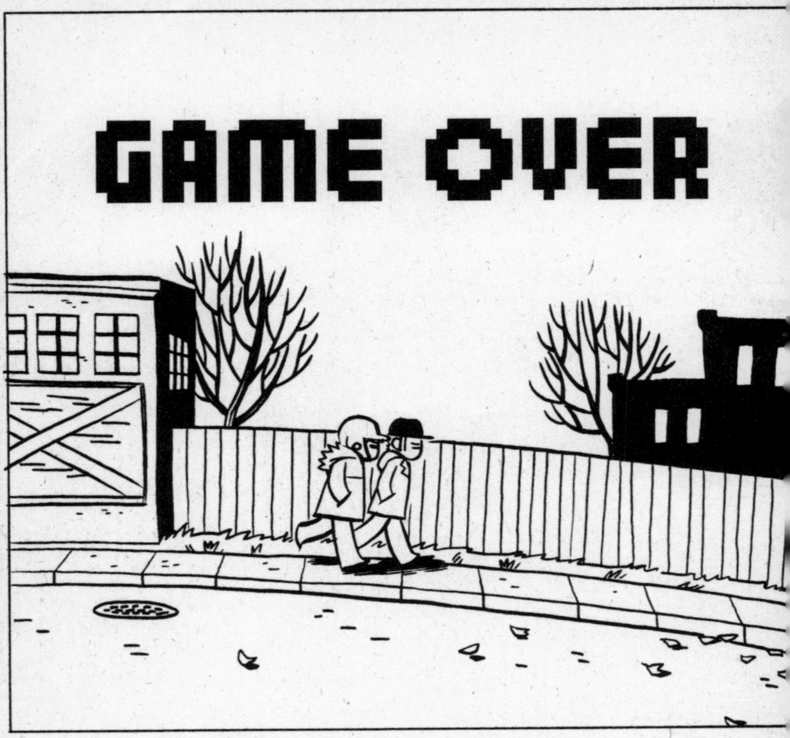
GAME OVER

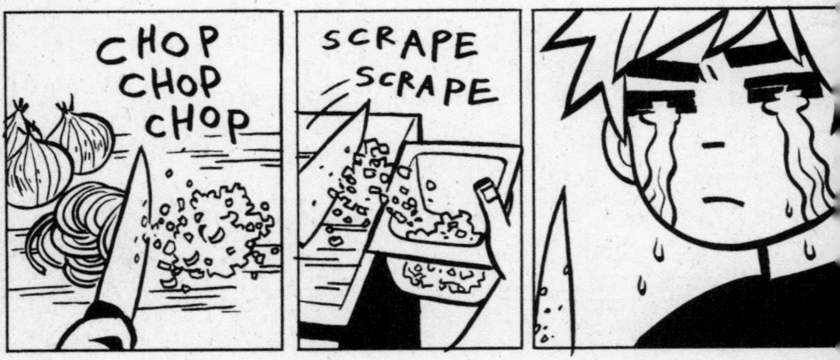
CHOP
CHOP
CHOP
SCRAPE
SCRAPE

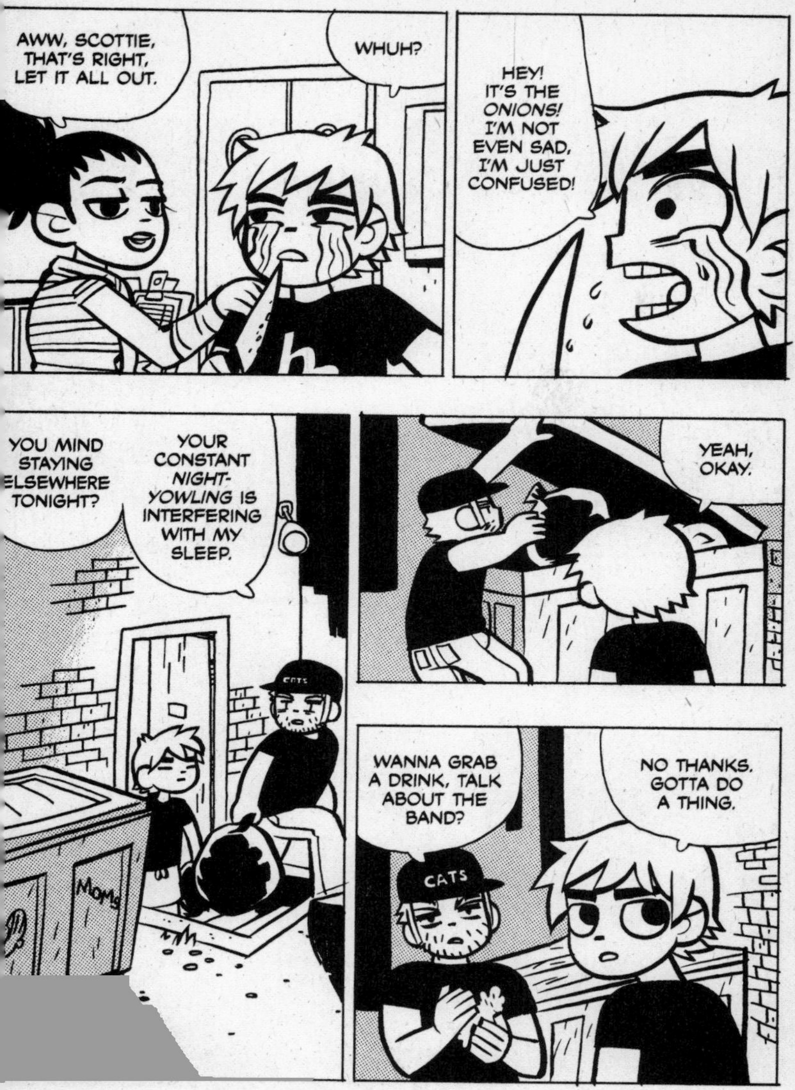
AWW, SCOTTIE, THAT'S RIGHT, LET IT ALL OUT.
WHUH?
HEY! IT'S THE *ONIONS!* I'M NOT EVEN SAD, I'M JUST CONFUSED!
YOU MIND STAYING ELSEWHERE TONIGHT?
YOUR CONSTANT *NIGHT-YOWLING* IS INTERFERING WITH MY SLEEP.
CATS
YEAH, OKAY.
WANNA GRAB A DRINK, TALK ABOUT THE BAND?
NO THANKS. GOTTA DO A THING.
CATS

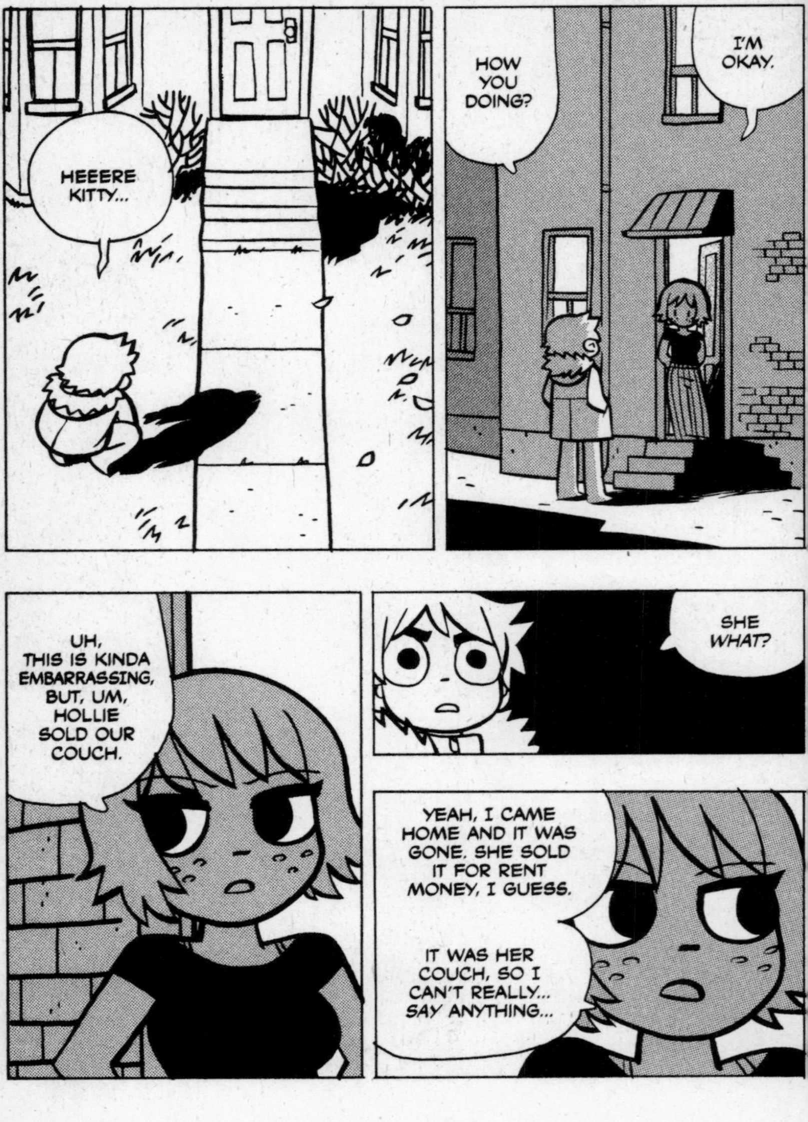
HEEERE KITTY...
HOW YOU DOING?
I'M OKAY.
UH, THIS IS KINDA EMBARRASSING, BUT, UM, HOLLIE SOLD OUR COUCH.
SHE *WHAT?*
YEAH, I CAME HOME AND IT WAS GONE. SHE SOLD IT FOR RENT MONEY, I GUESS.
IT WAS HER COUCH, SO I CAN'T REALLY... *SAY* ANYTHING...

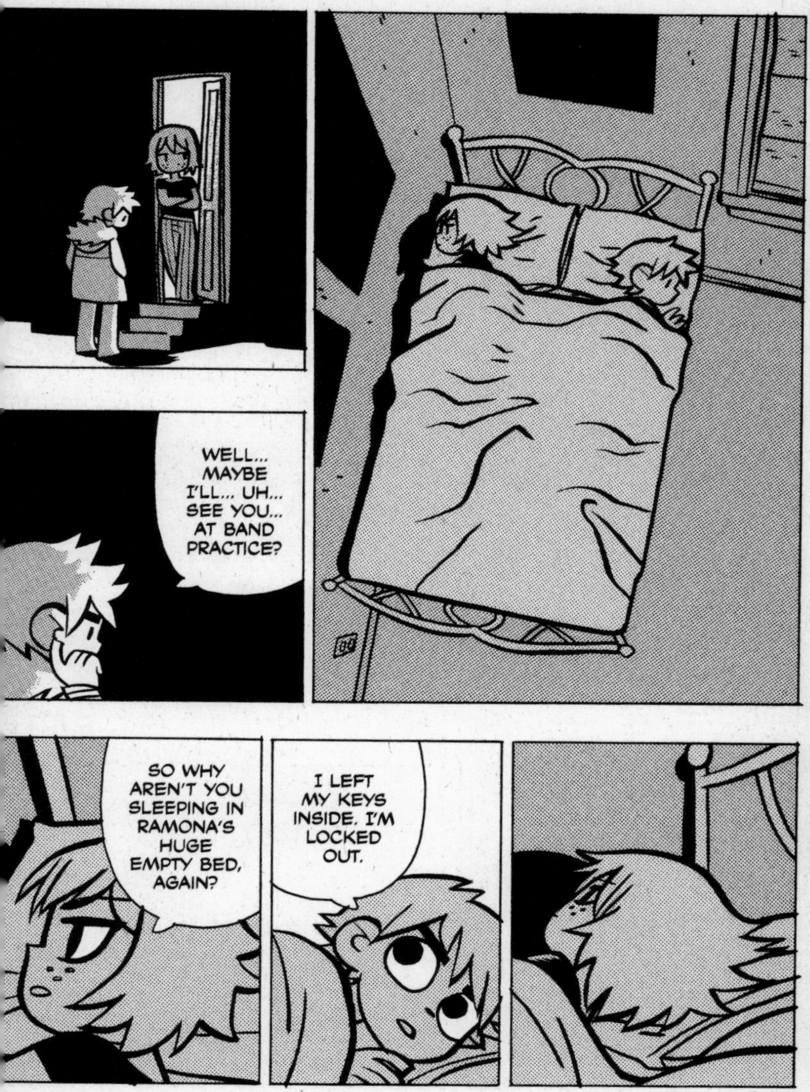
WELL... MAYBE I'LL... UH... SEE YOU... AT BAND PRACTICE?
SO WHY AREN'T YOU SLEEPING IN RAMONA'S HUGE EMPTY BED, AGAIN?
I LEFT MY KEYS INSIDE. I'M LOCKED OUT.

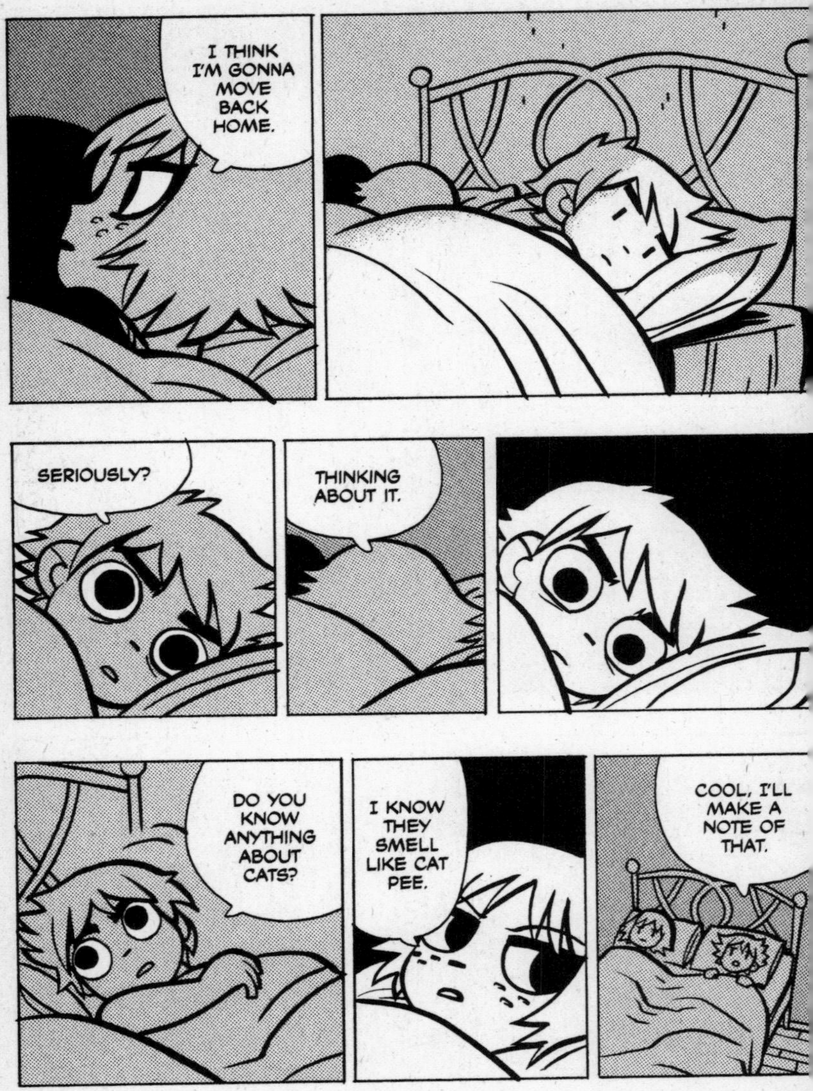
I THINK I'M GONNA MOVE BACK HOME.
SERIOUSLY?
THINKING ABOUT IT.
DO YOU KNOW ANYTHING ABOUT CATS?
I KNOW THEY SMELL LIKE CAT PEE.
COOL, I'LL MAKE A NOTE OF THAT.

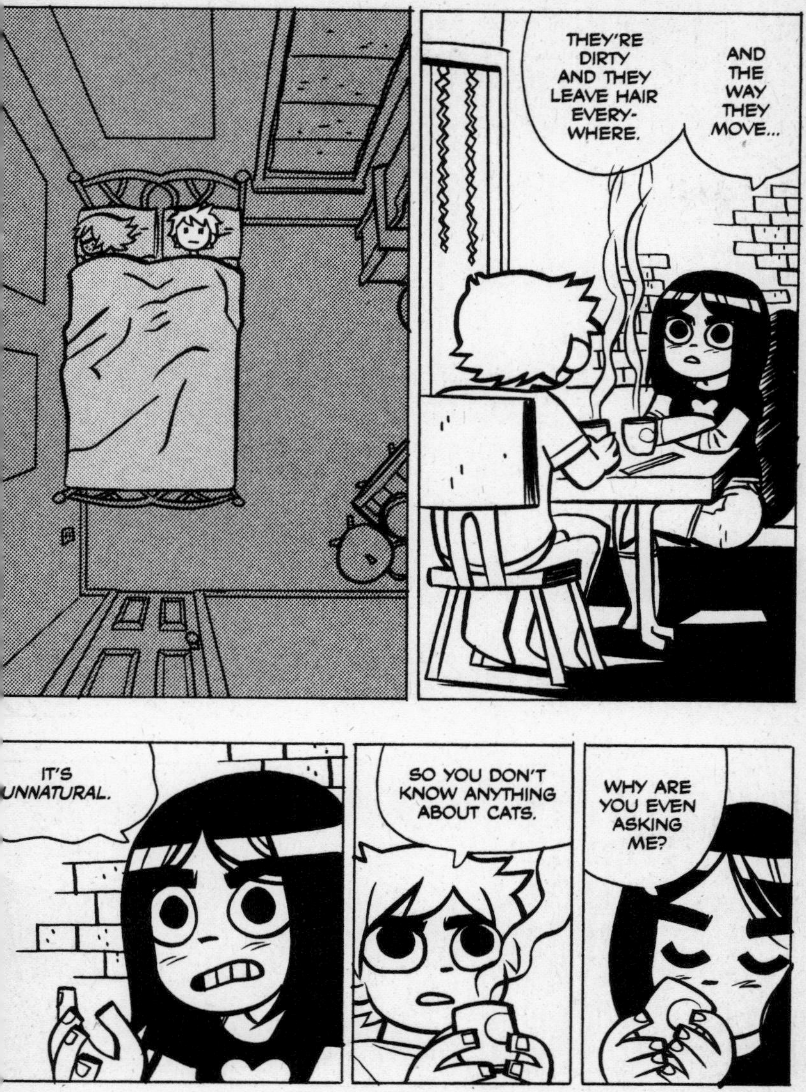
THEY'RE DIRTY AND THEY LEAVE HAIR EVERY-WHERE.
AND THE WAY THEY MOVE...
IT'S UNNATURAL.
SO YOU DON'T KNOW ANYTHING ABOUT CATS.
WHY ARE YOU EVEN ASKING ME?

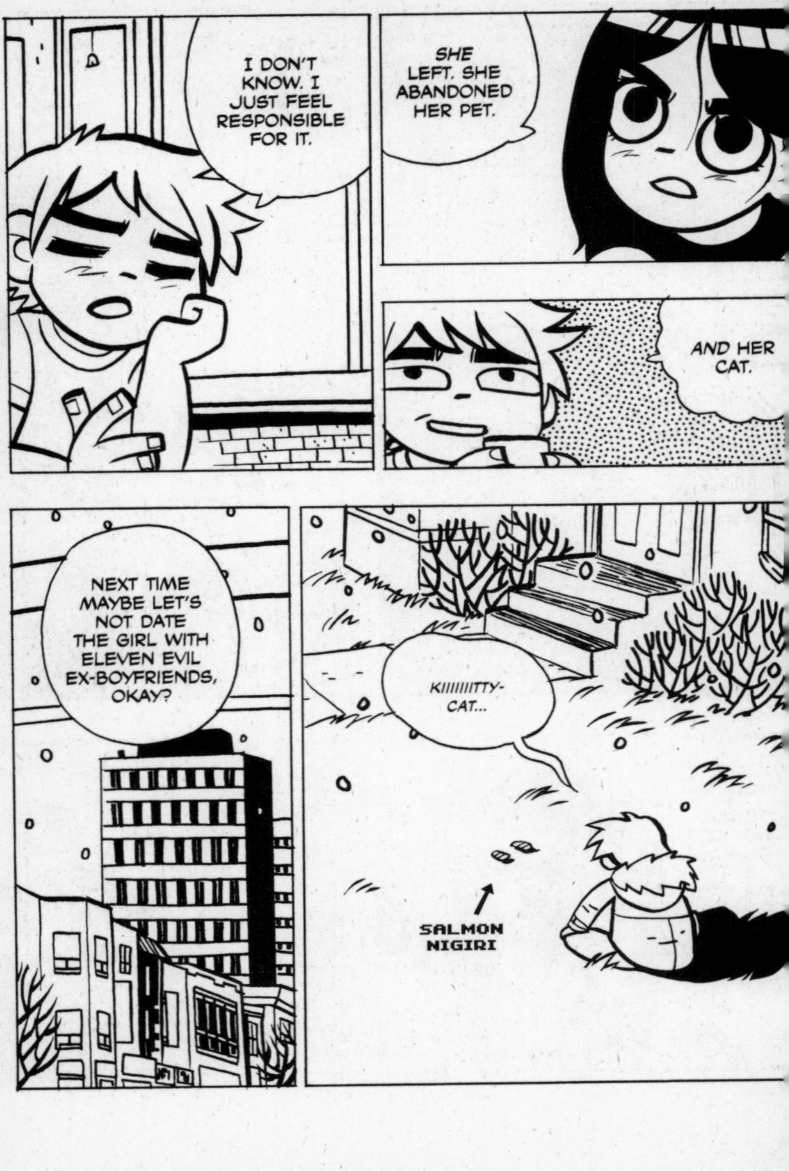
I DON'T KNOW. I JUST FEEL RESPONSIBLE FOR IT.
SHE LEFT. SHE ABANDONED HER PET.
AND HER CAT.
NEXT TIME MAYBE LET'S NOT DATE THE GIRL WITH ELEVEN EVIL EX-BOYFRIENDS, OKAY?
KIIIIIIITTY-CAT...
SALMON NIGIRI

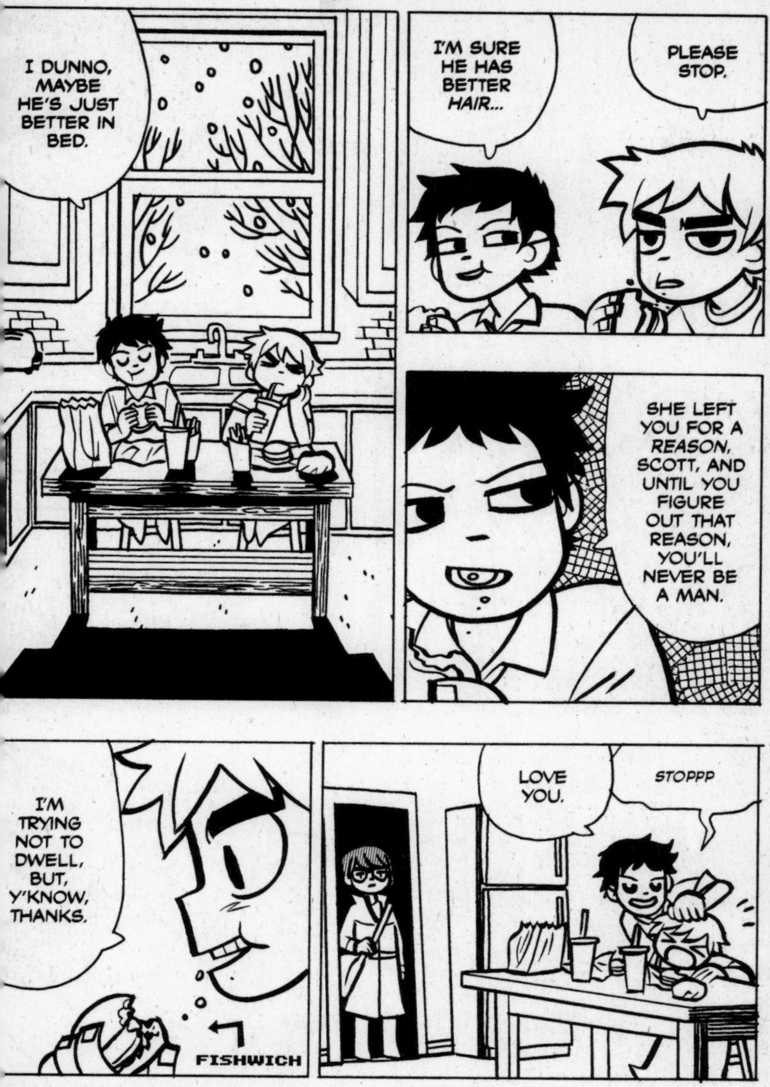

I DUNNO, MAYBE HE'S JUST BETTER IN BED.
I'M SURE HE HAS BETTER *HAIR*...
PLEASE STOP.
SHE LEFT YOU FOR A *REASON*, SCOTT, AND UNTIL YOU FIGURE OUT THAT REASON, YOU'LL NEVER BE A MAN.
I'M TRYING NOT TO DWELL, BUT, Y'KNOW, THANKS.
FISHWICH
LOVE YOU.
STOPPP

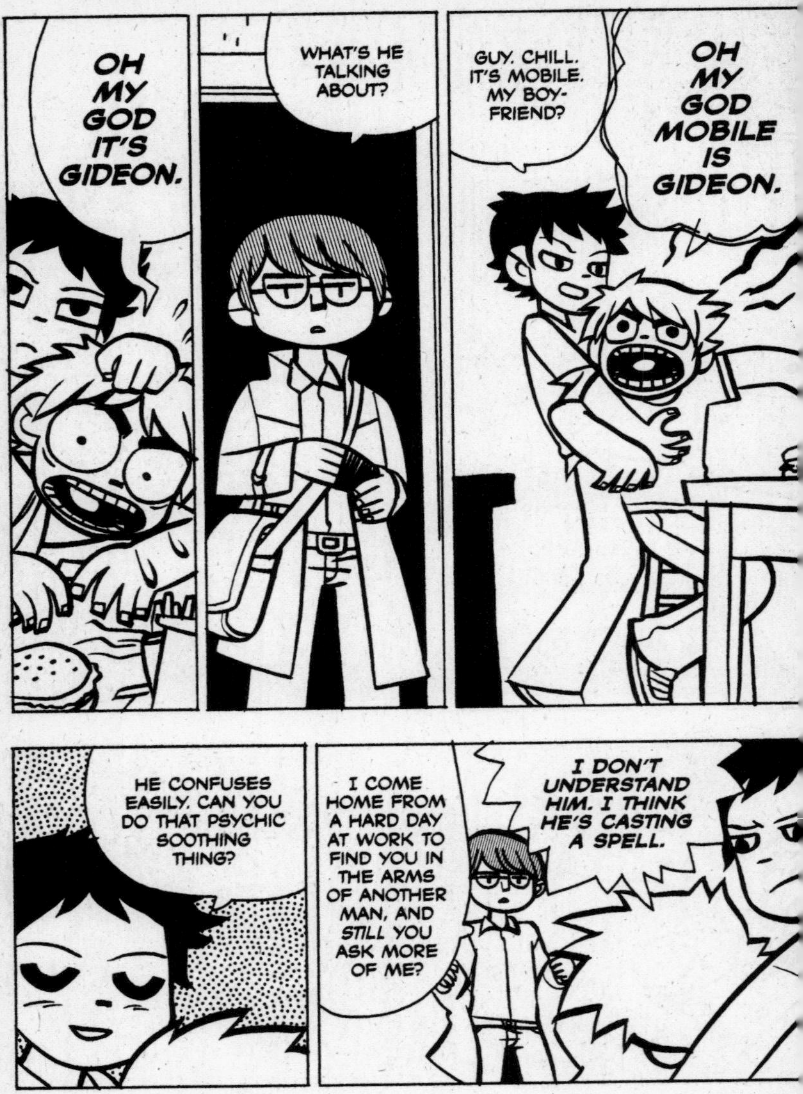
OH MY GOD IT'S GIDEON.
WHAT'S HE TALKING ABOUT?
GUY. CHILL. IT'S MOBILE. MY BOY-FRIEND?
OH MY GOD MOBILE IS GIDEON.
HE CONFUSES EASILY. CAN YOU DO THAT PSYCHIC SOOTHING THING?
I COME HOME FROM A HARD DAY AT WORK TO FIND YOU IN THE ARMS OF ANOTHER MAN, AND STILL YOU ASK MORE OF ME?
I DON'T UNDERSTAND HIM. I THINK HE'S CASTING A SPELL.

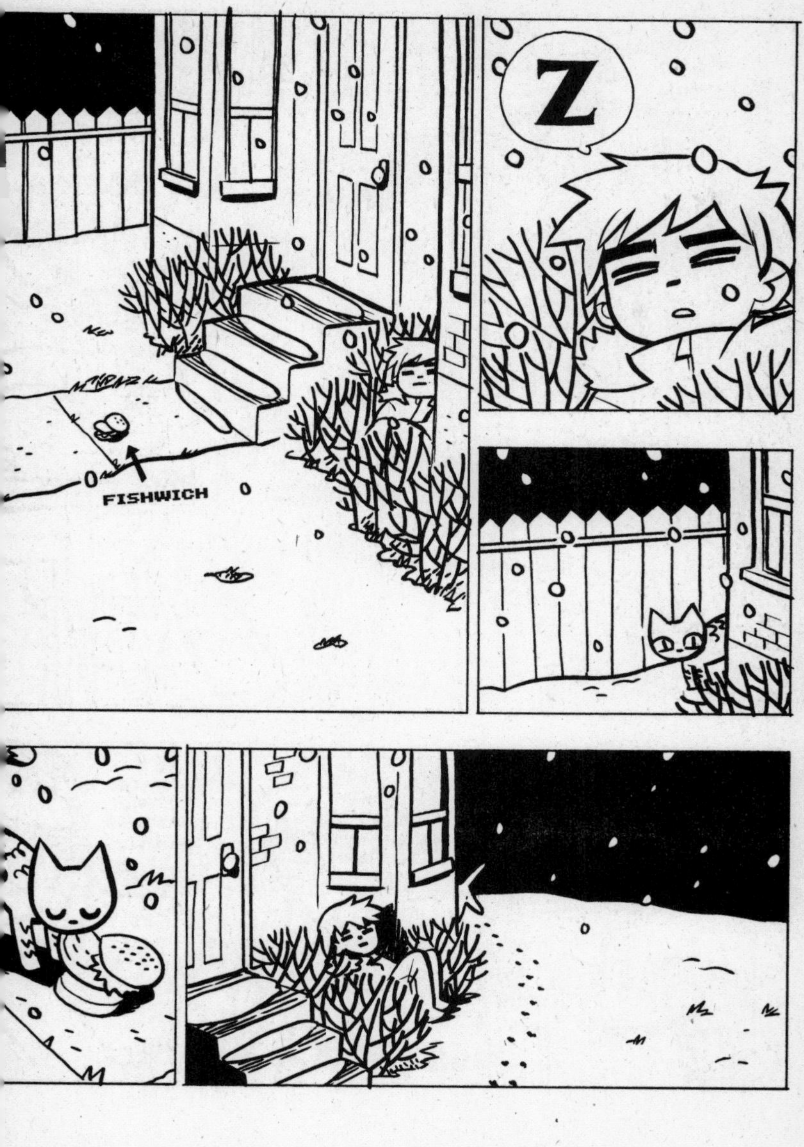
FISHWICH
Z

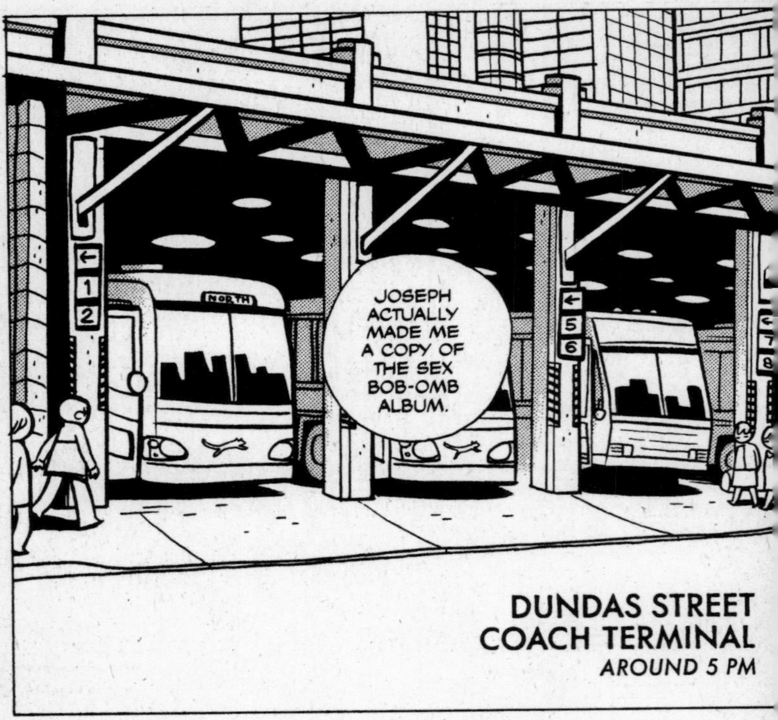
JOSEPH ACTUALLY MADE ME A COPY OF THE SEX BOB-OMB ALBUM.
DUNDAS STREET COACH TERMINAL
AROUND 5 PM

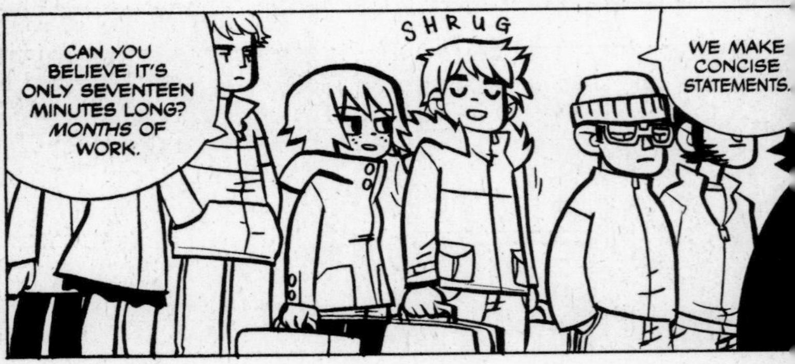
CAN YOU BELIEVE IT'S ONLY SEVENTEEN MINUTES LONG? *MONTHS* OF WORK.
SHRUG
WE MAKE CONCISE STATEMENTS.

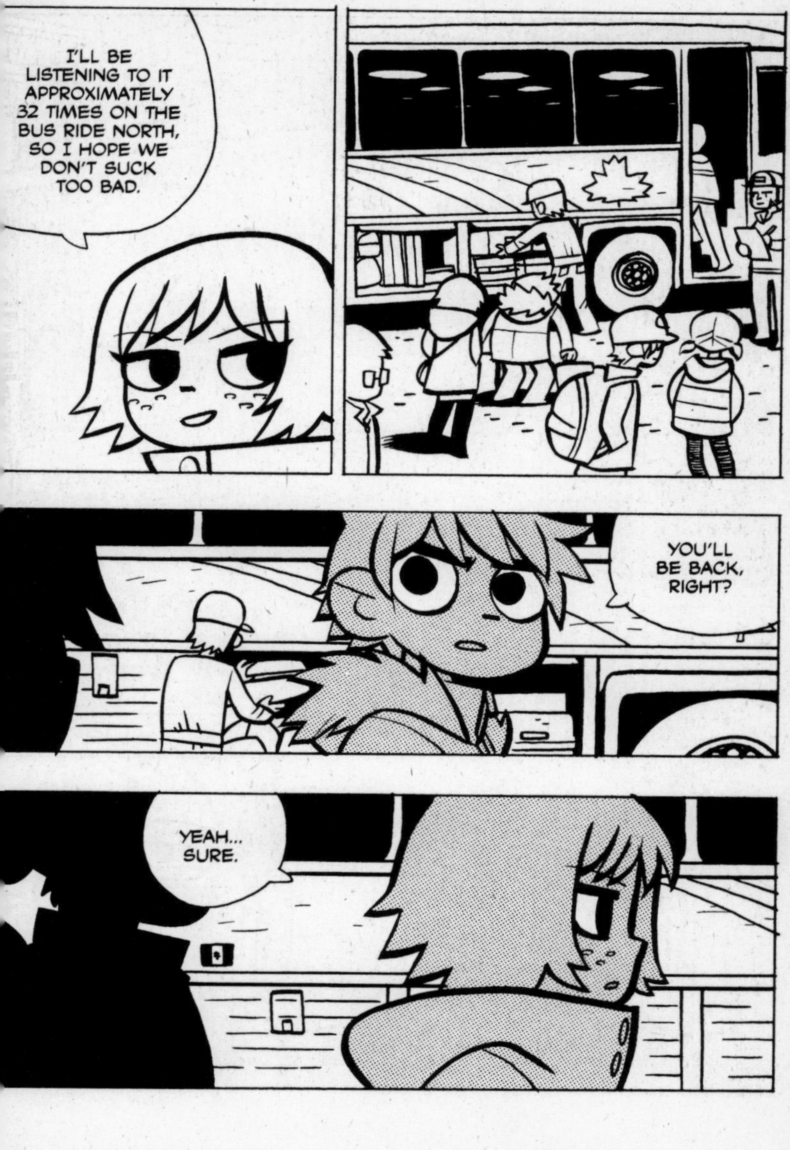
I'LL BE LISTENING TO IT APPROXIMATELY 32 TIMES ON THE BUS RIDE NORTH, SO I HOPE WE DON'T SUCK TOO BAD.
YOU'LL BE BACK, RIGHT?
YEAH... SURE.

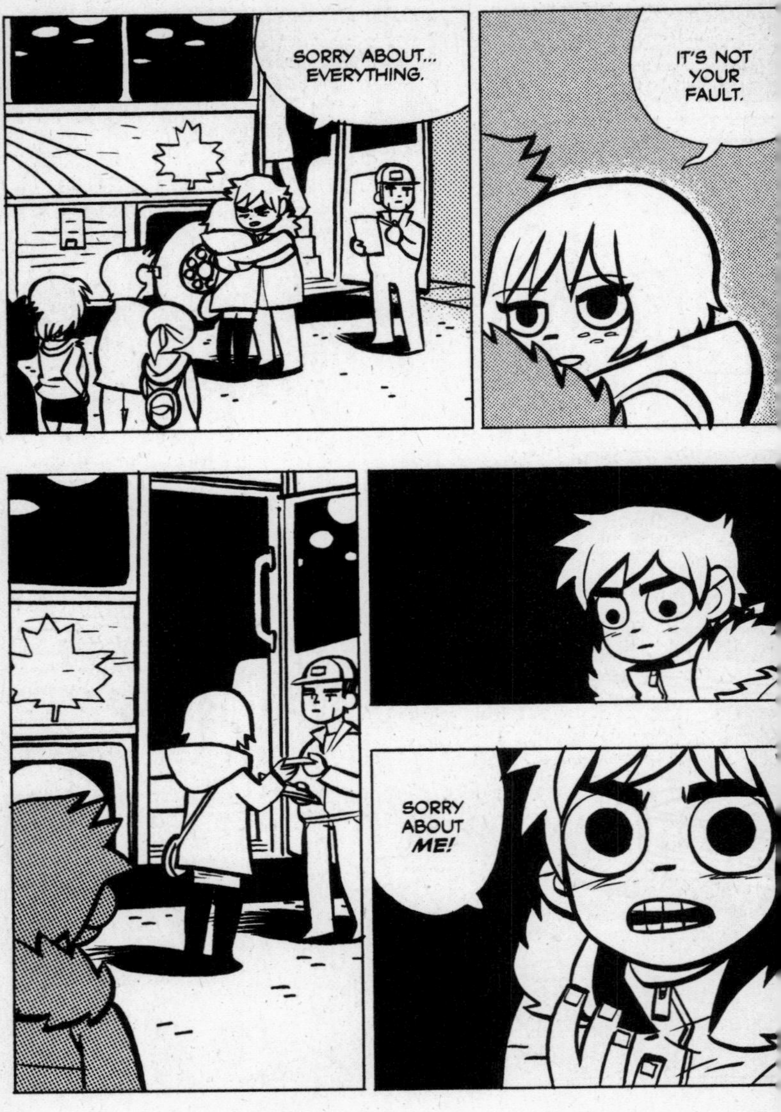
SORRY ABOUT... EVERYTHING.
IT'S NOT YOUR FAULT.
SORRY ABOUT ME!

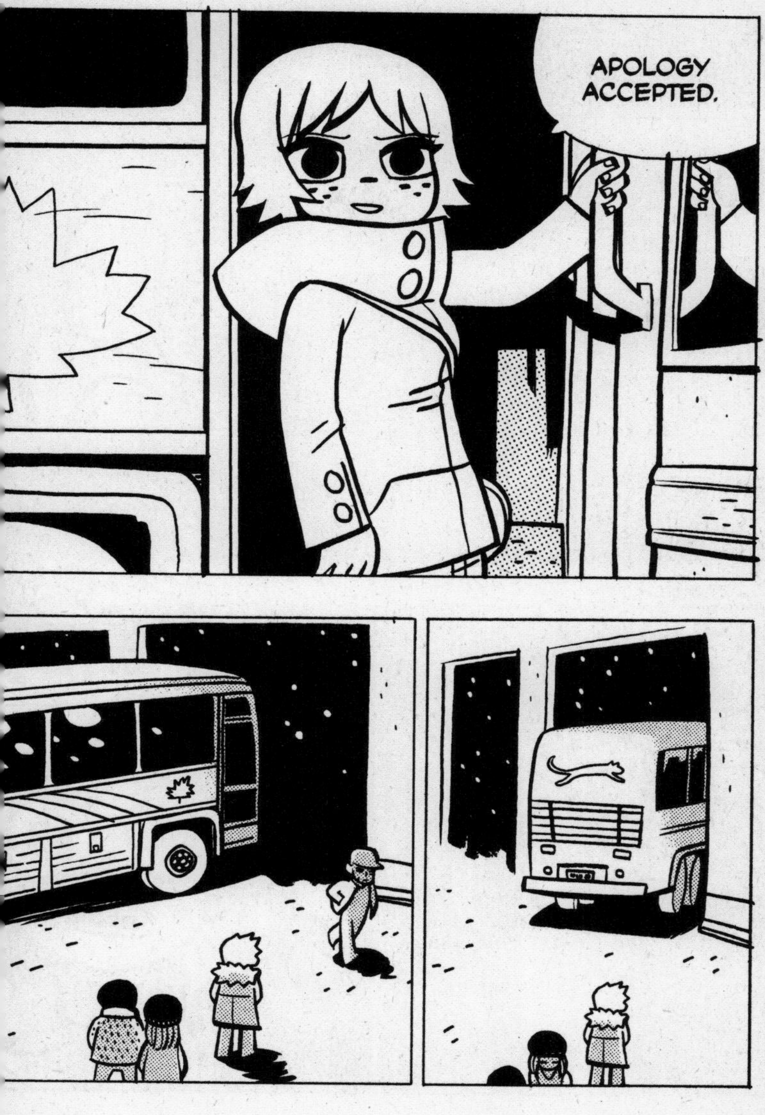
APOLOGY
ACCEPTED.

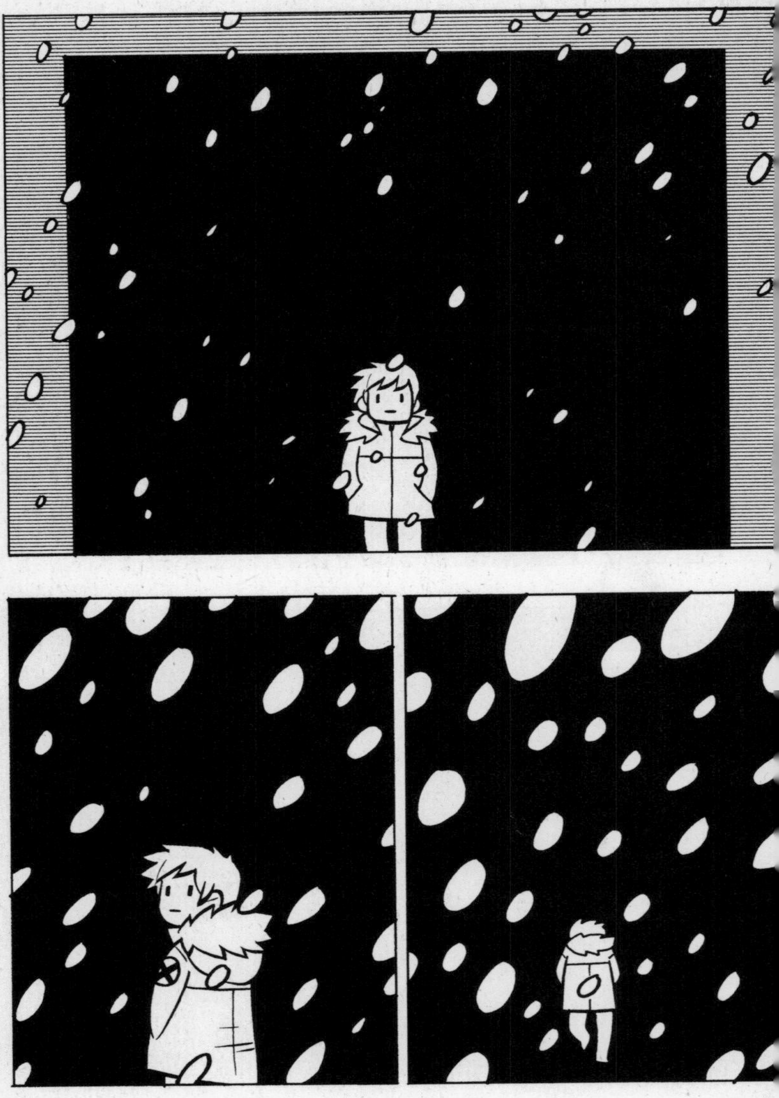

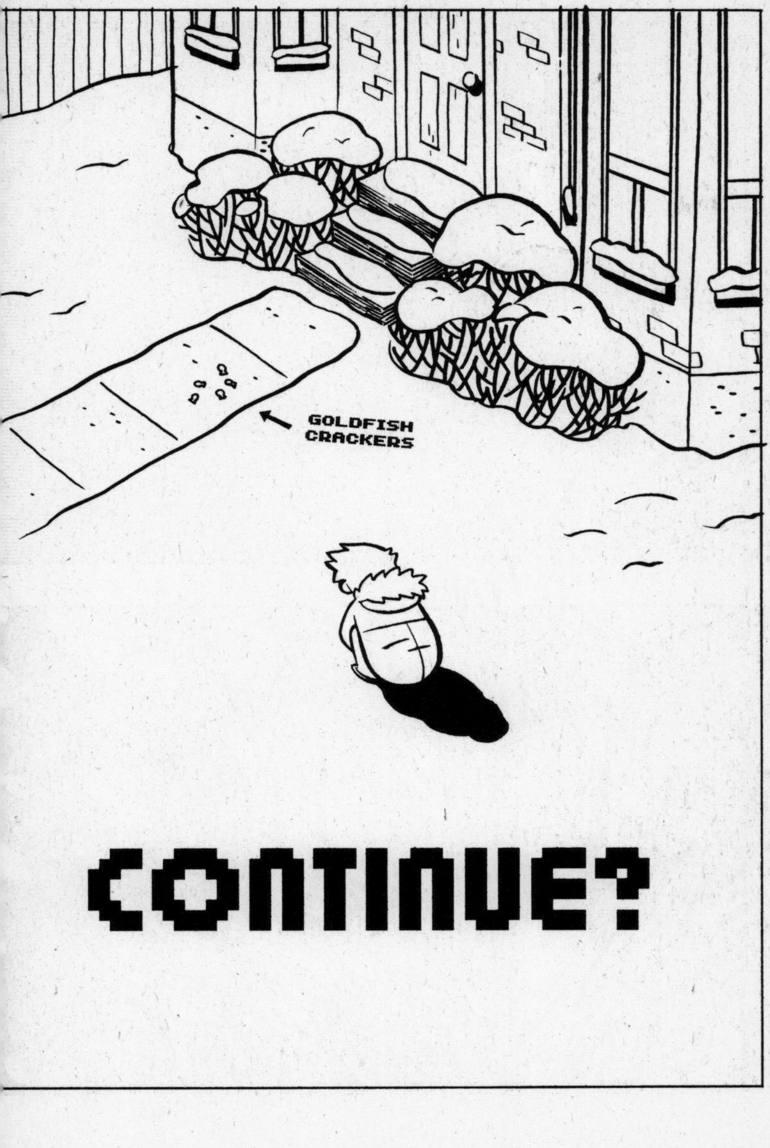
GOLDFISH CRACKERS
CONTINUE?

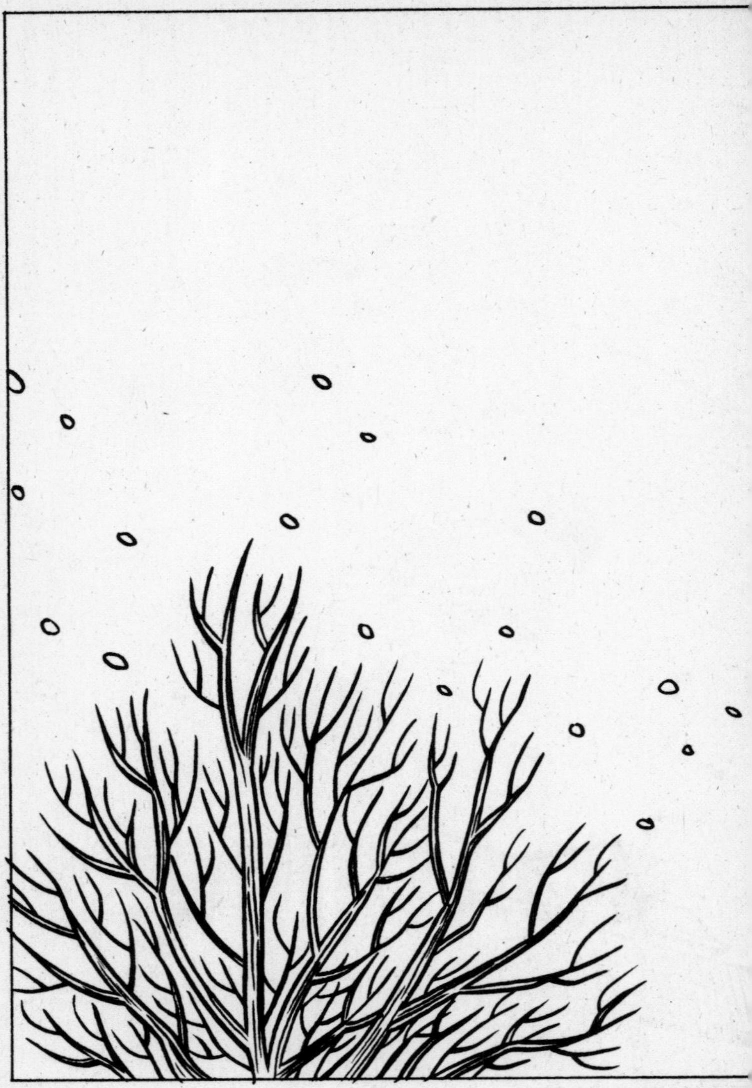

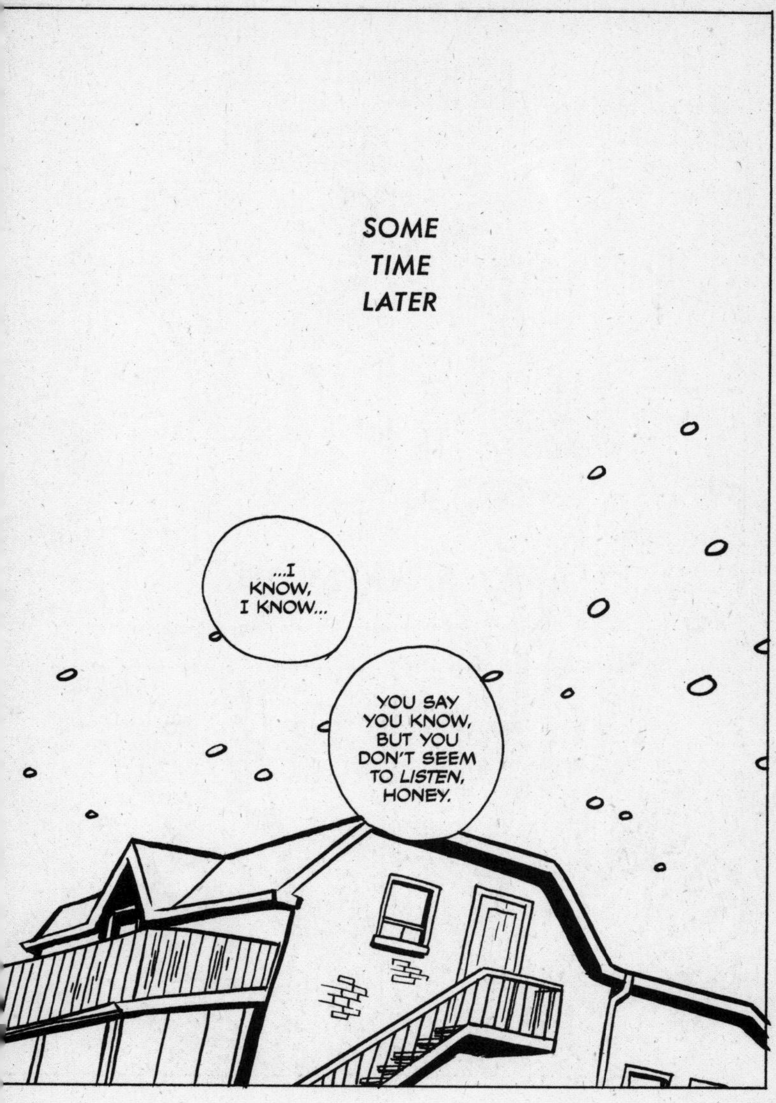
SOME TIME LATER
...I KNOW, I KNOW...
YOU SAY YOU KNOW, BUT YOU DON'T SEEM TO *LISTEN*, HONEY.

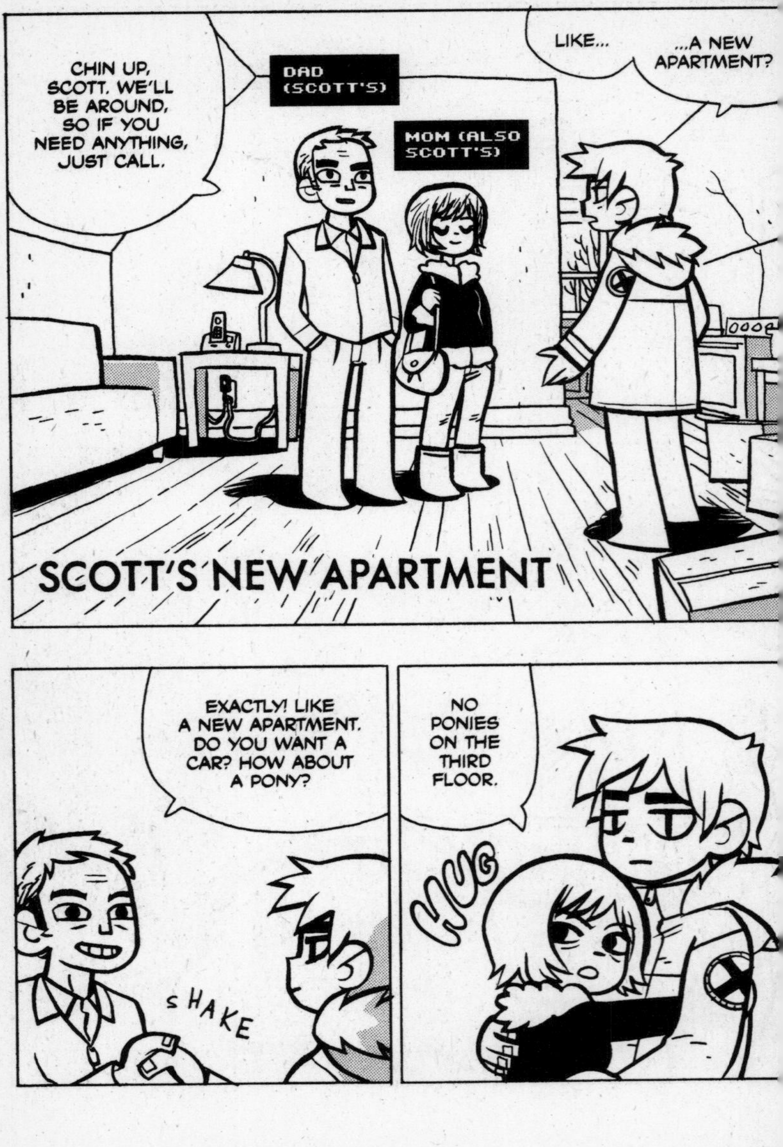
CHIN UP, SCOTT. WE'LL BE AROUND, SO IF YOU NEED ANYTHING, JUST CALL.
DAD (SCOTT'S)
MOM (ALSO SCOTT'S)
LIKE...
...A NEW APARTMENT?
SCOTT'S NEW APARTMENT
EXACTLY! LIKE A NEW APARTMENT. DO YOU WANT A CAR? HOW ABOUT A PONY?
SHAKE
NO PONIES ON THE THIRD FLOOR.
HUG

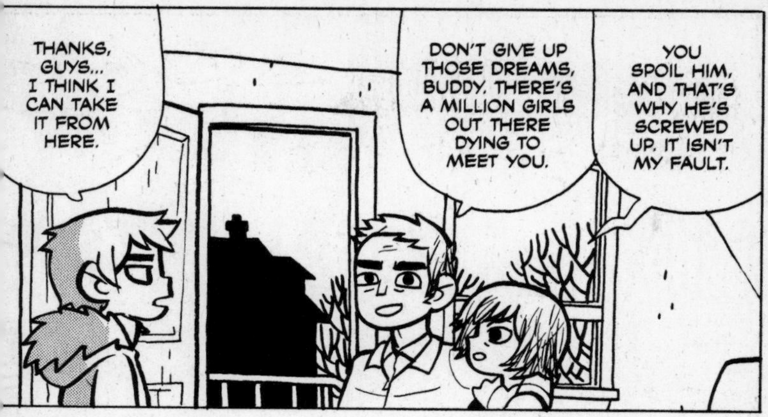
THANKS, GUYS... I THINK I CAN TAKE IT FROM HERE.
DON'T GIVE UP THOSE DREAMS, BUDDY. THERE'S A MILLION GIRLS OUT THERE DYING TO MEET YOU.
YOU SPOIL HIM, AND THAT'S WHY HE'S SCREWED UP. IT ISN'T MY FAULT.

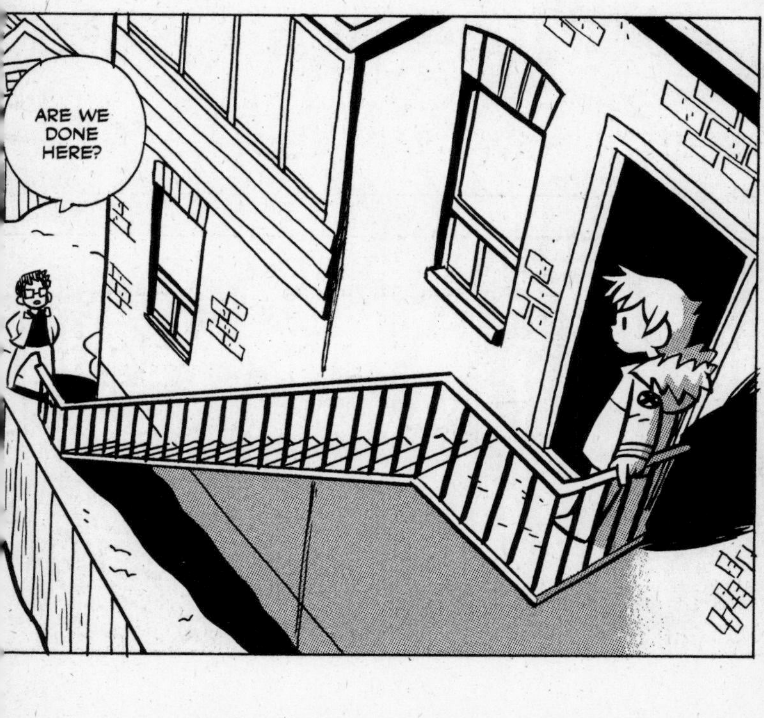
ARE WE DONE HERE?

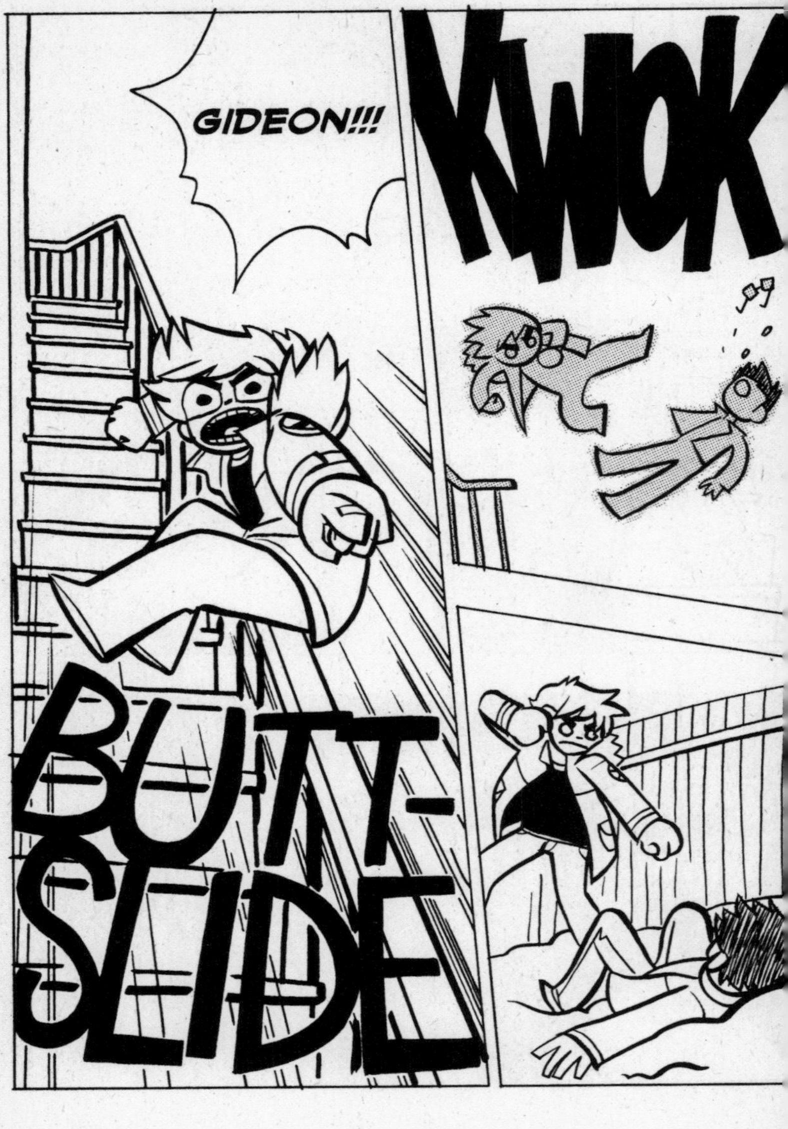
GIDEON!!!
BUTT-SLIDE
KWOK

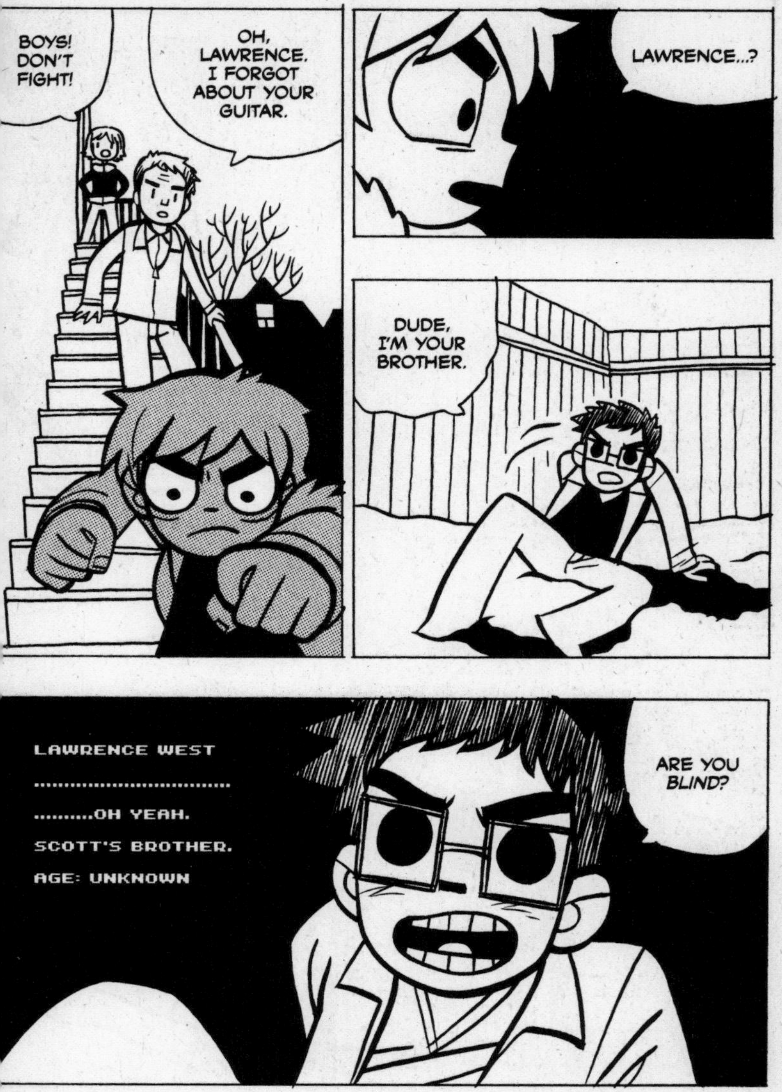
BOYS! DON'T FIGHT!
OH, LAWRENCE. I FORGOT ABOUT YOUR GUITAR.
LAWRENCE...?
DUDE, I'M YOUR BROTHER.
LAWRENCE WEST
....
..........OH YEAH.
SCOTT'S BROTHER.
AGE: UNKNOWN
ARE YOU BLIND?

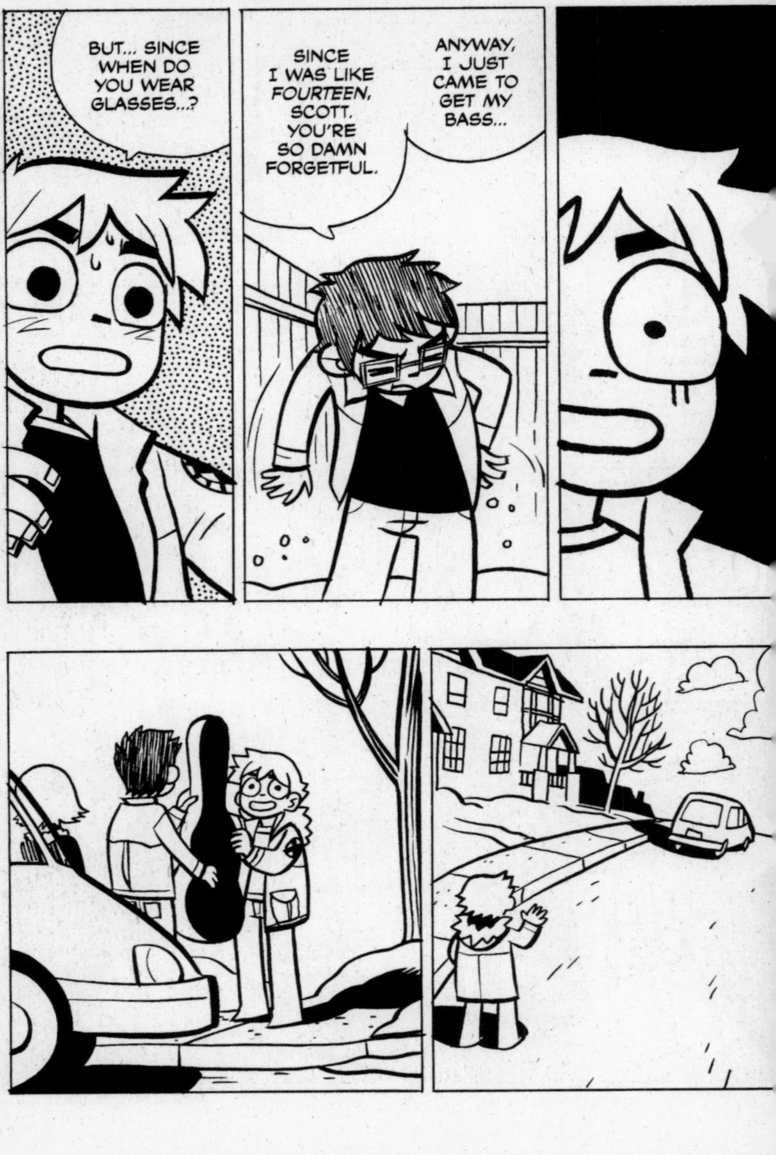
BUT... SINCE WHEN DO YOU WEAR GLASSES...?
SINCE I WAS LIKE *FOURTEEN,* SCOTT. YOU'RE SO DAMN FORGETFUL.
ANYWAY, I JUST CAME TO GET MY BASS...

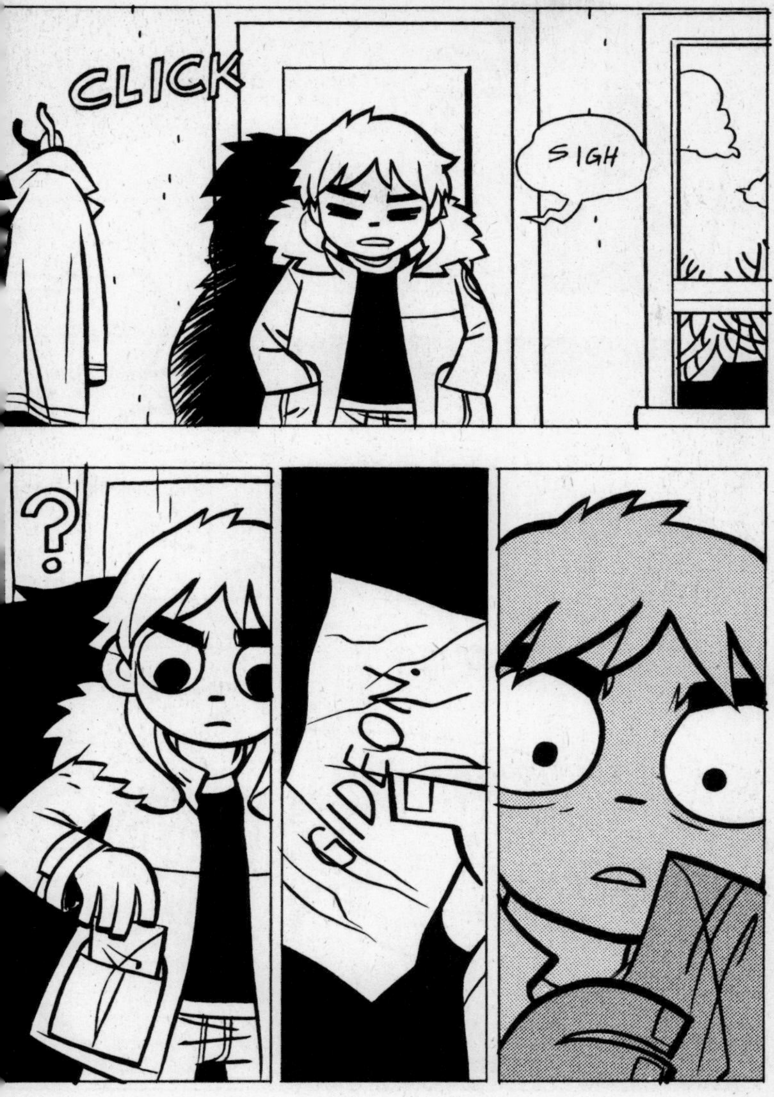
CLICK
SIGH
?
GIDEON?!

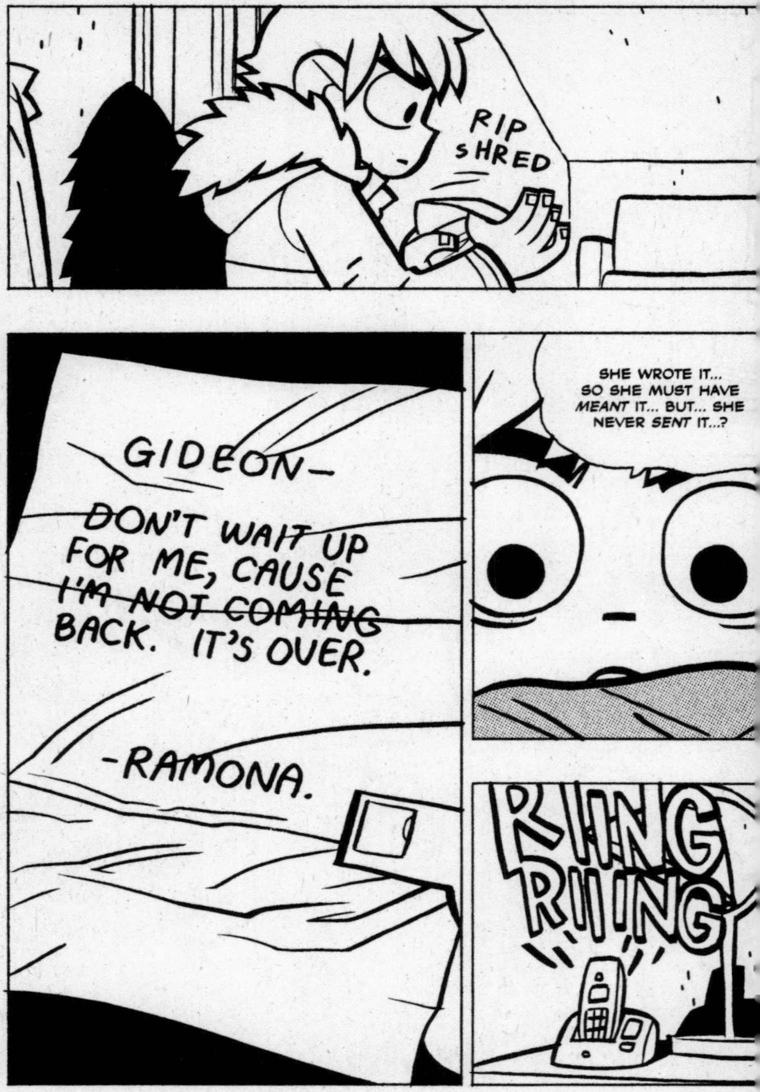
RIP
SHRED
GIDEON-
DON'T WAIT UP FOR ME, CAUSE I'M NOT COMING BACK. IT'S OVER.
-RAMONA.
SHE WROTE IT... SO SHE MUST HAVE MEANT IT... BUT... SHE NEVER SENT IT...?
RING
RING

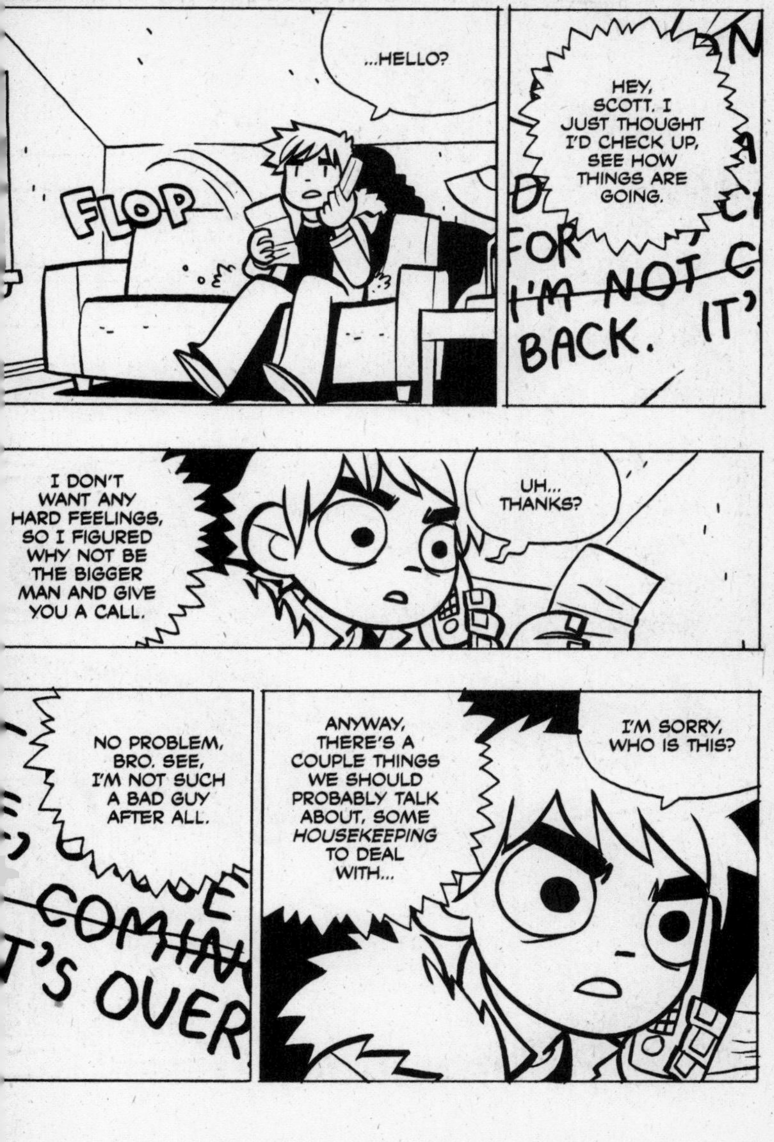
...HELLO?
FLOP
HEY, SCOTT. I JUST THOUGHT I'D CHECK UP, SEE HOW THINGS ARE GOING.
I DON'T WANT ANY HARD FEELINGS, SO I FIGURED WHY NOT BE THE BIGGER MAN AND GIVE YOU A CALL.
UH... THANKS?
NO PROBLEM, BRO. SEE, I'M NOT SUCH A BAD GUY AFTER ALL.
ANYWAY, THERE'S A COUPLE THINGS WE SHOULD PROBABLY TALK ABOUT, SOME *HOUSEKEEPING* TO DEAL WITH...
I'M SORRY, WHO IS THIS?

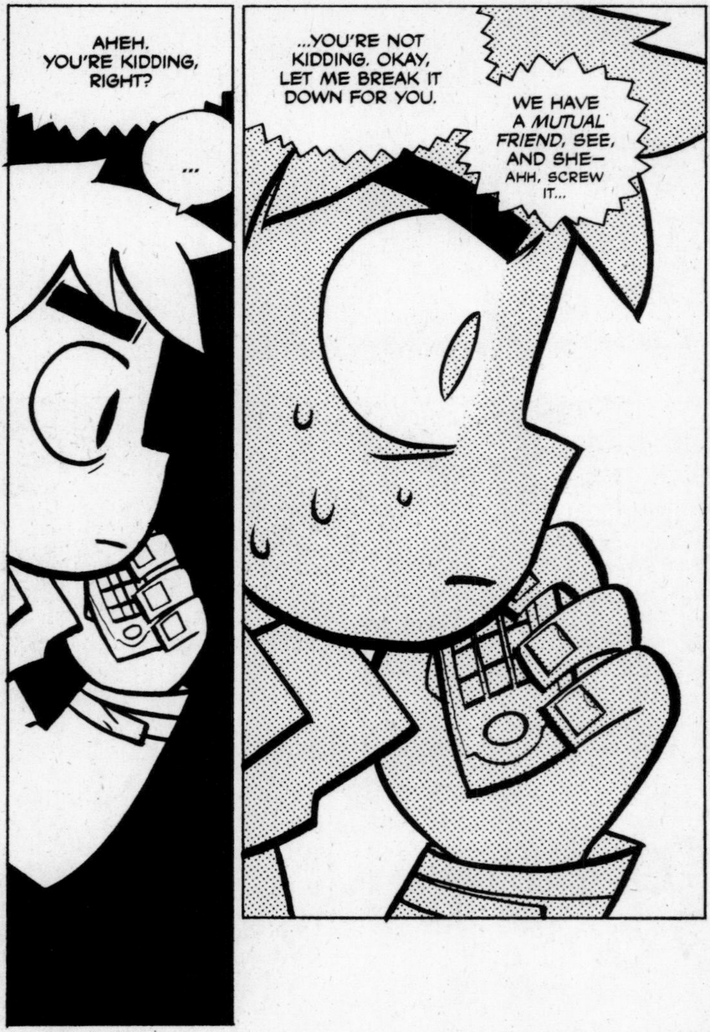
AHEH. YOU'RE KIDDING, RIGHT?
...
...YOU'RE NOT KIDDING. OKAY, LET ME BREAK IT DOWN FOR YOU.
WE HAVE A *MUTUAL* FRIEND, SEE, AND SHE— AHH, SCREW IT...

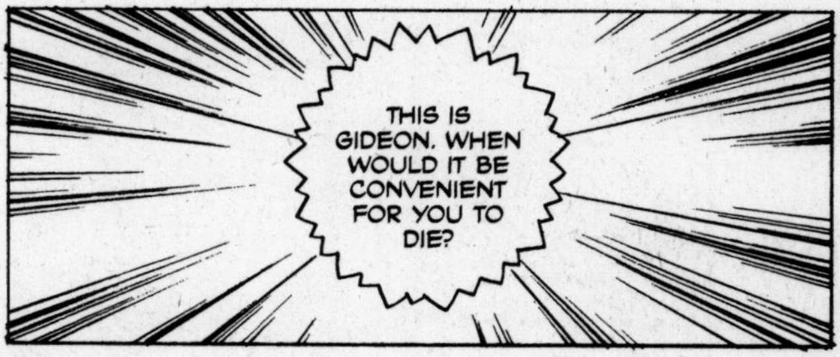
THIS IS GIDEON. WHEN WOULD IT BE CONVENIENT FOR YOU TO DIE?

NEXT:

ONE MORE TIME!

CREATING SCOTT PILGRIM FOR FUN AND PROFIT

By Bryan Lee O'Malley

SCRIPT

I like to write a full script for my books before I ever start drawing them. It looks kind of like the screenplay for a movie. A lot of cartoonists don't script this way, but I feel that I'm, ironically, not very visual-minded. I like words.

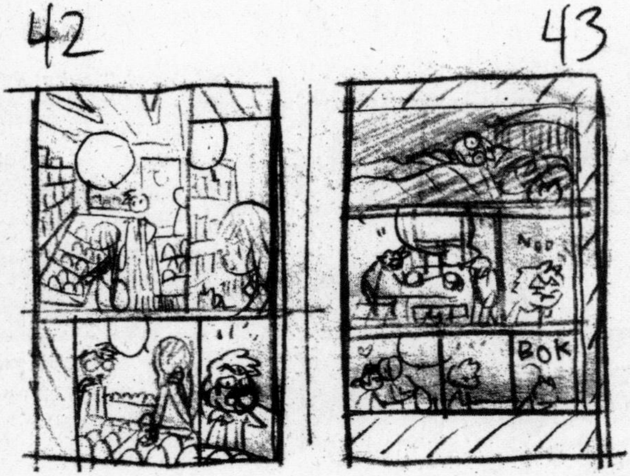
42
43
BOK

THUMBNAIL

After the script is totally finished (which in this case took a shockingly long time), it's time to break things down into comics. First I roughly determine how much content is going to fit on a page, and then I decide how the information will be laid out on the page. I like to draw these thumbnail sketches at a ridiculously small size, maybe an inch and a half high, otherwise I fear I'll spend too much time rendering them. The simpler they are, the better.

LAYOUT

I transfer the layout to a full-size page. I'm working at 9.5" x 14", which involves ruling and cutting a strip from an 11" x 14" sheet. I use Strathmore bristol and lately I like the vellum finish. I generally ink all of the panel borders before any actual drawing.

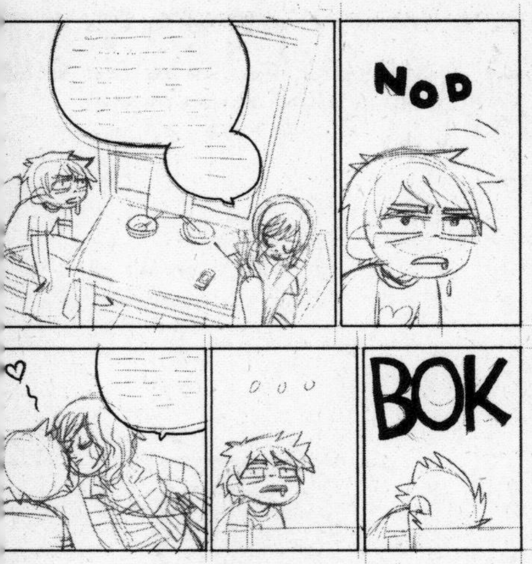
NOD
BOK

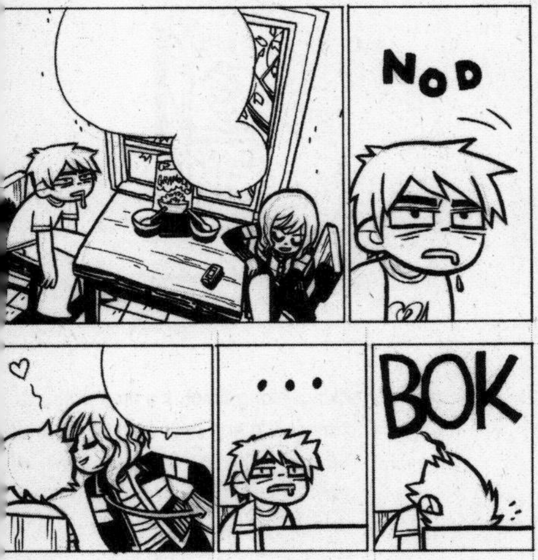
NOD
• • •
BOK

PENCILS

I work pretty roughly, with a light blue Col-Erase pencil. I like to place my word balloons as soon as possible - I already know where they'll be, from the thumbnail sketch, and often I can just put a balloon in the corner before I even begin to draw the figures.

The final lettering in the book is done with a computer font, and I space out the word balloons with a combination of letters, scribbles and straight lines. It's not the most scientific method, but I'm used to it by now.

When the pencils are done and I'm satisfied, I immediately ink in the word balloon outlines, using a cheap Pilot pen. I like those pens because they have a sharp point with great flexibility. They don't last very long, though.

Sometimes I will end up re-penciling a whole panel after having inked in the balloon outlines, trying to keep the figures in roughly the same location. Sometimes I have to paste in a new panel, when things get really bad.

INKS

Mostly done with a brush and ink (Rosemary & Co, #3 Kolinsky Sable, with Koh-I-Noor drawing ink). Small details are drawn with the cheap Pilot pens again — things like wood grain, branches and leaves, floor tiles, etc.

I add or change certain things without re-penciling at all, like the angles of facial features, decorations and textures that I left blank, and shadows on the furniture and floors.

POST-PRODUCTION

Scanning, lettering, and screentones. Like everything else, these processes have been cobbled together from years of experience, tips and tricks learned from all over the place, and so they're difficult to explain. I use a variety of screentone effects, most of which I created myself in Photoshop, and which I've struggled to master the use of over the years. I'm definitely still struggling, and it'd be great if I had about twice as much time to really do a good job on toning.

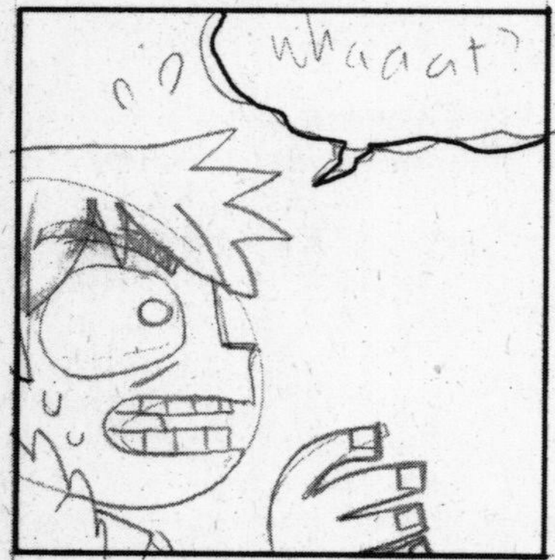
whaaat?

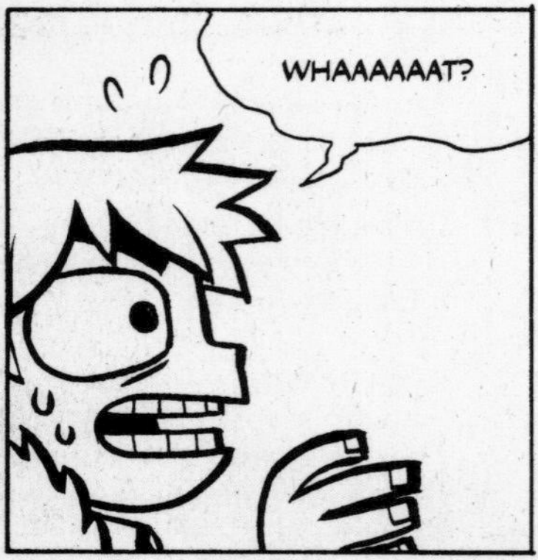
WHAAAAAAT?

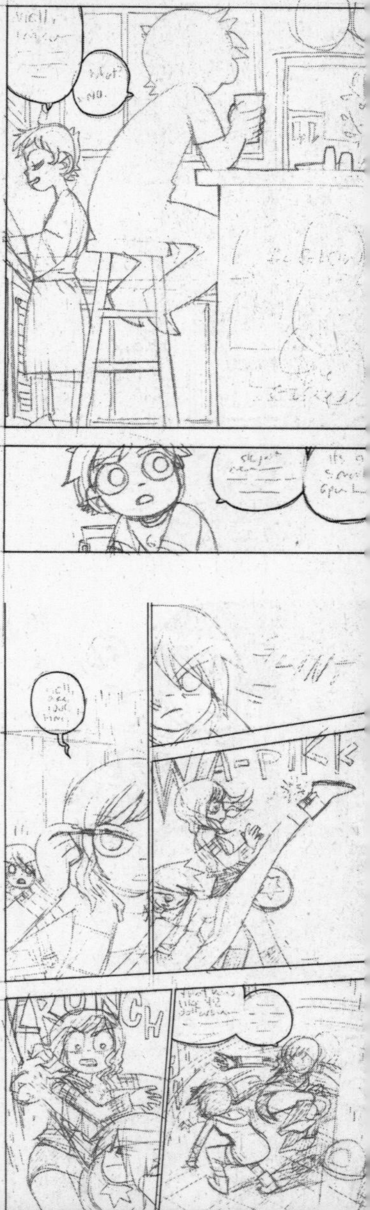